"RUN!" RUTH SHRIEKED AT THE UNICORN. . . .

She threw her bundled cloak at the creature with all her might.

The unicorn reared and fled. Ruth turned and ran at right angles to its path, into the brush where—please, God—a horse couldn't follow.

But she was leaving Nic behind. Terror and self-interest screamed at her to keep running; unwillingly Ruth stopped and looked back.

She saw a flash of metal. Nic had one of the enemy's spears in his hand and one of the attackers was on the ground. As she watched, the spear began to spin in Nic's hands—like an airplane propellor but faster, and glinting with that deadly gleam of metal.

Quarterstaff, Ruth realized in wonder. *He's using the spear as a quarterstaff.*

The others realized it, too. They spread out, trying to surround him. Ruth watched, knowing she was their next target once Nic was down, dry sickness in her throat as she realized this was not a dream, not a hoax, not a special effect. The blood and broken bones would be real. . . .

THE CUP OF MORNING SHADOWS

The Second Book of
The Twelve Treasures

Rosemary Edghill

DAW BOOKS, INC.
DONALD A. WOLLHEIM, FOUNDER
375 Hudson Street, New York, NY 10014

ELIZABETH R. WOLLHEIM
SHEILA E. GILBERT
PUBLISHERS

First Printing, December 1995

1 2 3 4 5 6 7 8 9

DAW TRADEMARK REGISTERED
U.S. PAT. OFF. AND FOREIGN COUNTRIES
—MARCA REGISTRADA
HECHO EN U.S.A.

PRINTED IN THE U.S.A.

THE CUP
OF
MORNING
SHADOWS

Contents

When the Magic's Real

The way to Elfland was neither easy nor straight, nor yet easy to find, but it was a road he could travel. He had paid the price.

How many miles to Babylon?
Threescore miles and ten.
Can I get there by candlelight?

And never go home again.

He lit the first candle, and the world warped; a bright flash like a coin dropped into water. He lit the second, and there was a sizzle like ice and boiling oil.

Perfect. He left them where they were, reflecting light from their pedestals of silver and crystal, and shouldered his pack. Leather, and custom-made, and it and its contents together weighed over eighty pounds.

He was glad he'd done so much weightlifting. He was glad of everything; of all the skills he'd had to master.

And now intended to use.

He ran his hand over the hunting knife strapped at his thigh.

Cold iron breaks all magic.

Then he stooped, carefully, and picked up the first candle.

The vertigo hit like an attacking shark. Cold wind whipped up from nowhere, threatening the flame of the second candle. Quickly he grabbed that one, too. It jiggled; hot beeswax spilled out over the back of his hand. It hurt, but not enough to make him drop it.

He'd learned to live with pain.

The pain of stretching his body beyond its limits. The pain of forcing his mind beyond its boundaries. The pain of having no heart—no, not any more, his heart had been cut out with a magic knife one night and he hadn't even been there.

But he was going to be there now.

And return the favor.

He lifted both the candles; five pounds each, confection-ery-grade beeswax with red linen wicks. As they were in the *lais,* the *gestes,* the old tales—

The truth.

The wall shimmered liquidly and seemed to tilt drunkenly askew in every dimension at once. And beyond it, he saw the road. The High Road. The Iron Road. The Road to Fair Elphame. He tightened his grip on the candles. He set his foot on the road.

One step, and he was already gone from the World of Iron. Two steps, and the ghost-wind had sharpened to a tidal roaring, insistent as the calling of his blood. Three steps, and the road began to slant upward, toward the Morning and the Lands Beyond the Morning.

Four steps, and the iron in his bones was an aching weight, calling him back to the Last World, the World of Iron.

Five steps, six, and the Road was the only reality; the Road, and the clamoring darkness on either side.

The Road, the fire, the pain. And the chill ache where his heart used to be.

But he was used to pain.

Chapter 1

The Game of Kings

The chess set was quite old; so old, in fact, that the pawn pieces were carved in the likeness of elves. The great pieces were the Treasures, twelve in coral, twelve in amber—a lie, in a way. There were only twelve Treasures, unique and irreplaceable. But vulnerable. Very.

No one now living knew how the Seven Houses of the Twilight had come to possess the Twelve Treasures. They had come with the Folk of the Air into the land they had renamed Chandrakar, and forever after had been the cornerstone of the Morning Lords' power. The tales of their wielding were many, but it had been long and long since Chandrakar's borders were less than secure, or since the title "Marchlord" had been anything other than a convenient honor to bestow upon an eldest son.

Even the long war following Rainouart High King's death had not changed the essential security of Chandrakar—not a small thing in a universe where worlds and lands were made and unmade in a careless thought. That the Treasures had the power to shatter worlds was understood by all.

What was less well known was that the majority of each Treasure's unique abilities were lost beyond the power of their Keepers to regain them. Only the least of the Treasures' gifts—formidable in themselves—remained: the power of the Sword to see into its opponent's heart; the power of the Cup to brew a posset that would kill or cure. These small tricks, and the mandate to guard the Treasures carefully, lest Chandrakar itself be lost, were all that was left.

Rohannan Melior of the House of the Silver Silences sat in his father's solar in his father's castle, both of which he must learn to think of as his own, and brooded, wine cup at his elbow. One day's work was done, another would soon begin. In a few days he must leave for the Twilight Court, to be confirmed by the Lords Temporal in his succession, to make known the recovery of the Sword of Maiden's Tears, to. . . .

To tell them that Eirdois Baligant, their new High King, was trying to kill them all?

Melior set out the chess pieces. Each Treasure—and its shadow-self. Conscientiously Melior lined them up in pairs down the jade-and-silver board. The pawns he left in their case.

The Sword: Line Rohannan, and safe. The coral sword and the amber one he placed to one side. They glinted in the varicolored light of candles and fire, so unlike the cold white light that came at nightfall in the World of Iron.

The Cup: Line Floire, and . . . in doubt. Jausserande had not spoken to him of her attempts to regain the Cup, but if they had been successful, she would not still be here.

And that they had not been successful in three full moons gave Melior even greater worry.

She is too young for this burden! Melior protested. But in Chandrakar that was all that was left: children—and survivors.

Like me. Melior took a sip from his goblet and wondered how the grape harvest fared on his southern holdings. You couldn't just let a vineyard lie fallow for a handful of seasons and have anything you wanted at the other end.

He hoped, nevertheless, for a good harvest. More than half the grain would have to be reserved for seed, which would mean a shortage of beer and ale, but they should at least be able to drown their sorrows in the new vintage.

Rohannan Melior of the House of the Silver Silences; Swordwarden and Marchlord; with his mind as earthbound as any of his human serfs'. Amusing in a quiet way, but not really helpful.

And what of the other Treasures? Melior sighed. Every day brought new reminders of what the war had taken from them. In the reign of King Rainouart, everyone had known who held which Treasure—it was a source of pride. But now?

Lines destroyed; cadet branches ruling; Treasures hidden for safety and their guardians slain before passing on the secret . . . Melior wondered if the Burning Lance and the Horse of Air were anywhere in any of the Nine Worlds: Line Rivalen and Line Tantris, which had held them, were gone to the last fighter. Even the peace-bonded women and children of Rivalen had died in the Red Peace; surely at least one mother would have taken her children and fled if Tantris had still possessed the Horse.

Perhaps Baligant already held the Horse and all the rest.

Chandrakar's High King had died, and Eirdois Baligant had been chosen to succeed him, but that was not where the tragedy lay. The tragedy lay in the fact that Eirdois Baligant had been chosen by the Lords Temporal to become High King over the Seven Houses of the Twilight much too late. For Baligant, passed over as a claimant before, shunted aside in the endless intriguing for alliance and advantage, was not now willing to forgive. And despite the fact that law and custom both decreed that the High King might not go to war with any of the Great Houses, nor condemn a Son of the Morning without a trial before all his peers, Eirdois Baligant had found a way to punish those he would not forgive.

Sword and Cup, Lance and Shield, Harp, Mirror, Cauldron, Comb, Cloak, Horse, Book and Crown. The Twelve Treasures of Chandrakar, each separately entrusted to one of the noble families of Chandrakar for safekeeping. All of which must be present at the crowning of the High King— and the lineage that did not come before the High Seat upon that day with the Treasure entrusted into its care would never come before it again: all rank and seizin were forfeit, and that line forever banished from the Twilight Lands.

And Baligant, it seemed, meant that to be all of them: Line Rohannan, Line Floire; all the Treasurekeepers. Driven from the land. By law.

Carelessly Melior swept all the pieces back into the box.

The safety of the Realm Eternal hung teetering in the balance, and what occupied his time? Farming and tax-collecting. . . .

But if the crop is not gathered and the rents distributed, we shall all starve come winter, and that with no help from Baligant. If only there were some proof to show. . . .

But there *was* proof. Melior straightened in his chair.

And slumped again, passing a hand over his brow. His proof was where he couldn't possibly reach it—trapped in the World of Iron.

Ruth. *Ruth.*

Chapter 2

The Glass Ceiling

"Christmas just won't be Christmas without an alarm call from the library," Penny Canaday grumbled.

She was one of those people who appear self-contained and self-consistent: plump, nonthreatening, and brown all over: brown skin, brown hair in a restless ponytail, brown eyes. Reminiscent of a gingerbread woman, and of that intermediate age (as she said) between graduation and death. Penny was wearing a set of grass-green Osh Kosh B'Gosh overalls with a white cotton shirt and bore a faint but determined resemblance to Mr. Greenjeans.

She was also the Chief Librarian at the Ryerson Memorial Library in beautiful downtown Ippisiqua (Queen City of the Hudson) New York, at which Ruth Marlowe had been the newest librarian for the last three months.

"Try to imagine it," Ruth coaxed automatically, although the thought of the last three months—and all the three months' to follow—was almost enough to send her out into the storm and back to her own apartment. Interpersonal relationships were not her strong suit these days, but Ruth dutifully did her best. And now it was Christmas, and she'd been dragooned into spending it with Penny and Katy and Nic.

Ruth wasn't sure she wanted to be here, even as insistent as her new friends had been. There were too many different horrible Christmases in her past for her to want to add one more.

Her first Christmas after coming out of the coma, spent in the nursing home. Braces on her legs and a body that wouldn't obey her—and a mind rebelling against the knowledge that it had been eight years—all her life from eighteen to twenty-six—since the last thing she could remember.

Her first Christmas after Naomi died. Spent even more alone, in a hastily-rented studio apartment in Brooklyn.

She'd lost track of Michael—she didn't even know if he'd graduated—but Philip and Jane were only a phone call away, finishing up their degrees at Columbia Library School.

She hadn't called them. Naomi's death had driven the once close-knit group apart, as if they were all co-inheritors of some ghastly guilty secret that made them unable to face each other. Naomi's cheerful tolerance had been what bound them all together. Without it, there had been nothing left.

Pulling her mind back into the present, Ruth looked out the window of Penny's and Katy's neat, restored-Victorian living room at white horizontal streaks of unseasonable late afternoon wind-driven snow. No, Christmas was not an especially good time for Ruth these days, but then, face it, the other three hundred sixty-four days were no picnic either.

"C'mon, Ruth, smile," Penny urged. "Katy's cooking dinner, the library isn't open, and we're going to have a white Christmas."

Ruth shook herself out of her reverie and forced the real world into focus. There was no point in pining after things she couldn't have. After things, in fact, that she'd thrown away with her own lily-white hands. Love and honor, courage and loyalty. . . .

Love.

"And anyway, if there is an alarm, you can pretend you don't hear it," Ruth said, valiantly keeping the conversational ball in play.

"Why bother?" Penny groaned theatrically. "Nic's going to have to go, and if Nic goes I might as well go, and that leaves you and Katy here."

"With a twelve-pound goose and a plum pudding with hard sauce," Ruth said, trying hard to make it sound as if they were something she wanted. Naomi had cooked, and the memories roused in Ruth by the kitchen aromas were not kind.

"But really, Penny, if the alarm goes off, it's sure to be a false alarm, and it's only two blocks away, anyway. We can all go," Ruth said, trying to keep herself firmly anchored in the here and now. She couldn't spend the rest of her life in mourning, however justified.

"It's the principle," Penny told her loftily.

Ruth was saved from riposte by Katy Battledore, Penny's clerk and—library gossip had it—the secret master of library services in the five-county area, who paraded out of the kitchen, bearing a large platter.

"Announcing the turkey," Katy said, with pardonable pride.

"It's a goose, actually," Nic Brightlaw added apologetically. He entered behind Katy, shirtsleeves rolled up and collar buttons undone, holding twelve pounds of thoroughly-cooked goose on an Armortel platter.

Nicodemus Brightlaw, the Ryerson Library Director, was one of those librarians who, Ruth thought, existed only in the fevered imaginations of Hollywood casting directors. Nicodemus Brightlaw was at least six foot two, and had eyes of blue, hair the shade of rich insistent gold rarely achieved without reference to Lady Clairol, perfect white teeth, and muscles in places most other men only had T-shirts. By rights he should have been drop-devastatingly handsome.

Ruth had distrusted him on sight. Nicodemus Brightlaw, the Library Director from Central Casting. The man with a past and no future—or possibly that was the other way around. In any event, it was pretty obvious after the first week that it was Penny, not Nic, who was running the library. The only useful function Ruth had yet seen Nic perform was to sign her paycheck. Now, three months later, she liked him (it was hard not to at least put up with the friends of your friends) and still didn't trust him.

It was puzzling.

"It's delicious," Penny prophesied. "Dinner, then presents. Yum."

"I thought you just said that Christmas wouldn't be Christmas without—" Ruth began.

There was the sound of a beeper.

Penny swore. Nic headed for the phone.

"You had to say it," Katy said to Ruth. Katy's mop of bright yellow curls and big brown eyes—and five foot two frame—always gave Ruth a shock when combined with the voice of Lauren Bacall and the diction of a cigar-smoking carnival barker. She looked like the star of the Shirley Temple remake of *The Exorcist*.

"You had to go and say it. If you hadn't said it—"

The secret of Katy's survival into adulthood was that she was also a world-class cook who felt unable, so she said, to cook for less than six people at a time. Since she lived alone with Penny in a restored Victorian on the edge of the Historic District, this meant the two of them ate a lot of left-overs. It was Katy's avowed hatred of leftovers (she said) that had first caused her to badger Ruth until Ruth accepted a dinner invitation. After that, it had simply been taken for granted that Ruth's place was at Penny's and Katy's house, for as many meals as Katy could wangle excuses to cook.

Nic came back from the phone. "It's the library," he said with a sigh. "It's just a false alarm, but. . . ." He shrugged. "You guys start without me; I'll be right back."

"Yeah, sure," jeered Katy. "C'mon and help me carry this damn bird back into the kitchen, and why they couldn't have called ten minutes ago and saved us all the trouble I'm sure I don't know."

The weather was settling down to snow in a sullen determined manner as the three librarians (and one clerk) walked down (mostly deserted) Market Street in the direction of the library. At this time of year, even four o'clock in the afternoon was twilight time. The front of the library was nearly the same color as the sky.

"Looks okay to me," Ruth said.

"Fine, let's go home," said Katy.

"It won't take that long to reset it," Nic said pacifically.

"Come on," said Penny.

Nic pushed open the inner door of the library and flipped on the first bank of lights. Ruth and the others followed. The familiar scent of wet boots, chalk, and sweetly-decaying books filled her nose. Library smell.

The Ryerson was a library of "a certain age"—about a hundred years old, Ruth had once guessed, looking at the ornate plaster medallions of the cupola—and dated from the first great flush of the American love affair with public works and high culture. Buildings like the Ryerson were the legacy of Rockefeller, Carnegie, Mellon, Vanderbilt: conscienceless robber barons who had lived like princes and acknowledged no law but themselves—and despite this had left their country an enduring heritage of public sector Arts. Many lesser plutocrats had imitated them: almost every city in America could boast a turn-of-the-century culture temple like the Ryerson.

And it hasn't gotten a good square endowment since, thought Ruth automatically, looking at the missing patches of plaster and the rusty watermarks that stained the plaster that *was* there. When the Ryerson was built, the area beneath the rotunda had probably been meant to be gracious and spacious; an architectural overture to the literary treasures within. Now it was jammed with desks, files, on-line catalog terminals, and tipsy racks of paperbacks. Study carrels vied with a massive oak card catalog for floor space on Ruth's left, and the charge desk at her right was almost completely concealed behind book racks, CD cabinets, and importunate signs listing the variety of late fines for assorted media.

Not much, but I call it home. At least I do now, Ruth said to herself, even while an inner voice told her that she lied. Home now was where Rohannan Melior of the House of the Silver Silences was, but Chandrakar was worlds and lifetimes away.

Ruth hadn't set out to befriend a lost elvish prince—but then, she hadn't meant to turn thirty either, and the two things had happened more or less simultaneously. She'd been living in New York City, going to Columbia Library School, all set to graduate and unleash one more overqualified hyperlexic on the world, when she'd tripped over Melior.

Literally.

He'd been mugged.

Welcome to New York, now go home, Ruth had thought. She'd also thought he was a lost-stolen-or-strayed medievalist, but one look at his pointed ears—and pointed teeth—had cured her of that hopeful notion. But by then it was also too late to step back into the safe normal world: she'd already offered to help him, and that impulsive offer of aid to a wounded stranger had become an adventure that Ruth, all things considered, would rather not have had.

Ruth, Naomi, Philip, Michael, and Jane. Five unlikely friends, student librarians drawn together by a mutual sense of not fitting in. And before they had completed Melior's quest, and retrieved the beautiful and deadly Sword of Maiden's Tears, one of them was dead.

There were days when Ruth felt that it would have been better for everyone if she had died in Naomi's place. Or, at least, better for her.

Because she had fallen in love with Rohannan Melior, and he with her. And when the Sword was safe, he had wanted her to walk the Iron Road with him, back to his elvish land. And Ruth had agreed to go, settled her affairs, said good-bye to her friends.

And then had been forced to choose. Melior's magic, taxed by the battle to regain the Sword, was too weak to open the Iron Road enough for Ruth to pass. And Ruth faced a simple and terrible choice: between keeping Melior with her, in the World of Iron so deadly to his kind, or tricking him into returning to his land alone, knowing that when the Iron Road closed behind him, it would separate them beyond all power of elvish magic to reunite them.

"Come on," Penny said. "Let's round up the usual suspects."

"Because the sooner we do," Katy said sepulchrally, "the sooner we can get back to the goose."

Her comrades' voices jarred Ruth back to the present once more. They fanned out, not bothering to turn on most of the lights. As she walked deeper into the library, Ruth could hear Nic in his office, flipping switches to clear and then re-set the alarm system.

Sixty thousand dollars. Twenty-four hours notice of battle, murder, and sudden death. Not to mention notice of changes of humidity, trespassing mice, trucks rumbling by in the street outside, and any of a number of other interesting ephemera, necessitating midnight visits from Nic, or, failing Nic, Penny, at least once a month.

Given the approximately fifty false alarms in the three years of the system's installation, it was hardly surprising that Nic Brightlaw maintained such a cavalier attitude toward it.

Ruth went down the stairs toward the Children's Room. False alarm or no, a good check over in bad weather wasn't a bad idea. If a window had come open—or been forced—or if, God forbid, the ancient roof should start leaking, it was better to catch it now rather than after a hundred thousand dollars' worth of books had been ruined.

She took a quick tour of the Children's Room: the bricked-up fireplace with the painting of the *Half Moon* floating at anchor; the half-height bookcases with row after row of beloved classics—Eager, Nesbitt, Norton (Mary and Andre both). All windows closed, no suspicious drips. All right and tight.

Then, as if compelled by the sort of literary device found in bad fiction, Ruth's attention slid unwillingly toward the door to the Second File.

She really ought to check the Second File.

She should.

There were windows down there, too.

Ruth hesitated. She'd been in the Second File. Once.

A long time ago—say, a year and a half or so—Ruth had been a normal student librarian. She hadn't had any fear of dark enclosed places or what might live there.

That was then.

Oh, don't be a walking cliché! Ruth told herself furiously. *You know what's down there: spiders, snakes, and rats. Nothing to be afraid of.*

She walked out of the Children's Room, through the Meeting Room (in one door and out the other), and down the hall that led to the Second File.

Nothing to be afraid of. After all, you've already faced the worst Life has to offer, right?

Too true. And capitulated utterly. There was a certain dour comfort in that, come to think of it.

The Second File was—more or less, and rather less than more—in the basement, down the hall that ran behind the Children's Room. Up three stairs, open the iron door. There you were, down in the basement.

Welcome to the M.C. Escher Memorial Library. . . Ruth thought in wry self-mockery. She propped the iron door open with a brick. With an expert flick of her wrist she twisted the timer on the light switch to its ultimate max and then stepped inside.

Ruth tasted acid and copper as the smallness and darkness pressed in on her like wet rancid velvet. But there was no Sword, no *grendel,* no slain friend. There was only the solitary dark, and the memory of the cold equations that had led to the murder of her best friend.

Naomi's dead. You're alive. Act like it, Ruth told herself brutally. She took another step inside, keeping a wary eye on the door.

The basement—idealistically called the Second File, though not even Penny had been able to tell Ruth where the First File was—was illuminated in its entirety by one forty-watt bulb suspended in the middle of the space, giving the

entire basement the indefinable air of a Ridley Scott movie.
Piled tangles of ancient fixtures made inkblot shapes in the
wan winter light from the high, narrow, and filth-opaqued
windows at the back of the room. Ruth looked around, duck-
ing her head to avoid being brained by a couple of low-
flying pipes.

The basement of the Ryerson Memorial Library was, like
the library, in Ippisiqua, New York, and (again, like the library) of an 1890s vintage. In the case of the basement, this
meant that it was dug, unfinished, into the rocky bank of the
Hudson River. It was cold, damp, and dirty, infested with
bats, squirrels, and God knew what else.

For all of these reasons, the Library Gods had chosen to
store their bound copies of old magazines and newspapers
down here; hundred-year-old copies of the *Hudson Eagle*
going to mold and dust alongside seventy years of *National
Geographic,* proceedings of the State Legislature, random
government documents, antique maps, and other exciting
ephemera.

*They said we had to have them. They didn't say they had
to be accessible. Or usable,* Ruth thought, staring at the
shelves of magazines stored against what had been the back
basement wall of the original library building; half-
smoothed rock evened in places with plugs of brick and
(now crumbling) mortar.

The ceiling was low here; the beams of the first floor sup-
ports just scant inches above her head. In the farthest corner,
where ceiling and wall made a mad rush at each other and
met in a non-Euclidean tangle, several volumes of *Life* magazine lay stacked in the middle of the floor, gathering more
damp (if possible) than they would elsewhere. Ruth, a librarian to the roots of her soul, went over and picked them up.
Yes, here was the space on the bottom shelf they'd come
from, but what moron had pulled them out and left them on
the *floor?*

Ruth reached to put the books back and stopped. The light
shifted, and suddenly there was sunlight spilling into the
room where she stood.

Hot summer sunlight in the dead of winter, from a direction that ought to be solid rock.

Suddenly Ruth's heart was hammering and her mouth was
dry. And memory, unbidden, rose up to remind her why.

*In memory it was always raining, although Ruth knew that
May evening had been clear. Clear and cool, and the present
dissolved and left her in what Ruth thought of as the last
real moment of her life.*

*Hand in hand and each carrying a flickering beeswax
candle, Ruth and her elphen prince, Rohannan Melior from
the Morning Lands, stood in a rail yard in Brooklyn, spinning the magic that would take Melior home—and take her
with him. Melior started down the tracks, toward the tunnel
at the end of them, and his hand burned like cold fire over
hers. Melior, who had fallen out of his world into her own,
and now was climbing back.*

*Soon the Iron Road was steeper and the air was winter-
chill. Ruth's head spun giddily, and each step was a lead-
weighted effort to defy gravity. Her mouth tasted of rust,
metal, and salt, and her eyes stung with sweat. The way was
hard for one. Impossible for two?*

*Melior would not leave her. Did she have the courage to
leave him? Or would she, through inertia and moral cowardice, condemn the man she loved to a slow death in the
World of Iron?*

*No. Ruth knew she wasn't a heroine, but she had enough
courage for this.*

She dropped the candle that bound her fate to his.

*And suddenly there was a roaring void, chill blackness,
and the sensation, more terrifying by far, of her fingers slipping from Melior's grasp. . . .*

And so Melior was gone, and Ruth was left behind, and
the knowledge that Melior would come back for her if he
could was balanced by the cold truth that he could never
reach the World of Iron again. And she, she had thrown
away her one chance to reach Chandrakar.

But now here was a second chance. Maybe. There
wouldn't be a third. Ruth knew it in her bones.

With trembling hands she tore at the hardbound volumes
of *Life 1920-1950*. Hot summer sun played across her hands,
light from a land where it was always summer.

The half-remembered sensation of Magic tingled along
her bones. Yes. Here it was. Yes.

"Ruth!" Nic's voice, raised behind her in a horrified bel-
low.

A second chance. Never a third. Ruth dropped to her belly and began to wriggle through the opening.

Darkness and sunlight, and the tang of the salt sea. A roaring, and a chill burning, and as vertigo tilted down to up and Ruth felt herself slide forward in the grip of no earthly gravity, cowardly sweet reason reasserted itself and yammered that there were far, far worse things than anomie.

But it was far too late for a thirty-one-year-old librarian whose soul had been stolen to guard a magic sword out of Elphame. Ruth felt the grasp of fingers on her ankle slide free as she tumbled inexorably into magic.

Chapter 3

In Your Heart No Love Is True

Floire Jausserande of the House of the Silver Silences, Warrior and Treasurekeeper, had been born and bred for war, and in the seventeen years of the warrior's lifetime which was all she had to measure time by, Jausserande had learned more than the casual observer might think about the rhythms and textures of waiting.

She knew good waiting from bad waiting, the unbearable from the merely boring, and, most subtle of all, the necessary from the entirely useless.

This waiting felt like useless waiting.

In the New Peace, Jausserande had no duties for her Line but to recover the Cup of Morning Shadows, hidden in the Vale of Stars. Dawnheart was the nearest castle to the Vale, and so she was here: had been since Floire Glorete had passed the Cupbearing to her, the oldest in Line Floire willing to live untouched that she might touch the Cup.

She had been here to see Rohannan Lanval die and his death barge launched upon the river. She had been here to see Rohannan Melior return from the World of Iron a month later, bearing the Treasure he had been sent to recover and a mare's nest of allegations against their newfound High King: allegations he would not repeat to anyone with more political power than a middle daughter of a subordinate Line of a House now in eclipse. Would not repeat, and could not prove.

Jausserande leaned her chin on her arms and gazed out over the battlements of the castle. The wind blew her shoulder-length silver hair against its confining golden fillet.

Jausserande was tall and fair-haired, as all of Melior's House were, and her eyes were the hot jewel-violet of twilight over the Vale of Stars. Despite her youth she was a blooded warrior, a captain of cavalry. Jausserande's Ravens had led many a charge in Chandrakar's civil wars, where loyalties shifted like shadows in candlelight. Born in war, she had never known what it was to spend a summer other than in arming for war.

Until now.

Harvest Home began in just two weeks; one of the reasons Jausserande had chosen this windy perch was to evade the hordes of guests and visitors that filled Dawnheart nigh to bursting. Every reaped field for half a league was filled with pavilions, tents, and lodging carts, and even at this height the uneven music of the carpenters hammering together the booths for the Harvest Fair on the meadow below reached her ears. In a fortnight the Home would begin—just as the Twilight Court would convene at Citadel—but this year the games and gauds of neither Court nor Home would mask the maneuvering for advantage and alliance that was prelude to a winter's war.

This year they had peace.

And they would have peace, Jausserande realized with a frustrated uneasiness, even if everything Melior said about Eirdois Baligant of the House of the Vermilion Shadows was true and he could prove it at the Twilight Court.

Jausserande shook her head sharply, refusing to follow that train of thought to any conclusion. She would leave the cloud-castle building to her strange cousin, and thank all the vague lucks and soldiers' gods that the House of the Silver Silences did not look to Line Rohannan, but to the Regordane of Line Regordane. And Regordane would choose the next head of Line Rohannan, if Melior held to his mad fancies that the High King chosen by the barons after a century of war was a murderous lunatic who wished to see the land laid waste.

But her cousin's sanity was not Jausserande's immediate problem. The Earl of Silver, the Regordane of Line Regordane, had bid her make sure of her Treasure before Twilight Court convened. For the last three months she had been frustrated in every attempt she had made to reach the Vale of Stars and work the small spell that would deliver the Cup into her hands, and now her time was running out.

Tomorrow would be her last chance.

And that was all very well, and no more than she had expected from a short life spent learning that luck could not be trusted and fortune was a myth, save for the fact that, like all the heaven-born, Floire Jausserande had her rightful inheri-

tance of the elphensight that allowed her to look a little way
into the most probable of all the possible futures.

Not for her was her cousin's greater gift, that could show
more futures than one, nor yet an Adept's pitiless Sight, that
showed all the possible futures sharp and clear and allowed
the sorcerer some chance to choose which of these futures
would become the only reality. Jausserande could see only a
little way, before the fog of "might be" closed in and left everything as mazy as it would be to one of the humans who
followed the plow on Line Floire's demesne.

But the little way that she could see did not contain anywhere within itself the recovery of Line Floire's Treasure,
nor, indeed, anything other than a peculiar tangled suspicion
of battle, murder, and sudden death.

Which was ridiculous. They were at peace. The rulers of
the Seven Houses of the Twilight—Silver, Vermilion, Saffron, Azure, Crystal, Indigo, and Emerald—and their vassal
lords—Rohannan, Floire, Rivalen, Gauvain, Amarmonde,
Eirdois, Calogrenant, and the dozen-something others—had
sworn. They had all chosen Eirdois Baligant of the House of
the Vermilion Shadows for the High King, and bound themselves with fearful oaths to support him and no other.

The thin shouts of the laboring mud-born on the field below drifted up to her. Happy mud-born, to have no cares
beyond the next full meal and a warm place to sleep, both
provided by their elphen overlords. For a moment Jausserande almost wished she were human: finite, limited, untroubled by such dreams or visions as made even Jausserande's
waking hours restless.

The Morning Lords had sworn peace. And as that had
been only a few seasons ago, and Baligant was not yet even
crowned, it was a bit soon to be looking for treachery, in
Jausserande's opinion.

Thus, there could not be war from within.

And Chandrakar was fortunate in its location among the
Morning Lands: it lay between no two things of any strate-
gic importance whatever, nor held any Gate that led so. Any
invader of Chandrakar would do so for what lay within it,
not through it. And at the moment, Chandrakar was much
too poor to tempt even the most whimsical empire builder.

Thus, there would not be war from without.

But there was going to be trouble from somewhere. And
all Jausserande could do was wait. Knowing that waiting

was the wrong thing to do, and knowing there was nothing else she could do.

But if waiting perturbed Jausserande's mind, she was nearly unique in her ability to do nothing but wait. This was the height of the harvest; the grapes, the barley, the wheat, and the apples—all the produce of the Rohannan lands needed to be harvested, the herds thinned, preparation for winter made.

And when that preparation was done, the Home would begin: the fair that had been the prelude for war since Jausserande's earliest memories, but which this year would bring peace instead. Delegates to the Twilight Court, Advocates to the High Court . . . and no war.

Why, then, did her memories of the future hold the clash of steel?

Jausserande shrugged and turned away. The battlements had brought her no peace, and so her frustrated ramblings brought her at last to a room that, no matter how overcrowded the castle became, would remain unencroached upon.

The door swung inward before she had a chance to knock.

"A small magic, but still impressive, do you not think, Jauss?" said the voice within. Jausserande shrugged and stepped through the door.

Dawnheart was a castle built for war, without any large windows in its outer walls, and so the windows in this curtain-wall tower were narrow unglassed slits barely a handspan wide. The sun's rays struck through them for only a few brief minutes each day; for all the rest the sun fell at a slanting angle upon all the three-foot thickness of good white granite that formed Dawnheart's outer walls, spreading its light a little way along the stone and leaving the room itself in darkness.

The room's occupant did not mind.

It was always night here, in the small room to which the Lady Vuissane had withdrawn after her last battle; Rohannan Vuissane of the House of the Silver Silences, Adept and Scout of her brother's infantry.

Like most of the elphenkind born during the wars, Jausserande had little training in the Great Art; enough to avoid ruining a spell, or becoming trapped in one, but that was all. Vuissane had been Adept of the Low Magic, with only the simplest tricks of fire and wind available to her from the High. The Low Magic was, so Vuissane had said, so nearly indistinguishable from common sense that it had been no burden to her to let it merge with her huntscraft and that with the ability to walk softly in another's footsteps to make her the most valuable of her brother's spies. Vuissane had been able to walk into an enemy camp and spy out its disposition down to the last barrel of ale on the sumpter's wagons, and slip away as silently as she had come.

But then, once the Lady Vuissane had been able to walk.

"Come in—and sit down—and stop jittering—and tell me what is going on in the world."

The door behind Jausserande closed with a thud. Jausserande stepped forward into the room.

There were coal fires burning at each end of the small room, and the light they shed was further augmented by the illumination from two bronze candle trees, each as tall as a standing man. One stood at each end of the high carved bed that, save for a chair, two stools, and a low table covered in books, was the only furniture in the room.

Lady Vuissane lay upon the bed, propped upright upon a mound of brightly-colored pillows. Her useless legs were stretched beneath a dyed fur coverlet, carefully bolstered with pillows to keep them straight.

"Well, here's a surprise," Vuissane said. "Three months in Dawnheart and this your second visit. What marvels may attend upon this rare visitation, eh, Equitan?"

The immense human in Rohannan livery stood impassively in the corner, saying nothing. Castle gossip said that he was as much jailer as servant; certainly Vuissane had tried many times to end her life when she saw what she had become.

To lose the use of one's limbs was, alas, not unique in Chandrakar, in all the years of war. Even elphen magic could do little to palliate the pains of those who suffered maimings and worse. Only the far frontiers of the High Magic, where such regeneration could be purchased at the cost of lives, and the twisted labyrinth of the Wild Magic, where the price was even higher, offered repair, and there were many who wouldn't—or couldn't—pay the price demanded to be whole once more.

But for the Adepts of High and Low Magic, there was not even that chimerical hope of renewal. Their years of study and sacrifice barred them by custom and oath from ever accepting another's magical help, and their training held that the powers they wielded were focused through the lens of the body—

And a broken body meant powers broken forever, beyond all hope of mending.

Vuissane shared her brother's pale silver hair and cat-green eyes. Younger than he, she was still some years older than Jausserande, and where Melior's face showed the stamp of a wary kindness and acceptance of the folly of elphen-kind, Vuissane's fox-bright eyes and pain-grimmed mouth seemed to say that the worst her people could do was only what she expected.

"Wine for the guest," Vuissane said, and Equitan went to fill his mistress' command. "Sit," she said, and Jausserande moved uneasily toward the stool indicated.

The close heat of the room made Jausserande profoundly uncomfortable and if it disquieted her, how much more must it grate upon Vuissane, who had been as free of wood and forest as any wild thing.

Before the House of the Saffron Evenings' one unwise experiment with cannon had ended all her freedom.

"Well?" Vuissane said.

"Everything's going all wrong!" Jausserande burst out. She drew breath to say more, but at that moment Equitan returned and Vuissane held up her hand for silence.

"Go outside and close the door," Vuissane told him. "As you can see," she said, making a bitter face, "I shall be well guarded in your absence. And *you* may serve us," she added to Jausserande, as Equitan set down the tray.

Jausserande poured wine into both cups, wondering why she had come. There was little enough Vuissane could do for anyone, and her company was not exactly cheering.

"But speak to me of the greater world," Vuissane said, taking ruthless control of the conversation. "How is my brother?"

"He swears he still pines for the Ironworlder—Heruthane?— and that the High King lusts to kill us all."

"Ruth, not Heruthane. And Baligant need not kill, when all he need do is follow the law."

"That the Line which cannot produce its Treasure at the Kingmaking is tainted and banished? That would—" Jausserande's brow furrowed with thought.

"Destroy twelve Lines, among them the ruling Lines of

six of the Seven Houses of the Twilight: Regordane is the only ruling Line which does not ward a Treasure. And for that matter, who has the others now?"

Jausserande had no idea; so many Treasurekeepers had died in the war. She concentrated on the immediate fact that Vuissane seemed to take Melior's nonsensical theory seriously.

"It's nonsense," Jausserand said bluntly. "Baligant's the High King—what would he gain?"

"Maybe he's bored. But undoubtedly you're right, Floire Jausserande. Baligant Baneful makes no designs. His honor is pure. And you have already reclaimed the Cup from the Vale of Stars."

Jausserande flung herself to her feet with a hiss, her hand upon her dagger.

"No?" Vuissane's smile was bittersweet. Jausserande sat down again, slowly. It would not do to let Vuissane bait her.

"I do not have the Cup," Jausserande admitted reluctantly, although it was no secret. "But that is nothing to do with the High King! The roads are filled with bandits, and every wood and coppice holds some bully who would rather pillage honest men than do honest work!"

"It must be hard, when one has been a captain of hundreds, to meekly bow your head to some unblooded clerk not even of your own race," Vuissane said.

It took Jausserande a moment to realize that she was not being agreed with.

"If they dispute their rightful overlords, then they are criminals and should be punished as such! If they prefer a kingdom where humans rule, they're certainly welcome to look for one—if they can find the Gates, or use them," she added, sneering.

"Oh, do be reasonable, Jauss. Humans have no magic—how do you expect them to go Gatewalking?"

"If they have no magic, then they should do as they are told and like it," Jausserande said stubbornly.

Vuissane sighed.

"Very well. Humans are all that you say they are, and it is their malice, not Baligant's, that has kept you from the Cup. And doubtless you, now being prepared, will achieve it on the morrow."

Jausserande hung her head, and Vuissane regretted, if only a little, her biting tongue. It was true that Jausserande's sublime faith in her present virtue and future victory could wear down a sword blade's edge, but Jausserande was Cupbearer, and that was more important than her infuriating arrogance.

Besides, if she lived long enough, she would learn that Life betrayed everyone in the end. That would be revenge enough, if Vuissane wanted any.

"I don't know," Jausserande said in a low voice. "I cannot See."

"You see well enough to find tomorrow's sunset," Vuissane pointed out, kindly enough for one whose own elphensight had been broken to meaninglessness.

"Nothing I like," Jausserande said, and managed a wry smile. "Nothing that makes any sense."

There was a scuffle at the door, and both women's heads turned toward it.

"My lady is therein, churl, and do you not afford me entrance I shall prove your discourtesy upon your body!" The young voice was raised with cockerel outrage; furious with entitlement.

Jausserande coughed. Vuissane held her countenance still with an effort.

"Let him in, Equitan. I should so hate to replace you." Vuissane snapped her fingers and the door flew inward, revealing Equitan and his assailant.

Gauvain Guiraut of the House of the Crystal Wind was Jausserande's squire. He was young enough to have been too young for the battlefield, but like all the children in Chandrakar, Guiraut had been born into a land at war.

He took three long steps into the room and flung himself at Jausserande's feet. His dagger—for Guiraut was not yet a knight, and thus could not bear long steel—grated lightly upon the tiles of the floor.

"My lady!" he announced, and Jausserande ruffled his pale hair.

"Guiraut."

The boy darted a wary glance at the Lady Vuissane, whom everyone from the chief cook to the stable boys *knew* to be an Adept of undimmed and malevolent power.

"My lady," he said again. "All is prepared for our journey tomorrow. A party of the Guard will ride with us to the edge of the Vale Road and wait there until our return."

"You—" Jausserande said, and stopped. There was no reasonable reason she could give to forbid Guiraut to go, and he had done nothing to deserve so visible and humiliating a mark of her displeasure. "You've done well," she said at last.

"There is a tisane I can brew to mend that other matter for you," Vuissane said. "But it will leave you with a dreadful headache. And if you ride tomorrow. . . ."

"I will have it," Jausserande said shortly, almost as if she still ordered her Ravens into battle. "I thank you."

Vuissane looked from Jausserande to Guiraut. "I wish you fortune on the morrow," she said, in tones that dismissed Jausserande from her presence. "You will come again," she added, and it was impossible to tell if it was request or prophecy.

Chapter 4

Between the Darkness and the Light

Sick. The car. Jimmy— Aching fragmented memories blurred and danced, masking pain. Ruth. Her name was Ruth, and—

And what was she doing here? There was no car. That had been fourteen years ago. Ruth opened her eyes, and felt a sliding disorientation in her stomach as her preconceptions rearranged themselves.

This was none of the places she had expected to wake up in.

Half an inch from the end of her nose, an iridescent beetle climbed a stalk of green glowing grass. The hot green scent was strong in Ruth's nostrils, and sunlight made rainbows in her eyelashes. She moved her tongue experimentally. There was earth in her mouth.

Not earth. Ruth, ever scrupulous, made the last connection as memory fell into place. Not earth. Not *Earth.* Elphame.

She tried to move, and couldn't. Laggardly sensory information, checking in from the jumbled array of her body, announced that her legs were pinned under a crushing weight.

Ruth kicked. And struggled free, panting, from beneath the prone body of Nicodemus Brightlaw. She got to her knees, then to her feet, and stood there, trembling.

For a moment the sight of him blotted out everything else. She was baffled; she was indignant; she was jealous at the thought of having to share her adventure; she was glad to have someone familiar with her.

She wondered what the hell he was doing here. By a number of the cardinal rules of magic, he shouldn't have been able to follow her through at all.

Never mind that now.

Ruth brushed her long light-brown hair back out of her face. She'd lost one of her thick winter gloves going through the Second File to Elfland and this wasn't really the weather for them anyway. She pulled off the other glove and, lacking pockets, dropped it on what Ruth, a stickler for accuracy, felt one must really call the greensward.

Next, she undid the clasps at the neck of the dull green wool Inverness cloak she wore. The cloak joined the scarf and glove on the ground. The summer sun, no matter how untimely, was glorious.

Belatedly, Ruth realized she ought to see if Nic was all right, but just as the thought came to her, he rolled over onto his back.

He must have left his trench coat and gloves in his office back in the library; he was dressed as always in a conservative wool fade-to-black suit and forgettable silk tie. The tie was askew; the white oxford-cloth shirt was streakily gray with Second File dust.

He did not groan and mutter his way into wakefulness. His eyes came open, their stare as sudden and fixed as an awakening vampire's. There was a moment of nerve-stretching stillness. Then the muscles of his face came into play, assuming an expression, Ruth suddenly knew, that was both false and practiced.

There was a moment while she watched him evaluate the impossible: the noonday sun, the faery glade. Ruth, watching him watch the world, heard birdsong somewhere behind her and the murmurous plash of a running stream. Her skin prickled stickily beneath the baby-blue vintage cashmere twin set and wool Black Watch plaid kilt she wore. Her heart fluttered with emotions too complex to be named.

"Ah." Nic seemed to be trying out his voice. He arched his back and caught sight of Ruth, and got to his feet as it was occurring to Ruth that it might actually have been better to ditch her companion and take her chances on her own.

"Ruth," said Nic Brightlaw, and paused.

As if she were observing an actor preparing to go onstage, Ruth watched Nic armor himself in amiable vagueness, and the sight unnerved her far more than naked threat might.

He smiled. "Ah, any idea where we are?"

"I don't know if you're going to believe this," Ruth began in careful tones.

There was a large-animal-sized crashing through the wood.

"Damn," Nic said conversationally. Without seeming to hurry he crossed the clearing toward Ruth, scooped up her scarf and cloak from the ground, and grabbed Ruth herself with his free arm. Her squeak of surprised protest was cut short when he thrust her cloak at her; blinded by winter-weight wool she followed where he dragged her.

"Down. Don't move," Nic said softly in her ear. Ruth sank to hands and knees in the second-growth scrub that ringed the clearing, willing for the moment to do what he said. But there was no command that could keep her from looking.

She saw something large and white moving through the wood at the other side. Saw it turn, in her speculation, from bear, to deer, to—

Magic.

The unicorn was a little larger than a white-tailed deer; horse-shaped (as much as anything) with a mane that stood on end like a white silk Mohawk and a tufted lionish tail that it lashed as if it were a cat about to be bathed. Its hooves were pink and cloven.

And its horn, set with taxonomic irregularity in the center of its forehead, was spiral pearl and white gold, opal-shot.

Ruth made a sound in the back of her throat. Nic's hand pressed down hard between her shoulder blades.

The unicorn stopped in the middle of the clearing, head up, pink nostrils flaring. Its head swung from side to side, questing.

It found Ruth's glove, lying on the ground where she'd dropped it. Ruth heard Nic draw breath in a frustrated hiss.

The unicorn nuzzled the glove, pawed at it, and finally picked it up in its teeth and shook it, giving itself a momentary ludicrous resemblance to a terrier.

It dropped the glove and bugled plaintively.

It's looking for me. Ruth knew this with the certainty of a suspension of disbelief that had strained to its limits and then snapped. *It's looking for me.*

She started to get up. Nic shoved her down.

Ruth struggled. The unicorn cried out once more, then bounded away.

"*Let* me go!" Ruth demanded in a furious undertone. Nic released her, and she struggled to her feet, but the unicorn was gone. "Don't you *ever* grab me like that again!"

"That was a unicorn," Nic said in a flat voice.

Ruth stared in the direction it had gone, longing supersed-ing all other emotions. "*The silken-swift . . .*" she quoted from some long-ago fantasy. "*The gloriously fair . . .*"

"Ruth, we have to talk," Nic Brightlaw said, in a voice that was not quite steady.

Ruth wadded the cloak she carried into a more practical bundle and tied it up with the scarf. Ignoring Nic, she walked back out into the clearing. The croquet-course smoothness of the grass was scarred by the unicorn's hooves, and Ruth, who should have been numb with shock, found herself thinking clearly for the first time since she could remember.

Forget the question of how she and Nic had gotten here; those answers could be found later. Meanwhile, they were here. What exactly had Melior told her about his world? Ruth furrowed her brow, racking memory.

Melior's land, Chandrakar, had just achieved a shaky peace after a generation of civil war. Chandrakar was one of the Morning Lands, which Ruth vaguely construed to be something on the order of a collection of little Graustarkian kingdoms. All were connected by the Iron Road which led to the World of Iron or, as its inhabitants called it, Earth.

She knew she wasn't on Earth right now, but that didn't necessarily mean, Ruth realized, that she was in Chandrakar—Melior's conversations had implied that there were a number of mail stops between his world and hers.

So where was she? And how did she get to where Melior was, without falling back to Earth?

How, in fact, did she get anywhere at all from here? Especially since the people she met here were likely to be both strange and overexcitable, as well as living in universal ignorance of the fact that she, Ruth Marlowe, was the heroine of the story.

Added to which, she didn't know what enemies Melior had made lately, let alone how to recognize them if she met them.

Ruth gazed around the clearing, excitement cooling slowly toward puzzlement, when there were more sounds from the woods. She turned hopefully in the direction the unicorn had gone.

It was back.

But it wasn't alone.

"Get back," Nic said, at a volume meant only for her to hear. Ruth edged behind him, trying to watch two fronts at once. On her left hand, the unicorn sprang and skittered at the edge of the glade, its dark blue gaze fixed unwaveringly on Ruth, but unwilling to approach any closer.

There were five men. Three on foot, two on horses, dressed in a mock-medieval style straight out of Maxfield Parrish. The ones on foot carried nets and spears. Ruth was painfully aware of her bare knees and sensible shoes.

"A maid!" one of the riders exclaimed, jerking a thumb at the unicorn in clarification. His companion laughed.

"Come here, pretty maidey, we won't hurt thee," the one who had spoken coaxed unconvincingly.

Ruth looked at the unicorn. It flung its head up and down in an agony of indecision, frantic to flee but obviously not quite able to bring itself to.

"Come, maidey; a gold ring for a few moments' work."

Ruth took a step toward the unicorn. It crouched on its haunches, poised to run as soon Ruth had reached it.

She sensed as much as saw the riders shift their weight; to run her down; to run *it* down.

"Gentlemen," Nic began.

"Get her now; talk later." The second rider spoke.

"Run!" Ruth shrieked at the unicorn, and threw her bundled cloak at it with all her might.

The unicorn reared and fled. Ruth turned and ran at right angles to its path, into the brush where—please, God—a horse couldn't follow.

But she was leaving Nic behind. Terror and self-interest screamed at her to keep running; unwillingly Ruth stopped and looked back.

She saw a flash of metal. Nic had one of the spears in his hand and one of the footmen was on the ground. As she watched, the spear began to spin in Nic's hands—like an airplane propeller but faster, and glinting with that deadly gleam of metal.

Quarterstaff, Ruth realized in wonder. *He's using the spear as a quarterstaff.*

The others realized it, too. They spread out, trying to surround him. Ruth watched, knowing she was their next target once Nic was down, dry sickness in her throat as she realized this was not a dream, not a hoax, not a special effect. The blood and broken bones would be real.

There was a scream, following a movement that Ruth, watching closely, still hadn't been alert enough to see. One of the footmen staggered back, clutching his arm. There was a second blow, a baseball-sharp crack of wood on bone. The wounded man went down.

The second footman closed, jabbing with his spear in a fashion even Ruth recognized as amateurish. The horsemen spread and circled, but one of the cardinal tenets of war is that a man on horseback is at a disadvantage against the close work of a man on foot.

Ruth saw the flash of teeth and realized that Nic was smiling. Then—again she did not see the actual moment of the move—he was in beneath the spearman's guard. She saw the flicker of the falling spear, and then Nic was lying on the ground, one leg raised, and the ex-spearman was flying ludicrously and theatrically through the air. Nic bounded to his feet again.

One of the horsemen rode forward, leaning sideways out of the saddle. Nic moved, not fast enough, and went down. They were both on him now, blocking his attempt to rise with their horses' bodies.

And Ruth, in despair, knowing this could not end other than badly, was running through the brush toward Nic.

"Stop it— Stop— Leave him alone!"

She'd had to take her eyes off them to run; as she burst out into clear sunlight she could see that Nic was on the ground, lying still and twisted; and that one of the horsemen was afoot, and stood with a naked sword in his hand.

"Leave him alone!" Ruth screamed with all the volume she could muster. Her voice stuck and cracked, and her throat felt raw. Nic was lying very still, eyes closed.

"I'll do what you want," Ruth said in a small voice.

"No point to it now," one of the riders said. "The *losel* beast's probably halfway to the borders."

The other rider studied Ruth. His eyes were mismatched; pied; one blue, the other a brown so pale it was almost amber. His skin was a coarse, leathery, outdoor brown, deepfurrowed about the mouth. And he was regarding her, Ruth realized with a sick chill, the way she was used to regard a package of pork chops at the supermarket: was this worth the trouble?

He turned his head to speak to his companion, confident she wouldn't run. And where, exactly, could she go, anyway?

Ruth knelt by Nic's side, not knowing what else to do. He wasn't dead, and the relief of knowing that was so great she nearly wept. But he was hurt—how badly Ruth couldn't tell, but the skin was broken and the blood was a shocking scarlet against Nic's blond hair. Gingerly she touched the side of his head. She got blood all over her hand and achieved no other particular result. Ruth gulped back nausea.

Head wounds bleed a lot. It doesn't mean anything, Ruth told herself desperately. *He could still be fine.*

"We've two men dead and nowt to show for it."

A conversation she ought to have been paying more attention to broke into Ruth's consciousness at last.

"Take the gel. Have the beast at least; there's a round *thaler* on the nail head."

The local dialect seemed to be Monty Python Northumbrian, Ruth noticed with shocky indignation. And it looked like they'd kill the unicorn after all. All her brave mad gesture of defiance had done was get Nic hurt, maybe even killed. Ruth blinked back tears and looked back down again.

Nic's eyes were open. His gaze held hers. And slowly, making sure she saw, he moved his hand down toward his belt.

She didn't know how she could have missed it before. What had to be the handle—the butt—of a gun nestled, small and brown and deadly, in a flat leather holster tucked inside Nic's waistband. The jacket had covered it.

What kind of library director packs a piece? Ruth silently demanded of the universe. But she reached for the gun.

"Come on now, maidey; fair is fair. We'll even give you a *pfennig* or two of the horn price to holpen you on your way—aye, and feed you, too. Come now, maidey, don't be shy. Leave the *jarl* for wolf-bait; that's fair, too."

Ruth, staring up at the horseman, felt the gun butt hard under her hand. She curled her fingers around it and the gun slid into her hand as if it belonged there. She pulled; it resisted for a moment then came free of the holster. Nic nodded ever so slightly.

Ruth stood up and backed away.

"I want you both to go away now. I said I'd help you, but you hurt my friend and you were going to leave him here to die. I've changed my mind. Go away."

As speeches of heroic defiance went, it wasn't much. Pied-eyes laughed and growled something to his companion that Ruth felt fortunate not to be able to hear. He flicked his reins at his horse and moved forward at a walk, obviously intending to make a game of running her down.

I am tired of being moved here and there and treated like a china doll as if what I want doesn't matter! Sudden alchemical fury—witch-fire struck alight by lucifer matches—rinsed through Ruth's veins like a drug. She brought the gun up threateningly in hands that shook, even though she hardly knew where she pointed it.

The gunshot was loud and flat; deafening, and apparently all the gun's own idea. She nearly dropped the little pistol in surprise.

But surprised as Ruth was, she was not nearly as surprised as the hunters' horses. They didn't stop to rear and whinny; they simply sought the straightest path away from the noise and took it, running flat-out and heads down. Within moments they were lost to sight, then to sound. She was lucky, Ruth supposed, that their riders had stayed on and not remained behind to make trouble.

Later she would discover that what she had fired was a double action Colt "Bulldog"; a .38-caliber revolver that would cock and fire just for pulling the trigger. Now she only wanted to find some place to ditch the noisy dangerous thing.

"Ruth, do me a favor . . . point that thing somewhere else."

Ruth looked back at Nic, and realized she was pointing the gun right at him. Nauseated reaction replaced the hot bright anger of a moment before. Carefully she placed the gun on the ground and stepped back from it.

"Good girl. Now come over here, and let's see how hard they hit me." His voice sounded frayed around the edges, but not nearly as frightened or angry as he had a right to be. Correction: as a *normal* person had a right to be.

Her sweater was ruined, Ruth thought with gloomy relish a few minutes later, but at least Nic was sitting up now. Beads of perspiration stood out all over his face, and his mouth was very set, but he was halfway to his feet and had assured her he was fine.

"I've been hit that hard before," he said wryly, "but usually with a chair. Never mind now. One question, Ruth, and I'd like a straight answer: do you know where we are?"

She met his eyes. Their gazes crossed like a romantic

cliché with nothing of sex in it; only knowing. Knowing that Nicodemus Brightlaw, boy library director, was something from which all human contradiction had been carefully edited away, leaving behind something powerful and focused . . . and perhaps not quite human any more.

She wondered what he saw when he looked at her.

"No," said Ruth. "I don't know where we are. Would it help at all if I said I think I know how we got here, and where we ought to be, but not how to get there?"

"You forgot to say that it's a very long story," Nic added. He smiled as if it hurt, which it very likely did.

"Well, it is that," Ruth admitted.

"Fine. You can tell me while I recuperate. C'mon. I think I heard water over that way. Help me up. You can catch me when I fall over."

"Sure," Ruth said, relieved, all things considered, to be let off so easily.

"And, Ruth? Get the gun. We're going to need it."

Ruth went back to where she had laid it down and gingerly picked up the gun. She slid it carefully into the pocket of her skirt, hoping it wouldn't go off and shoot her in the foot. Or worse.

Then she went to see if the man that Nic had thrown was all right.

Part of her knew already what she was going to see. Hadn't Pied-eyes said Nic had killed two of their own? But part of her hoped it wasn't true.

It was. The man who lay on the emerald greensward stared sightlessly into the sun, mouth agape. His neck was broken. Ruth turned away.

Nic had killed him. Nic had killed both of them. And it didn't matter whether they were in Elfland or Ippisiqua, it was still murder.

She turned back to where Nic sat. He was looking at her.

"Yes, they're dead," he said, as if she'd spoken. "I intended to kill them, I used deadly force, and they died. Once I'd seen the unicorn, I didn't think they'd recognize the threat of a gun. Shaving the odds until they ran was the only other choice." His voice was neutral, as if he were discussing the weather.

"You could at least be sorry about it," Ruth said weakly.

"I'm not sorry about it," Nic said flatly. "I didn't care whether they killed the unicorn or not, but when you scared it away, they were set to ride both of us down. That isn't the behavior of the rule of law."

"So you killed them." Ruth hadn't intended for it to sound so much like an accusation.

"I defended the . . . personal integrity . . . of both of us," Nic answered mildly. "If you didn't like it, don't use me as a playing piece next time." He shrugged.

Where anger and outrage—some honest human feelings— should have been, Ruth only felt sick blankness; the north-less spinning of a moral compass. She hadn't wanted to be hurt. Nic had saved her. To do that he'd had to kill two men.

Was the fair market value of her safety too high?

"Who . . . *are* you, actually?" Ruth said at last.

Nic smiled without joy. "The one who survived," he said. He began the painful process of getting to his feet, and Ruth, without further inward consultation, rushed to help him.

Chapter 5

Bad Blood and Risky Business

"I am sorry, Baron Rohannan." The speaker's voice was regretful.

"Are you certain?" He could not keep himself from asking, though Melior knew that Gislaine No-House—once, long ago, Rivalen Gislaine of Line Rivalen, of the House of the Saffron Evenings—would have made sure.

Rohannan Melior looked without seeing about the solar of Dawnheart. There had been peace in the land for long enough that the windows' bronze-bound wooden shutters had been replaced with airy winged glass shapes that filled the room above the Great Hall with autumn daylight—the room where rents and tithes were gathered and fee service was ordained, where one could have a private word or spy upon one's nobles with equal facility. His father's place—his, now that Rohannan Lanval was dead. And he had not even been here to lay the last-fruits upon his father's barge for its unaccompanied journey to the sea. . . .

Gislaine sighed, bringing Melior back to the here and now. "I am as certain as may be, my lord. Through all the wide Border, from Counterpane to Amalur—there is no passage to the World of Iron." He picked up the jeweled wine cup before him and stared into it as if hoping to find another truth there.

Involuntarily Melior looked to where the Treasuresword hung upon the wall of his solar. The enormous jeweled counterweight of the pommel glowed with more than the pale autumn sunlight that touched the stones of Dawnheart with gold. Ruth Marlowe's soul, wizard-bound into the Sword of Maiden's Tears, kept it balanced only precariously in Melior's world. At any moment the sword might slip free and back to its other self; to Ruth Marlowe in the World of Iron.

If only things were that easy. If only that were true.

The Sword of Maiden's Tears had fallen from Chandrakar into the World of Iron; fell because it was bound to the human soul of an Ironworlder: Ruth Marlowe. Her soul stretched between her body and the Sword; a bond unbreakable till her death. A wizard-forged bond.

A bond whose history could be resurrected, made visible for all to see. A bond whose forging might even implicate Baligant, or one of his favorites.

There were only two problems—or three, or half a dozen—with putting this plan into action.

"I do not know what else to try," Gislaine admitted. "As you know, my business lies along that border; my traffick in those things the Last World makes that the Morning Lands do not. Passage across the Border is an easy thing, do you merely know the trick of it."

"Until now?" Melior asked. Gislaine nodded sadly.

The moment Melior had reached Dawnheart's walls, he had sent a proxy back down the Iron Road, charged with a message that he prayed Ruth would believe and heed; a proxy mounted on a milk-white stallion, leading a blood-bay mare, and loaded down with encouraging gifts and suitable clothes for Melior's Lady, Ruth of the World of Iron.

He returned within a fortnight, to tell the story Gislaine was telling now; the story Melior had heard from Adepts of the High and the Low Magic; the most powerful whose service Melior could command. The way to the World of Iron was closed.

Gislaine had been his last hope—a hope that one whose trade lay along the Border could succeed where Melior's own vassals could not.

"If there is nothing more," Gislaine said delicately, rising to his feet. It was only a boyhood friendship, no longer acknowledged, that had brought him to Melior's aid at all, for Gislaine had lost more in the war than most.

And now he wished to be gone from Chandrakar again, and Melior could not find it in his heart to keep him.

Melior stood as well. "I thank you for all you have done, friend Gislaine—"

"Even though there was no issue?" Gislaine's voice was quietly mocking. "Well, and that is the way of the world in these dark times. Keep well, Baron Rohannan."

He turned and strode from the solar, a tall and slender figure dressed in a forester's dark leathers, both older and younger than his years.

Melior stared into the fire, barely hearing the door close. It had all been for nothing. Two interminable months since he had walked the Iron Road—away from Ruth—and come home to find his father dead, himself the head of his Line, and the situation more tangled than it had been when he left.

Two months. And how many months and years in the World of Iron, where time sped giddily and lovers were mortal? How long until Time wore Ruth away at last and his only link to his lady would be her soul burning brightly in the Sword of Maiden's Tears?

How could the Iron Road be closed; the World of Iron barred to them? It was madness. He had to believe what Gislaine and all the others had told him, and it was still idiocy. You could not close the way to the World of Iron. It lay at the bottom of the Nine Worlds; it was the place where all the roads of all the Morning Lands led to. A trap for the unwary, a snare for the careless, a dark eidolon that drew all light and life and magic into it, ever greedy. Sorcerers and morthworkers had been trying to seal the doors into it, for safety's sake, for years. Lifetimes.

And now that someone actually wished to go there, the way to the World of Iron was sealed.

Ruth would have seen the humor in that. Ruth, who more than his love, his heartsease, was the puzzle piece he could show to the Twilight Court that would prove the Treasures had been tampered with.

As always, his thoughts circled back around to that central problem—of proving what was now mere belief: that Eirdois Baligant, their High King-Elect, meant to compass the destruction of all the Seven Houses of the Twilight. The lady Ruth was his proof, trapped in the World of Iron, out of reach.

Or—Melior steeled himself to admit the worst—dead.

He put his head in his hands.

I cannot prove Lord Baligant's fell intentions without her. I can write to the others and tell them my fears, not that it will matter. They know the date of the Kingmaking as well as I; no doubt they hurry even now to find—or retrieve—their Treasures. We have all grown untrusting through the years. . . .

Untrusting or not, he must try to tell his truth. But there

was no point in asking the others to come to hear him unless he could produce his lady Ruth in proof of his accusations.

Ruth, lost beyond the power of elphen magic to retrieve— but not beyond the power of magic.

He needed a wizard.

A very powerful wizard.

Melior roused himself. There was one last hope. It was nearly as dangerous as Baligant himself, but it was the only thing left for Melior to try. He pulled inkstand and vellum toward himself and began to write.

Chapter 6

Cold Steel and Loaded Pistols

The brook was right out of a storybook, or one of those slices of English countryside now found only in dreams. It was about three feet wide and not more than a foot deep where they were, and mossy grassy verges overhung it. Its course was starred with large round boulders green with algae, but the water was clean and fast-running over a bed of colored stones.

The sight of the clear purling water made Ruth suddenly aware of how thirsty she was. She helped Nic sit down against the bole of a large tree on the clover and knelt beside him, then looked around for something to serve as a cup.

There wasn't anything, unless she used her shoe. And questions of delicacy aside, it wouldn't be any good to walk in afterward. She knelt beside the stream and scooped up several handfuls of the water, drinking and washing her face. The water tasted wonderful, and even the specter of cholera, typhus, and dysentery didn't slow her down much. If they even had them here.

Oh, God, she knew nothing at all about this mystic fun house that she and the mysterious Nic Brightlaw were trapped in. Was she really any closer to Melior? And did it actually matter? Maybe he'd written her off and settled down with a nice elf Valley Girl.

"Help me get my jacket off," Nic said, breaking into her thoughts. "It's ruined anyway. You're going to have to make a bandage out of my shirt, or I'll be leaving a blood trail a blind man could follow."

"If he was you," Ruth muttered, moving forward to help.

"Or someone who—ow! Let that be a lesson to you, Miss Marlowe, never ask strangers to share their toys; they won't play nicely."

Ruth eased the jacket off Nic's brawny shoulders. It was heavy, but appeared to contain only the normal mundane

male impedimenta of wallet, checkbook, notepad, pens. . . .
His glasses were there, thin glass lenses cracked across. All
useless here, as Melior's possessions had been in the World
of Iron.

Their positions were reversed now—at least Ruth hoped
so. Melior was safe and in his own place, and she was somewhere outlandish, hoping for the kindness of a passing stranger.

Only the last strangers they'd seen hadn't been very nice.

Nic dragged the useless tie from around his neck and
dropped it on Ruth's knee.

"Here," he said. "You might want to tie somebody up with
it."

"Wrong movie." Ruth carefully rolled the tie into a ball
and set it aside. Nic leaned back against the tree with his
eyes closed, unbuttoning his shirt. Blood had dripped down
his neck and face and soaked the collar and neck of the shirt.
He looked like a bad special effect in a splatter-movie.

"It comes and goes," he said without opening his eyes. "I
only hope the next outtakes from *Lord of the Rings* we meet
are more inclined to be reasonable."

"It was my fault," Ruth said miserably. "If I hadn't—"

"To hell with 'if.' 'If' will kill you," Nic enunciated, very
distinctly. Ruth shut up.

"Now, if you can just help me get this off, you can soak
it in the stream and see what we can do to make me less a
sight to frighten children with."

Ruth plunged the shirt into the river as if she were drowning delinquent borrowers. Blood made theatrical swirls in
the rippling current, leaving behind only pale pink stains in
the oxford-cloth button-down shirt from Earth.

She came back to Nic holding the sopping mass in two
hands. The undershirt he wore did little to conceal the long
bruises from the attacker's weapons that barred his shoulders, angry red welts darkening slowly to purple. She knelt
carefully beside him and began dabbing blood off his face
and neck with her makeshift sponge.

"Arrgh," Nic said on a rueful sigh. "I should know better
than to do things like this at my age." He took the shirt away
from her and pressed it gently against the back of his head,
closing his eyes. Ruth glanced away.

The summer sun filtered in long gold bars through the leaf
canopy. The brook's song was a rhythmic noise in the back-

ground, and hesitant birdsong began again around them. As her eyes sharpened, Ruth could see flowers everywhere; tiny ones in the moss-covered bank; bolder ones peering out in hot summer hues from the gorse. As she stared, a butterfly in violent purple bumbled through the air and vanished in the leaf canopy.

All of it might be as mundane as a *National Geographic* special or as strange as *The Twilight Zone*. Ruth didn't have enough experience with even normal Earth-type flora and fauna to know.

Except, of course, for the odd unicorn or so.

And what if this was as far into the Morning Lands as she was ever going to get—stuck playing Girl Medievalist in some place that both wasn't home and didn't have Melior?

And not only her. There was Nic to consider.

"Do you think you're going to be all right?" Ruth asked, forcing her voice to steadiness.

"Um, well, no, actually," Nic said apologetically. His eyes were closed, and his voice was slightly muffled by the mass of wet cloth. "I'm going to have one hell of a headache. Could you soak this again?"

Ruth went back to the stream—only a step and a half, really, Nic's feet were almost in it—and soaked the shirt again, as requested. So this was Elfland. And here she was, Ruth Marlowe, stuck here, like a mirror, for reflection.

Reflecting on how she, no matter where she was, was caught betwixt and between. Not alive, not really, and no chance of a life until she gave up hope of Melior. Unless— until—she did, there was not only a glass ceiling between her and the rest of the world, but glass walls and a glass floor as well. Glass coffin, in which this new improved Snow White slept on, with her awakening only a dream.

What am I going to do? What am I going to do? The idiot plaint circled round and round in her mind. Here in this strange place, cut off from everything familiar, she had no idea what she ought to think or feel, and one course of action began to seem just as reasonable as another. *God, you're morbid,* Ruth chided herself. The bleak thoughts lifted themselves to flight, and, like vultures, circled only to return. *Later,* Ruth told them firmly.

She turned, wet shirt in her hands. And froze when she saw the knife.

It was only a little knife. About as long as her thumb, all

in all, with a cheerful red plastic case with a white cross on
it. A penknife. Nic brandished it.

"Unless, of course, you'd like to tear my shirt into strips
with your teeth?" he said politely.

It was with a certain effort that Ruth refrained from simply tipping the sopping shirt into his lap. She took the knife,
and discovered that a wet, well made cotton shirt resists
retailoring with an inch-and-a-half blade.

Eventually she whacked enough of it apart to make a pad
for the back of his head, and used the despised silk rep tie
to bind it on with. The finished result was rather festive and
piratical.

"Better," Nic said when she was finished. Moving carefully, he maneuvered himself to the edge of the stream,
washed his face, and drank. Then he sat up again and held
out his hand.

"The gun."

Wordlessly Ruth dug it out of her skirt pocket and handed
it to him. He inspected it closely and slid it back into its
concealed holster, then leaned back against the tree.

"Conventional wisdom says that, lost in enemy country,
we should make tracks for our extraction point or at least
find shelter for the night. But before we do that, I'd kind of
like to hear your life story, Miss Marlowe," Nic said with
elaborate casualness.

"Me?" said Ruth, staring at him with wide blue eyes.

"Let me put it this way: I'd just gotten the alarm reset
when it started going crazy all over again, so I cut the power
and went looking for what caused it. When I got to the Second File, I found you staring down the throat of a genuine
Spielberg special effect and not looking very upset about it.
The next thing I know, we're here in an MGM remake of
Robin Hood, and you don't seem too surprised by that either.

"So I think I'm entitled to an explanation—at least before
you start defending any more unicorns."

Ruth winced. But if he were as right as common sense indicated, why was it so annoying? She took a deep breath and
tried to feel cooperative.

"Okay. In twenty words or less the story goes like this:
about two years ago in New York, I rescued an elf who'd
gotten lost on Earth. They call it the World of Iron," she
added, reluctant to come to the point. "He was looking for
a lost sword. My friends and I helped him find it."

This was the stupidest story she'd ever heard, Ruth realized, and she'd been there.

"And?" Nic prompted.

Ruth closed her lips on the rest. He'd laugh, and then she'd have to kill him, and she didn't have the energy for it just now. "So then he found the Sword and went home. Or at least went away. End of story."

"Except that there seems to be a mouse hole to Elfland in the basement of the Ryerson Memorial Library," Nic pointed out.

And Penny and Katy must still be there looking for them, Ruth realized. What a dreadful Christmas present. She ought to be horrified or something, but thinking about them only made Ruth tired. Two more people whose lives she'd ruined, just by being alive. She closed her eyes.

Her eyes flew open again a moment later as Nic flicked water at her.

"Don't spend so much of your time on vain regrets, Miss Marlowe; nobody ever appreciates it. You haven't told me half the story, but it'll do for now," Nic said. "But you don't think this is the world your traveling elf-errant came from?"

"I don't know," Ruth said, conscious only of a vast, dragging weariness. "He said there were a lot of, um, lands on the High Road to Chandrakar." *And you're remarkably unsurprised to be here, too, Nicodemus Brightlaw, to coin an observation. I'd say you aren't what you appear to be either, but I'm not quite certain what you* do *appear to be.*

A twig cracked, sharply, somewhere nearby. Nic sprang to his feet, reeled, swore, and grabbed at the tree. When Ruth started to get up, he waved a minatory hand at her.

"Stay there," he said through gritted teeth. "I'm going to use you for bait." Still holding one-handed to the tree for support, he slipped around it, hidden.

Ruth sank back into a sitting position. There was a sound of something moving through the brush.

I could really, really, get to dislike that man, Ruth thought, holding very still. Was it the hunters coming back? Nic had killed the two footmen and she'd run the horses off. Maybe Pied-eyes wanted revenge.

There was a glint of sunlight on metal as Nic drew the little gun.

Now Ruth could hear the direction of the sounds clearly.

She swore she would not look as they came closer, but at the last moment nerve and resolve both broke, and she turned.

The unicorn stepped through the stream and laid its head in her lap.

Chapter 7

Fancies and Goodnights

Floire Jausserande of the House of the Silver Silences, Cupbearer and once Captain of Jausserande's Ravens, sat in the small elegant tower room that custom and courtesy appointed to the lady-cousin of the Master of Dawnheart whenever she should choose to visit there. She wore a loose short tunic over wide ankle-gathered trousers tucked into soft short velvet boots, every item shades of the same violet as her eyes. The tunic and trews were hand-painted in eye-teasing variations—light to dark and light again—as if all the world were purple and she a Scout who needed to hide in it.

She wished.

Though she could see the sun was setting through the room's wide windows, and fire and candles alike stood waiting, she did not call for light. Before her on the table were a battered tin cup and a squat bottle of violet glass with Vuissane's seal pressed into the wax at the stopper. The bottle held the draught that Jausserande had asked the Lady Vuissane for; the draught that sharpened the kenning of the world-*leys*. Equitan had brought it just a few moments before.

Jausserande fidgeted in her chair, sick of her own company but unwilling to seek the company of others. Once again, unwillingly, like telling over an old scar, she picked up the cup on the table before her.

It was a footed cup, of rough workmanship, such as was turned out in the marketplace by the dozen for the use of serfs and soldiers. Crudely formed of disks and triangles of rough-soldered tin, it was already pewter-black with tarnish and age. Jausserande turned it in her hands. The mock-Cup, the *tainaiste*-Cup, worthless except for the simple spell laid on it: to show the presence of the true Cup and, being thrust into shadow, bringing the true Cup visible.

But it couldn't do it from here. It could only do it in the Vale of Stars, the place where the Cup of Morning Shadows was hidden, and only on the second day of the full moon, at moonrise. Conditions finicking enough to satisfy any Adept, set around the Cup like wards to assure that it was not taken lightly from its resting place in the Vale of Stars.

A place less than a day's ride from here, that Jausserande had not reached in three moons full of days. Almost as if someone prevented her.

Jausserande shook her head angrily, banishing fancy. Oh, for her lance and bow—for a good warhorse beneath her and her Ravens around her! They had never been beaten, never left one of their own in enemy hands, and the tales of their prowess had made fine songs for the fireside at the day's end.

But no one wanted to sing those songs now. And the Ravens were gone; dispersed to home and fireside, to marriage. Miralh even had a child, and another on the way, and no time for retelling old glories with her former captain.

And in the end, they hadn't even won the war. They'd just . . . stopped. And now she was supposed to bend the knee to Baligant No-House when he set his clerkly arse in the High Seat, with that white ferret Hermonicet beside him, gloating over the way she'd been dangled like a gobbet of meat over a kennel of starving dogs and then flung to the noisiest.

It was beyond Jausserande's understanding. She tilted the *tainaiste*-Cup in her hands, so that the last rays of sunset ran round its rim like wine. All she had to do was reach the Vale of Stars with it by tomorrow's sunset, and it would call the other Cup forth. And Line Floire, Cupbearers, would have that which it must bring to the Kingmaking—or be banished, down to the smallest babe, beyond the borders of Chandrakar.

Jausserande returned the cup to the table with a snort. Melior swore that Baligant No-House was trying to gather all the Treasures to himself and then declare their erstwhile guardians attainted. She'd like to think he was. Seven, eight, ten Lines—half the Houses of Twilight—try to strip them of everything they held and drive them out of the land and there'd be a fight.

There'd be war.

Whereas, as seemed more likely, if Baligant Baneful's plot existed only in her cousin's mind, the others would present their Treasures on the day of the Kingmaking, and only Line Floire would come empty-handed.

And only Line Floire would be driven away.

Everything depended on her.

In the war Jausserande had been a warrior, not a planner of high strategy. And though she might—by right of birth and of what she held—claim a seat at the councils of her House, Jausserande had no interest in endless weary talk of marriages and dowries, taxes and *teines,* of who to send as Advocate to the High Court and who to send as Speaker to the Twilight Court. And while her sister, who had been Cup-bearer before her and was now head of Line Floire, would willingly advise her, even in wartime Glorete had been too prudent for Jausserande's taste.

It was Jausserande's task alone. She would get the Cup of Morning Shadows tomorrow moonrise. She must. She would not fail Line Floire.

There was a knock on the door.

"Go away!" Jausserande exclaimed.

The door opened. Guiraut appeared, bearing a tray large enough to hold a whole roast deer without crowding. Steam and savory odors rose from it.

"Your dinner, my lady."

"I'm not hungry," Jausserande said sullenly. Guiraut, conveniently deaf, set the tray on the table before her. He looked around and noticed the darkened condition of the room. He snapped his fingers.

Nothing happened.

He muttered an oath copied from the chief groom, and violet blood rose to the tips of his pointed ears. Jausserande stared out the window, keeping her face expressionless with an effort. Guiraut wanted to impress her, and she would not mock him.

After three more tries, Guiraut snapped hearth and candles ablaze.

"You've been practicing," Jausserande said, making sure the approval was plain in her tone. Guiraut had more aptitude for the Art Magical than she did, but aptitude was nothing without practice.

He blushed again, this time with pleasure. "I have laid out your armor for the morrow, my lady. You must eat, and then away to bed," he said with as much severity as his youth would allow.

Jausserande looked at the food with faint repulsion. The
sense of doom she had felt all day was back now, stronger
but still as nebulous. Would Vuissane's potion buy her any
clarity? Or would it simply befuddle her mind with a garden
of bright images?

"I will eat if you will join me," she said finally, gesturing
at the stool that stood beside the leaping fire. As Guiraut
turned away to pull it forward, Jausserande picked up the violet flask and broke the seal. The liquid inside bore the cloying scent of too many flowers. She poured it into the
tainaiste-Cup, and added wine to fill the cup to the brim.

"To success," Jausserande said, when Guiraut had filled
his own cup with watered wine. And though he echoed the
toast, he could not begin to know how passionately she
meant it.

The predawn air was breathtakingly chill. She could almost imagine she was setting out on a daybreak scouting
raid; the lightest armor, the fastest horse, and the barest sky
glow differentiating the castle roofs from the sky. Almost,
Jausserande could forget the Cup, the Line, and the wretched
unheroic Peace.

"Art ready, Guiraut?" she cried, joy at their freedom ring-
ing through her voice. The mouse-gray mare Sparrow
danced with muffled hooves on the dew-wet courtyard cobbles.

"Ready," Guiraut answered. But it was not Guiraut at all,
but her cousin Melior—to be named, by later generations,
Melior the Mad—who swung into the saddle of his big gray
cob, his deep-hooded traveling cloak making him hard to see
in the morning twilight. The Sword of Maiden's Tears, slung
over Melior's shoulder in a traveling baldric, gathered all the
light in the courtyard to itself.

That was when Jausserande knew that this was a dream.
She glanced around, searching for signs and portents, and
saw that instead of Dawnheart's silver stone, the living red
granite of Citadel surrounded them. Citadel, where the High
King was made and the Twilight Court met.

Was this her future?

The mare danced; hot-blooded and impatient to run.
Jausserande set that question aside. She spurred Sparrow on;
the mare leaped forward like a doe before the hunters, and
in moments she had left Citadel and Melior behind.

The countryside was familiar, though nothing that belonged near Citadel. Ahead the white clay road ran twisting through the valley, until the valley became a canyon and the pass too narrow for even a single armored warhorse. Beyond that pass was the Vale of Stars, and in the Vale was the Cup of Morning Shadows.

So intent was she, even in the dream, on what *ought* to be that it was not until Sparrow slipped and barely recovered herself that Jausserande took a good look at her dreamscape.

The road beneath her mare's hooves was not white, but red. Mud-red. Blood-red.

"Hold it right there, Miss."

The voice came just as Jausserande was reining in. Sparrow stopped. Ahead, Jausserande could see the pass into the Vale of Stars, and just outside it, barring her way, was a man on a horse.

The horse was the dazzling frost-on-snow color that shouted magic—a legendary, wizard-conjured beast. The rider was not like anything Jausserande had ever seen before. He was dressed in outlandish dull-colored armor pied black and green. After a long moment she realized with a shock that he was human.

"Out of my way, earthling," Jausserande snapped.

"I don't think so," the human observed politely. His hair was the yellow of the gold that humans prized so highly and his eyes were a bright jeweled blue.

"Insolence! We'll see what taste you have for insolence after being run at my horse's stirrup for a mile or two!" Jausserande loosened her sword in its sheath and reached for her mace.

"With all due respect, Miss," the human said, with just enough emphasis on the "due" to make Jausserande grit her teeth, "aren't you forgetting that you've come for the Cup?"

At this new insolence Jausserande ground her heels into Sparrow's flanks and the mare bounded forward. Jausserande crouched low on her neck, the battle cry of the Ravens on her lips.

But as hard as Sparrow strained, and Jausserande with her, they came no closer to the false knight or the pass into the Vale of Stars.

"You're what's standing in the way of your getting the Cup, not me. And if you can't get past me, you'll never get it," the human said in tones of scholarly reproof.

The words echoed, reverberated, took on form and solidity, and caged her with bars of burning fire. Then her horse was gone, the road was gone, her dream was gone and the knight with it, and Jausserande was alone in her bed, staring out at false dawn and listening to the sentry cry the hours.

As Vuissane had promised, her head hurt abominably. And she was no closer to seeing a true future than she had been the night before.

Chapter 8

Into the Woods

The unicorn refused to leave. It didn't like Nic though it tolerated him, but it positively doted upon Ruth. Its improbable coat was as thick and soft as a cat's fur and its long-lashed eyes were bright lapis blue. It was the size of a small deer, or a very large dog—its shoulder came as high as her ribs—and it would not go away for any money.

"Tears, threats, pleas, entreaties, vain, all vain," muttered Ruth. The unicorn nudged at her elbow hopefully. "Oh, what do you *want?*" Ruth wailed, ruffling the downy neck. All she knew about unicorns was that people hunted them.

"A maiden?" Nic suggested.

An hour's rest on the stream bank had done him a lot of good; his color was better, and the gash on his scalp had finally stopped bleeding. It was cool enough under the shade of the trees that he'd put his suit jacket back on. Worn over the wet, bloodstained T-shirt, with his head garlanded in a necktie and the remains of his shirt, it gave him a particularly raffish look. *Miami Vice* for the Hyborean Age.

"Very funny," said Ruth crossly. She was hot, tired, hungry, and lost in the woods without a yellow brick road in sight. She looked at her watch. 7:30—at least it was back home in Ippisiqua. *My, what an interesting Christmas* this *is turning out to be.*

"Well, what do unicorns usually want?" Nic went on patiently. "You're the one with all the *Twilight Zone* experience."

The unicorn nudged her again.

"My experience does not include unicorns," Ruth said brusquely.

Her eyes prickled and her mouth went wry. She took a breath and held it, fighting back tears. She'd come here of her own free will; sniveling about it now was stupid. But at this precise moment she couldn't really remember *why* she'd wanted to come here so badly.

And badly was certainly the way she'd come.

Ruth took a deep breath. "Unicorns. Their horns are supposed to be proof against poison, they represent purity, they symbolize Scotland in the royal arms of Britain. . . ." She stopped. None of that seemed to be of any particular use at the moment.

"Go on," Nic said encouragingly.

He's humoring me, Ruth realized in sudden indignation. *Well, I suppose he dislikes screaming hysterics as much as the next man.* She tried a smile, carefully. "I'm afraid that's your lot. Nothing I ever read mentioned *live* unicorns."

"Well," said Nic, leaning back against the tree trunk. "It looks like we're stuck with Fluffy here for a while. The next question is: Where are we going to go?"

"Go?" Ruth echoed blankly.

"Unless you want to stay here and learn to fish," Nic pointed out. "And so far we've seen unicorns and unicorn hunters, which doesn't rule out lions and tigers and bears, oh my—or a dragon."

Ruth contemplated the thought of a dragon and wished she could feel more hopeful anticipation at the prospect. She wished, in fact, that she could feel anything, instead of assembling her emotions by guess and by gosh and by deduction.

Maybe if she got her soul back. Yeah, right.

"You're right," Ruth said. "But I'm afraid I'm not much help. What do *you* think we should do?"

What Nic thought they should do was nothing Ruth had any stomach for, though it made perfect sense. When the three of them (Nic leaning on Ruth, the unicorn following) made it back to the clearing, their approach startled a cloud of rooks that flew up from the bodies, cawing derision.

Ruth saw what the birds had left behind and turned away, gagging.

"Wait here," Nic said firmly. "And don't look."

She would have argued, but she hadn't the stomach for it; the animal depredations of the helpless dead were etched upon her mind's eye with remorseless clarity. Nic relinquished her support and shuffled off. Ruth knelt in the grass, one arm around the unicorn.

Is this all I'm good for—to be the hapless, helpless, faint-ing heroine? To let Nic protect me—and get hurt because of me? That isn't fair. He didn't ask to come here. He didn't know what he was getting into (well, neither did I, but I thought I did). And this isn't even dangerous. It's just icky.

She opened her eyes. Nic was on his knees beside the nearest body, pulling at the clothes. Ruth got to her feet and walked over to him.

"I guess you could use some help with that, right?" she said in a steady voice.

Above the trees, the false-lying sun of Elfland was sliding toward the West. Ruth, no expert, placed the local time at anywhere between two and four. She knelt beside the stream, sluicing armloads of rough woolen cloth through the icy water, frightening the fish and hoping the wool wouldn't shrink too much. The dead footmen's clothing was a far cry from the expensive and exquisite traveling garb that Melior had worn when Ruth had first seen him. Baggy undyed homespun trousers were meant to be tucked into coarse knit-ted socks, while a wrapped breechclout and a sleeveless slit-necked singlet protected the cloth of trousers and the green-dyed T-tunic of heavy fulled cloth from the sweat and dirt of the skin.

Heavy leather belts with horn or wooden buckles and sheepskin spats cross-gartered over stiff boiled-leather shoes completed these less than haute-couture outfits. Ruth wasn't looking forward to wearing this stuff, but Nic felt if the two of them wore the local clothes they'd be safer.

Just who is this guy, anyway?

Ruth shoved her nagging worries about her traveling com-panion to one side and tried to think of something useful. The unicorn (still with her) had thrown her mental balance off badly. Who'd written the rules for this place, anyway: J. R. R. Tolkien or the Brothers Grimm? Ruth breathed a brief bibliophile's prayer that it wasn't Angela Carter, but there were no guarantees.

That was the difference between Elfland and Real Life. There were no guarantees either way, but in Real Life you pretended there were. Elfland stripped away that pleasant fiction.

Ruth added yet another length of cloth to the sopping pile. Done.

* * *

She emerged into the bright late-afternoon summer sunlight, blinking owlishly. While she'd been gone, Nic had dragged the dead bodies off into the woods. Now he sat, back braced against a rock that had been padded with Ruth's discarded Inverness cloak, sorting through the contents of the dead men's belts.

Ruth chose a patch of sunlight and began to spread the clothes out to dry. The trews and undertunics might make it, but the heavy green knee-length tunics definitely wouldn't dry in the few hours of sunlight left.

And that raised the interesting question of where—and how—she and Nic were going to spend the night. She'd done some camping, true, but previous experiences had involved such comforts as a tent and a battery-powered microwave. She walked over to Nic and sat down beside him.

"So," Ruth said, by way of a conversational opening.

"So," Nic said. His plunder was spread out in little patterns beside him.

Two crude general purpose daggers, bone-hilted and slightly rusty, were laid carefully upon their sheaths. At first Ruth thought the blades were copper, but the metal had a brassier sheen. Bronze. No cold iron in Elfland. She turned to the rest of the loot. Two belt-pouches, of differing sizes and design. One drinking horn, rimmed and tipped in leather, with a loop and a bronze ring to hang it from a belt. An empty waterskin.

And, laid out carefully on Ruth's muffler, the contents of the belt-pouches. A pair of dice, crudely hand-carved. A tin spoon. A box the size of Ruth's palm, purpose unknown. A handful of copper or bronze coins, small change in any universe.

And among all these items, flagrantly, the one that did not fit.

Fine silver is as different from sterling as gold is from brass. Soft, perishable, white as moonlight, too soft for use in jewelry without the adulteration of baser metal that turns it from fine silver to sterling, few moderns have ever seen it.

The ring was fine silver, thick and wide-banded, set with a gemstone the size of an apricot pit glittering transparent and opaline in all the hot plangent spectrum of the dragon's eye.

"Don't touch that!" Ruth cried, her voice raw with fear, as

Nic, following the direction of her gaze, reached to pick it up.

He stopped.

"Don't touch it," Ruth said hoarsely. "That's . . . I think it's magic." Sunlight and fire; its gemstone the chatoyant witch-fire rainbow of the jewels in the Sword of Maiden's Tears.

The sword that had killed Naomi.

"Magic." Nic's voice was neutral, neither accepting nor denying. "It's a valuable ring. What was our friend doing with it?"

Magic . . . Ruth reached for the ring indecisively. What spell, what horror, was this stone designed to release?

"Ruth? Have you seen something like it before?"

Ruth withdrew her hand. "In a sword," she managed to say. "Melior's sword. It . . . killed somebody."

Nic picked up one of the daggers and slipped its point through the ring. He lifted the ring off the muffler. The band was open behind the stone, allowing the light to pass through. The sun shining through it made a small hot point of whiteness on the muffler beneath and threw the curious carvings on the band into sharp black-and-white relief.

Ruth Marlowe was a realist, a rationalist, born into a clockwork universe that kept all its magic safely between the covers of YA fiction. Her adventures with Melior had been strange, but not enough to shake her faith in cause and effect, a world defined by objectivism.

The ring seemed to shimmer against the knife blade, saying it was a mere artifact, saying its artifactury was a lie. Malignant because unnatural, supernatural, *magic*.

"And you think this is more of the same?" Nic asked, as even-voiced as if inquiring about the possibility of rain.

"I don't know." Before she could censor herself, Ruth plucked the ring from the knife blade and held it in her hand. A cold uncanniness seemed to radiate from it into her bones, but it appeared that the message—or the spell—that it held was not strong enough to affect her.

"Magic," Ruth repeated uncertainly. She closed her fingers over it. Hard and chunky in her palm, it burned as cold against her flesh as it ought to have been hot. After a moment she dropped it to the scarf again. "Yeuch." She rubbed her palm against her skirt.

Nic picked up the ring and stared at it suspiciously, but it didn't seem to trouble him even as much as it had Ruth. His mouth set in a dogged line. "Not a piece of junk," he pronounced. "And nothing like anything else that bozo had. Why did he have it? Loot? Payment?"

"A plot device?" Ruth suggested. She'd long since discarded the bloodstained cardigan portion of her twin set, but even the short-sleeved cashmere shell was too hot for the weather. And blood-spotted as well, damnit; blood was hell to get out of woolens. "I don't know, Nic, maybe they come in gumball machines here."

"Somehow I think we'll find out," Nic prophesied. "All roads lead to Amber. Or to Oz," he added.

Chapter 9

High Noon in Elphame

The Vale of Stars and its surrounding woods were supposed to be the among the most beautiful places in all Chandrakar, but all its new denizens knew or cared about was that the area was easily defensible. There was only one path a horse could follow; the narrow riverine track that led between the steep hills covered in birch and pine. The road ran straight and smooth, and the trees on either side grew dark and thick.

A perfect site for an ambush.

As it had been.

The other rider had turned and fled at the first sign of trouble. The riderless horse of their victim had bolted ahead; they would find it later. Scholars in a hard school, they held their places until the birds had resumed their untroubled calling before moving out to claim their prey.

Fox reached the body first. His knife flashed, bright and quick, cutting the arrow loose from the throat and letting the dead elf's blood ooze onto the track. The edges of the wound blackened and smoked; Fox's blade was iron.

"Defiled for at least a month; let those cat-eyed weasels think about that," he said with satisfaction.

Fox got to his feet and began cleaning his knife. The others, as frightened of cold iron as any elphenborn, closed in and began stripping the body of everything useful. Fox turned his knife so its blade flashed in the sun. *Iron, cold iron, the master of them all*: a thing not easily come by in Chandrakar, where iron blistered the flesh of its privileged, silver-blooded princes.

And confounded their magic.

"Fox, what if they come for us? An open killing—that's different than a little thieving," Raven said.

And God knew, it had taken him long enough to give them the stomach for it. Fox turned toward the man who had spoken. And Raven was the best of them; wasn't that a joke? A handful of apologetic cowards to topple an empire.

"Of course it's different, Raven," he explained with a reasonable amount of patience. "It's better. When that pointy-eared bimbo gets back and puts out the word that—*quelle horreur*—elf blood has been spilled in the Vale of Stars, they might not even come back next month. If they don't come back, they don't get their Cup."

Raven's brow bent with the effort of following Fox's train of thought. Fox sighed inwardly. He'd thought it would be so easy, once. Before he'd seen what he had to work with—the outlaws of Chandrakar.

There were disaffected men—outlaws—living in every forest of Chandrakar; yes, and starving there, too, since their elphen overlords had the magic to hunt them down with no more aid than a lock of hair or a drop of blood any time their depredations became seriously annoying. The elphenborn spent magic with the profligacy of those expending an infinitely renewable resource. Everywhere but here, in the Vale of Stars.

Here, humans were safe to come and go and hunt and eat their fill as they pleased. All it had taken was the courage—and the brains—to come here. And that Fox had given them.

"And if the highborn don't reclaim their Treasures, there won't be a Kingmaking. There'll be another war," Raven said dutifully, in the fashion of one telling back a hard-learned lesson.

Raven towered over his companion by a good two hands' worth, and with flowing black hair and curling beard—and branded cheek—Raven looked far more likely to lead a band of human outlaws than Fox. But then, Raven had been a blacksmith, once upon a time.

And Fox had not.

"Another war. And this time, humans won't fight it for them, dying for some damned abstraction. Baligant will banish most of them and we'll take care of the rest. More humans than elves equals no elves. Simple." Fox smiled up at his companion. He would be short in any company; slender and pale and quite as dangerous as a type of blade that did not exist in this or any nearby world.

Tempered steel. Tempered in flame.

"All we have to do is hold this road a year and a day," another man—Yarrow—said.

"That's right." Fox's smile was as sweet as it was infrequent. "Hold this road, keep them out of the Vale of Stars."

And drag Line Rohannan down with Line Floire, lose Baligant two of the most powerful Treasures . . . it would be Chaos come again. *"Disorganized chaos is the worst kind,"* echoed a sudden memory voice. Absent friends, dead loves.

"C'mon," Fox said, a few moments later. He took a last look at the body, at the dull violet bloodstain in the white clay roadbed that would keep any "highborn" who saw it from setting foot on such unlucky ground, let alone using magic to find the killers.

There were some things about magic that Fox liked just fine.

Chapter 10

A New Way to Pay Old Debts

Melior heard the footsteps a scant instant before their cause entered the room.

"I give you good greeting, Cousin—and bring you the Cup of Morning Shadows!" the Lady Jausserande cried. Her spurred and booted steps rang harshly on the inlaid stone floor of Melior's solar. And then she threw it.

Melior did not duck; the missile was not meant for him. It landed with a dull unmusical thud on the carpets at the center of the room and rolled in a forlorn half-circle.

Melior turned away from the standing desk beside the tall narrow window. The late afternoon sunlight struck through the high windows and scattered prismed reflections across the floor and tapestries as Melior walked across the carpet. He bent down and picked up what Jausserande had thrown.

"This," Melior said neutrally, "is the Cup of Morning Shadows."

It was not, of course; merely the shadow of a shadow which—if pushed into the Otherworld in the right time and place—would bring the Cup of Morning Shadows into the world of Chandrakar once more.

As it should now have done.

Jausserande shrugged her saddlepouches to the floor with a thump more eloquent than mere words and began to unbuckle her gorget.

Melior watched as his cousin shrugged her gray-dappled travel cloak to the floor. In peacetime, in a land at peace, she wore no plate, only a sleek white doeskin tunic beneath a shirt of fine-linked silver mail. The mail gleamed silvery in the light as she worked the heavy armored collet free and dropped it, too, on the floor before she spoke.

"No ... just a little something I picked up in the Bazaar for the douce amusement it would give Baligant High Prince when I present it instead of the Cup."

Her words were honeyed-sweet, and her tone the sweet singsong of murderous fury held barely in check. She picked up the decanter from the side table, saw the cups sitting innocently beside it, and lost what was left of her temper.

This time Melior did duck. The wine-filled flagon barely cleared his head, and with marksmanlike accuracy sailed out through the open window. There was an instant's silence, then a distant sound of shattering.

"If you misliked the vintage, Cousin, you had only to say," Melior observed mildly. A low growl was the only response.

Melior turned away, bearing the *tainaiste*-Cup back to the high desk by the window. He looked out and down, to where the decanter was a glittering crimson smear on the courtyard flags. The servants clustering around it looked up, saw him looking, and scattered. Melior continued gazing idly about his demesne, giving Jausserande time to recover herself. His eyes flickered to where the Sword of Maiden's Tears hung upon the wall.

"Oh, yes. Very well for you." Jausserande crossed the room, stray bits of half-unbuckled armor jingling, and took the cup from him. She slid the battered tinny thing inside a fold of her surcoat. She could not meet Melior's gaze, and began to pluck at her gauntlets.

"Well for you," she repeated. "Line Rohannan will appear at the Kingmaking, and all will be well—for Line Rohannan."

"And how long do you think Line Rohannan will stand alone?" Melior asked.

"If Bastard Baligant is what you say, challenge him and make an end to it." One heavy elbow-length gauntlet of gold-stamped scarlet leather fell to the floor, then the other. *Hard work for her squire,* Melior thought to himself, following Jausserande's back trail to collect and restore all her possessions. But Guiraut worshiped her; he'd think the duty no hardship.

"Where is Guiraut?" he asked without thinking.

"Feeding the rooks on the Vale Road," Jausserande said harshly. "He took an arrow through the throat. Meant for me, I think, but in the end it doesn't really matter, does it?"

"How—?"

"There are outlaws living in the Vale, Cousin. And I did not imagine they could be so bold." Jausserande's proud head bowed. She had hoped to award Guiraut his knightly spurs at Midsummer. "We'll try again, Line Floire and I. Next moon, and the moon after that. Until the Kingmaking."

When Line Floire—without the Cup—would be attainted, and the Cup, present or absent, would fall to the High King's hand to bestow upon a more worthy Treasurekeeper. Somehow, Melior doubted that Baligant would be generous.

"I share your sorrow, Cousin," Melior said formally. "And I have made up my mind that I can delay no longer in dealing with that matter of which we spoke. I shall be leaving on a journey tomorrow dawn. You are, of course, welcome to guest at Dawnheart for as long as it takes you to achieve the Cup."

"I shall achieve the heads of those mud-mannikins first," Jausserande said in low tones. "Of your charity, Cousin, a detachment of the castle guard to sweep the forests and the roads. Your outlaws and beggars have become far too bold of late."

"Granted," Melior said, "but only as far as lies between Dawnheart and the Vale. Little though you may credit it, Cousin, they are *my* outlaws and beggars, and I hold myself rather fond of them."

Jausserande made a face of eloquent disgust. "What of Harvest Home? What of Twilight Court?"

"I imagine my tenants can celebrate the Harvest without me. As for the Court, it hardly seems necessary in this time of peace to meet one's enemies beneath the branch of truce and plan the coming slaughter, does it? I have considered how I may best serve the Realm, and there is only one truth I see: I must bring the lady Ruth of the World of Iron to my side."

The calm matter-of-factness of Melior's madness swept Jausserande's grief momentarily aside. To think that Melior set so much store by some mud-born leman that he would—

Do what?

"And how, Cousin, will you bring Ruth from the World of Iron, when you have said that all that way is closed?"

"I shall seek out a wizard."

"A *wizard?*" If anything in Chandrakar could have the power to rouse Jausserande from the contemplation of her own problems, it was such a declaration. Adepts in the Art Magical were one thing: elphen scholars as loyal and trustworthy as any fighting man, masters of the High and Low

Magics both Right and Left, who walked in sunlight, order, and law. Wizards were something else entirely: masters of the Wild Magic who bowed to no law save their own desires. A wizard might belong to any of the Five Races, though it was rare indeed for one of the Sons of the Morning to follow the Wild Magic's path.

"You're going to seek out a *wizard?*" Perhaps she had misheard him.

"Not merely any wizard, but one with whom I have had dealings of old. I know his price; it is high, but I think now that I have no choice but to meet it. I think he will accept my promise as sure coin."

"Bargaining with a wizard!" Jausserande burst out, "For a— A—"

"For the proof that Baligant has tampered with the Treasures," Melior said before Jausserande could say otherwise.

But his cousin was as stubborn as he. "And would this *'proof'* be so desirable, my lord Rohannan, were it not the earthling that you have sworn to be your heartsease? A pretty package, Cousin, when duty is so neatly yoked with expediency."

"And what course would you suggest, Cupbearer?" Melior's tone was distantly formal.

Leave it alone. Baligant's scheme is the air-dream of one on fire for a mortal maid. Jausserande bit her lip, unwilling to speak so plainly. She already knew it would do no good. Melior wanted the mortal for his heart's-bride, even if it was idiocy.

Marry a mud-daughter?

"I would not presume to advise Line Rohannan, my lord," Jausserande said, equally formally. "I wish you a safe and pleasant journey."

Now, if only the wizard would do as he asked, and open the Iron Road so that Ruth could come here. Melior's sturdy dappled gelding, a mount chosen for its steadiness and endurance, stood quietly in the chill of the early morning courtyard as its master made his last minute preparations.

Melior dwelt for a pleasant instant upon the thought of his lady Ruth here in his own world. But more than that, Ruth's arrival would undo the trap that bound the Sword of Maiden's Tears, and reunite Ruth with her pilgrim soul. And in that unbinding and reunion allow Melior to prove how that binding had first been done, proving Baligant's treachery to all who were willing to see.

Melior frowned. For the first time since he had hit upon this certain proof, he was close enough to gaining it to think about what having it might mean. Eirdois Baligant of the House of Vermilion Shadows, High Prince and High King to be, had been the only claimant of the High Seat all the Morning Lords could agree upon; the only one all could bear to gift with, not only the Kingship, but the white body of Hermonicet the Fair. Remove him, and war began again.

Fail to remove him, and see the Seven Houses of Twilight destroyed.

It was not a decision that Melior had a right to make alone, and so he had held his peace even after he knew the truth. But now there was proof to present to the Twilight Court, to set the yoke of this vendetta squarely upon the shoulders of them all.

It was not a vendetta, Melior assured himself. Not yet, at least. He gave one last tug to the girth, not wanting to leave that homely task to his groom.

Melior set his foot in the stirrup and vaulted into his saddle. The groom at the gelding's head released its bridle, and another waiting servant unbolted the postern gate. Melior shrugged the folds of his travel cloak more warmly about himself.

First Ruth, he promised himself, *then all the rest.*

Melior headed his gelding up into the hills, away from the plowed fields and terraced vineyards of his demesne. He did not have far to go—in Chandrakar, at least. The wizard that he sought was not here, though the way to his tower was not hard to find—once you had the key.

Reflexively Melior touched the object hung on the cord about his neck: a little knife barely a hand's width in length, with a hilt of clear amber and a blade of black glass.

A key, if you knew how to use it.

At midday Melior stopped to eat and to give the gelding a rest. He would not reach the place he sought before sunset, and there was no point in reaching it before sunset in any event: this Gate was a complicated one, opening to time, location, and proper tools.

As was the Gate the Cup of Morning Shadows lay beyond.

Would he, Melior wondered, have done any better than Jausserande, were the Cup his quest? She was young, and touchy about her autonomy; newly come to her Wardenship. Floire Glorete had never sought the Cup through all the long years of war, knowing it to be safe in the Vale of Stars. Line Floire had held the Cup since time out of mind; it had been Floire Bertraine who put it there when Rainouart the Beautiful had died, and charged no Cupbearer to come near it until the war was over. Glorete had served her entire tenure without having held her Treasure in her hands.

And now that Jausserande went to claim it, there were brigands in her way, brigands who had slain Guiraut—mostly likely by sheer accident—and now undoubtedly cowered half-mad with terror at their ill fortune. Assuming they were, in fact, honest villains, and not more of Baligant's mischief. Since the peace had been declared and the great armies of each side disbanded, such feral lostlings had become an all-too-common problem for the Morning Lords. Landless, masterless men—human men, whose sires and grandsires and great-grandsires had been raised to war—what was there for them, without place or occupation, but to roam the roads, taking what they could?

Melior shook his head sadly. No matter the reason, he could not permit it. And if the ambush on the road to the Vale of Stars was something more than honest brigandage, he could not permit that either. Baligant would not play his games in Melior's demesne.

Why? It was the question Melior always returned to in the end, the question that eternally baffled him. Baligant already had everything, and still he fought on.

Why?

Melior was not of the generation that had striven so bloodily for those twin prizes: the High Kingship and the white body of Hermonicet the Fair. The earls and barons who had battled for such riches were his uncles and cousins: even Rohannan Lanval had possessed ambitions in that direction, although it was more accurate to say that Melior's father had had firm notions of who should *not* be High King.

Yet he had lived to see Baligant chosen, and said nothing.

Melior frowned, staring unseeing at the half-eaten apple in his hand. Rohannan Lanval had said nothing, but perhaps his reasons had more to do with the reasons for Melior's silence now than with blind cowardice. Perhaps Melior's father had also held his suspicions yet had no way to prove them, and found himself forced to choose between an unjust peace and a just war.

There was no way now to know.

It was, as Melior had intended, just sunset when he arrived at the place of the Gate. The long day's ride had brought him to a place where the grass and trees were replaced by dust and rock—too companionable to be called desolation—and the eye was drawn to the horizon by the first promise of the great mountains to the north. There was nothing on this side of the wizard's Gate to make the location particularly memorable; only four boulders of a mottled dark granite arranged in an irregular circle in a place where the trail widened to obscurity.

Melior dismounted, keeping a firm hold on the gelding's reins. This Gate was one through which a mounted man might pass, and he had no intention of doing any more walking than he had to. He looped the reins about his arm and took the glass and amber knife in his right hand. The gelding nudged at his shoulder curiously as he pulled off his left gauntlet and pushed up the sleeve of his tunic.

Melior glanced around, taking his bearings. The long sunset shadows of the boulders reached out to him, straggling and elongated with the same tricky sunset light that turned the knife's golden amber hilt red.

At the last moment before darkness Melior used the little knife to make a long cut in his left arm.

The wine-violet elphen blood welled up and began to run. Melior caught the first drops on the knife blade, and at once time seemed to stop, and Melior was wrapped in the chill uncanniness of the High Magic.

He made certain the blade was well coated before shrugging his sleeve back into place. Then he sketched a door in the unchanging twilight: high enough for a rider, broad enough for a horse.

Within the area he had marked, Reality fell away as if he had cut a hole in a painted canvas backdrop. The space beyond was jarringly unlike the world he stood in—the sky the wrong blue, the soil the wrong brown. Melior unlooped the reins from his arm and remounted, pressing the cut on his forearm closed before tucking the little knife away against future need. And the gelding stepped, with only a little hesitancy, through the Gate.

* * *

At once everything changed. A thin chill wind plucked at his hair, and Melior pulled the deep hood of his cloak forward to shield himself. It was brighter here than in the day he had just left, but the sky was a deep indigo, crossed by impossible auroras, and Melior had never seen either sun or moon here.

Melior glanced over his shoulder as his mount—steady, dependable, not given to nerves—picked its way along the downward-sloping trail.

Behind him was a cyclopean jumble of white granite cast down from the cliffs above, among which two slabs had been raised as Brobdingnagian gateposts. Beyond them the wide road seemed to roll onward forever, though Melior knew that he had but to ride on for a few leagues to find himself upon it, approaching the Gate again from the direction he had come.

The land around him was mountainous and barren, a place where nothing grew. It ought to have reminded him of the World of Iron, but if it did it was only because of the differences. For the World of Iron was . . . iron, while this was a world whose very bones were made of magic; the small kingdom of an Adept of the Wild Magic, to be entered at one's peril.

Was Ruth worth it? Or Baligant's defeat? Could anyone, could any*thing* be worth coming here?

"Yes," said Melior aloud.

The tension lifted: a soap bubble vanishing. There was the scent of laughter upon the wind. Melior rounded a bend in the trail and saw his goal.

Ahead the road stopped abruptly at the base of a sheer cliff. White as everything was in this world; bone-white and all the colors of shadows. But the cliff was not in shadow. Whatever source this world's light had, the light itself shone full-face upon the cliff.

About halfway up the cliff face there was an opening in the stone; a smooth and regular arch filled with sooty and indigo shadows.

"I am waiting," Melior observed into the emptiness.

"Don't get your bones in an uproar, Child of Air," a voice answered from the air around him. "I'm coming."

But no entity appeared. Instead, the blowing wind stopped and the light shifted, and in that still silence Melior saw the ghostly outline of a phantom staircase, curving upward to the stone doorway.

Melior shrugged within himself, and dismounted. He flung the loop of the horse's reins over the finial of an ornate and barely perceptible newel post and began to ascend the stairs.

Only a soap bubble iridescence betrayed the existence of those stairs; that, and the solidity of the treads beneath Melior's feet. The jagged boulders at the base of the cliff were starkly visible between his boot toes; the balustrade, hard and slick beneath his hand, held all the insubstantial character of water to his eye.

Ophidias had always had a sense of humor, Melior reminded himself. Of a sort.

As he reached the top of the staircase, the wind returned full force. His cloak unfurled with a snap that nearly strangled him, dragging him backward, into the empty air. He pulled it around him, and that, too, was a mistake; the wind found every entrance, filling the fabric as if it were a ship's sail and hauling at him with invisible hands.

Clutching the balustrade with one hand, Melior clawed at the throat latch of the cloak until he had worried it loose. The wind took the cloak with almost sentient glee, snatching it from his shoulders and bearing it off with a long whistling howl.

"You owe me a new cloak," Melior said, taking advantage of the respite to struggle inside.

It was warmer out of the wind, though not by much. The chamber he had entered was long and straight, the walls curving upward and inward until their meeting, if any, was lost in shadow. There was no light. The only illumination came from the tatterdemalion sky behind and the firelike glow ahead.

Melior walked toward the light and entered a chamber of gold.

The walls, floor, and ceiling were made of gold; gold polished mirror-bright, gold wrought in a thousand styles of ornament. The floor of the room was heaped with treasure; treasure spilling carelessly from casks as valuable as their contents; the plundered excellence of a thousand worlds. But the light did not come from the walls, nor from the treasure.

The light came from the room's occupant.

"It took you long enough to think of me," the wizard said.

The wizard Ophidias was not elphen. There were Five Races in the Morning Lands which had the Art of Magic, and of these, Ophidias belonged to the oldest: the People of Fire, who shared with their namesake element the native power to change . . . and to be transformed.

"I thought of your price longer," Melior responded.

The firedrake half-spread his vast wings. His throat and stomach were the pure hot gold of embers; his sides and back the same color but slightly silvered, as if with a fine coating of ash. A pleasant warmth—at least at this distance—radiated off his skin in waves.

"You wrong me, Child of Air," Ophidias commented.

"Then, of course, you'll do what I ask without cost?" Melior responded.

"No," Ophidias said simply. "But you've had a long cold journey—and without a cloak, too. You might as well have some wine and tell me what you want."

One opal-webbed wing spread and gestured to a jade table balanced precariously upon the golden hoard. Atop it was a blue glass beaker webbed in jeweled silver, and a carven pearl cup that could ransom a hundred queens.

Melior unstopped the one and poured its contents into the other. He drank, suspiciously at first, then with real pleasure.

"Did you know," said Melior with as much artlessness as he could muster at short notice, "that the Iron Road is sealed on the Borders?"

"Ridiculous," said the firedrake. He changed position on his treasure and stretched luxuriously. Gold coins shifted and spilled beneath his weight; a cup rolled free with a clinking sound.

"Nearly as ridiculous as this mummer's play of yours. I have seen more convincing deceits on *television*," Melior said, drawing on a term from his recent excursion to the World of Iron.

"Ah, well, if you don't like it . . ." Ophidias waved one polydactyl foreclaw and everything—save the wine table and its contents—vanished.

Including the light.

Considered as a dragon, Ophidias was not especially large; perhaps as large, if you compressed the serpentine neck and the barbed whiplike tail and the vast veined wings, as one of the drafthorses that tilled Melior's acres in Chandrakar.

But a dragon Ophidias was not, any more than Rohannan Melior was human. And considered as a wizard, Ophidias was formidable.

"I thought she'd like it, you see. The expected thing," Ophidias said out of the darkness.

Light reappeared, and now the room was such as might grace any of Melior's own castles. The walls were hung with dark claret velvet. The wizard lay curled on a couch constructed to his special requirements, and regarded Melior from a glowing eye set in a long narrow head of flanged and sculpted chitin.

"Better?" the wizard purred.

"Your skill is, as always, most impressive, Ophidias, but I have not come for entertainment."

"No. You've come to ask a boon. It is a great pity you're going to ask for the wrong thing, since as high as you say my price is, you'll only be able to meet it once."

Melior stood very still. Nothing that a wizard said was idle chatter, and the aid of an Adept of the Wild Magic, bound to no law, was never free. They delighted in tricking any of the Five Races who dealt with them by speaking nothing but the truth, only in a fashion so obscure that their victims never recognized the warning until far too late.

But Ophidias was his friend, and was speaking plainer than most. What Melior had come to ask for—Ruth's summoning into the Lands Beyond the Morning—was the wrong thing to ask for. Ophidias had just said so.

Thus, there must be a right thing to ask for, if Melior could only figure out what it was.

"Then perhaps we should settle on your price first, before we come to the small matter of my request," Melior said with forced ease. He wondered how long he could stall for time.

Ophidias flicked his tail. "Now, how are we to do that, Child of Air, when you haven't told me what you've come for?"

"Surely so great a wizard—" Melior began, and stopped. Surely so great a wizard could indeed peer into Melior's mind and see what he *thought* he had come for—and sell it to him, too, even though what he had come for was the wrong thing.

And asking the wizard what he ought to want would be

just as expensive, Melior suspected, as getting the thing itself.

"—will give a great vintage the respect it deserves?" Melior finished smoothly, sipping the wine.

"Of course," the firedrake agreed, a draconian rumble of mirth in his voice.

Melior reflected with well-concealed irritation that riddling with wizards was nearly as low on his list of fun things to do—as his human friends might have said—as was visiting the World of Iron.

But was that, perhaps, the boon he ought to ask? To go to the World of Iron, and this time bring Ruth away with him? Melior considered that for only a moment. He had failed once and had no greater expectation of success this time, even with his own Adepts to lend him the power to walk out of that most treacherous of all worlds. And the way was now sealed besides, beyond the power of any, Adept or wizard, to unseal it. Which must mean—

"I trust that Ruth will reach Dawnheart in time to enjoy the Harvest Fair?" Melior observed politely.

Ophidias opened his jaws wide, and light poured from his throat. The velvet he lay upon emitted a faint curl of smoke. "Oh, very good, Child of Air. Of all your line, you are the least stupid. Now ask your boon."

The whiplike tail lashed again and the opal-webbed wings mantled. Melior was to be given no more time for delay.

So. Ruth was already in the Lands Beyond the Morning and, all things being equal, could be found with the arts available to Melior's own Adepts, now that he knew where to look.

So what must he ask of Ophidias? Proof of Baligant's treachery? Once he had Ruth, he would have that; with an Adept to unbind her soul from the Sword—

Melior took a deep breath and wished he did not know how plainly Ophidias could see his fear. Ask the boon and he was pledged to pay for it, whether it was something he truly needed or not. The price might be agonizingly high, and he was bargaining with Ruth's life.

"Come once into my land, at a place and time appointed by me, and there unbind Lady Ruth's soul from the Sword of Maiden's Tears, restore her soul to her entire, and make plain to all who watch the Adept who performed the binding." *And*

*let me hang Baligant No-House from Dawnheart's highest
tower. Better death in war than this ravening treachery.*

"A clever little elf," Ophidias said. He spread his wings
and cupped the air, rising from his couch as the room around
him vanished like sands through an hourglass.

Now the room was dark again, the wine cup, the treasure,
the world—all—vanished into this formless potential creation. This was the true state of Ophidias' world: magic
shaped by will.

"Now hear me, elphenborn." The wizard's voice was everywhere: the world was made of words whose power was
greater than swords, and Melior saw Ophidias at their heart
like a bright flame of *logos*.

"What you ask I shall accomplish, but at the price of a
life. For what I do, you will bring a human bride who comes
freely and of her own will to wed with me."

Melior nearly protested aloud. Humans had no magic and
thus were fearful of it; and to become the bride of a wizard,
an Adept of the Wild Magic and a Child of Fire besides, was
a *geas* so daunting that even many an elphen heart would
quail.

Freely. Willingly. Human. Where in all the Lands Beyond
the Morning would Melior find Ophidias' price?

Never mind.

"This I promise to bring you before the day that my first-
born son weds," Melior said, tempering his promise as much
as he dared.

Slowly light returned, until Melior stood once more in the
chamber of golden mirrors that he had first entered. Ophidias stared at him, reptilian muzzle inches away from
Melior's face. Melior felt his skin tighten with the heat that
radiated from the firedrake's body.

"And so you shall, elf-child—because if you don't, your
son's bride will become mine, and everything you hold mine
as well," Ophidias told him. "In this I have no choice,
Rohannan Melior, so mark me well."

"How shall I summon you?" Melior said, ignoring the
wizard's closeness—and as far as he might, the doom he had
bought for Line Rohannan.

The fire-glowing head on the sinuous neck was withdrawn. Ophidias blinked once, causing a momentary flicker
in the room's light.

"A ring is traditional. Cast it into fire, and I will come."
A wing spread, pointed.

A ring lay upon what appeared to be a cloth of finest scale mail. It was a domed band of red gold, and set into it was a smooth-surfaced gem that was the bright clear flame color of the firedrake's eyes.

Melior picked it up. It was almost painfully warm, but he slipped it on his finger anyway. It slid on loosely, then seemed to strop itself against his skin like a contented kitten, settling to a perfect fit.

"Since you seem to have lost your cloak, take this as well. Give it to my bride, when you find her."

Ophidias was enjoying himself hugely, but Melior could not bring himself to object. He turned his back and picked up the armored cloth the ring had rested on.

Ophidias' skin was smooth, but this was not. Melior could not imagine what animal the skin had been taken from, that the perfect pearlfire golden scales should all be the same size, delicate as gilded fingernails. The cloak was not hooded, though heavy enough and more for outdoors. It had a high stiff collar ornamented with more gems of the sort in the firedrake's ring. Melior shrugged it over his shoulders and found that, like mail, the weight was not as great worn as when carried. It was lined and edged with fur softer than *vair* and as red as human blood, and it brushed the backs of his boot heels. Whoever Ophidias' future bride might be, she had better be both tall and strong.

"And now, O great wizard, have I your leave to go?" Melior said. Dealing with wizards was a tricky business, and although he seemed to have survived it, his temper had not.

"Oh, go by all means, Child of Air. Do come again, it is always delightful to see you." Ophidias lay back, fanning himself with lazy wings.

Melior swept the cloak around himself and left the chamber.

Chapter 11

Adventures in the Greenwood

As Ruth had predicted, the heavy green tunics were nowhere near dry when lengthening shadows forced her to admit that they were certainly as dry as they were going to get.

"They'll have to do," Nic pronounced, shrugging into the larger of the two. The trews and clogs that were the rest of their gruesome salvage were hopelessly too small; he settled for the green tunic and the sheepskin leggings gartered over his suit trousers.

The unicorn regarded the transformation from library director to rogue with skepticism. It shook its head and creeled, an odd, unruminant sound.

"I think I agree," Ruth said. She looked at her intended wardrobe of damp scratchy homespun with distaste. Still, her kilt and cashmere shell were almost an invitation to assault from uncouth passersby. For Nic's sake as much as her own she didn't want to get into any more fights. Traveling with the unicorn would draw attention enough.

"All right, all right—I'm going."

Fifteen minutes later Ruth stumped back out of the woods to which she had retreated for privacy. A damp baggy pair of brown homespun trousers were cross-gartered over sheepskins that nearly concealed her brown-and-bone saddle oxfords. A thick leather belt with a carved bone buckle cinched in the soggy wool tunic enough to help the drawstring waist hold the trousers up. She only hoped the things would finish drying quickly—she felt like the Second Murderer; a spearcarrier from any play you cared to name; unkempt and ludicrous.

She hated it.

"Now what?" Ruth said, more than a little crossly.

"Now we follow the stream and see where it takes us. We'll be sure of water, at any rate."

"Travel at night?" Ruth was dubious. Beside her, the uni-

corn's coat shimmered like a silver flame in the dusk. It nuzzled her hand and Ruth patted it absently.

"There's at least an hour of useful light," Nic said ruth-
lessly. "Enough to find a place to bivouac."

But the unicorn, it turned out, had other ideas.

Nic had made himself a staff from one of the spears and
used it to lean on. If the blow to his head still bothered him,
he didn't show it.

He started into the woods in the direction of the stream.
Ruth took one last longing glance behind her at the brighter
open spaces and followed.

The unicorn stood its ground, looking after them beseech-
ingly. And then it—

Well, Ruth wasn't sure how to describe it, but it was loud.
It yodeled like a cat in the throes of a hairball, like a beagle
with its people away for the weekend, like a lovesick pea-
cock and an entire cote of pigeons.

It shut up as soon as Ruth came back.

"I wonder what unicorn steak would taste like?" said Nic,
with admirable restraint but perfect seriousness.

"Come on, Daisy," Ruth said to the unicorn. "We're going
this way."

She put her hand on its neck and tried to lead it. After a
few steps it broke away and skittered to the opposite side of
the clearing, gazing at them reproachfully.

And then it began yodeling again.

Ruth tried making her muffler into a noose and dragging
the unicorn on a leash. Same result.

"Leave it, then," Nic said. "I don't recall asking to travel
with a unicorn anyway."

Ruth hesitated.

"It'll probably give up and follow if it's going to, Ruth."

Reluctantly, Ruth allowed herself to be persuaded. She
followed Nic into the forest. The birds were twittering their
birdish evensong high above, where the topmost tree
branches still caught the last rays of evening light. Under the
forest canopy it was nearly dark. Progress was slow, and
Ruth began to doubt Nic's assertion that they would get any
distance at all. Behind her the unicorn's cries grew louder
and more frantic, and finally stopped. Ruth felt like the sort
of monster usually found tying orphans to railroad tracks for
her desertion.

There was a sudden crashing in the brush ahead. Ruth heard abrupt sibilants as Nic said something rude and heartfelt.

The unicorn stalked out of the thicket before them.

Like any wild thing, its eyes flashed in the half-light: not the silvery-green of the headlight-dazzled deer, but a deep, burning, predatory red. Its silky fur was fluffed out like an angry cat's; its neck stretched long and snakelike as it menaced them in weaving darting motions with its spiraled, dagger-sharp horn.

It was growling.

The unicorn advanced, growling and twisting its neck. Nic began to back up, very slowly. Ruth backed up a bit faster.

It took them very little time to reach the clearing once more, and there the unicorn, like a cat, pretended it had never been the spiky fiend of moments before. It stropped itself against Ruth, crooning its pleasure, and tugged coaxingly at her tunic with teeth sharper than any herbivore should reasonably possess.

Ruth took a couple of steps in the direction of the pull. The unicorn released the cloth and danced away cajolingly, looking back over its shoulder.

"I think it wants us to follow it," Ruth said needlessly.

"Do tell," Nic said. "I don't see a lot of choice—but if this thing is leading us into a trap, I *am* going to have that steak.

Ruth made a strangled sort of half-laughing noise. Shaking her head, she followed the white beacon of the unicorn's body into the woods on the other side of the clearing. And *they'd* been trying to save *it* from hunters!

Nic intended for them only to put a half mile or so between themselves and the unicorn hunters before stopping for the night. The unicorn had other ideas, and wasn't shy about enforcing them.

This left Nic and Ruth with a choice between following the unicorn blindly through the pitch-dark forest, or camping next to something that was howling like a defective smoke alarm and incidentally pointing them out to every emissary of the ungodly within earshot.

They followed. Until, some fifteen hours after seven o'clock Christmas Eve night, the unicorn vanished.

* * *

"I'm immoderately delighted," Nic Brightlaw said in an acid undertone.

"What?" Ruth said. Her hunger had subsided to a slow resentful rumble long since, but lack of food and lack of sleep and the clammy awfulness of her clothes combined with good old-fashioned shock to lend everything a giddy unreality.

"Your damned pet fire siren's gone," Nic said shortly. He took a step forward, and then another. "And so's the forest."

Ruth, leaning wearily against a tree that seemed to be revolving slowly about the Pole Star, decided she couldn't possibly have heard him clearly. "What?" she said again.

"We have reached the end of the forest. Stumps and second-growth ahead, then road, I think. And Fluffy the Wonder Caprid is nowhere in sight."

This seemed to call for more than another monosyllable. "What do we do now?" Ruth asked after a long pause.

"What I wanted to do in the first place," Nic said crossly. "Wait for morning."

Chapter 12

When the Deal Calls for a Sacrifice

The castle was a pale tower of shimmering stone. Once it had belonged to the husband of Hermonicet the Fair. Its name was Mourning.

From a distance the castle bore the appearance of a child's toy discarded thoughtlessly in the marshes that marked the eastern border of Chandrakar. It was the single vertical line in the flat marsh landscape, and what it guarded would be safe forever.

Eirdois Baligant sat within Mourning's walls upon a most comfortable chair of state in a private chamber to which he had brought the most expensive, if not the most tasteful, of his newly-won treasures. The High King-Elect was a little below average height, and his hair was a color that an inhabitant of the World of Iron would not have hesitated to call gunmetal. Before he had been acclaimed High King by the Twilight Court, he had not been accounted handsome, the elvish beauty that was his birthright marred by the decades of dissipation, greed, and anger that had carved his face into the permanent frozen snarl of a cheated bird of prey.

He no longer wore the armor of the soldier's life that had occupied all but his earliest youth. Eirdois Baligant was High King-Elect, and wore silk trousers and jeweled slippers, a velvet robe and furred mantle and rings for every finger. Delicacies from all the world—and worlds beyond—graced his table, and nobles who had once dismissed him as inconsequential now bent reluctant knee at his demand.

Eirdois Baligant was High King-Elect, with the lady Hermonicet the Fair to his wife. He had everything it was possible to want within Chandrakar's borders. The Kingship, Hermonicet—and soon enough his enemies would be gone, on the very day of the Kingmaking that would set the seal on his triumph.

If only there weren't something he felt he might be forgetting.

It was not that he was not content—or rather, it was not that his discontent was disturbing to him, for Baligant knew himself better than some, and knew his appetites could only be deadened for a time, never slaked. That the High Kingship itself would not content him he knew; but he knew also that the High King has endless opportunities for fresh, inventive revenges, and Baligant was by nature vindictive.

He knew these things about himself and many more, having lived quite long enough to become well acquainted with his own measure of what other men called faults. To avarice he would also admit, and held that such admission rendered him superior to those who lusted and coveted and swore that they did not. In his own narrow fashion, Baligant was a shrewd and honest prince, and if Fate had fitted him admirably for a pawnbroker and then turned him loose upon the stage of greater events, this was not his fault.

Baligant rose from his chair and began to pace about the room, marking his path by the treasures which lay along it. Each of them had once belonged to someone else, and not one of their former owners would have had an approving word to say of Eirdois Baligant were he not the High King. Elect.

But at the moment Baligant felt very much like the laborer who, having worked long and hard, discovers that the coin he has been paid in is false. Baligant was honest enough to assign that fault to no one—he was to be High King, and it would be foolish to complain that the High King was ruler of a land spoiled by three generations of war.

And besides, he would tax it as if it flourished.

Baligant smiled. Let them complain—the alternative to obedience was war.

And Baligant had seen the war, every year of it—from the beginning, when every lord called up his *meinie* to wage what would surely be only the briefest of battles, to the end, when even the slights and cruelties and betrayals of a century of war could not keep the earls from negotiating their secret treaties of peace. Even the loss of the white body of Hermonicet the Fair could not incline them to battle once more.

And if they would not fight for her, they would not fight.

He could do as he liked, until the grandchildren of this generation were grown.

And by then it would be too late for the Seven Houses of the Twilight. Far too late.

Baligant smiled.

"Lord Baligant?" The voice was hesitant, but that was as it should be. He was in his private chamber, and no one would disturb him there without overriding necessity.

That was power.

He turned, prepared to show a terrifying arrogance.

"My lord?"

It was his wizard. His *pet* wizard.

Her name was not Amadis, but it was what he had been given to call her. Her hair was long and silken, and her form was slender and lithe, and these, too, were not necessarily truth.

What was true was that Baligant didn't care. For someone who trusted all his plans to his captive wizard, Baligant truly knew very little about her. But he knew the two things that mattered. He knew she was an Adept of the Wild Magic.

And he knew about the flowers.

He let her wait for his pleasure, studying her while he wondered—not for the first time—how it would be to be more to her than her master. But he was smart enough not to attempt it. That small thing might be the one thing that would tip the balance of binding and obligation and free her.

And he meant never to free her.

Amadis swayed in the doorway, and Baligant noted with pleasure the green shadows beneath her skin; the hollowed, fever-bright eyes. She had been too long away from the flowers.

"Yes?" he said at last. "I hope this is important."

Fury gave her strength; Baligant saw it flare in her eyes as it brought her body rigidly upright. Her eyes were a brilliant copper a few shades darker than her hair; Baligant wondered (again, not for the first time) if the elphen form she wore were her own. So few Daughters of the Twilight had any talent for the Wild Magic.

But if Amadis were truly talented, mere elphenborn would not have been able to trap her.

"You may find it so," Amadis said briefly. "The soul-anchor I set upon the Sword of Maiden's Tears has broken

loose from the World of Iron. The Sword has been carried
out of this world through a Gate that is not charted in my
ephemeris. If both the Sword and the soul-anchor are in motion through the Lands, they will meet. That is the Law."

"What do I care if one vermin-infested mud-daughter
finds her way out of the World of Iron?" Baligant blustered,
beginning to fear.

His wizard didn't answer—didn't need to answer, because
Baligant already knew. In tampering with the Sword, perhaps the greatest of the Treasures, Amadis had left evidence
that tampering had been done. And the heart and triumph of
Baligant's plan lay in that his wizard's meddling should
never be discovered by the elphen Houses that it doomed.

"Kill her," Baligant said simply.

The wizard did not answer. The hot bright anger that had
animated her had ebbed. She put out a long pale hand to
steady herself, the gesture echoing the unfolding of a drag-
onwing.

"But perhaps you'll want a stirrup cup to speed you on
your journey?" Baligant smiled, unease dissolved in cruelty.
This was his private chamber. The flowers were here.

He went to his desk and opened a jar. The moment he did,
sunlight and high summer seemed to radiate from it, warm-
ing the chill autumn day. He plunged his hand into the jar,
pulling out a fistful of dried flower heads.

"Is this what you want?"

He held them out. The wizard drifted closer, an unwilling
serpent drawn to his piping. She stared at the crushed flowers with hungry despair.

"Not to your taste?" He held his hand over the jar, preparing to drop the flowers back in, and was rewarded by the
sound of a whimpering gasp from the wizard.

"If you'd control your temper better, Amadis, you'd get
more of what you want." He smiled, feeling the heat of the
wizard's hatred wash over him like the wave of a summer
sea. She wanted his death. But she didn't want it quite badly
enough.

"On the other hand, you did tell me about the Sword," he
said, relenting.

Baligant picked up a small dagger from the table. He cut
the hand that held the flowers once, very carefully, and
watched as his blood welled up and began to soak the crum-
pled petals.

Let no man say I have not shed blood for Chandrakar.
"Is this what you want?"

He held his hand out to her. The dried flowers were saturated and sticky with his blood, their pale ivory petals stained a swollen blood-red.

The wizard Amadis snatched the flowers from his hand and crammed them into her mouth, gulping and choking on them. A thin trail of bloody saliva flowed down her chin and dripped onto her long white gown. She held both hands over her mouth, hiding behind them, licking them clean.

She turned away.

"Amadis? Kill the Ironworlder before she reaches the Sword," Baligant said genially. He wiped his bloody hand upon his tunic, staining the costly delicate fabric.

Chapter 13

Traveling in an Antique Land

The world was called Counterpane.

Ruth sat on the bench outside the country inn, quaint as a Brothers Grimm woodcut, and let the pale morning sun bake the midnight chill out of her bones. Counterpane. Her store of local information was increased by one hundred ludicrous percent. It was—she sought through a jumbled trove of J-book memories—straight out of *A Child's Garden of Verses*. Something that started "I used to go to bed by day ..."

Which did not, at the moment, seem like a bad idea.

She and Nic had slept the few hours until dawn huddled against each other for warmth like the proverbial Babes in the Wood. They were awakened by the sound of cart wheels rumbling along the road, and in the early daylight the two of them crouched in the underbrush at the side of a road and watched as a barrel-filled, wooden-wheeled cart drawn by four oxen rolled magisterially past. A drover dressed much as Ruth and Nic were walked at their heads.

Almost as soon as it had rolled out of sight, another party came down the road, this time on horseback.

The two in the lead were riding gray horses the improbable color of polished steel. In contrast to the earth-toned world Ruth had seen so far, the knights—somehow they looked to Ruth like knights—were in technicolor: their horses' reins were tasseled with bright multicolored flags that matched the colors in their long fringed saddlecloths, and their riders were bright and brave in sweeping feathered hats, long colored boots, striped hose, and brilliant silken tabards over white shirts trimmed in lace. Behind them, on a horse of a different gray and far less fine, rode a bare-headed young man with a plain dark vest over his laceless shirt, leading a white mule piled high with wrapped bundles, including two long canvas-wrapped ones that Ruth thought looked like skies but considering everything were probably lances.

"They look like what the SCA would do if it had money," she muttered half aloud. Nic nudged her warningly.

One of the knights reined in and stared in their direction. His companion, finding himself riding on alone, looked back and said something that Ruth was too far away to hear. After a moment more, both knights rode on.

But the squire, too, paused to stare. And without a floppy hat and trailing feathers to get in the way, Ruth could see that his ears rose to delicate points and his slit-pupiled eyes were cat-green.

Nic gently but firmly put a hand over Ruth's mouth.

The party of elphen knights rode on.

When it was entirely quiet once more, he let her go.

"Vulcans," Nic said.

"Elves," said Ruth.

"Whatever."

After that they had cautiously taken to the road themselves—once Nic had unwound the bandage around his head and scrubbed away as much blood as he could with the heavy morning dew. Half his blond hair was stained a rusty brown, but he looked much more conventional without the bandage than with it.

Once they began, Ruth discovered how many aches and pains you could have after walking all night and sleeping in a ditch. Her only consolation was that since she never wore makeup, leftover mascara was not now making dark rings under her eyes.

"Ah-hah," Nic said, after about an hour's walking. Ruth looked up. He pointed, and Ruth's gaze followed the direction of the pointing finger.

If there were buildings in Elphame at all, Ruth imagined they must be tall, airy Gothic cathedral structures entirely constructed from gleaming white marble with tasteful accents of granite and maybe rock crystal, with silk pennons flapping in the breeze and every single copper-sheathed turret roof foiled in gold.

Of course, if that were true, this wasn't Elphame.

"The Last Homely House," Nic said.

"Get real," Ruth said weakly. But the building did bear a

weird and irritating resemblance to a Professor Tolkien set piece.

The building was set back a few hundred yards from the edge of the road on the right side, with a wide beaten-dirt courtyard before it. The building itself was made of wood planks weathered to gray, with a flat turf-covered roof that angled sharply backward, giving it an outline not inconsistent with that of certain Dairy Queens in Tulsa, Oklahoma. There were no windows at all in the front wall, just a whitewashed door beneath a carven lintel. There was a bench on either side of the door, each rough-hewn from a single plank. Both were empty.

"Give me all your money," Nic said.

Ruth obediently dug into the belt-pouch that had come with her new outfit, rummaging until she retrieved the handful of chump change bequeathed her by its previous owner. She held it out to Nic.

He turned over a couple of the coins as dubiously as if he'd never seen them before, and slid the whole into his belt-pouch. He looked at Ruth and shrugged.

"Let's go buy some information."

They crossed the road and the inn yard, and stopped a few paces away from the door.

"You stay here," Nic said, pointing to the bench. Ruth—much against her inclinations—began to protest. Nic put a hand on her shoulder, shoving until she sat.

"Look," he said. "I can't watch you and them at the same time, Miss Marlowe. If this turns out to be more unicorn hunters, you're the one with the allies and connections here in Wonderland. So if I don't come out . . ."

"What?" Ruth asked, because he'd stopped.

"Run like hell," Nic said, and grinned.

Ruth sat down, and within a few minutes found herself fighting not to fall asleep.

A few minutes later Nic came out again. His hair was wet and slicked back, all traces of blood removed, and he carried a battered leather mug and a slab of coarse dark bread that had a slab of soft white cheese balanced on top of it. He handed them to Ruth.

"Welcome to the canton of Counterpane," Nic said, "which is one of the Borderlands—I hope I have the emphasis right—that the Iron Road runs through. This is the Merry Grigot, and its main business is serving traders. Business has been bad this spring—no caravans—and the innkeeper isn't sure why. What he does know is that some lord from one of 'the inward lands' has been crossing borders in a rather high-handed fashion, throwing his weight around."

"My, haven't you been busy," Ruth said peevishly. She took a hesitant drink from the quart-sized leather mug. It smelled like apples and had a vinegary, bubbly taste with a burning afterkick. Hard cider. She followed it with a bite of bread and cheese.

"Basic recon. Apparently they're used to all kinds of strangers through there, so neither of us should attract much attention. The name Counterpane mean anything to you?"

"A counterpane is a bedspread, if that's what you mean," Ruth offered. "Melior said he came from Chandrakar. He didn't exactly run through *Baedeker's Guide to the Perplexed.*"

"Cheer up, Miss Marlowe. Apparently you *can* get there from here," Nic said, before going back inside.

Ruth sat and drank her cider, wishing for a number of things that started with a shower and clean clothes and ended with her toothbrush. And now, because it had suddenly become possible, and because it didn't look as if she and Nic were going to get thoroughly killed any time in the near future, she thought about what she was going to say to Melior the next time they met.

She loved him, and she was pretty sure her feelings hadn't changed. But while feelings didn't change, situations did.

He hadn't come back for her, though it had taken her a long time to give up hope. Had Rohannan Melior accepted that he would never see her again, settled down with a nice second-best elf-princess, and gotten a steady day job, whatever his sort of day job might be?

Or had he not come back for her because he was dead? He'd said he had enemies. One of the traps they'd set for him had dumped him onto 116th Street in little old New York. The next might have been fatal.

These thoughts were not new, but always before Ruth had been able to bury them deep beneath the impossibility of ever finding out the end of the story. But now she was here in the Morning Lands, and it seemed very likely that she'd find out.

And which of the three possibilities—married, dead, or

ready to take up where they left off—distressed her most, Ruth was not prepared, at this time, to say.

She wondered if a real person—with a whole soul—could have made an easier choice.

She finished her bread and cheese and cider, and set the leather mug beside her on the sun-warmed bench. After a while a boy appeared from around the back of the inn, collected it, and skittered off again. He returned a short while later leading a saddled horse, and a traveler in a dark cloak came out the front door, mounted, and road away. No one gave Ruth any more notice than if she had been a part of the wall.

Eventually she did fall asleep.

A hand on her shoulder woke her. Ruth started awake with a gasp to find Nic Brightlaw gazing mildly down at her. The sun was higher in the sky; nearly noon.

He placed a cloth-wrapped bundle on her lap.

"Your lunch, Miss Marlowe. C'mon, let's move."

Ruth opened the bundle. More bread, more cheese, a couple of apples and a slab of over-roasted meat.

It looked delicious. She extracted the meat and shoved the rest into a vest pocket for later.

"Yeah, right. Where?" She stood up, biting into the meat.

Nic started for the road. He gave her time to catch up before he answered.

"Oh . . . you might call it the Unfair Faire Affair."

Chapter 14

The Fox and the Hounds

Poets might have called it the greenwood, and maybe a hundred years after the event a highly-colored romanticized version of events would make its way into the popular songs. And then again, maybe not.

Fox was bored.

He lay at full length among the birches that covered the ridge and looked down on the pass into the Vale of Stars. The noonday silence was broken only by the chirr of cicadas, and the deep blue unpolluted sky was occupied only by a pair of soaring hawks.

Several hundred yards behind him and down the ridge was their village; half a dozen rude structures made of green birch saplings bent into semicircles and then covered over with peeled bark and animal hides. Warm enough, even in winter, with half a dozen fellow sleepers, but Fox was fastidious by nature and craved more solitude than this rusticity was likely to give him.

Nominally he was on watch. And should anything in fact appear on the road that led to the Vale of Stars, the willow whistle he wore on a cord around his neck would gather his men around him soon enough.

Absently Fox scratched himself inside the leather jerkin where the summer sweat made a tingling itch along his ribs. Leather might be fine to pick up girls in, but it wasn't as comfortable as a cotton shirt. Even homespun would be better.

But outlaws couldn't get cloth at all, even the coarse homespun that the cottage weavers made. And as for cotton and linen, silk and velvet, they were woven on giant waterdriven looms in the market towns of the north for the sole consumption of the elf-lords and their favorites.

Fox sighed for what he couldn't have, and returned his mind to his current problem. He'd been slow enough learning the lesson that all good generals knew—that the bone and sinew of an army is people. Fox hadn't had much use for people—before. To be perfectly frank, he'd always thought most of them were extremely stupid, and in this belief he had not been disappointed by later experience. His merrie outlaw band, Fox estimated, was about as thick as two short planks. And that was on a *good* day.

But never mind. He needed them. And he had a much better idea now than he'd once had of how to make people do what he wanted them to.

Up to a point.

A waiting game was the strongest tactical position, and all very well for fellows like Wellington and Alexander who commanded a paid army that actually wanted to be there. Fox had a collection of followers who were with him only because they couldn't be somewhere else. They'd been taxed out of existence, driven from their homes, and generally disenfranchised—and far from having instilled in them by these vicissitudes a steely spine and a martial nature, all they really wanted was to be left alone.

But even if he were willing to let them sit in the shrubbery and rot, he didn't have that luxury. Without a goal, his semblance of leadership evaporated, and without leadership, the Merries would just wander off and get caught—or be sitting ducks when their numbers became too large for their former masters to ignore.

And that time—despite all Fox had done to delay it—was coming soon. His fame was spreading. Every month brought a scattering of new recruits. If his outlaws could not manage to fight when they were attacked, he had called them together only to see them slaughtered.

And though that thought would not have bothered him before, it bothered him now.

They had to be able to fight—and more than that, they had to be willing. He needed some cheap and easy victories to weld them into a unit. And it wouldn't hurt, not at all, if this cloud-castle victory allowed them a change of fare from venison, rabbit, and dandelion greens.

Besides, he thought the point-ears were getting it a bit too much their own way. He was keeping the blonde elf-bimbo away from the Cup, true, but what if he could do better than that?

What if he could *get* the Cup?

* * *

"Okay, is everybody clear on what's going on here?" Fox squatted on his haunches over the improvised sand table and pointed at the diagram with a peeled twig.

"Dawnheart's here. The village is over here. The market sets up in this flat place between the village and the castle, but the Harvest Fair won't be there—it's too big. It's going to set up over *here,* on the water meadow just beyond the castle."

He'd made up his mind to raid the Harvest Fair because his skittish band of rebels needed a cheap and easy victory, and what could be easier than pillaging a bunch of unwarlike merchants? Besides, Fox had found out that there was something called the Harvest Truce, which meant that nobody on the Fair's grounds would be armed.

Except Fox. And his band of merrie men, of course.

"What if they open the dyke?" Raven asked.

"The river's too low to flood the meadow this time of year. Even if we're close to the castle, we're out of bowshot—and even if they could get siege engines up onto the catwalks, they won't be able to fire into the middle of the Fair without fragging a couple hundred civilians. Which I don't think they'll do."

"What about magic?" another man asked. He was branded on both cheeks—poaching, a first offense.

This was something Fox had worried about himself, being largely ignorant of the workings of magic. But most of his outlaws had seen service on a battlefield where magic was in use, and he had listened carefully to their talk.

"They aren't expecting trouble. Magic takes time. As long as we're fast, we're safe—and once we're back to the Vale of Stars they can't even track us."

The others laughed at this, and Fox felt their tension ease, to be replaced by confidence. And once they saw that a strike at their former overlords brought no reprisals, they'd be bolder.

And so would every other human in Chandrakar.

Yippee, thought Fox dourly. *We're finally going to do something.*

"Okay, guys. We'll move out as soon as the moon is up. We hit the Fair tomorrow at dawn. And remember—the goal is a horse for every man."

The gathering around the sand table broke up. Fox took a

last look at his careful map, running one more time over escape routes and pitfalls, before scrubbing the sand smooth again. By this time tomorrow he'd either have proof that he was as good as he thought he was, or he'd be dead.

Of course, maybe he'd be both. There was always that possibility.

Fox sighed. None of this was going quite the way he'd planned, back when he'd begun. He'd wanted some basic surgical first-strike revenge against elvenkind in general and Rohannan Melior of the House of the Silver Silences in particular.

So you build the tools to build the tools to build the weapon to wage the war. And if it takes long enough, you can even forget what you're fighting for. Isn't that fun?

Chapter 15

The Road Goes Ever Onward

He was lost.

Ridiculous.

Nonetheless.

Rohannan Melior—Marchlord, Swordwarden, Treasure-keeper, Baron Rohannan of the House of the Silver Silences—reined his gelding to a halt yet again.

Lost. Lost, and the Sword of Maiden's Tears with him. Lost somewhere. Lost some*when*.

To pass through any of the Gates was to play with time. At its simplest, Time ran faster the closer one came to the World of Iron, and slower the farther away one got, until one reached the Timeless Lands where Time did not exist at all. Pass through a Gate and gain—or lose—a day, a week, a month—or more. And when dealing with the Wild Magic, be grateful it wasn't still more.

But he had thought to lose those days to threshold-*teind,* and not to a wizard's prank that seemed neatly designed to make him take the long way home.

And he had been so sure that Ophidias stood his friend.

Melior had left the wizard's lair wrapped warmly in his borrowed troth-cloak, the bargain-ring on his finger. He had ridden through the ice-pale world with its lying sky and back through the hills to the bleached bone Gate. He had seen the Gate, and clucked encouragingly to his mount, and ridden through the arch at a jog-trot.

And come here. Wherever it was. It was not Chandrakar in autumn, nor any of her neighboring Lands. Nor yet did it seem to be any of the Borderlands—Cockaigne, Broceliande, Amalur, Counterpane—that lay along the Iron Road to Earth. Gislaine had said that road was closed anyway; there was nothing for him there.

Yet if Ophidias had not lied—and no wizard, whose magical Self was created entirely through the Word, *could* lie—

then Ruth had crossed that border before it closed, and wandered now in the Morning Lands.

Perhaps she was here?

Melior gazed about the wholly unfamiliar countryside, nameless and unknown despite his magical attempts to find one of the *leys;* the power-lines that would lead him to a Gate or to the Iron Road itself. A fair land, a pleasant land—but not the one he wanted, unless it held his lady.

Melior frowned. Ruth was no longer in the World of Iron. Ruth was here. Here, lost, alone, and—if he knew his Ruth—highly indignant about it all.

And so easy to kill, did anyone know who and what she was. And if she died, far more than Melior's heart would die with her. The chance to publish Baligant Baneful's treachery would die as well, and that must not be.

A man who made slow decisions would not have lived to grow older in wartime. Almost as the thought came to him, Melior had drawn the Sword of Maiden's Tears and held it before him. The bare blade shone blue in the daylight as Melior balanced it cautiously upon his gloved palms.

Perhaps he was foolish in thinking that the Sword could help him now. He was no magician, nor, it seemed, was he adept in dealing with wizards.

But for good or ill, the Sword was linked to Ruth Marlowe through her stolen soul. And Ruth was freed from the World of Iron, and walked a world as filled with magic as the Ironworld was filled with electricity.

The pommel-piece of the Sword glinted, a giant drop of frozen fire. Melior breathed a Word across it, his breath misting the polished steel on its blade. He felt the *dweomer* gather power as it left his lips, and slowly the Sword swung its ponderous weight gracefully upon his hands, until the pommel-stone pointed distinctly in a direction it had not pointed before.

Melior marked it, then flung the Sword up and caught it by the hilt in a theatrical gesture that would have much surprised his lady-cousin, who thought him dull and peace-bound. And then he clapped his heels to the sides of his surprised mount, and took off across the meadow, once more upon a quest.

Chapter 16

The Unfair Faire Affair

"If you don't mind a little vulgar curiosity," Ruth said, "just what *is* the Goblin Market? Other than a poem by Christina Rossetti, of course."

It was late afternoon on the High Road. Ruth's feet hurt, but not to the exclusion of rational thought. Their superfluous garments were bundled in Ruth's cloak and Nic had lashed it across his shoulders like a pack. Life was good. In fact, nothing had tried to kill either of them since, oh, this time yesterday.

After leaving the inn, they had walked in what seemed to Ruth to be a more-or-less easterly direction. They'd left the road three more times to make way for parties of travelers, but no one had stopped them or tried to question them.

"The Goblin Market, according to mine host," Nic replied, "is something supposed to be so well known in these parts that you'll appreciate that I couldn't ask too many questions about it. The caravans travel with special scouts whose specific job is to guide them away from it. From what I gathered, it's some sort of navigational hazard that dumps you off course and slides you across Borders."

"Which would make it pretty ideal," Ruth said slowly.

Nic smiled without humor. "If crossing Borders is what you're after, the Goblin Market sounds like the place to go. The only question I have is how to find it. By the way, we're being followed."

Nic spoke so casually that by the time the words sank in Ruth didn't react at all—which had probably been his intention, damn him anyway. Just let them get somewhere safe and she was going to have a number of tough questions for Nicodemus Brightlaw, Boy Library Director.

Of course, she had no idea how she could make him answer them.

"Followed," Ruth said, in admirably even tones.

"In the woods, off to the left."

His voice was pitched lower now, so that only Ruth could hear.

This time she did look, as casually as she knew how, and saw nothing but what she had seen all along: the beige, slightly-rutted dirt of the road, the grassy verge with its sharp drop-off into the reed-filled ditch, the expanse of grass on the other side, now mixed with bushes and skinny trees that became bigger trees with no bushes until the forest proper began. All the trees were in the full leaf of summer; you could hide two armies and a three-ring circus in that woods in perfect concealment.

I don't see anything, Ruth thought of saying, and rejected the remark as idiotic. "What are you going to do about it?" she said instead.

"That looks like a nice place to have lunch," Nic said irrelevantly. He gestured at the road ahead, where the grassy verge widened into a semicircle bordered by the forest. Wagon ruts and burned circles on the grass showed where other travelers had taken advantage of this Otherworld rest stop.

"Yeah, sure," Ruth said under her breath. But dutifully she followed Nic off to the side of the road.

He untied the improvised pack from around his shoulders and spread it out on the ground for a blanket. "Miss Marlowe," he said, and Ruth bobbed him a mock-curtsy and sat down.

She dug out the remains of the lunch Nic had bought her at the inn and bit into an apple. The taste was sweet and tart, mouthwateringly strong, and Ruth suddenly remembered something else about the poem "The Goblin Market": the warning it contained against eating Otherworldly fruits.

But it doesn't matter. I'm not going back to Ippisiqua no matter what happens. She took another bite of the apple and bent to unlace her shoes.

"If you take those off, you'll never get them back on," Nic observed. He squatted on his haunches, watching her. Ready to move in any direction. "Your feet will swell."

"I don't care," Ruth said, trying not to sound sulky about it. He was only annoying because he was right, of course.

She unlaced the furry cross-gaiters and pulled off her bone-and-brown saddle oxfords, and then, for good measure, the blue cashmere argyle kneesocks that went with them.

Her skin was winter-white, unseasonable. She took another bite of her apple.

"Have it your way. I'm going for a walk."

Nic's voice was bland. As always. Ruth watched him amble away toward the edge of the wood, the picture of unconcern, and wondered what it would be like to hear real emotion in his voice. She wriggled her toes defiantly in the grass, savoring the coolness, and finished her apple. She flung the core in his general direction, careful not to come remotely close. Emotion scared Ruth. It always had.

Not always.

As if it had only been waiting for this break in her concentration, her mind directed Ruth's attention back to that eternal sore spot: the years Ruth had spent . . . asleep. The nothingness after the accident that had stolen eight years of her life.

She did not remember how it had happened. That had been left for others to tell her, and none of them could tell her how she had felt, what she had thought.

1981. Ruth had been seventeen. She—and Jimmy, and Allen, and Kathleen—had been going to the Senior Prom. Jimmy had his father's convertible. There was dinner before, at an expensive restaurant, then the Prom itself, and afterward about twenty of them had been going back to Kathleen's house to party till dawn.

Or so Ruth had been told afterward. She didn't remember the month before the Prom; her graduation; or even why she'd bought the dress she had. She had a picture of it; a Polaroid her folks had taken when Jimmy came to pick her up. Yards of pink tulle, in every shade from baby's breath to flamingo. Fourteen years later she still wore her hair the same way; long, parted in the middle.

The need to know the truth ground against the unshakable reality that she would never know the truth. Those memories were gone, destroyed by the same thing that had pushed her into the coma.

Because somehow, somewhere, between the Prom and the party, there was a car accident, and nobody ever knew why for sure. There was no other car, no sign of anything except that Jimmy Ramirez had put the pedal to the metal and rammed a tree at something over sixty miles per hour.

Everyone else was killed. Ruth had been thrown clear, to

dream the next eight years of her life—all her young adult-hood—away.

The newspapers Ruth read ten years later said Jimmy must have been drinking. When she'd come out of her coma, her father had said the same thing. At the time, confused about so many things, she accepted what she was told. Ruth's memories of Jimmy were vague, like old photographs seen through carnival glass, but one thing she eventually remembered with certainty was that he couldn't have been drinking. Jimmy Ramirez' older brother had been an alcoholic. Jimmy didn't smoke, didn't pop, didn't drink anything stronger than Coca Cola.

And this was a hell of a time to dredge up ancient history.

Except that it wasn't ancient history, according to Melior. According to Melior, Ruth's soul had been stolen while she lay in that hospital bed, stolen and used to tie the Sword of Maiden's Tears to the World of Iron, so that it would fall into that last of all possible worlds, unrecoverable.

Only Melior *had* recovered it, and without enough magic to repair the damage, had taken the Sword—and, Ruth supposed, her soul—away with him again.

What could she say to him when—if—she saw him again? What could she say?

Ruth lay back, staring up at the wispy cloud trails in the sky. It was just for a moment. She should keep a lookout for Nic, and for whatever was following them. If anything.

Ruth slept.

"C'mon, Jimmy—we're going to be late!"

"Party can't start till you get there, Kath!" Jimmy shot back, laughing. He made a great show of searching for the car keys through all his pockets—the cummerbund and bow tie of his rented tux in his other hand—and then when he found them, tossed them up in the air and made a production out of scrambling to catch them. Ruth snickered.

Ruth Marlowe was sure that Jimmy Ramirez was the handsomest man she'd ever seen, and even though they knew perfectly well they didn't love each other, they both enjoyed the looks they drew as a couple. After tonight their paths would diverge: Ruth to college, Jimmy to work in his father's gas station. But tonight that didn't matter.

Jimmy finally opened the car—it didn't matter, really, since it was his dad's almost-a-classic-car convertible and

*the top was down, but Kathleen's dress fit like one of her
mom's old panty-girdles from her armpits to her knees and
she couldn't exactly climb over the side of the car. Allen
handed Kath in and she slid across the seat and then Jimmy
walked around the car and opened the door for Ruth.*

*She tossed her head, flirting with him, both of them know-
ing it was all for show. He'd brought her a corsage of white
roses to go with her dress and Mom had pinned it into her
center-parted hair. Her ombréd-tulle dress swirled around
her calves, and her satin pumps were dyed to match the
darkest shade of pink in it. They had glittering rhinestone
buckles on them that matched her earrings, and Ruth could
not imagine a future occasion on which she would be so perfectly dressed. She got into the car. Jimmy closed the door.*

*There was a shortcut to Kath's place—a back road, not
very well lit, not exactly two lanes wide, although everyone
pretended it was. It was one in the morning, and real unlikely that anyone else would be on it. Ruth held her hair in
place with her lace shawl and shivered deliciously in the
whipping midnight slipstream.*

There was a flash of light in the road ahead.

*"Shit," Jimmy muttered, thinking of cops, of tickets, of his
dad's refusal to ever let him borrow the car again. But the
lights weren't flashing red-and-blue. It was a coppery fiery
light, and Ruth, straining her eyes, suddenly saw—*

"Nuh—*oh!*" Ruth struggled awake, pulled by terror and a
feathery, whiskery touch on her cheek. She opened her eyes,
and the meaning of the dream dissolved into spangled fragments, leaving only the fear behind.

Her unicorn was looking down at her, blue eyes wide and
pink nostrils flaring. Around its neck it wore a garland of
flowers, each bloom the bright intense improbable color of
one of the Crayolas in the Deluxe 64 Color assortment. The
scent pouring off them suggested that someone had
machine-gunned the perfume counter at Bloomingdale's. It
nuzzled her again.

"Yag," said Ruth, and forgot her dream entirely. She
struggled to a sitting position. The unicorn backed up politely and sat down, looking rather like a large friendly dog
that happened to have hooves and a single horn growing out
of its forehead.

"Where have *you* been?" Ruth asked it. She stood up, wincing as she put weight on her bare feet. Nic had been right, of course; her feet were swollen. If she'd known she was coming to Elfland, she would have worn hiking boots.

The unicorn got to its feet and shook itself all over. It trotted a little ways away and looked back over its shoulder hopefully.

"Oh, no. Not this time." Ruth looked around. Where was Nic? "Hello?" she said tentatively.

The unicorn trotted back to her and nudged her arm. Urgently.

Oh, the hell with it. "Nic!" Ruth shouted at the top of her lungs. The unicorn added its trilling bugle to her shout and then looked at her expectantly. Ruth shook a minatory finger in its face.

"We are not going anywhere without Nic. We started out with Nic, and we are finishing up with Nic, whether you like him or not. And, really, you ought to be a little grateful."

The unicorn was unimpressed.

"And where did you get those flowers anyway? A secret admirer?" Ruth reached out to touch the flowers. The unicorn skittered back just out of reach.

Ruth looked around, turning her whole body to do so. Where was Nic? If what had been following them was the unicorn, then he wouldn't have been able to catch it, but he would have come back. And if it hadn't been the unicorn that was following them, had Nic met up with what was?

And what happened then?

"Damn," Ruth said inadequately. And everything had been going so well just five minutes ago.

With quick angry motions she bundled the cloak and its contents back together as she'd seen Nic do and yanked on her socks. Getting her shoes back on took more determination, but Ruth was mad enough now not to care how much it hurt.

Or, to be honest, scared enough. But mad was better. She'd rather be angry than scared, any day.

"*Nic!*" She looked around hopefully, but he didn't appear. It was, to coin a cliché, later than she'd thought. The sun would be setting in a few hours, heralding the start of another wonderful night spent sleeping on the ground in her clothes with no blankets. "Nic! Nico*demus*!"

She'd give him one last chance to show up before she really lost her temper.

But he didn't, and secretly she'd known he wouldn't. Nic Brightlaw thought she had survival skills one notch above those of free-range linoleum. He would not leave her alone for this long if he'd had a choice.

Unless, of course, he's simply abandoned you.

"Cute, Ruth. Real cute. C'mon, Fluffy. Let's go hunting."

Chapter 17

Midnight Is a Place

The tower was in no place, at no time. And that was precisely the way its lady liked things. To age meant to change, even for the Sons of the Morning and the Daughters of the Twilight.

And the lady liked herself just the way she was.

Here in her tower, time passed just as she wished it to. Quickly, slowly, backward . . . or not at all. Here she dreamed and made her plans, and wielded the small subtle weapons that bent the great and powerful to her will.

A small thing, in the midst of war, to single out Baligant No-House and put into his mind the thought to hide the Treasures. Easier still, to direct him to the Adept who could aid him in this—the Adept whose weakness she had discovered.

And no trouble at all to conceal from Baligant the fatal idiotic flaw in his ambitious plan—that even though their absence would allow him to attaint and destroy the seven unruly Houses of Twilight, without the Treasures, Baligant could not be made High King of the land, much less hold its borders. No trouble, because Baligant was . . . dazzled.

The lady regarded her image in a mirror and allowed it to reflect a faint expression of contempt. A fool, a greedy and jealous mediocrity who might never have been noticed all the days of his elvish immortality, save for the war that had cast him upon his betters' regard just as if he were some deep-sea refuse tossed ashore by a storm.

Weak and flawed, but those very qualities were what made Baligant No-House such an able tool of destruction.

Her tool. And when this working was done, nothing would be left—not High King, not Morning Lords, not the very boundaries of Chandrakar itself.

Hermonicet—called the Fair—regarded her image in the mirror. And smiled.

Chapter 18

The Broken Swordsman

Nic moved into the forest, letting it close around him like the sea, touching him all over. And, like the sea, a disturbance in any part of it would be transmitted to him here.

He did not think about Ruth. He did not worry about the impossibility of their arrival here by way of a haunted bookshelf in a library basement, or about her half-told tale of sorcery and power politics. Nic Brightlaw had learned in a very hard school to focus his mind in a deep and narrow track, avoiding speculation about things he could not affect.

Just now, his mind was focused on achieving the Objective: ID-ing the stalker who followed them.

He wished, momentarily, for the toys that belonged to another world and another life: grenades, rifle, LAW. Then he put them from his mind. He had a knife.

At first he headed away from the direction of the presence. He intended to circle around, and if he drew the Unfriendly away from Ruth and toward him, so much the better.

He stopped, sheltered by a stand of trees. He stood until the birdsong resumed, and knew by its resumption that his quarry was either equally motionless or absent entirely. He continued his sweep. Neutralization would be second best. Live capture and interrogation would be better. Who were they, who did they report to, why were they following him and Ruth, what did they want—

Ahead the forest thinned. Second-growth vegetation, legacy of a recent fire. A clearing. The sort of place he'd wanted to look for so that he and Ruth could camp for the night. He saw a flicker of color and movement in the clearing ahead. He moved closer, and stopped.

A horse. A roan mare.

In the afternoon sunlight her coat blazed like polished copper. She swung her beautiful sculpted head toward him and flicked her ears back and forth. The sun turned her eyes as red as her coat, and her mane and tail fell in a long silky curve, fine as a woman's hair.

Nic's lips curved in a sardonic smile. He had a certain amount of experience with horses. Enough to tell him that the presence of this one was suspicious.

"The *phooka*," he announced in loud, conversational tones, "is an Irish fairy able to take three forms: dog, human, and horse."

And to tell him that there was no more point in playing hide and seek. He couldn't break a horse's neck. And a horse couldn't talk.

Scratch Objectives One and Two.

On the other hand, the knife in his hand was iron.

"Iron, Cold Iron, the Master of them All." I hope.

"I'm not a *phooka*," the woman said. She was red-gold and ivory, and she was absolutely naked. Her ivory body shone like every dream of goodness and honor he'd ever had.

"All hail, O mighty Queen of Heaven—isn't that how it goes?" Nic said. If she'd expected her magic to unnerve him, she was doomed to disappointment. *Du ma nhieu, Charlie.* Goodness and honor were dreams. And dreams were lies.

She shook out her hair and it fell over her shoulders, highlighting her nakedness instead of concealing it.

She was alone. If she weren't, she and her partner would have tried a flanking maneuver against him and Ruth on the Road long since. The only question was, were they after him or after Ruth?

The smart money was on Ruth. She had a history with the local politicos.

"And then I am to tell you that name does not belong to me." She smiled. The effect was heartbreakingly beautiful, meant to keep his eyes riveted to her face.

Nic looked past her, moving his gaze without moving his head. Beyond her, at the edge of the clearing, he saw the unicorn. Its head was down, neck extended, the very picture of a dog trying to pull its head out of a too-tight collar. There was a black strap digging into the flesh just behind its head. The other end of the strap was looped around a tree. The creature struggled in desperate silence.

Nic looked back at the Queen of Air and Darkness. He focused all his attention on her, banishing the unicorn from his mind. He took a step sideways, as if trying to get a better view of her.

"What do you want with me?" he asked, because it was the next obvious stupid civilian question.

There was an infinitesimal pause, a ball-lightning crackle of electrical potential on his skin. *She's checking something.* He took the opportunity to shift position slightly.

"You are a great warrior, Nicodemus, unjustly betrayed by your leaders. There are those among the worlds who have noted that betrayal, and would give you the means to set it right."

"You can't know what you're talking about," Nic said pleasantly.

"But I do," the Lady said. "Time is mine to command. I can give you a sword to shatter worlds, and return you to your own place at any time you wish."

She waved her hand, and hanging in the air was the image of a sword. A Prince Valiant, King Arthur, Conan the Barbarian wet dream of a sword, with a blade as long as his thigh and an edge sharper than a razor.

"Yeah, I can just see me walking into Firebase Delta carrying that."

"It is invincible," the Lady purred, and whether she was lying or not, he believed her. It would chop through the barrel of an AK-47 like it was balsa, and go through a man like he was made out of Jell-O.

She waved her hand again, and a doorway appeared beside the sword. Rank, fleshy, yellow-green vegetation filled the opening, and the light was the shadowy bluish light that was all that filtered through the jungle canopy.

It was the place that had become home, because it had burned away the memory of any other place. He smelled cinnamon and burnt rubber, the rank brackishness of canal water and the glass-house humidity of the jungle.

"Take it," the Lady said. "Go." She gestured toward the doorway. Offering him life. Offering him the real world.

One step forward, one to the side. "I like it here," Nic lied.

She snapped her fingers, and sword-image and doorway both vanished. She turned toward him, just as he wanted. If you moved slowly enough, most people would turn to face you without really noticing.

"Then stay. I'll sponsor you." She held out her hand. "I can promise you adventure beyond imagining, and—" she dropped her eyes demurely, "—other things."

Her hand was white and soft, the nails gleaming seashell pink. And the glamourie she was exuding would have melted the tires on an eighteen-wheel semi tractor trailer.

But not Nic Brightlaw, who believed in neither Beauty or Truth in any possible combination.

"The trip down Memory Lane was really special, but if there wasn't something you wanted, we wouldn't be talking." He took another step. The unicorn's tree was almost within reach.

The woman stretched, raising her arms and pushing the copper-gold mass of her hair off her neck. Nic felt power and intention reach out for him—and miss, as if he had almost intercepted a message meant for another.

Interesting.

"You didn't come here willingly. It was an accident, in fact. Come with me, and I will make it right."

Almost there. Time to set off the fireworks.

"And Ruth?" Nic said.

"Ruth has her own destiny to follow," the Lady said glibly. She smiled, and her teeth were long and white and sharp. "Come to me, Nicodemus Brightlaw. I have waited for you for so long." She held her arms out to him, welcoming him.

He knew who she was now. She was Death, and he'd strung her about as far as he was going to be able to.

He threw himself sideways, toward the tree. The penknife in his hand sliced down at the strap circling the trunk. He'd expected a struggle, but when the blade touched it there was a recoil sharp as an explosion, and the little knife flew out of his hand. The strap parted with a teeth-setting scream, and the unicorn plunged free.

He rolled to his back just in time to meet the leopard's rush. She hit him like a football player going for the winning tackle and her open jaws stank of blood and roses. He kicked her off him and knew he couldn't do it twice. He scrabbled to his feet, back against the tree.

She crouched, sleek and beautiful, her copper coat spotted with improbable vermilion florets. Her ears were flat and her jaws were open, and her beautiful eyes flared as red as dashboard warning lights.

The jaws could grind his bones to powder. The foreclaws could lay him open like a fistful of razors. But the hind claws would kill him fastest, disemboweling him with unstoppable force.

But whatever she was, she had wanted the unicorn trapped, and he'd freed it. Maybe that gave Ruth a chance.

"Nice kitty," said Nic. He bared his teeth in an expression that had very little to do with a smile. He knew someone who'd killed a leopard bare-handed. He'd died, but then so had the leopard.

And she deserved something for waking up the memories he'd buried so carefully.

The leopardess sprang again. Nic flung himself away from the tree, and she slammed against the trunk with bruising force. He saw what he wanted, half-buried in the mulch of the forest floor, and dove for it. The cat came up in a blinding flurry of fur and fangs, and a small dispassionate timekeeper in the back of Nic's brain told him he had only a few more seconds before she tried something more effective.

But now he had a rock in each hand. And when she launched herself at him again, he brought both hands up, trying to make them meet in the middle of the big cat's skull. His fists struck with a hollow wooden sound, and bounced away again.

She flung herself away from him in mid-leap, defying all the laws of physics. Nic scrabbled backward, adrenaline obliterating weakness. His feet skidded and slipped on the leaf mold of the forest floor and he saw, for only a moment, the image of the copper-fire witch-queen, her face bloody and bruised.

You will die a thousand deaths! screamed the voice inside his skull.

She flung her arms skyward as if summoning heavenly vengeance, but instead her body rippled, pulled like taffy. A wave of furnace heat tightened his skin. The dragon-thing spread her wings, blotting out the sun.

Maleficent. Jesus, I always hated that movie.

She reared back to strike, all beauty and inevitable grace. First him—because he'd made her mad. Then Ruth.

Only he didn't give a damn whether she turned into a dragon or a two-car garage. She wasn't getting Ruth.

The gun was small. A pocket pistol. The noise it made

would scare horses, not dragons. But the load was steel-jacketed hollowpoints.

Steel. *Iron.*

She swung a head the size of a Japanese sedan at him, mouth wide with rows and rows of teeth. The scent of blood and roses was enough to make him gag. He thrust his arm down her throat and pulled the trigger.

The jaws closed. Oblivion for Nic Brightlaw came with the speed of a collision.

Chapter 19

Shop Till You Drop

The Goblin Market was one of the most dangerous places in all the lands, and in the end, it was inevitable that every Gatewalker should find himself there at least once. If dealing with a wizard took all one's skill, surviving the Goblin Market without loss took all one's skill—plus luck.

The rules of commerce there were simple: you could only sell what you wanted to keep, and purchase what you already owned.

Melior, on horseback, sat on the crest of a hill and looked down into the Market. Painted tents and ribbon-decorated stalls spread out across the floor of the valley. Gypsy wagons occupied the edges of the pitch, and also on the perimeter were the horse-copers' lines, filled with horses worth—well, what you paid for them. Literally.

Every road out of this valley led to a different Land. No road led to the same destination twice. Even experienced travelers, when caught in the Goblin Market's turbulence, let its power fling them where it would, and made their way home from that more stable Land with gratitude for the ability to do so.

Power and opportunity. Or, in other words, danger. The Goblin Market.

The Goblin Market never closed, but its character changed sharply with nightfall. It was safer, by far, to chance the Market during the day.

Melior looked at the sun, balanced a bare hour's worth of daylight above the mountains. Go down the path to the Market an hour from now, and there was every chance he'd lose the Sword again. And Ruth was not worth that, no matter what his heart told him. That cold equation had been solved before, and nothing yet had changed. He would die to save Ruth. But he would not give up the Sword.

But it was only a chance he would lose the Sword, not a

certainty. And Ruth *was* there. If he waited for her to pass through the Market and enter a less hazardous Land, he might lose her forever.

There were no certainties.

Melior clucked to his tired gelding and urged him down the path to the Market. In its sheath upon his back, the Sword of Maiden's Tears flamed palely.

"What—to coin a phrase—fresh hell is this?" Ruth demanded of the unicorn. It had been willing enough to follow her into the forest in search of Nic, but inevitably she'd gotten lost. The unicorn had brought her to a trail, and the trail had brought her here.

If the inn this morning had been vintage Hildebrandt, the scene before her now was pure Howard Pyle.

There were wooden stalls, some with bright-colored cloth awnings. The counters were piled high with all sorts of things—hats, it looked like over there, and those were gloves. . . .

"Whoa," Ruth said. "It's the Hollow Hills branch of Nieman Marcus."

And it was filled with people, more people than Ruth had seen in one place since she'd fallen through the bookcase. Some behind counters, more—far more—strolling the lanes between the stalls in garb from every possible historical period and fantasy kingdom.

Here was a lady wearing a gown that Ruth could reasonably assign to fourteenth century France—save for the fact that the gown was made from layer on layer of sea-green gauze, and the lady's headdress was a cone-shaped *hennin* of spectacular height, swathed in more sea-green veiling.

There she saw a man whose silky black hair hung nearly to his waist. He did not look toward her, but shouldered his way through the crowd, wearing full plate armor of breathtaking rococo splendor that looked as if it had been emitted from a cake decorator, chrome-plated, and then Turtle-Waxed. A tiny woman with hair the bright improbable blue of Egyptian faience darted up to him from between two stalls. He bent his head toward her, listening, and they went off together.

Ruth hesitated, then stumbled forward as the unicorn nudged her—hard—in the back of her knees. Ruth swung toward it and it bounced sideways, out of reach, shaking its head at her in silent laughter. It tossed its head, and the wreath it had worn lay in the road at her feet.

Then it turned and trotted off, back the way they'd come. In a few moments the white flash of its body was lost to sight.

"Abandoned," Ruth said out loud.

She took a step in the direction it had gone, and stopped. It obviously didn't mean to be followed, this time. The bushes closed behind it, and the path she'd followed to come here looked narrow and unappealing.

Ruth blinked hard against tears. She'd miss the silly thing. She supposed it was gone for good this time. She stooped and picked up the flowers it had dropped. Something to remember it by, at least.

She'd expected it to be rigid, like a horse collar or a wreath, but instead the flower garland was as flexible as a lei. She draped it around her neck. The perfume radiated from it like a more benignant form of a particularly virulent Air-Wick.

Ruth turned back to the fair. Was this Nic's Goblin Market? Probably.

And because it was as likely that Nic was there as anywhere, she walked toward it. Ruth Marlowe had faced hordes of sixth-graders with an assignment due tomorrow and five minutes until the library closed. A Goblin Market full of elves, fairies, and little men shouldn't faze her in the least.

The race is not to the swift, nor the contest to the strong, but that's the way to bet. James Thurber.

There was no formal entrance to the Market, only two posts about eighteen feet tall and slender and straight as teenaged telephone poles, striped black and white in a cognitively-dissonant symbolic blend with railway-crossing barriers. Ruth passed between them and into the colorful, noisy, busy babble of the Goblin Market.

The setting sun gave the place the fluorescent jewel-brightness of a medieval Book of Hours. And, as in a Book of Hours, there were small cylindrical tents of bright-colored felt flying pennants of gorgeous, rippling, many-colored silk, banners on poles, and liveried lackeys of every stripe. There were piemen in motley hawking their wares, pushcarts draped with brightly-colored banners, strolling minnesingers; the New York City bustle that Elfland had so far lacked.

It took all Ruth's attention just to navigate through the press of crosstime patrons without trampling or being trampled. Fortunately she didn't have to worry about getting her pocket picked. She didn't have anything worth stealing.

"What d'ye lack?"

Ruth swung around again, menacing oblivious fairgoers with the bundle she carried over one shoulder. While she'd been staring, one of the wandering *handelsmenchen* had waylaid her.

He was wearing red and gold striped hose and purple velvet boots with tiny golden bells sewn around the dagged cuffs. His shirt had billowing white sleeves, and over it he wore a quilted vest of deep green leather.

Ruth regarded this vision with fascination. His hair was red and his wide eyes were a green-hazel, and when he saw that he had Ruth's attention, he smiled more broadly. His wares were piled on a tray he carried hung from a strap that went around the back of his neck.

"What d'ye lack?"

"Everything," Ruth sighed with weary comprehensiveness. "Have you seen—"

"Old loves, lost causes, true dreams, new hope—tell me what you lack; for I've the key to every lock and the word to every riddle."

"I'm looking for my friend," Ruth persisted. "He's tall—" but there were any number of tall men in the Goblin Market "—and he was hit on the head. Have you seen him?"

"Friends, ah, lost loves are the sweetest. The Market has what you lack if I do not—but before you go on, won't you buy a faireing from me?"

"I haven't got any money," Ruth said apologetically.

"Barter me, then—the knife at your belt, useless thing, for any piece on my tray. No, better yet—any two." He smiled coaxingly.

Ruth considered, staring at the tray. There was no reason not to, after all—and though she was probably going to be cheated of the real value of the dagger, she didn't have any use for it anyway. She took a closer look at the items on the peddler's tray.

There was a red glass heart on a chain of pearls, a gossamer scarf in grays and blues, a mirror the size of a half-dollar with a silver frame shaped like a snake swallowing its tail. There was a set of what first looked like bondage gear for hamsters but which Ruth eventually identified as a hood and jesses for a hawk. Glass bracelets, gilded nutmegs, embroidered ribbons ... an entire jumble of possibilities.

"Choose what you lack," the peddler urged.

Ruth pulled the dagger from her belt and handed it—still in its scabbard—to the peddler. He inspected it briefly and slipped it into his vest. Around them large competent-looking men in more sober dress carried baskets of torches, stopping at intervals to set one in a socket on pole or stallside and light it. The warm scent of burning resins tickled Ruth's nostrils.

"Any thing—any two things—that you see," the peddler urged.

She plunged her hand into his tray almost at random. Beneath the jumbled surface of ribbons and silks, her fingers hit something hard. She pulled it out.

Scissors. Well, that's useful. Maybe I can cut my hair. Or my throat.

The scissors looked as perfectly ordinary as any Ruth had in her sewing basket back in lost New York: about four inches long. The eyes were gilded, and textured with some sort of design that Ruth couldn't make out in the twilight. The blades gleamed needle-sharp; embroidery scissors.

Tangled through the scissors' eyes as if it belonged there was a long red ribbon with a tiny gold bell at each end. Gold embroidery on the ribbon glittered in the torchlight.

"I'll take these," Ruth said. "And if you see my friend—"

But the man with the tray was already bowing his way out of her presence, searching for new customers. Ruth found an unoccupied pouch in which to stow her purchases, and walked on into the Market.

She had not had time to see much of it in daylight, but it seemed to Ruth that the character of the Market changed perceptibly in torchlight. All the middle ground in shapes and colors vanished, and all that was left were the brightest brights and the darkest darks.

And it was no longer possible to fool herself that Nic was here. She was the one who was here, in the place that people paid good money to stay away from, so Nic had said. She'd lost him—and the unicorn—and herself—and she felt not so much threatened as maddeningly ineffectual.

"Ruth!" A voice called her name.

* * *

They would say, when it was time to compose his epitaph, that Rohannan Melior was a fool. So be it. He was a fool. The sun's light had fled the Goblin Market and he was still here.

A wise man would not try to ride his horse through the twisting maze of alleys and fairways that made up the Market, and so Melior had left his in the place provided, bribing the attendant suitably to assure that he came back not only to *a* horse, but to the same horse he'd left.

He carried the Sword of Maiden's Tears upon his hip; an awkward position for a sword of that length, but it enabled him to use it as his compass in his search for Ruth.

And either its magic had failed entirely, or Ruth was dead, or she was here.

What a comforting selection of possibilities to choose from.

But the flame that was Ruth's soul burned clear and bright in the pommel of the Sword, and while there was a chance of finding her, Melior knew he would not leave, fool though that marked him.

He paced through the Market, oblivious to its temptations. Scraps of music and conversation swept past him like clouds scattered by a storm wind, and Melior ignored them all. Natives and visitors alike spared him a respectful distance, for the sword that Melior carried held one-twelfth the magic of an entire Land, and such power commanded respect even here.

He was so focused on finding Ruth before the Market did her harm that the sound had been in the air for several seconds before he noticed it. The sound of wings. *Large* wings.

He looked up. The bowl of night was filling slowly, pale stars visible only at midheaven in a sky only just darker than an October day's. The flying thing could be seen against that background quite clearly, the last rays of day striking greenish-copper light from its hide. Its wings were a dark insectile blur about its torso.

Warwasp. Not a natural creature. A form assumed by wizards and Adepts Major for the damage it could do. Created for war. Faster than a dragon, more poisonous than a manticore, able to burn with the lethality of a salamander. Melior had seen a warwasp destroy an entire unit of cavalry once.

Around him others who had seen it too were spreading the

news; in moments this collection of unrelated people would be a mob. Or a riot.

He looked down, choosing his retreat. And then he saw her.

"Ruth!"

He recognized her even through the motley rags Fate had dressed her in. For some impossible reason she was wearing a Gate-garland—the ornament that assured you exited through the same Gate you had entered by—around her shoulders.

She swung toward the sound of her name and stared straight at him. Above him, he heard the thin song of the monster's flight change pitch as the warwasp prepared to dive.

She wasn't ready, was Ruth's first thought. She'd turned at the sound of her name, thinking Nic had somehow found her after all, and seen him. Rohannan Melior of the House of the Silver Silences. And she found she was nearly as afraid of him as in love with him.

He was wearing a cloak the metallic orange-gold color of enameled monarch butterfly wings. It glittered in the torch-light, and in his hand he held the Sword.

The Sword of Maiden's Tears.

The Sword that had killed Naomi.

As she stood, indecisive, the press of people that had seemed pliable and permeable suddenly took on solidity and direction; a solid mass of people, pushing her away from Melior. She struggled against them, trying to go the other way, and then at last she heard the sound that everyone else had heard before her Ironworlder ears had.

A dive bomber? Don't be—

Ruth looked up.

A nightmare, vexed to madness by a thousand Japanese monster movies: a wasp the size of a subway car, glowing dull red as if stoked by hell's own furnace. Its giant bubble-eyes gleamed wetly with unclean phosphorescence, and when Ruth looked up she knew with a sick certainty transcending logic that it was looking at *her*.

Melior drew his sword; a white-hot neon blur that bleached his surroundings to a ghost of daylight brightness. And the determined self-interested exodus around Ruth became a full-scale rout.

She struggled to keep her feet, knowing that if she fell she would be trampled. Reaching Melior, finding him, was abruptly less urgent than surviving to find him again.

Melior took a step toward Ruth, knowing that he could never reach her through this mob; that by the time he might search for her again she could be half a hundred Lands away. Then he drew the Sword of Maiden's Tears and pushed Ruth from his mind.

The Goblin Market was sacrosanct: to use sorcery near it—or *in* it—was a violation of custom and treaty so vast that Melior could not begin to imagine the retribution that would be exacted. And the warwasp was a creature of Chandrakar and those Lands near it. Paranoid intuition indicated that the creature was here for him.

Or for Ruth.

To save Ruth; to deflect the Heartlands' retribution from Chandrakar, Melior had to kill the warwasp. Here. Now. Quickly.

The Sword flared nova-bright in his hands, heterodyning magic from the creature above him. He saw the nightmare yanked from its intended path by the compelling magnet of the Sword's power, and took the last moment before it reached him to feel fear that for the first time the Sword's hidden weapon was his to wield.

Each of the Twelve Treasures was more than it seemed. The Sword of Maiden's Tears was unstoppable, unshatterable—but more than that: the Sword of Maiden's Tears gave its wielder the opportunity to know the mind of his opponent.

As Melior would know the mind of the warwasp.

He unclasped the hindering cloak and flung it away.

Then the warwasp was within reach.

Against beasts, spears and bow. Against men, the sword. Against a true dragon, the only defense was prayer. And the warwasp was none of these.

It hovered above him, as large as three cart horses and their wagon. He slashed upward, and it dodged out of reach, nimble in an element Melior couldn't enter. Heat radiated off it like a furnace. The body was scaled; six grasping legs ended in claws, and mandibles glistened like black glass. It descended on him and this time Melior retreated, hampered by close quarters and the inability to bring the Sword to bear. The mandibles clicked, inches from his face.

But he had seen something. Behind the head, high in the chest between the two forelimbs, was a tiny fleck of blue-white light, as if there were something inside the warwasp, burning.

That was its vulnerable part.

Melior backed between two market stalls, hoping the warwasp would follow. The intuition granted him by the Sword assured him that it wouldn't. The monster snatched itself into the sky again on its black gauze blur of wings.

It wanted Ruth, not him, and now Melior knew it. But the wizard whose creation this warwasp was couldn't search for Ruth, not while the Sword of Maiden's Tears flared magic like a balefire, eclipsing all lesser lights. The warwasp would attack the Sword until the Sword was destroyed, or until it gave up and left without its prey.

So he was risking the Sword after all.

He looked around, trying to find his enemy. The space he was in was a narrow alley between two rows of stalls. The top was covered with canvas. He saw a clear space ahead, and started to move toward it.

The canvas above him bulged inward. The stall timbers edging it began to groan and splinter. The canvas smoked, catching fire, and black mandibles sliced though it, seeking him.

Melior cut upward, and the canvas split with a high buzzing shriek, dropping the hindquarters of the warwasp into the alleyway with him. The barb in its tail dripped greenish vitriol that smoked and stank.

The Sword bit into the creature's thorax. Only a glancing blow, but enough to make the warwasp disengage. Only this time, when the monster tried to rise into the air, it was tangled in the burning canvas. It thrashed like a dying horse, spraying poison from its trapped hindquarters.

Melior ran. Behind him the walls of the market stalls began to burn.

He heard the crashing as the warwasp floundered free, and a distant, bookish part of his mind wondered what indemnities the Heartlands would ask against Chadrakar for the bringing of its war into the Goblin Market. He wondered what coin his pillaged kingdom could find to pay in, after a century of war.

But what he wondered most was if he could find a clear area ahead so that he could seduce the warwasp into another attack.

Buying time, so that Ruth and the other innocents here could flee.

And Ruth would be lost to him again.

Ahead, the alley opened out into another thoroughfare. There were still people here, cowering or merely watching. He saw a blue-eyed lion the size of a pony regarding him unblinkingly.

Melior turned back the way he'd come, and saw the warwasp rise into the air again. Bright gold blood dripped thickly from its torso, setting fires wherever it dropped, and the werewizard itself glowed like a stoked kiln.

The night was full dark now, illuminated only by torches, random fires, and the light that flamed from both combatants. The monster sighted the radiant Sword and flew toward it.

Its heat sucked the breath from his lungs and pulled his skin taut. Melior raised the Sword for the downward cut—through the shoulder, into the spine—that experience and training swore was the surest kill. The bright blade flung itself forward.

And the lower part of the warwasp whipped forward like a second attacker, and a chitinous barb the size of a boar-spear slashed at Melior.

Its venom had been expended in the first encounter; the droplets remaining were only enough to burn, not kill. The barb struck his thigh and stuck, then tore free to drag a smoking furrow up his body before Melior flung himself out of reach.

The Sword passed cleanly through untenanted air as the warwasp reared back. A miss. And the swift instants in which Melior might have won the fight through surprise and misdirection were gone, and all that was left was a war of attrition. A war that Melior Treasurekeeper, elphenborn or not, would inevitably lose.

And though the roads through all Lands crossed here, by the time another warrior came to his aid it would be too late.

He would be dead.

And Baligant would have the Sword.

The wound in his side burned, poisoned and seeping. Melior's vision blurred. His body shook with waves of hot

and cold, and not even the incandescent insectile proximity
of his foe could warm him. It seemed there had been poison
enough remaining, after all.

The warwasp hung in the air before him, just out of reach,
savoring the moment. It was a tactical advantage Melior had
been taught to look for—that those creatures who loved
slaughter often stopped to admire their work. It would not be
enough to save him, but if he could cripple it, another might
finish the task.

This, too, Melior had been taught.

He slashed down. The Sword hit the barb in the
warwasp's tail with the sound of an ax hitting wood. And the
barb broke and the Sword did not.

But the Sword was so heavy. . . .

Up again, with the weapon that now felt as awkward as a
bar of farrier's bronze clutched clumsily in his hands. Stroke
to the midline; open the belly.

He missed.

And while his clouded senses were still registering the
fact, the warwasp closed on him. He brought the Sword up
barely in time to save himself, all the while knowing it was
only a temporary respite.

Through a hot poisoned fog Melior felt himself falling
backward, felt the dulled impact as he struck the street. He
saw his hand clasped around the hilt of the Sword, and the
warwasp's maw upon it. His fingers lay just outside the flex-
ing mandibles; safe. But the blade was being pushed back
toward Melior's own throat, and his other arm was trapped
beneath him.

And through the Sword he felt his opponent's intentions.
No ambiguity there, only madness, blood, and flowers. And
the furnace heat, beginning to sear.

"Father!"

The shout cut through Melior's concentration, forcing him
to look. A brown-haired girl, her face a subtle blending of
Ruth's features and his own, stood in the street behind the
warwasp.

His daughter.

And in her hands she held a sword that was twin to his
own—that *was* his own, duplicated by Time refolded like a
silk ribbon to touch itself. It was not the warwasp's poison
alone that had sickened him; the air was glutted with the

magic that had let this be; a stifling rarified atmosphere that choked the breath in Melior's lungs and made his vision dim.

Not what will be, but what may *be.*

The Sword in his hands vibrated like some mad Ironworld machine, threatening to tear itself apart through proximity to . . . itself.

The warwasp turned, sensing, impossibly, the magic that bespelled it, redoubled. It lifted off him to confront this new threat, and Melior freed his trapped arm and snatched the Sword from its jaws; felt his hands, burned and cut to the bone, slide upon the sharp dimpled substance of the hilt.

Then the warwasp jerked and reared up, screaming silently as it was attacked from behind. Melior felt the blow that had struck it vibrate through its body and into his, and at last he had the clear target he had been trying for.

With the last of his endurance, Melior thrust the Sword of Maiden's Tears, point first, into the glowing patch in the warwasp's throat.

He felt the Sword turn icy and sullen in his hand as it transfixed the node of molten iron burning in the warwasp's breast. Reflexively he jerked it sideways, clearing the blade with a snap-wristed jerk, and fell to the street, sick and dizzy.

The warwasp flung itself into the night sky, body rippling as it threw off the form that had served it so ill. Melior didn't need his Sword to tell that it was abandoning the attack.

And it hadn't killed him.

But the riptide of Wild Magic might.

He scrambled to his knees and looked through the veils of shifting smoke to his daughter. The daughter who had not yet been born, who might never be born, despite her appearance here today. Who had saved his life, at the cost of a greater magic than Melior thought there was to buy.

She smiled at him, pushing her hair up off her forehead in an achingly familiar gesture. He could see the street beyond through her body.

". . . *Father* . . ." her voice was faint, as the Time River that had never been meant to merge here separated itself again before the worlds tore themselves apart.

"Your name! Child, your name!" Melior shouted, willing

her to hear him. Suddenly it was important to know, to properly honor this spirit-daughter.

He saw her lips move in answer as she faded. No sound reached him, but he didn't need to hear to know.

"Naomi. . . ."

Chapter 20

For the Love and for the Glory

A plan. I need a plan.

Ruth Marlowe was no ordinary interdimensional traveler. Possibly unique among the visitants of the Goblin Market, she had survived rush hour in the New York Subway. In the crowd that swept her away from Melior she kept both her feet and her head, looking for an alley to dodge down.

She worked herself to the edge of the press of bodies and pulled free, the force of the maneuver sending her sprawling into a display of baskets. As she fell, the scissors jabbed her sharply; Ruth swore and tucked them somewhere safer, rolling into concealment. No one saw her here, no one was idiotish enough to stop and "rescue" her. Ruth tried to catch her breath and think sensibly. Melior was back there. And it would be vapor-brained to the ultimate max to do anything but get back to him as soon as possible.

There was a blinding flash of light and Ruth cringed instinctively deeper into the baskets. She thought about that *thing* that Melior was currently fighting and shuddered, a mutinous panic building in her. It belonged in a monster movie, not in Elfland.

She didn't like adventures. She didn't like surprises. And most particularly she didn't like monsters, whether they flew, shambled, or swam. She closed her eyes tightly, stricken paralytically by the certainty that twelve-foot wasp knew who she was, knew she was here, and was coming for her.

And someone showed up to rescue her after all.

"—shut up. Your pardon, demoiselle, can we be of assistance?" A man's voice, light and amiable.

"We. I like that." A woman.

Ruth opened her eyes and looked up. Two of the people she'd seen before—the man in the wedding-cake armor and the woman with the blue hair—were standing in front of the stall. The man was looking at her. His companion was looking at him.

He looked like a sword and sorcery pinup designed by a particularly vindictive armorer. His hair was black, his eyes were blue, and his strong sculpted face had a faintly Oriental cast to it. His hair was longer than Ruth's own and straight, caught back in a jeweled ring and falling free over his shoulder. His armor was intricately jointed and elaborately chromed. He had an earring, equally bright, in his left ear, and the open, friendly expression of an All-American Hero from a thirties pulp magazine.

His companion barely came up to his elbow. Her hair was shoulder-length, a bright false cerulean blue that clashed weirdly with her old-ivory skin and slanting amber eyes. She was wearing a fussy, elaborate costume that incorporated every form of dagging, slashing, trapunto, bead, button, and ribbon ornamentation of Western Europe from the fourteenth to the seventeenth centuries, inclusive, but far from making her look ridiculous, it simply increased her resemblance to some fabulously expensive jeweled clockwork doll. Her boots had curled toes and her cape resembled a fuschia suede artichoke that someone had edged heavily with gold bullion fringe. Her gloves had lace trim.

Ruth took a deep breath and tried not to surrender to an hysterical urge to laugh.

"Might you perhaps have a particularly large can of Raid?" she asked carefully.

The man smiled, an especially dazzling smile on an entirely human face. "No," he said, "but I'll happily stand you a cup of wine. No obligation."

His companion made a noise like an enraged cat sneezing.

There was another flash of light. Ruth flinched. The man's expression sobered slightly, then lightened.

"Oh, don't worry about that—just some local elf-lord bringing his war to Market. One of them'll kill the other, and everything'll be fine. I'm Perigord, by the way, and this is Azure Bowl." He held out his hand and Ruth took it. He helped her to her feet.

"You don't understand. That's *my* elf-lord, and—"

"I knew it!" Azure Bowl shrieked. "Peri, you inbred son of a peripatetic sphinx, I *knew* she was trouble!"

"And I suppose I should have just stepped over her and gone on?" Perigord shot back. He looked over his shoulder, and Ruth followed the direction of his gaze. Fires. He turned back to her.

"If the elf-lord's your friend, then I hope he wins. But he's going to have to win without me." Perigord shrugged.

"No money in it—and too much trouble," Azure Bowl snapped, but unease radiated from her.

With an effort alien to her nature Ruth shut her mouth on her next remark, which was that if the giant bug killed Melior, it would be coming after *her* next. Why should she tell these people that? She didn't know them.

And they might decide that it *wasn't* too much trouble to simply hand her over to the wasp-thing in the name of peace and quiet.

"The offer of a drink still stands," the man—Perigord—said, and Azure Bowl threw up her hands in the universal gesture of one who has nothing to do with events. She regarded Ruth with a measuring eye.

"Maybe you should buy her some clothes instead, Peri," she purred.

Pure irritation wiped every other thought from Ruth's mind for an instant, and she took a quick self-inventory: borrowed clothes, the wrong size to begin with, that she'd worn for two days; her hair full of brambles; her possessions much the worse for wear. And her cloak—Naomi's cloak—was gone.

"It's been a long day," Ruth said tightly, and didn't add: *"Just who's calling who a fashion victim? I've seen better dressed Macy's Thanksgiving Day Parade floats."*

"Don't mind my charming companion," Perigord said, with a haste suggesting this was a speech he had to make frequently. "She used to be a librarian and she's never gotten over it."

"Better a librarian than a prince," Azure Bowl rejoined. Perigord took Ruth's arm and led her in the direction in which the crowd had been running.

Librarian? Ruth wondered.

It was perhaps fortunate that visitors to the Goblin Market were a uniquely sophisticated clientele. Most of them were only interested in getting out of the way of the immediate danger. Though half the Market seemed to be burning, the customers grouped around the wine seller's stall were completely nonchalant.

Perigord handed Ruth a battered tin goblet full of wine.

She started to raise it to her lips, trying to phrase some graceful way of thanking him for such disinterested kindness, when suddenly the ground . . . shimmered.

"Magic!" shrilled Azure Bowl. Perigord clutched her in his arms, which would have surprised Ruth if she'd had any inquisitiveness to spare.

The world had taken on a form only seen in nightmare, where there was vision without light, sensation without perception. Everything seemed both distorted and horribly clear; vertiginous, hot, cold, greasy, and dryly gritty. Ruth felt as if the air had turned to rubber cement, gelid and chill. In her sight the objects around her pulled like taffy and flickered like a riffle of playing cards.

The Market was there. It wasn't.

It was a forest.

A city inhabited by huge insects.

A featureless plain.

The Market.

And Ruth felt the shock wave strike her, as personal and intended as if someone had found the loose trailing ends of her nerves and yanked on them. It was terrifying enough to numb her entirely, and without a backward look for her new friends she ran toward where she had last seen Melior, though the ground beneath her rippled and bucked like a fun house attraction.

I have to get out of here, was Melior's first clear thought, and then: *The cloak. Not mine. Ophidias' gift to his bride. I cannot leave it.*

But where was it? And was it, for that matter, still there?

He got unsteadily to his feet and looked around. The Market was burning. The smoke hung in a low pall, reflecting back the light of the fires. Several of the stalls were smashed, their inventories strewn about the street. In a few moments their owners would return, and Melior hoped to be gone by then. Or, at least, to blend into the crowd.

Small chance of that, battered as he was, and with the Sword he carried. Melior grinned mockingly at that, and winced, and staggered as the world did another slow revolve. Now distinct from the disorientation of High Magic, the warwasp's poison burned in Melior's veins. He looked down at tunic and trousers shredded and soaked with blood.

He could still die here.

With flayed and shaking hands he sheathed the Sword of Maiden's Tears. He drew breath to voice the Word that would show him Ruth's location, and realized that to expend even so little magic would use all his remaining strength.

The cloak. Then his horse. If either was still there.

Now. He had come out of that alleyway. . . .

The alley was smoldering and venom-fouled, but Melior didn't dare choose an alternate path, lest he lose his way entirely. He was rewarded by the sight of Ophidias' cloak just where he'd left it, and risked losing his balance completely to bend and retrieve it.

New strength seemed to seep into his bones as its scaled golden folds settled about his body. There was a wine seller's stall across the way, and Melior stopped to retrieve an unbroken flask from the wreckage, carefully putting a silver penny in its place. Another wave of dizziness roiled through him and he clutched at a wooden pole for support. Still gripping the pole, he broke the wax seal on the bottle and drank. Brandywine, spiced and potent.

False strength surged through him with the liquor's heat— enough, perhaps, to get him to his horse, but far from enough to allow him to pass through a Gate of his own choosing, or to find Ruth. That much, at least, the warwasp had succeeded in accomplishing.

He had hated Eirdois Baligant before. But now Melior swore that he would kill him, no matter what else happened, no matter what the consequence to Line Rohannan. For forcing Melior to abandon Ruth here, Eirdois Baligant would die.

Childish runesinger nonsense, Melior scolded himself. A battle was not a campaign. And Ruth was not lost, nor was he.

He hoped.

But Baligant would still die.

Grimly, Melior set himself to reach the horse lines.

"No!" Ruth screamed it in pure terrified fury. She skidded to a stop, the leaf-and-pine-needle-strewn track treacherous beneath her saddle oxfords. She spun around, glaring behind her, already knowing what she'd see.

Or wouldn't see.

The Goblin Market was gone. And here, where simple

physics and the logic of Ruth Marlowe's top speed, even terrified, both assured her should be approximately where
Melior was fighting the Return of the Creature From Beneath the Id, wasn't.

It was as if she'd run *through* the Market, unheeding, but
even so she should see it behind her.

I HATE magic! Ruth stamped her foot, and rejected every
swearword she'd learned in a lifetime of obscure reading
as simply ... inadequate. The Market—and Melior—were
gone.

It was night, and Ruth stood just inside a forest, on a long
straight track that, looking back, she could see led out into
a gently-sloping meadow lit a bright unreal blue-silver by
the full moon. In the distance were more trees, and beyond
that a different darkness that could be mountains or clouds
or both.

No Goblin Market.

Ruth walked out into the middle of the meadow, finding
that moonlight was everything its detractors had ever said it
was: tricky and lying and full of illusion. Though the light
seemed nearly bright enough to read by, objects seen by
moonlight seemed to possess a sort of insubstantial vagueness that made it difficult to navigate, even if she did stay on
the path.

And she couldn't see the Goblin Market from here either.

By the time she reached the middle of the meadow Ruth
realized she was still clutching the wine cup. It had long
since been emptied by her headlong flight, and whether it
had been Prince Perigord's or belonged to the Market wineshop, Ruth saw precious little hope of returning it.

She thought of throwing it away, but a lifetime of reading
Andrew Lang's fairy-tale collections stopped her. Whatever
else it was, the cup wasn't *hers.*

And besides, that would be littering. She stuffed the cup
into her tunic and hoped she wouldn't lose it, too. She'd lost
Nic, she'd lost the unicorn—*Oh, I've lost Britain and I've
lost Gaul and I've lost Rome, but most of all*—she'd even
lost Melior, although she hadn't really had him, and although she now knew that he'd gotten home to Chandrakar
alive, she didn't know if he was alive *now* and had a number
of reasons to think he wasn't, so she really didn't think she
was ahead on points. . . .

And she was lost, with no idea of which way to go, a

pretty good idea that there were people and *things* around that didn't like Ruth Marlowe very much at all, and no basis for choosing a direction.

That, at least, was solved for her with the first cold drops of rain, falling miraculously out of a sky still moonlit and star spangled, but even as Ruth stared upward indignantly the question of whether the dark shapes on the horizon had been clouds or mountains was answered as the clouds slid across the sky like scenery being changed between acts, blotting out the moon and bringing rain in earnest—wet, soaking, cold, pneumonia-producing rain.

Ruth ran for the nearest possible shelter: the forest she'd just left.

The rain became a full-fledged downpour, complete, suddenly, with thunder and lightning and noisy whipping wind. And while the forest canopy was a roof of sorts, it was a very leaky one, and the gusting air was damp and chill.

The thought of holing up in a hollow tree with a woodland assortment of spiders, woodlice, and rabid squirrels actually began to take on a certain charm as Ruth stood, shivering, in the dark. After standing there long enough to realize exactly how miserably uncomfortable and out of alternatives she was—about two and a half minutes—Ruth began groping along the path that led deeper into the forest, guided by intermittent spasms of lightning, seeking some place drier and out of the wind.

Navigating by lightning was exhausting enough that Ruth stopped at the first halfway suitable spot. She sat down among the gnarly sheltering roots of the enormous tree and set her back firmly against its trunk, and vowed to sit there forever, or at least until a kindly old fairy godfather came along with a pair of red shoes.

And what would I wish for and where would I go? Ruth wondered. Then she thought about Melior, and put her head on her knees, and wept.

She thought she'd probably dozed, because when she roused the storm had spent itself, and the only sound was a faint but constant dripping as the rainwater spilled from leaf to leaf in search of the forest floor. She was so cold that everything hurt; her fingers felt as if they'd been boiled, and if she wasn't as wet as she would have been out in the meadow, she was at least much wetter than she liked.

And there was a light.

Ruth stared at it for a while, numb-brained and fuzzy, and tried not to think that it was what it so very much looked like: a porch light, or one of those retro coach lanterns people hung on their gates or over their garages.

But it didn't move, and it didn't vanish, and eventually Ruth got wincingly to her feet and tottered off in the direction of the friendly yellow light.

He was, Melior realized, in what his cousin Jausserande would have called real trouble (to distinguish it, Melior had always supposed, from the numberless samples of unreal trouble she was constantly exposed to).

The Goblin Market was deserted. And that could not be the case, nor ought it be that the Market's rulers would hesitate to make their feelings known to him, and that at once. Yet he saw no one and heard nothing, only the crackle of the fires that burned in half a hundred locations.

Even the gypsy wagons were dark and silent when he reached them. Melior shook his head, wishing he could be more regretful of the unpleasantness his future undoubtedly held. He clutched at the side of one of the gypsy carts, using it to hold him upright as he made his way past it and to the horse lines.

Ah. So that explains it, Melior thought with light-headed clarity. At least it would save him the sorry task of informing Line Rohannan of this latest disaster. He tried to remember who was next in the succession at the moment, and failed. Was it Rollant? Acevelt?

All the horses were gone—the horses for sale and trade, the pack animals with their watchful trader masters, the light, long-legged couriers and the savage, heavy-boned warhorses. Even the donkeys, mules, and oxen. All of the animals were gone.

Save one.

It advanced upon him with a slow, measured gait—but this horse was not one which had to run—or that any in the Morning Lands wished to hurry.

It was pale gray, this horse, its mane and tail a darker gray than its coat. Its long hooves were unshod, yet Melior could hear each step that fell upon the soft turf clearly. Around its eyes, and at its muzzle, its coat was soot-dark, and out of that darkness, its long-lashed eyes flared red.

Melior knew this horse. He had seen it on innumerable battlefields. Some called it beautiful, and some hideous, but it had never been his to ride.

Until now.

It walked toward him without hurry, and when it reached him, it stopped.

"Now?" Melior said. "But I have suffered deeper wounds than this—"

And why, he thought with regret and indignation, should he still suffer all the hurts of the body, when the presence of this new mount showed that Rohannan Melior was beyond them?

The horse nudged him with its nose, soft and implacable. Melior stretched his hand out toward its mane.

No! If he must choose to mount this horse, then it followed that he could still choose otherwise. He recoiled from the pale horse and stumbled away, toward the forest.

Behind him, he heard the footsteps of Death follow patiently after.

Ruth stumbled creakingly toward the light at the aching pace of an arthritic snail. If the storm had not passed, she could not have managed, but the blue bars of moonlight filtering down through the leaves gave just enough light to move by.

As she got closer, the one light became two, and once she was closer still, Ruth saw that the light came from two lanterns hung one at each side of a set of wooden gates.

The forest path branched there; one path leading on into the forest, one leading toward the gate. Two carved posts, each with an iron hook to hold a lantern. Between them the gates—about five feet high; low enough to peer over without too much difficulty. Gates of what must be a purely ornamental nature, because anyone who chose to leave the path and step into the bramble of the forest for a step or two could simply walk around the gates: there was no fence.

Ruth did not leave the path. She tottered up to the gates and looked over them. As she pressed close, she felt the soggy wreath she still wore around her neck squish against the wood, pressing water into her clothes. She pulled back and hung it over one of the gateposts, then gripped the top of the gate with blue and aching fingers and peered over.

On the other side of the gates the path was graveled, wide

and silver in the moonlight. The forest receded from the sides of the path until it was gone altogether; the path itself ambled on for a little distance until it reached the house.

In the pale moonlight what Ruth saw was a house that could very well have come out of her own world. It was a Tudor manor house, with a half-timbered, lime-washed second story, and high narrow windows set with diamond-shaped panes of glass. The flagstone path spread out to a courtyard that ran the length of the front of the house. Beyond the house Ruth could see a low stone wall and the regular planting of trees that meant an orchard. There was a lantern burning over the front door, but all the windows were dark.

Ruth hesitated, wanting to run to the safety and normalcy the house proclaimed, but knowing that here, in Melior's world, things were ... different. The householders might welcome her with open arms. Or chain her in the basement. Or serve her for dinner. And there were no cops to call, and she didn't think the American Library Association would take much of an interest either.

She might be much better off just staying with the forest, and starvation, pneumonia, lions, tigers, and bears.

In the end it was the homely ordinariness of what she saw that persuaded her to risk it. Surely people who lived in a house that looked like that would at least be ... civilized.

Jennet Jourdemayne Memorial Society, here we come.

Ruth ran her hand down the front of the gate, looking for a latch, and one wing of it slid inward under her hand.

Ruth was cold and wet and hungry and tired and not in the mood for extended debate. She stepped through the gate, stopped to close and latch it carefully—*but if the latch is on this side, and it was closed, how come it came open?*—and hurried on down the path.

It was, if anything, colder out in the open than in the forest, and the air had the crystal-bright stillness of long after midnight. Ruth walked as quietly as she could, but her progress was marked by the sharp crunching of saddle oxfords on gravel.

Then she stood at the house's front door and tried to gather up enough nerve to knock. At least, if you were meeting someone under normal circumstances, you had a hint of what you should say, and some idea, however unfounded, of what sort of person they were. Not here.

And it was late, and she was a stranger knocking on a country house door. And bringing trouble with her. Ruth had to admit that here even if she hadn't admitted it to her new acquaintances at the Goblin Market. Trouble was following her.

She stood in front of the door for a long moment in silent frustration, then finally grabbed the dangling chain of the bell that hung beside the door, and pulled.

There was no sound. *I HATE magic.* Instead, the door slowly swung open.

It was warm inside, and light. Ruth hesitated only a moment before walking in.

"Hello?"

Profoundly disinterested silence answered her.

Ruth stood in a front hall facing a staircase. The hall was dimly lit by candles in glass bowls in sconces on the wall. The floor beneath her muddy shoes was polished wood, and Ruth conscientiously backtracked to wipe her feet clean on the rag rug just outside the door.

"Hello?" she said again, a little louder this time. There was no sound from deeper in the house. She glanced around the hallway nervously, wondering what she was looking for and how she'd know if she saw it, anyway.

No one and nothing. An empty house.

The wall on her right was half-timbered; golden wood below, whitewashed plaster above. The staircase took up the left wall, its newel post fancifully carved with leaves and acorns. There were sliding parlor doors—closed now—in the wall to her right, and straight ahead a half-open door led to a parlor with a fireplace. Ruth could see the shadows the firelight cast upon the wall, and went toward that source of light and warmth as if drawn by a magnet.

This room was empty, too, but Ruth didn't care. She huddled in the arch of the fireplace, hands nearly in the flames, and winced in silent discomfort as the blazing fire baked the bone-deep damp from her body. A few minutes later, the worst of the chill gone, Ruth gave the room a careful inspection.

Not a modern house after all. Something more in the Colonial Williamsburg line, from the high-backed settles on each side of the fire to the high, narrow windows swathed in velvet curtains worthy of Scarlett O'Hara's dressmaking abilities. There was a narrow, brocade-covered couch, two deep padded chairs, and, to one side of the room, a table swathed in white linen upon which two candelabra burned.

Ruth left the fireside and advanced upon the table, an unsettled feeling of triumphant dread in her throat. She knew what she was going to find.

On the table was a glass goblet, a pewter bowl, a silver spoon, and a folded square of white linen. There was also a green glass carafe filled with red wine, a loaf of bread on a wooden dish, a wedge of cheese on a patterned china plate with a silver knife beside it, a wooden bowl of apples, and a blue and white china tureen with a silver ladle beside it. Ruth lifted the lid of the tureen. It was warm under her fingers, and the tureen contained steaming hot stew.

I know where this is.

Abruptly Ruth wondered if she would have seen a rose garden if she'd walked all the way around the house. Was there a garden here, in which the roses bloomed even in winter, and was one of them a blue rose, fairest of the fair?

I know where this is.

The Beast's castle, to which the weary traveler came in the dead of night and found food and drink, clothes and shelter—and no master. The house was familiar in the way dreams and childhood are familiar. No wonder she had recognized it.

Ruth considered her options. Suppose this was the Beast's castle—or house—just as advertised? If it was, she should be perfectly safe, providing she stayed out of the garden and didn't steal the spoons.

But what if it wasn't? What if—

Oh, God, she was so tired. And there was one thing left to do. To make the proof that she needed, because Ruth had no faith left in her to give to anything.

She picked up one of the candlesticks from the table and left the room. She slid open the doors to the parlor—cold fireplace, more Jacobean furniture—then climbed the stairs.

On the second floor she found two bedrooms, a dressing room, and a study with shelves of books and a writing desk. She did not stop to look further, because all of them were empty of inhabitants.

The last room she entered—a back bedroom—was not dark like the others.

She opened the door into light. Burning candles on the table, well-made fire in the grate. The room contained a large four-poster bed with carved walnut posts and garnet velvet bed curtains fringed with bullion, a dressing table, and a clothespress. There was a patterned carpet on the floor, and a fireplace with a roaring fire built up in it, and in front of the fire, sheltered by canvas-covered crewelwork screens from the draft, there was a copper hip bath full of steaming water.

Beside the hip bath stood a narrow can shaped like a cone with the point sliced off, also filled with water. There was a stack of fawn-colored towels with a square cake of orange soap and a wide-toothed comb lying upon it. There was a puffy yellow bath sponge, and, best of all, on a bench near the fire was a long soft heavy gown very nearly the color of the firelight with a pair of fur-lined soft boots beside it.

That does it. Ruth surrendered to her fate with a sigh. She could pass up any number of roses, and she could even, with an effort, pass up dinner, but she could not bear another moment of being filthy and unwashed and grubbing around wearing a dead man's clothes.

She kicked off her oxfords and began to undress.

Some minutes later, a pink, wet, and naked Ruth sat in the bath and gouged the last of the burrs and elflocks out of her hair with the sandalwood comb. She was warm—really warm—for the first time since she'd fallen through the bookcase in the Ryerson basement, and clean besides. And now she was going to wash her hair.

If she hadn't been stupefied with exhaustion, stress, and unaccustomed exercise she might have thought twice about participating in this setup for a Masterpiece Theater remake of *Psycho*. But Ruth was numb past hysteria, and so she bent her head between her knees to wet her hair, and then lathered it thoroughly with the soft orange soap.

Afterward there remained the problem of getting it really rinsed, but with the aid of the second can of water Ruth managed to get her long brown hair "clean enough for government work," as she thought of it. Then she rubbed off another layer of unwanted skin with the hot rough towels and picked up the robe.

It was a simple T-tunic, generic to the point of parody; the garment all moderns thought everyone in "The Middle Ages" wore and none of them actually did. The tunic had a close round neck with a short slit in front to let the head through, fell to just below the calf, had slightly-flared three-quarter-length sleeves and otherwise fit like a unisex sack of potatoes. The fabric had a close smooth hand and was the color of pale apricot flame; a color that Ruth was quite certain could not be achieved in Nature before the introduction of coal-tar (aniline) dyes in 1857. It was thick and rather stiff, the way wool blankets or drapery fabric are stiff, and reminded Ruth vaguely of one of those one-piece acrylic fleece sleepers for infants.

It was also clean and soft and she hadn't had to peel it off a corpse. Ruth put it on. The slippers were soft suede fur-lined ankle boots, obviously meant to be worn indoors, and Ruth put those on, too. Then, compulsively and apologetically tidy, she shook out and folded the clothes she had come in, and spread the towels she had used over the fire screens to dry. Then she sat in front of the fire and combed her hair until it fell in a soft, loose light brown curtain. *Clean.*

Ruth braided her hair in a fat tail over one shoulder, and was standing there, holding it, and wishing in frustration for her long-lost purse or even one good rubber band, when she remembered the hair ribbon she'd bought at the Market. That sent her on a (one-handed) search through her possessions until she unearthed it.

She found more than that, though.

Ruth stood, absentmindedly tying off her braid with the red silk ribbon with the tiny golden bells and looking at the object now lying on top of her discarded clothes. She'd forgotten all about the ring.

Ruth's worldly goods as of this moment, exclusive of clothes, consisted of a battered tin cup stolen (probably) from a Goblin Market wineshop, a pair of golden embroidery scissors, Nic's wristwatch (how had she gotten that?), and a ring, a silver ring with a golden stone that glittered uncleanly of magic. The ring the dead man had been carrying, back in the meadow where she met the unicorn.

Nic had said it was out of place where it was, and Ruth could only agree. She also knew that it made her profoundly uneasy. She was tempted to throw it into the fire, but the firm resolve not to trespass against her unseen host's graciousness stopped her.

With some reluctance, she unearthed the one remaining belt-pouch in her possession and shoved ring, scissors, and goblet into it. She hesitated for a moment more, looking about for something to hold it on with, then went over to the bed and unhooked one of the golden ropes that held back the curtains. It had a heavy fringed tassel at each end, and easily went round her waist with a good deal to spare. She slipped the strings of the pouch over one of the fringed tasseled ends and tied the makeshift belt tight over the housegown. She didn't want any of the pouch's contents, but she didn't think it was fair to leave them lying around loose for someone else to trip over.

She snuffed all of the candles in the bedroom except the one she'd brought with her from downstairs, and went back down. Her soft booted feet made no sound on the oak-planked floors of the empty house.

In the parlor the stew was still steaming hot, just as it had been an hour before. The candles were no lower, nor were the logs on the fire any more consumed. It was as if, in this room, time had stopped while Ruth was elsewhere.

The thought made her uneasy, but not profoundly so. Not after however long it had been since Christmas Eve.

She tried to remember exactly how long it had been, how many days she had been here, but the only thing that came to mind were scraps of misplaced poetry about a sleep and a forgetting.

She wished she *could* forget. Or remember. Or something.

The stew was very good, and the wine had spices in it. Ruth finished both. Sometime tomorrow she'd have to try to find the kitchen. But somehow it didn't seem like a very good idea just now, so Ruth finished her stew and her wine and then, like a good actor patiently following his assigned if rather bewildering role, Ruth took her candle and went back upstairs to bed.

Here, however, things were not just as she had left them. The hip bath and towels were gone, the screens were folded and stacked against the wall, and there was an enormous marmalade cat sitting on the pile of Ruth's neatly-folded clothes.

He must weigh twenty pounds! was Ruth's first marveling thought. As if it had heard her, the cat turned its head and regarded her, unwinking butter-yellow eyes fixed on her with a feline look of disdain.

"Hello, moggie," Ruth said. "I'm Ruth Marlowe, the tra-

ditional benighted traveler who comes to the house in the
woods and doesn't ask awkward questions about where
the owners are."

The cat closed its eyes and began to purr, kneading the
fabric beneath it with its paws.

"I'm going to bed," Ruth added, feeling only a little silly
to be having this one-sided conversation. "You're perfectly
welcome to join me. In the morning, all things being equal,
I expect to be on my way. Even if I don't know where I'm
going. Or how to get there. Or—" Ruth yawned, hugely.
"G'night, moggie."

The bed was already turned back, revealing an expanse of
white linen sheet trimmed in French point lace. Ruth sat
down on the side of the bed and kicked off the house boots,
curling her toes at the cold before sliding them beneath the
covers. There was a hot brick wrapped in flannel at the foot
of the bed; Ruth wrapped her toes around it and sighed. All
the comforts of civilization.

Civilization. And in the word the edges of some larger
concept than could be embodied in flush toilets and tax col-
lectors; something about expectation and reason and the rule
of law.

She unknotted the curtain tieback from her waist and
pulled the leather pouch off of it. She put the tieback on the
table beside the bed and the pouch (with reluctance) on the
pillow next to her. She snuffed the candle, but the room
remained rosily lit by the fire on the hearth. She lay down
and pulled the covers up to her neck.

There was a thump on the bed as the marmalade cat joined
her. It walked the length of the bed, toward the pillows, and
stopped as it encountered the pouch. It regarded it for a moment, sniffed at it, and sneezed. Then it began pawing at it,
making the universal "cat covering up something" motions
on the pillowcase.

"Oh, for heaven's sake," muttered Ruth. She snatched at
the pouch and moved it to the night table. The cat settled
into the pillow with a deep-voiced purr.

Time slipped from his ordering like a willful serpent, and
if anyone knew when and where he was, it was not Rohannan Melior of the House of the Silver Silences.

Head of Line Rohannan. Was that event far in his past, or
still yet to be?

At least the Sword was with him. It had been Melior's task and obsession for a human lifetime, and its absence would have left him more than restless.

He stood in his father's solar in Castle Dawnheart. A wild witch-storm battered the walls; cover for Arneis' and Gratien's move of troops along the border of the Vale of Stars, so Rohannan's scouts had said. As soon as the storm died, Rohannan Lanval and his son would be after them with two troops of horse and Jausserande's Ravens—if she got back here in time—and hope to pin them at the edge of the Vale until Rohannan infantry and Adepts could come to support them. At any cost, Arneis and Gratien must not be allowed to come to Medraut's aid with fresh troops.

"Melior." His father's voice recalled him to himself. He turned from the window. Rohannan Lanval was staring at him intently.

"Father?"

"You know that our Covenant forbids us to use that which we guard against one another—"

Melior frowned. Of course he knew it. They all knew it. With every hero-tale and elementary lesson in simple magic came the lore and warnings surrounding the Twelve Treasures. They must be kept. They must be presented at the Kingmaking. They must not be set against the other Treasures, for the Twelve Treasures were only vulnerable to themselves, and the destruction of any of them was the death of all the Seven Houses of Twilight.

"—yet I would have used it tomorrow."

Melior stared at his father in shock and felt disjointed time slide around him like chill oil.

"The Sword of Maiden's Tears is gone, my son. Find it. Find it. Find—"

Where was he? In the middle of some retreat, but the Sword of Maiden's Tears was with him, and Melior had never carried it in war.

The rain fell in distinct echoing *pock!* noises through the canopy of trees, and Melior was soaked; his silver hair sleeked dripping to his skull by the rain that slid down his skin and beneath the collar of the ornate cloak he wore to soak the clothes beneath. His boots, too narrow and high-heeled for this activity, squished soddenly with each step. There was nearly enough water to wash away the blood, until he felt life flow out of him with the trickling rain.

It seemed, however, important to go on.

Chills and fever racked him alternately, and Melior knew his senses could no longer be trusted. He was giddy with blood loss; unbearably thirsty. He had stopped once, to inspect the wound and bandage it as best he might, with strips dagger-cut from his undertunic, and then he had seen that the edges of the long slashing wound were iridescent and slimy, glowing with the residue of poisoned magic that would finish him, with time.

He paused, leaning against a tree, and a chilling douche of water from above caused the time-ocean to recede momentarily and beach him in the Now.

He was Melior Rohannan. His father was dead and he was alive, and lost somewhere in the Heartlands with the Sword of Maiden's Tears.

He looked over his shoulder and saw the gray mare. Her mane and tail fluttered in the breeze as if no rain reached her, and she walked in a shaft of moonlight reserved for her alone.

He would not ride.

Melior turned and stumbled on. And once more the world slid away, until he was only a soldier in an endless war, slogging through the rain without knowing why.

"C'mon, Jimmy—we're going to be late!"

Ruth tossed restlessly in the strange bed. Sleep had hit her like an auctioneer's hammer coming down on a quick sale, but it hadn't brought oblivion. Lost in the Lands Beyond the Morning, Ruth dreamed.

There was a shortcut to Kath's place—a back road, not very well lit. It was one in the morning. Ruth sat beside Jimmy Ramirez as he slewed the Oldsmobile around the curve.

There was a flash of light in the road ahead; a coppery fiery light, and Ruth, straining her eyes, suddenly saw—

It was in the middle of the road, and she saw—

She saw—

It was gold, copper and gold, and she saw—

"Oh, please, no," Ruth said in a tiny voice. She was awake, sitting bolt upright, staring into the embers of the fire. The marmalade cat was curled in her lap.

And this time she remembered her dream. For some unreasonable reason, here in Elfland the memories the doctors had told her were gone forever, destroyed by accident and trauma, were hers again, at least in dreams.

She would remember the moment of the accident soon. She knew it.

And she couldn't bear it.

Ruth took several deep breaths and tried to stop her hands from shaking. Horrible as the nightmare was, it wasn't what had awakened her. Something else had.

What?

There was no point in trying to go back to sleep, and for Ruth the question of whether she would like to sit in the dark and brood or do it by candlelight was easily answered. She gently set the cat aside and groped around the edge of the bed until she found her boots. Then she put them on, slid out of the bed, and took her bedside candle to light at the hearth.

Naomi always said the SCA'd come in useful some day. For the first time in a long while, thoughts of her dead friend didn't bring pain. Ruth held the lit candle aloft, feeling absurdly like a remake of the Statue of Liberty, and watched it chase shadows back to their hiding places in the corners of the room.

Then she went back downstairs.

The marmalade cat followed her, complaining volubly: it was too hot, it was too cold, what was she doing up at this time of night?

Ruth didn't know. She was still tired from the long walk that day and all that had followed it; exhaustion thrilled in her bones like a stubborn vibration. But the hope of sleep was gone.

The parlor that was her first entry to the house was dark; there were banked coals on the hearth, but everything else was tidied away, waiting for morning. Even the remains of Ruth's dinner were gone, and the white linen cloth of the table as chaste and unsullied as ever.

Simple tricks and nonsense, Ruth thought wearily, pleased through it all at her lack of reaction. Why, magic was becoming just as ordinary as ordinary to her.

There was a coruscating flash. Multicolored light forced itself through the chinks in the curtain in a neon Armageddon, as if someone had just detonated Times Square outside her window. Ruth yelped and flinched backward, to tangle herself inevitably with gown and cat and go sprawling.

The candle and its silver candlestick sailed in a wide arc toward the hearth, where the candle struck, broke, went out, and began slowly to melt in the greater heat of the fire.

The fall hurt, even though *she* was not hurt. The cat was all solicitude, stropping and purring and favoring Ruth's chin with a few random licks.

"Moron," Ruth muttered, pushing it away.

There were no further explosions, and after a moment to collect the shreds of her courage, Ruth limped over to the window, and pulled back the drape.

The moon was a ghostly galleon that illuminated the scene in monochrome clarity. Beyond the windows, a terrace; beyond the terrace, a garden. Nothing to frighten. Nothing to call her up out of bad dreams.

No source for the Filmore East Revisited light show, come to that.

The cat jumped up on the sill and thrust its furry face against her shoulder. Ruth stroked it absently. *Poor thing. It must be lonely. I wonder if—*

She jerked as if someone had shouted her name, and stood baffled the next moment, the cat in her arms. Nothing. No sound.

Something is going on, Ruth thought with grim certainty. But what?

If she were one of the peculiar natives of this place, Ruth had no doubt, she could simply whip out some highly enchanted mathom from her strait-waistcoat and thole the whole situation to the ultimate max. Hefting her handy crystal ball or notebook computer, she—

She was in a terrible mess because she didn't know the local rules, and it was about to get worse.

"Help me get out of this, Jonesey; there's a good moggie," Ruth whispered to her furry companion.

There it was again. The sensation that someone was shouting for her—someone in terrible danger. Only she didn't hear anything.

Any number of Ruth's acquaintances back in college would have been happy to suddenly manifest psychic powers at a juncture like this and be perfectly certain they knew what was going on, but Ruth was not so made. She liked her facts manifest and incontrovertible. Or at least visible.

She didn't hear anything, and she couldn't force herself to

pretend that she did. And that stubbornness, Ruth realized with a sinking feeling, might very well be the death of her.

Or of someone else.

He was lucid enough, in his periods of lucidity, to know that they were infrequent and becoming rarer. He might as well have mounted the nightmare back at the Goblin Market and saved himself all of this. It wasn't as if there was anywhere for him to go, or anyone who could help him. Chandrakar was worlds away, and Melior had no allies here. He didn't even know where he was. Some forest. Broceliande. Avingnon. The Forest of the Night. The Wherewood. Somewhere.

His feet slipped on the muddy forest path, and Melior staggered, working desperately to keep his feet. Fall and he would never get up again.

He shook his head to clear it, and the pain washed his senses clear for a moment. And he realized that here, in this rain-damp autumn forest, he smelled flowers.

Flowers. A moment later, looking for them, he saw them; a garland of many-colored blossoms hanging on a post. A Gate-garland. Ruth had been wearing a Gate-garland in the Market.

A small eternity later he reached it; hewn wood, a gate, and on one gatepost a garland—

Melior lost his balance and fell against the wood, crushing his wounds against the planks and smearing the wood with his blood. He groaned, sliding to his knees. Only his grasp on the Sword kept him from falling on his face.

The horse was closer now. And he had no more flight left in him. He reached behind himself, and pounded weakly upon the gates. No matter whose dominion lay beyond them, entrance to it was better than death.

The gates didn't open.

Reason, sweet or otherwise, was a poor substitute for faith or intuition. Either of those could have told her what to do, but Ruth lacked them utterly, and all that Reason could do was grant her answers that were some sum total of information she already had.

GiGo. Garbage In, Garbage Out. Ruth paced the parlor in frustration. In here she was warm, safe, fed, and protected. Out there it was the middle of the night. It was cold. It could rain. The house might vanish the moment she was over the doorsill. There was nothing out there, no reason to go out there, nothing out there that she wanted, come to that.

But at last Ruth realized that the choice boiled down to this: be stupid or go mad. And with this paradigm defined, she picked up a fresh candle and headed for the front door.

Instantly the cat was underfoot, explaining loquaciously to Ruth that there were needs, urgent needs, feline needs that must be addressed upon the instant. Needs in favor of which Ruth's petty priorities must be set aside. Surely she could not abandon a cat, a small and lonely cat, in a large empty house in the woods, could she?

Yes.

"I'm sorry, moggie, I really am—and it's undoubtedly the wrong thing to do, and I can tell my own self I told me so, but I haven't got any choice, you know," Ruth told it. With gentle firmness she scooped it out of the way and opened the front door.

The night was still out there, black and chill. And it came to Ruth, with the blatant irresistibility of the Improving Homily at the end of some nineteenth-century Moral Tale, that she was turning her back upon Safety and Normalcy to forge off into Chaos and Uncertainty.

"Crap," muttered Ruth under her breath. She pulled the door carefully shut. She was going up to the gate, and then she was coming back—if she could. And then she was going to find the wine cellar and get royally drunk.

She was heartily kicking herself for even this much of an indulgence in hysteria by the time she got to the gate. The candle had blown out before she'd gotten two steps, she was just as cold as she'd expected, and the soft slippers had introduced her to every sharp flint pebble in the path.

But she ran the last few yards to the gate—almost, Ruth thought self-mockingly, as if she knew what she was going to find.

She peered over the top of the gates and then wrestled them open, dragging one wing inward. It grated on the flagstones, creaking in protest. She hadn't recalled it making so much noise the last time.

Melior lay upon the threshold, looking like a high Victorian knight back from a seven-year party at Elf Hill. His skin was pale and rain-soaked, and his lips were blue.

He didn't seem to be breathing.

"Melior? Mel?" Ruth's voice was an overwrought croak. *Oh, Jesus—*

There was the sound of a hoof striking against stone.

Ruth looked up and saw the pale horse, and abandoned Reason and Logic in a rush. The horse was Death, and if it reached Melior, he would die. It stepped forward slowly, neck stretched toward Ruth questioningly.

"Get away from him." Even at the time Ruth had difficulty believing it was her own voice. Fury and adrenaline banished cold, pain, and common sense. "Get away from him, you bitch."

Its head snapped up—almost as if she'd insulted it, Ruth thought, stifling a suicidal impulse to laugh. She paid no more attention to the nightmare; there was nothing she could really do to stop it, except, perhaps, get Melior through the gates. She grappled awkwardly with the dead weight of him, trying first for a grip under his arms and flinching back when her hands came away wet with blood.

The horse took another step. Ruth gritted her teeth and plunged her hands into the blood-soaked cloth, grabbing and dragging and pulling Melior's body in through the gate and down the gentle incline of the flagstoned path that led back to the house.

The moment she was through them the gates shut with a snap, as if spring-loaded. Ruth heard the clatter of the mare galloping off and drew a breath that sobbed with the force of her relief. The she looked at Melior.

"Oh, God," said Ruth. "What a mess."

Chapter 21

The Fall Is All That Matters

And so, in the end, the Lady Floire Jausserande of the Silver Silences was back once more where she had begun: upon the walls of Castle Dawnheart without the pleasant serenities of grace that had lapped her as little as a week before. Guiraut was dead, and the castle's lord, Rohannan Melior, was gone, and that he had not returned home again argued persuasively that he had found his wizard—the one who would bring him his human concubine at whatever price Melior was willing to pay.

Human.

The upwash of fury was as perilous and irresistible as the flames of a spring balefire. Jausserande yielded to it even as she recognized the danger. Coolness, unemotionalism, were the hallmarks of a good commander. Detachment was what saved your life in battle.

But there had been no battle, and still Guiraut was dead. Struck to stillness between one breath and the next, all his might-have-beens forever unriddled. Dead. There would be no knighthood, no Adepthood for Guiraut now. He had ridden out with his lady on a bright fall morning and human brigands had squandered his blood in the dust of the Vale of Stars.

And she, his lady, had stayed not to defend or avenge him, but, burdened with the *tainaiste*-Cup that could not be lost lest the Cup of Morning Shadows be lost with it, had run.

If she had possessed the true Cup, she could have saved Guiraut. The Cup could cure. A formless murder coiled itself around Jausserande's heart, dark and subtle. The Cup could also kill.

The thought horrified her even while the fury whipped fire to ice and settled around her in seductively numbing armor. The outlaws who had killed Guiraut would die. Her Rohan-

nan cousin was not here to stop her. She would hang their
bodies in chains from the castle walls.

"First catch your coney," Jausserande whispered.

It could be done. She was Cupbearer and Treasurekeeper,
even without the Treasure in her hands. When she gave orders, there were few in the land that would say her nay.
What she willed would come to pass.

And was it so wrong, to sweep the land free of human
wolves that preyed upon their betters and upon Melior's
contented human sheep?

Yes, a last scrap of sanity protested.

But Guiraut had trusted her, and they had killed him—
now, in the New Peace, when through all the long years of
war Jausserande had not lost anyone she loved. But now she
had, and the pain was unbearable. The only refuge left to her
was in revenge.

The outlaws in the Vale would die. She would take them
by whatever means she must, and see every one of them
dead.

Jausserande took a deep breath, and felt cool clarity settle
over her like a cloak once the decision was made. A pretty
problem, this. How to proceed?

The villains were within the Vale of Stars. Magic did not
work in that sacred precinct; violence was forbidden there. It
did not matter that humankind broke that law. Elphenkind,
bound by magic, could not.

Very well. She must drive them *out* of the Vale.

What drove out vermin?

"Fire," Jausserande said softly, and began to sing, quietly,
under her breath.

His brain was on fire. Nic Brightlaw groped painfully
back to consciousness, afraid of what he would find if he allowed himself to reach it.

But against all expectation, the fire behind his eyes was
not a foretaste of crisped and suppurating limbs, shards of
candied white bone spangling the earth, silvery loops of in-
testine uncased and garlanding the jungle trail—

He opened his eyes, horror within banishing horror without. And found himself alive, intact—not whole, but not the
ruined meat-puppet of unimaginative memory.

He lay on his back in a woods. His clothes were shredded.
Blood made a sticky mask of his face, and the scalp wound

had opened again. He rolled over; every muscle protested and the crusted gouges in his arm began to bleed again.

He'd fought a dragon and lived. Nic gritted his teeth and sat up. Unfortunately, so had the dragon—since, looking around himself, Nic could see nothing, anywhere, that even slightly resembled a dead dragon.

And that meant that it was alive and after Ruth.

He tried to tell himself that it wasn't his problem. He tried to tell himself that Ruth didn't look for him to protect her. He tried to tell himself that it was far too late; that Ruth was already dead anyway; that once upon a long time ago there had been people who'd looked to him for rescue, for loyalty, and that all of them were dead.

Swearing, he dragged himself to his feet. Bone bruises were a dull ache, mixed with the bright heat of torn muscles and the sick damaged sense of open wounds. The head injury, gotten a day or maybe three before, throbbed chillily with this fresh mistreatment. He tried to close the hand the dragon had savaged, and watched the fingers clamp painfully into a half-numb unresponsive claw as the blood dripped brightly down. Torn muscles, damaged nerves. Impairment.

There was no point to this. It didn't matter how long he'd been unconscious. Five minutes or an hour, the dragon already had Ruth. There was no point. This wasn't his problem. This wasn't his fight. His war was over more than fifteen years before.

Ruth hadn't even wanted him here.

Nic drew a breath and found the strength to laugh. Don Quixote of the poisoned lance; he knew what he was going to do. There was no point in trying to bargain his way out of it. He was going to find Ruth if he could, save her if he could. And if he couldn't, he was going to kill her killer.

Or die trying.

Starting now.

"Courage, Miss Marlowe," Nic murmured. "One rather shopworn white knight, on his way."

The wood bordering the Vale of Stars was a ghostly monochrome in the dawn light. Fox's outlaws moved silently through their camp, gathering up their weapons: bows, staves, here and there a salvaged lance or sword.

This morning of all mornings there were no fires to warm

them. Better cold comfort than the risk of attracting unwanted attention here while they were most vulnerable.

And later?

Fox looked around at his men, wondering which of them would be dead by noon. He saw them watching his expression for some sign and smiled, as approvingly as if he thought they'd all live forever. Their tension relaxed, and Fox continued moving among them, making the last minute plans that would take them all to the Harvest Home by routes that would let them merge with the travelers, unremarked-upon.

One last time he coached Raven and Yarrow, his lieutenants, on what they must do and where they must go.

"Once you've got the horses, don't wait for me. You got that? Don't wait for anybody outside your group. Keep them together, keep track of them—and get out when you've got what you came for."

Yarrow was a tall sandy man missing both ears; a bit quicker than Raven to see the ways of the world, but too easily discouraged.

"And what if you don't come back?" Yarrow said.

Fox sighed inwardly. In the old days, he'd never needed to look at people and measure their capacities as if they held a list of ingredients for his recipe. Now things were different.

"If I don't come back, Yarrow, you and Raven will have to make up your minds what to do." Hopeless, when centuries of slavery had buried the human capacity for self-determination beyond Fox's ability to retrieve it.

"But I'll be back. You can bet on that." And if he didn't come back, he'd be dead, and would hardly be in any position to concern himself with broken promises.

Raven smiled brilliantly. "And if you don't come back, we'll rescue you."

Two chances of that. Slim and none. "Sure," Fox said.

He didn't like the way he felt; this treacherous sense of obligation and responsibility. But he didn't like most things in his life since the moment he'd first set eyes on Rohannan Melior, and for this thing, too, Melior was responsible.

"Come on, guys. Let's move out. Nobody wants to live forever," Fox the Outlaw said.

Jausserande had hoped, superstitiously, that Melior would return for the Harvest Home. She'd sat awake all night in his solar, watching the road that led up to the castle as intently as if it held her last hope of salvation. Watching, and not seeing him. Beyond the walls, in the Water Meadow, the circling sparks of torches told of midnight arrivals and late construction on the booths and dancing floors of the Harvest Home. Tomorrow, outliers from every corner of Melior's fee-lands would come to the Home, bearing samples of the harvest, the *teind* they paid to Line Rohannan. And Melior would not be here to receive it.

Nor, Jausserande realized with tardy dread, was Melior here to go to the Twilight Court to be confirmed by the Seven Houses as The Rohannan of Line Rohannan. It was custom that named him head of his Line as his father's inheritance, not law.

And the Peace had only ended the war, it had not healed the divisions among the Seven Houses of the Twilight. There would be those who would argue against Melior's accession for spite or advantage. Melior *must* be at the Twilight Court to speak for himself, else he would lose the guardianship of Line Rohannan to another.

He had known all that, and still he had gone to seek the wizard and be taken out of Time. For what?

Not for the mud-born, daughter of Earth. He had come back once without Heruthane—Ruth—and had not gone after her again. No, he had sent messengers, and mere common sense argued that now, when the stakes were so much higher and the penalty for absence so much more great, Melior would send messengers again, with gifts if needful, to the wizard whose assistance he desired to court.

Jausserande swung herself to her feet. Seven paces to the window, where the High Road gleamed white in the moonlight. Nine paces from that to the wall where Melior's Treasure, the Sword of Maiden's Tears, hung when its master was in residence. The empty pegs were black punctuation to the pale stone. Jausserande slapped the wall in pure frustration; the sound was muffled and flat.

He had gone for something more important to him than Ruth.

Jausserande stood in the middle of Melior's solar, the pale dawn light crowding around her like the enemy host. She must see Lady Vuissane at once. Perhaps she—

"So there you are."

Jausserande whirled to face this new threat. It was the human knight out of her dream, still dressed in his bizarre black-and-green armor, but even as she registered that, she understood that he was not here at all. An aftereffect of Vuissane's potion, or some baffling weight of futurity pressing its shadows into the real world.

"Who are you?" Jausserande said tightly.

"I'm nobody: who are you?" He smiled; teeth dazzling white against skin burned brown by the sun in human fashion. His eyes were cold as winter glass.

"Why are you here?" Jausserande persisted.

"You're supposed to be the ones so familiar with the unseen world, lady. I'm here because you keep calling me. You need me. Without me, you can't get the Cup."

Lies and illusion, Jausserande told herself firmly. "*I* need? And what do you need?"

"A windmill," the phantom answered maddeningly. "I need some tilting practice. A windmill will do."

Jausserande felt the anger take her, making her voice and movements abrupt and precise. So the *inconnu* wanted windmills, did he? When she found him in the flesh, she would chain him in a mill until he was sick of it. Sick to death. She took a step toward him, saw his smile widen with maddening mockery—

And then it was full day, the light of two hours past sunrise streaming in through the windows, and Dawnheart's steward stood where the apparition had been, holding a tray laden with morning bread and beer.

"A good day for fairing, Lady Jausserande," Arnaut suggested.

Jausserande blinked, the thoughts and visions of the night sliding and jumbling around each other until they were battered to fragments. She forced a smile, though she felt more like screaming.

"A good day, indeed," she answered, and every instinct told her that she lied.

She spoke with Arnaut a few moments more; small politenesses, forgotten as they were spoken. He was barely gone when she, too, left the chamber.

In her tower room, Jausserande dressed to go a-fairing. Perhaps her answers were there. At any rate, going to the fair would take her away from Dawnheart, with all its reminders of unkept promises. But the clothes she selected from her clothespress were not the garments of a young lady of fortune bent upon dalliance.

The doeskin trousers were soft and gray, molding to her skin like supple armor. She selected, and rejected, several pairs of boots before settling upon a high-cuffed pair in dark shagreen leather, broad-toed and low heeled and hobnailed for far journeying. The undertunic she chose was soft cream linen; nothing white to draw the eye; and over it a tunic of wool sheared black from the ram, a darker gray than her trousers. She pulled the laces at the neck tight and then let the ends dangle upon her chest.

The belt was the only touch of luxury to her outfit, buttery black leather studded with chased and enameled silver plates depicting ancient victories, its silver rings ready to hold a purse and dagger. Jausserande took neither: Lady Jausserande of Line Floire, Cupbearer and Treasurekeeper, would need neither to show coin nor defend herself at the Harvest Home. She picked up her cap from the windowsill and set it on her head. Soft dark leather, low and flat, and at one corner brooched with a red-eyed silver raven.

The badge of Rohannan's Ravens. Who had never left one of their own to the enemy—dead or alive. Who had never been defeated in battle. She had kept this one piece after all the rest of her battle livery was gone.

As she turned to go, she caught sight of herself in the mirror.

Where am I going and what do I seek? Jausserande asked her mirror. The image seemed almost about to speak, but Jausserande did not know what to say.

And if she could step through that mirror into the time before the New Peace, would she?

Jausserande turned and hurried from the room.

The Harvest Home was all that anyone could ask of it. Memories of childhood walked with Jausserande here, and she bought that imagined child fried cakes spangled in sugar and hair ribbons stamped with silver foil stars. But even the horse lines could not hold her attention for long; the animals were sleek and powerful, but Jausserande had no cavalry troop to buy for.

It was then that she saw him.

There were humans everywhere at the Fair. That was understandable; the Home was one of the few places where the

Sons of the Morning and their human vassals mingled freely. Humans came to sell. Elphenkind came to buy. This was as it had been all the autumns of Jausserande's life.

This year was different.

This human was different.

He was tall and gaunt, dressed in worn clothes and a hooded tunic. When he glanced in her direction, Jausserande saw pale sandy hair and pale eyes; an expression that made her think of a yellow dog kicked once too often. And when he turned away, a madcap flirt of autumn wind blew his cowl back and revealed the pale hair lying smooth and unimpeded along the sides of his head. He scrambled to pull the hood forward again, concealing his shame.

Both ears docked, Jausserande noted automatically. *Thieving.*

And as she began to wonder what fool had let such a man leave his master's lands to travel to the Fair, she saw the others.

They were not together, not taking overmuch notice of one another, but each one had the same air of subtle wrongness as Crop-Ears did.

Petty prigs, Jausserande thought, but even as she tried to convince herself, Jausserande's steps were taking her back toward Dawnheart and the guard barracks. Despite all law, custom, and the Harvest Truce, one of the outlaw bands that plagued Chandrakar in such numbers since the war had come to Rohannan's Harvest Home.

Dawnheart's main gate was closed, its master being absent and its steward a prudent man. Jausserande went in by the narrow postern gate.

Outer court. Inner court. The doors to the Great Hall were barred, and rather than summon someone to open them, she took a shortcut; up the outside stair to the second-floor gallery open to the air. The wall had a wooden walk behind it for archers to shoot from. Jausserande ran along the top.

Dawnheart had five towers set into its eighteen-foot-thick outer wall. In this time of peace, several of them were connected to the buildings of the inner castle by high-slung suspension bridges of ropes and planks, swaying and delicate. Jausserande found the one she sought and plunged down it without hesitation, her hobnailed boots catching and chattering on the smooth planks. The door at the far end was open to the warmth of early autumn. Jausserande lunged inside.

Nothing and no one. Nearly everyone was at the Fair, another reason to keep Dawnheart shut up so tight, that it could be guarded lightly, releasing its soldiers to their pleasures. But Richart, Captain of the Guard, should be here. She scanned the room, saw the down-flung quill spattering its ink across a curling sheet of vellum. Richart had left in a hurry.

She could not waste the time to find him. In the middle of the suspension bridge she looked out toward the Fair, and through the lazy curling of blue smoke she saw the flash and flicker of pikes and helmets. Richart did not need to be warned. Richart was at the Fair already.

The Harvest Truce was broken.

Melior was right! was her first outraged thought. But right about what, she could not say; all that Melior feared was Baligant No-House, and if the High Prince was bent on murder, he was hardly fool enough to tip his hand at a simple Harvest Home on Rohannan lands.

Across the bridge and down the wall. Back along the gallery, and this time her path took her along the hall and through the solar, the quickest shortcut to her tower room and weapons.

In the middle of the room she stopped, as abruptly as if the air before her had become stone.

Someone had been here.

She turned in a circle, looking around. The books on her cousin's desk had been moved. There were papers strewn around that she did not remember seeing. The bread and ale left for her this morning by Arnaut and left, by her, untouched, were half-eaten.

"Looking for me?" a voice said lazily.

Jausserande turned, scrabbling at her belt for the dagger she was not wearing.

The speaker stepped from behind a pillar. It was a man, blond as in her vision, but not that man at all. That one was an immovable barrier. This man was a stiletto, to break all locks.

"Or just looking around?" he went on. His hair was as long as any elf's, caught back with a leather thong to fall in a silky whip down his back, and he was dressed in the same shabby leathers as the outlaws she'd seen at the Fair. In his

left hand he held a stout staff several inches taller than he
was.

On his right hand was Melior's ring.

It flared with magic in the dim light of the room. This was
how this outlaw had bypassed all the castle defenses; the
magical traps and wards that should have alerted the guards
and kept him out. Melior's signet. The signet of Baron
Rohannan.

Was this why Melior had not returned?

"You are a dead man," Jausserande told him. But incred-
ibly, he did not seem afraid.

Watch me shake. You're Jausserande, right?" He took a
step toward her, and Jausserande's sight was drawn toward
the flicker in his right hand. A knife with a gray blade,
darker than silver and somehow harder.

Iron. *Iron.*

"Lord Arnaut!" Jausserande raised her voice in imperious
summons, and the intruder smiled.

"He's a little busy right now. Somebody seems to have set
a fire in the granary."

"A fitting place for rats—and mice. Run along, little
mouse, and perhaps you can still escape," Jausserande said
scornfully, but it was a bluff, and he seemed to know it.

"Maybe you can answer something that's been keeping
me up nights. How come you didn't go back after your
buddy on the Vale Road?" He took another step.

Jausserande had retreated from the iron that would burn
her before the sense of his words penetrated. The Vale Road.

He was the one who had killed Guiraut.

Red murder filled Jausserande's vision, driving out tactical thought and making it hard to breathe. Her eyes flicked
left and right, searching the room for a weapon.

"And while you're answering questions, Tinkerbelle,
where's Mel and his patented glow-in-the-dark Magic
Sword? I'm taking up a collection."

Jausserande turned and ran, for as many steps as it took
her to reach the hearth and the display of hunting weapons
mounted above it. She yanked down the first that came to
her hand. A boar-spear.

"Oh, very good, Tinkerbelle," the intruder sneered.

She grounded the butt of the spear and menaced him with
the fire-hardened point. "Tell me your name, before you die."

"Call me Fox. But I'm not going to die." The smile on

Fox's face widened, and became a burning, predatory thing. "And neither are you. Which is too bad—at least you're going to think so."

And then he lunged forward, knocking the point of the spear aside with his staff and lashing at her with the deadly iron blade. Jausserande leaped backward, barely far enough. The blade touched the sleeve of her tunic and the fabric began to spark and flare as the small magics in the weave guttered and died. She shifted her grip backward on her chosen weapon, trying to find the balance point that would let her lift and swing it. She backpedaled, lifting the spear barely in time to ward off a blow from Fox's staff.

"Historically," Fox remarked, "oppressed groups have not been allowed access to state-of-the-art military technology—in your case, Tink, swords and spears. Big deal."

The staff struck the heavier spear and bounced off, spinning in Fox's hands to strike again. Jausserande was barely fast enough to convert a blow meant to cripple to one that was only glancing. But even that glancing blow was enough to send bolts of tingling numbness down her arm.

"And also historically," Fox went on genially, his predator's smile wider now. "The oppressed people have managed to develop a pretty effective martial technology out of leftovers. Prepare to lose big time, elf bitch."

He struck, but Jausserande was not there. The spear clattered to the floor as she dropped it, and she sprang backward, gaining the refuge of a tabletop.

"I have not lost yet," Jausserande said, hefting a candlestick. "And you talk too much, Fox."

"Yeah, probably," Fox said. And threw the knife.

He aimed for none of the possible targets where a throw meant to disable could miss, and kill. The point of the iron hunting knife he carried sank into the meat of Jausserande's leg a little above the knee, sliding home as if it entered water, not flesh.

It felt to Jausserande as if every nerve in her body had been dipped in acid. She smelled the stink of her burning flesh in the moment before the pain hit, and as she drew breath to speak, the shock of raw agony slammed an iron vise around her lungs and throat, staggering her heart in its rhythm and blotting out every sensation except the pain. She did not feel herself fall from the table to the floor, nor hear the hard wooden sound of her solid impact. And when Fox turned her over and yanked the knife out of her leg, the blessed cessation of pain brought dreamless oblivion, and she did not hear the bitter sound of Fox's cursing.

Chapter 22

The Manor of Roses

It was wet, it was raining, she was kneeling in the mud over the bloody, dying body of a man who was not only her hopeful lover but a dead weight she could not possibly drag to true safety.

Ruth Marlowe had had better days.

"Melior," Ruth whispered under her breath. "Oh, God damn it to hell."

Rohannan Melior did not respond. He lay on his back in the road, wearing a gaudy fantastic scaled cloak the hot urgent color of monarch butterfly wings and holding the Sword of Maiden's Tears as if it were a walking stick. His face was pale as a beeswax casting; as still as if he slept.

And this would be a moment of high Victorian tragedy, except for the fact that Ruth's knees hurt from the gravel and her fingers ached with cold. The rain plastered her hair to her scalp and made it hang down her cheeks and back like dripping snake-locks, and there were urgent things to be done and no form of aid forthcoming anywhere.

But she could not simply let her lover die due to lack of imagination. The house held warmth and safety and a promise of life. If they could reach it.

If it would let them in.

Ruth rose stiffly to her feet and looked back the way she had come. The house was dark, and after a moment she realized she could not see the expected lights through the windows: the lights that had been burning when she left. Ruth set her jaw stubbornly. She would *make* the house let her in.

She turned back to Melior. The icy soaking rain still pocked noisily on the cobbled path around them. The edge of the forest still loomed just beyond the gate. The lantern at the gate still burned; light enough to show Ruth her lover. One hand was still clutched tightly around the hilt of the

Sword of Maiden's Tears. The other flexed feebly against the ground.

"Melior?" Ruth said quaveringly.

His eyes opened when she spoke. He saw her and smiled, an effortful redrawing of the lines of pain in his face.

"Don't try to talk," Ruth said hurriedly. "There's a house, I—"

He was already trying to get up, eyes closed against the pain. Ruth saw what he was doing and put her hands under his arms and pulled back and up, trying to get him on his feet.

He was taller than she was and heavy; the strain sent needles of warning pain down the long muscles in her back. But if she dropped him now, she would hurt him worse; Ruth clung to that thought just as Melior clung to her, grimly dragging them both upright. The point of the Sword grated along the cobbles as he dragged it, point first, to serve as a prop for his weight.

His clothes were soaked with blood and rain; the sodden front of his tunic was pressed against her, soaking the robe she wore and beginning to drip. She felt no warmth from his body; cold, sodden, and chill, he was a faery knight dragged from a watery grave, a burning brand bare in his hand. The strain of holding him upright was a tight fiery ache in her neck and shoulders, and ran quicksilver wires of strain down her back and leg muscles.

You're babbling, Marlowe. Get the lead out.

"Melior." She spoke his name loudly, willing him to attend. "Put the Sword away. Put it away, okay?"

She didn't know if he heard, but she knew that the touch of the Sword of Maiden's Tears would do worse than kill a human. She didn't need lamplight to see it; it glowed with a faint rotten phosphorescence—witch-fire and marsh gas; poison.

But he wouldn't leave it behind, and she didn't dare drag him toward the house while he clutched it naked in his hand.

"Melior!"

He heard her at last; with awkward, laborious grace he lifted the blade and slid it into its sheath. Deprived of its support he leaned even more heavily on Ruth; she felt her knees begin to buckle as he clutched at her again.

She felt her muscles begin to tremble as she forced her

legs straight. She had to get him to shelter or he'd die. To do that, all she had to do was walk there. With him.

She took one hand from beneath his arm and tried to unlock his hand enough to turn him. Finally he released his bruising death grip on her shoulder, only to transfer it to her hand, so that for one moment they stood poised like demented dancers in the rain. Slowly Ruth turned, moving with agonizing care, so that they stood side by side. Melior seemed to understand what she was doing; he let go of her and slid his arm across her shoulders, transferring his weight to that new support. With his other hand he clutched her arm. The fingers dug in cruelly, bringing first pain, then numbness, then, finally, a chill, bone-deep ache.

I can't move. The realization almost made Ruth laugh out loud, and only the fact that she would fall if she did stopped her. It was all she could do to stand supporting Melior's weight. Walking was impossible.

"Walking isn't impossible, Ruth. It's just going to be hard to learn."

A woman in white. The first of many days of mind-bending frustration and pain. But she'd learned. Ruth Marlowe had learned to walk once before. She could walk now.

First one step. She unbalanced them so that she could move. Heard Melior groan as his weight shifted. Slid her foot forward quickly. Caught her weight on that hip-knee-leg, and felt the muscles quiver and burn with strain.

A step.

Then another step. Legs heavy and aching and unresponsive, it was just like learning to walk again, wasn't it?

If she tore a muscle, if she hurt herself too badly, if she fell, it would be all over and Melior would be here, helpless, with no one to see if he lived or died.

A step. Then another step. Her feet pressed against the ground with more than twice her normal weight, and every sharp stone in her path was a possible assassin. But now the door was only a few yards away.

Locked and dark.

Unheeded tears ran down her face, mixing with rain and sweat. And Ruth, beginning to plea bargain with Fate in a rote litany of empty extravagant promises, stopped short with the chill certainty that here, in this place, words had meaning. What promises she made, she would be held to.

"Oh, please let us in," Ruth said very softly to the dark and shuttered house. Her words came in breathy staccato gasps of air drawn into lungs aching and strained with effort. "I don't have a kingdom and I won't marry some stranger and I won't work for a wizard for seven years." *I'm losing my mind.* "But there must be something you want. I promise to help—as much as I can and if it doesn't hurt anybody else. That's enough, isn't it? Please, please, oh, please—"

She was almost to the doorstep, and knew, with a soul-dead certainty, that she could not take the step that would lift Melior over the threshold.

The door swung inward. Faint and low on the wall inside Ruth could see the shifting glow of a chamberstick. In the open doorway the marmalade cat stood, looking up at Ruth accusingly.

Ruth opened her mouth to say something more, but all she could do was gasp for air with a ratcheting bellows sound. She had carried Melior perhaps a hundred yards, if that.

The door opened wider, and Ruth, determined to the point of madness, found the strength to drag herself up the one low step, and Melior after, and then pivot, swinging him around her and into the sure support of the door frame.

He slammed into it harder than she'd meant, and cried out as if the impact hurt him terribly. And then his knees buckled and he began to sink to the rain-wet threshold, and Ruth, all passion spent, slid down with him, unwilling to let go. Together they lay in the doorway, spent and shaking.

She must shut the door. The thought occurred to Ruth in a vague detached fashion. Melior's head was pressed firmly into the hollow between her neck and shoulder, and she was rain-chilled on one side and only slightly less cold on the other. The stiff immense sodden weight of Melior's cloak hung about them like a tent; Ruth smelled wet fur and leather and cinnamon, and even the trembling quivering aches of her shaking body were remote and forgettable. How pleasant to simply stay here until someone else solved all her problems for her.

There was a pat-pat-pat of a velvet paw against her face, and an outraged miaowing, as of a cat forced to stand in a cold and drafty hall when a warm fire was available.

Reluctantly Ruth opened her eyes and stared into the yellow eyes of the marmalade cat.

"I'm coming, I'm coming," she muttered hoarsely.

She crawled out from under Melior. Freed of her support, he slid the rest of the way down the doorjamb to sprawl on the stoop like an unstrung puppet. Ruth surveyed him for a moment and then grabbed him by the tunic and dragged him forward until his entire body was inside the house.

The latch was a carved wooden peg; she latched the door and slid the bolt home.

Now that Ruth was indoors again and safe, all the nagging annoyance of being cold and wet and dirty returned with full insistent force. Angrily she pushed the thoughts away and turned back to Melior.

In the shadows of the hall it was difficult to see how badly Melior was hurt, but she could smell his blood. She took the chamberstick and lit the hall lamps; in the pale candlelight, Ruth saw the outline of bones stark beneath his skin, the pale eyelashes wet and spiky and gilded with flame.

The cat wove back and forth around Ruth's feet, looking up at her with feline opacity and singing a constant chant-pleure of its needs and injuries.

"Oh, do be quiet, there's a good moggie," Ruth pleaded, and knelt beside Melior.

His eyes had opened, and his gaze was fixed, not on her, but upon the marmalade cat.

"I cry your pardon, Lord," Melior said, his voice thin and effortful. "I would not have come here had I known. But Ruth is my lady," he added, almost apologetically.

"Melior," Ruth said. He reached up and took her hand with fingers that were cold and trembling, then he closed his eyes again as if he had exhausted all his strength.

Ruth bit back a yelp of tearful laughter. His hand went slack in hers, and she laid it down gently. Her chest ached, and there was a lump in her throat that made it difficult to breathe. If this was love, she'd take a good book instead, thank you very much.

Because if Melior died, she couldn't bear it. And she didn't think there was anything she could do to prevent it. The realization made her hands shake even harder, and the tightness in her throat expanded in a burning, strangling ache.

"Mir-*RAO!*" The cat of the house was tired of being ignored. It sat on the newel post and wailed. Ruth jumped, and stared up at it guiltily before seeing what lay beyond it.

The parlor door was open.

Not the Parlor where Ruth had eaten her dinner, but the small one in the front hall that she had examined and dismissed; an odd unlikely room, useful mostly for spying upon the dooryard. Ruth got up and peered inside.

There was a roaring fire in the small fireplace. The heat tightened Ruth's skin and made her numb hands ache with returning life. There was a pallet of canvas-covered straw laid out beside the fire, and a pile of blankets beside, and on a nearby stool draped with a white cloth there were bandage rolls, lint, and cord, knives and probes and forceps. There was a squat green bottle of brandy and a wide copper basin of water.

"Thank you," Ruth whispered, tears prickling her eyes. She turned back to Melior. Warmth, and life, and everything else he lacked, only a few steps away. *"What d'ye lack?"* echoed the ghostly remembered voice of the redheaded vendor at the Goblin Market. If Melior died, Ruth would lack everything. Forever.

But she could help him live.

All she had to do was get him into the room.

"Only a little more," Ruth promised. She undid the beautiful jeweled clasps that held the golden cloak close about his throat and dragged him free of it, toward the safety and haven of the small front room. There was a rasping sound as the scabbarded Sword was pulled across the floor, but she did not stop until Melior lay upon the blankets in front of the fire.

In the bright hot light she could clearly see Melior's injuries at last; the slashes that crossed his leg and torso; the torn leathers and the ruined flesh beneath. Bile rose in her throat and she swallowed hard. But the bleeding seemed to have stopped, or slowed down at least, and if she could only get him warm and dry—

First she had to get the Sword away from him.

In a world not this, Ruth, whose hobby was costuming, had once had the opportunity of a long and detailed acquaintance with Melior's clothes. The straps and buckles were not unfamiliar to her now, and soon she had uncased him of belt and baldric. She unbuckled the high horseman's boots with their tassels and gilded spurs and pulled them off, and then eased the leather straps of the sword harness from beneath him until he no longer lay upon them.

To move them any further she would have to touch the Sword.

"No, no, no . . ." Ruth whimpered. It wasn't fair; she was willing to do anything else.

Anything but that.

Once there had been five friends: Ruth and Michael and Philip and Naomi and Jane. And they'd rescued an elf named Rohannan Melior, who told them his magic sword— the Sword of Maiden's Tears—would do worse than kill any human who touched it. The Sword would turn that human into a *grendel*, a mindless cannibal who lived only to kill, who could only be killed by the Sword. And Naomi had taken up the Sword. . . .

She stood in a tunnel far below the city, bleeding and gore-spattered, resting the tip of the Sword of Maiden's Tears upon the platform floor, the body of the slain grendel *liquifying at her feet.*

The last grendel.

Ruth ran toward her.

"Get back!" Naomi whirled around to face her, holding the sword en garde as if it were weightless. Drops of liquid flew from the spinning blade. Her voice was high, her eyes wide and mad.

"You can't have it!" Naomi shrieked.

Ruth stopped dead.

"Naomi!" Ruth said. "Don't do—"

"What you know damn well is the only thing I can do, now?" Naomi's voice was ragged; her breathing faster now than even exertion had made it. "God dammit, Ruth." The words were evenly spaced, inflectionless. "Melior was right. The sword wants—" She broke off. Ruth could see sweat trickling down Naomi's face, her teeth bared in a grimace of effort. "Get out of here. Go on."

Naomi had taken up the Sword. And died for it.

There was a poker by the fireplace. Ruth shoved at the Sword with it until it was safely on the other side of the room. She threw Melior's boots after the Sword and then crouched beside him, clutching the poker.

But she didn't have time for this now. She turned back to Melior. His eyes were open again; she smoothed his hair back from his forehead with a hand that trembled only a little.

"Everything's going to be fine," Ruth said.

"And so it is," said Melior, his voice a bare whisper, "I have rescued you, my lady Ruth. There is nothing to fear." The corner of his mouth quirked upward in a wry smile. "It is cold here," he added, in a tone of faint apology.

Cold? In front of a fire that baked Ruth's skin like custard and filled the room with the wet scent of stewed wool? Ruth lunged for the pile of blankets that lay beside the pallet and flung several of them over him. She remembered the brandy and uncorked it. There was no cup, but then she remembered the cup in the bag on her belt and pulled it out, filling it and holding Melior up to it to drink.

He drained it as if it were water. "Again," he said, and Ruth refilled it. "Better," he said, when it was empty again. She laid him down and sighed deeply, still holding her hand.

"There is so much to tell you," Melior said. Then his eyes closed, and he was unconscious again.

Ruth studied him with desperate attention.

His skin was pale, but it had always been pale. His hair was drying now in the furnace heat of the fire; Ruth smoothed his hair back; his skin was chill and clammy.

Was he healing? Dying? And if he was dying, what could she do? Ruth remembered the pale nightmare in the forest outside and shuddered. The nightmare would not have Melior.

If she could help it.

The only thing she could think of to do was to get his wet clothes off and bandage his bleeding wounds. And then—

What? Blood transfusion? Amputation? Antibiotics she didn't have? She couldn't imagine the extent of his injuries and had less idea of how to treat them. But she had to do something.

"You're going to be all right," Ruth said, wishing it were true. Then she set to work.

There didn't seem to be any place here for false modesty, but even so it was difficult in a purely practical sense, working with her hands beneath the sheltering blankets to remove tunic, mail shirt, jerkin, and undertunic—all sodden— without hurting him further. Melior stirred and muttered as she shifted him, and Ruth recognized at last that this was not healthy sleep, but feverish delirium.

Why? He was wounded, not sick. And it was only a few hours since she'd seen him at the Market—there hadn't been time for infection to spread.

She worked the soaked woolen tunic up under his arms at last and tossed it into a corner. The mail shirt beneath was a fine-woven silvery thing, but crumbling and discolored in places, as though—

Ruth dropped the blankets back over Melior and grabbed the tunic. It dripped as she shook it out and held it up. The gapes she'd thought were cuts were *burns*—something had eaten through it.

A horrible realization spread through Ruth's mind. She turned back to Melior. Where the silvery mail had been splashed, it was flaking and black, and she brushed metal ashes aside to expose rotting leather beneath.

She dithered for a moment before she used the knife to cut the leather thongs that bound the mail shirt closed and worked it off Melior's body. He stirred and muttered, but whatever he said wasn't in English. A ring with an orange-red stone gleamed on his left hand, brilliant and out of place. Magic. She left it alone.

The leather jerkin beneath the mail had been white once; now it was soaked, rotting away where the monster's poison had spilled on it. It was a tighter fit than the tunic and harder to remove; Ruth worked carefully to keep the rotted places in it from touching either Melior's skin or her own. Beneath it, the linen undertunic was yellowed and burnt, and even the skin underneath was faintly reddened. Ruth pulled the blankets down to Melior's waist to sponge him clean of the last possible traces of poison before swaddling him in blankets again. He shivered beneath them as though neither the blankets nor the fire were there.

"Oh, God," Ruth muttered under her breath. "Oh, God, oh, God—"

But the worst injuries were below the waist, where the armor did not cover him. The doeskin of his breeches was glued to his skin by the blood of reopened wounds, and she had to sponge, and cut, and sponge again, before she could peel them off.

But once she had, she could see the injuries Melior was dying of.

Whatever had wounded him had struck up from below. It had dug a deep gouge above his left knee before ripping free to slice a shallower trench across the front of the thigh and then, at last, to score a dark welt across the top of his right hipbone where the mail did not protect him. The splashes that corroded his mail followed the same trajectory, as if Rohannan Melior had been attacked by some mad mix of bayonet and acid-gun.

No. It was no use pretending she did not know what had made these wounds. Memory of the monster she had glimpsed at the Goblin Market made her shudder. It had looked like a giant wasp.

And a wasp's stings were poison.

Panicked hopelessness sluiced through her veins like ice water. If he was poisoned, he was going to die.

No. There was a chance. People survived wasp stings and even snakebites without medical intervention. If she could just keep him warm and safe . . .

The water in the basin was too bloody now to be of any use and her neck and back were a screaming knot of tension, demanding release. Ruth covered the exposed gashes with a square of bandage, then stood up. She could not think of anything else to do; it should be safe to leave him for a while. She stretched her cramped muscles gratefully.

She looked down at the basin. She needed somewhere to dump and refill it. She stood, and picked up the basin of bloody water and went out into the hallway again.

The cat was still sitting on the banister.

"Any suggestions?" Ruth asked it. Melior had spoken to it as if to an equal, but Ruth was too tired to manage more than simple politeness. That must have been sufficient, because the cat trotted off down the hall in a purposeful way, tail up and glancing back at her. Ruth followed, carrying the basin gingerly.

So this is the kitchen, Ruth said to herself a few moments later.

It looked like most English kitchens before 1750; a low room with small windows high in the walls; a hearth big enough to hold a whole roast ox and encumbered with a number of hooks and swivels that Ruth realized were bronze, not iron; a table or two in the middle of the floor and a whole catalog of hulking, unidentifiable furniture along the walls.

She located the back door and emptied the contents of the basin out it in a great watery crimson arc. The bloody water spattered on the stones of the walkway, and it was a shock to see, in addition to a well-tended kitchen garden, that the rain had stopped and the sky was lightening. Dawn.

The cat strolled in and out of the open doorway, looking up at her as if anxious she should approve the place. Ruth looked over her shoulder into the kitchen, worrying her lip in indecision. She didn't want to take anything from the house that wasn't freely given, but she needed water, water in quantity, and preferably hot. Finally she shut the bottom half of the door and went in search.

One of the cupboards Ruth opened held food. A half-cut wheel of yellow cheese, a bowl of white butter, a loaf and a cut loaf of bread, and a crock of milk.

Habit alone made her think of eating. Common sense and a lifetime of reading fairy tales was stronger. But the cat was winding around her ankles, prrt-ing and miouwrling just as if it were any kitchen cat, any cat that had never been fed in this or any other lifetime, and so she went and got a dish from one of the other cupboards and filled it from the crock. She set it down on the floor and the cat immediately deserted her, lapping at the milk and purring loudly.

Ruth continued her search. If she could just find one of those jerricans that had appeared at her bath, it would be practically perfect for what she wanted.

She located one eventually, and ten minutes of excruciating exercise with the pump enabled her to fill it. Every single one of her strained, abused, and exhausted muscles objected to their treatment, and once she'd filled the can, it was nearly too heavy for her to carry. But she managed to bring both it and the empty basin back to the room where Melior lay.

He'd thrown off the blankets. Ruth set down the can and basin hastily and hurried over to him. He thrashed back and forth, defending himself against some absent enemy, his eyes wide and unseeing. Blood soaked the cotton pad and spilled down his leg, soaking the pallet beneath him, a richer red than human blood. Ruth put her hands on his shoulders, trying to push him back down to the bed.

She hissed in pain as his fingers clamped on her arm, finding old bruises with unerring accuracy. She'd forgotten how strong Melior was. He struggled against her, and even leaning all her weight against him, she could not get him to lie still.

"Stop it!" Ruth cried in frustration. She would gladly have shaken him, if she could only get free to do it. At last she simply lay across his chest, trapping his body with her own.

He struggled against her for a few moments more, then subsided.

Ruth rose awkwardly off him and replaced the blankets, sopping up the oozing blood as best she could. It didn't seem possible that one person could contain that much blood, but on the other hand, look how much tea a teacup could be found to have contained once you spilled it. . . .

The sun was rising now, and the little room was filling with daylight. Ruth looked down at what she was wearing; the robe that had been so pretty when she put it on the night before; it was draggled with mud and blood, and still damp from the rain. She exhaled and closed her eyes, a weariness great enough to bring tears to her eyes dragging at her very bones. She felt like a swimmer, pushed beyond her strength, in that last moment before the ocean closed over her head forever. A small traitorous part of her mind assured her that no blame could come to her if Melior died, and then she could stay here forever, *free.* . . .

No.

She turned back to the doorway and picked up the can and basin. She found the hook in the fireplace that instinct had told her must be there, and hung the can on it to warm the water. While she waited, she retrieved the brandy bottle and the tin cup from the Market. She poured it half-full of brandy and raised it toward her lips, glancing down into it as she did.

The cup was filled with cool blue streamers of glowing light, coiling into the depths of the brandy, swirling down and and down, as if she stared into a tiny holographic maelstrom.

Ruth was tired and her reactions were slow, or else she would simply have dropped the cup. But as it was, she only quivered slightly, staring into the liquid. The fire seemed to drift out of the walls of the cup. It spiraled into the dark red brandy, turning it a rich, luscious, impossible purple. It might be a trick of the light, but now, dazed, half dizzy with the need for sleep, Ruth thought she recognized the faint unnaturalness of magic.

The cup was magic.

Whatever this was, it did not bring the instant lightning revulsion that the magic ring she had taken from the outlaw did. Good magic, then, if there was such a thing.

But what did it *do?* Other than make brandy change colors

and glow in the dark? Hesitantly she dipped a finger into the brandy and licked it dry. She felt no different, tasted no strangeness.

Recklessly, Ruth belted back a healthy mouthful of the brandy. Then she blinked once, very slowly, in astonishment.

It was like drinking sleep. Sleep, rest, health ... she felt like she'd had two Excedrin and a nice cup of hot cocoa.

Ruth looked at the cup and looked at Melior. There was no possible way she could get him to drink now. She took a tag-end of clean bandage and moistened it in the brandy, and wiped at the burned and poisoned skin on Melior's thigh.

Was it her imagination, or was the redness less red, the puffiness decreased?

Alcohol was a good antiseptic, anyway.

She filled the cup from the bottle again, and watched as cerulean witch-fire drifted out into the brandy. When it seemed to be about as magical as it was going to get, she went back to her task, drizzling brandy from the cup to the cloth and swabbing Melior's skin until she'd wiped all around the gashes in his leg.

But the wound itself still had to be cleaned.

And if she poured alcohol into an open wound, it'd hurt like hell, magic or not.

But would water have the same effect?

The water in the jerrican was pleasantly hot now. Ruth drank the last mouthful of brandy and dipped the cup into the water. The blue streamers of light were fainter now, or possibly only harder to see against clear water in full daylight. But after a few moments the liquid was perceptibly bluer.

Maybe the cup was running out of charge, or something. She'd have to be careful. Not waste it.

Carefully she poured the water over Melior's leg.

He jerked once as the water touched him, but almost as if he'd started in his sleep. Ruth's stomach clenched as she realized the water was literally filling the wound, the way rainwater would fill a rut in the road. An iridescent scum rose to the top of the water and Ruth swallowed hard, trying not to gag.

She poured another cup of water into the wounds on Melior's leg. It spilled over, carrying the scum-residue with it. Ruth mopped and swabbed, noting with resigned despair the growing pile of soggy, bloody, *messy* cloth. She blotted the gashes dry and then poured water over them a third time. This time the water ran nearly clear.

The bleeding had stopped.

She did not question her good fortune, but used the last of the dry pads and the bandage rolls, brisk efficient wrappings and tyings learned in what seemed another lifetime. She lifted Melior's leg carefully, propping it up against her knee so she could wrap the bandage all around his thigh, crisp and clean and sane and white. Then she covered him in blankets until he lay like a little hill before the embering fire.

There was nothing more to do. And Ruth, unable to push her mind past the moment, lay down beside him on the bare wood floor.

And slept.

"C'mon, Jimmy—we're going to be late!"

Ruth tossed and turned, realizing too late that sleep had been a bad idea. The dream that had followed her into the Morning Lands had seized her again and not let go.

And now they were on the back road to Kathleen's place, on their way to the accident that had stolen eight years of Ruth's life, and she could not wake. Jimmy Ramirez was driving, and Kathleen and Allen sat in the back, and in a few moments all three of them would be dead.

Desperately Ruth attempted to wrench her inner vision away from the sight of what must be. There were flashing lights around the corner of the road ahead, and at the moment Jimmy thought they were cop-car flashers, but the lights weren't red-and-blue. It was a coppery fiery light, glowing as balefully as the stone in the brigand's ring, and Jimmy, slowing, slewed the Oldsmobile around the corner and Ruth saw—

And Jimmy screamed—

The car jumped forward as he floored the accelerator—

"No!" Ruth jerked herself free at last. She lay on the floor, staring unseeingly at the legs of unfamiliar furniture, while her heart battered the inside of her chest like a demonic washing machine on eternal spin cycle.

A hand touched her shoulder. Ruth screamed and flung herself away, scrabbling at the floorboards like a maddened armadillo.

She looked back. Melior was staring at her with an expression of bewildered concern.

"Oh. It's you," Ruth said lamely.

"Yes," Melior said.

He was, if not completely recovered, at least *going* to recover. He was propped up on one elbow among the blankets in front of the ashes of the fire, one hand was still raised in the gesture of touching her.

He did not ask who it was she thought might have been in the room with her.

Ruth scrabbled to her feet and sat down on the settle. Heroines of fiction might have seized the moment to throw themselves into their lovers' arms, but she just didn't feel like it right now, she told herself crossly.

"You came back to me," Melior said marvelingly.

And it was true, she knew it was true; she remembered, vividly, Christmas Eve in Ippisiqua, and wanting him, and knowing there would never be any peace or happiness in the world again. And finding the door that had led her here.

Ruth began to cry. All that, and now that she had him, she couldn't think of a single thing to say.

She was so absorbed in blotting out the world that she did not hear him move. Only the faint unstartling susurrus of wool as he sat down beside her on the wooden bench and gathered her into his arms. He smelled of brandy and wood smoke and damp linen, and Ruth clung to him both as if she would keep him safe forever and punish him for unspecified wrongs.

"Your leg," she said, a long damp time later.

"Does not pain me so much as some wounds might. And as the dead feel no pain, I should be grateful for the discomfort," he responded.

Ruth looked at him with suspicious embarrassment. He had one of the blankets draped around himself. One fold of it covered her bandaging job. She scrubbed at her eyes with the back of one hand. He was well enough to have gotten over here, at any rate.

"How long has it been in the World of Iron?" Melior asked.

"About two years," Ruth said. "Well, a year and seven months. It was Christmas, when—" She stopped.

When she had fallen through a hole in the world with Nic Brightlaw right behind her.

"Nic! Ohmigod, I— How could I just have forgotten about him? We've got to find him. He's my boss, the library director at Ryerson; he fell through the bookcase with me and then the unicorn got me lost, and he's *out* there—"

Melior shook her gently. "The round tale, from the beginning. And—not following my example—omitting no details whose omission could prove inconvenient or fatal later."

Ruth stared around the room. Late afternoon sunlight streamed through the narrow windows, and the place looked as messy, rumpled, and disorganized as Ruth felt. There were piles of bloody rags everywhere, the scraps of Melior's clothes, and, abandoned in one corner, his riding boots and the Sword of Maiden's Tears.

"But perhaps not at once," Melior amended. "Lend me your aid, and we will see if my strength extends to leaving this room, and what generosity this house's master may be moved to. The magic that runs here is not to be accomplished in the sight of eyes," Melior added, as if annotating some guidebook for her benefit.

"There's a cheese in the kitchen," Ruth offered. Melior shook his head, saying nothing, and after a moment Ruth got to her feet and helped him stand. Then Melior pulled her toward where the Sword of Maiden's Tears lay on the floor.

Ruth dug in her heels, pulling them both to a stop.

"I must bring it with me," Melior said quietly. "It will not hurt you."

"It—kills people," Ruth said, from a throat drawn suddenly tight. *Naomi* . . .

"That is the nature of swords," Melior answered implacably. "But it lacks the particular power you fear while it is in my possession."

"You mean you can turn it off," Ruth said flatly. Melior sighed.

"While I am its guardian—while it is *mine*—it will not trap humankind into *grendel*form, nor will humans covet it. The sword is harmless now, Ruth, and I must keep it with me. It is my duty." Plainly this was not a subject for discussion.

And Ruth knew that Melior would not lie to her, nor lead her into any danger. But it was still hard to help him over to where the Sword lay, to pick it up by a loop of swordbelt and hand it to him. He looped the strap over one shoulder. The silver-chased scabbard dragged on the floor. Ruth turned to go, Melior's arm around her shoulders. Then she remembered the other thing that it would not do to abandon.

"My cup!" she said. "Oh, well, it isn't really mine, but—"
She stopped babbling with an effort, and guided Melior to
the door frame where he could stand supported while she
scurried back over to the hearth.

Ruth found the cup without difficulty and stuffed it into
the pouch with her other (wanted and unwanted) possessions, and returned to Melior. Together they went out into
the hall.

The back parlor where Ruth had eaten her dinner the night
before was sun-drenched and welcoming. Through the long
leaded windows she could see a flagstoned walk and a low
wall, and beyond the wall an entire orchard of apple trees,
bare-limbed in the fashion of early spring. Beyond the orchard was another low wall, and then a long meadow, punc-
tuated with stands of blue and yellow flowers. Hyacinth.
Daffodil. At the foot of the meadow, Ruth was certain, there
was a stream, and beyond the farther bank of the stream a
forest—

There was bread and wine laid out on the sideboard, and
Ruth consoled herself with the knowledge that a skimpy
breakfast was better than none. Melior sat on the sofa with
the Sword propped up beside him while Ruth cut bread and
poured wine.

"Tell me how you came to this place, Ruth," Melior said.
Ruth turned back to him, forgetting about the forest.

"It was raining—" Ruth began, and with the help of
Melior's patient questioning was able to tell him most of
what had happened since she fell through the enchanted
bookcase. Nic, the unicorn, the inn they'd found—and what
had happened after.

"He said there was someone following us. He went off
into the woods to look. I thought it might be the unicorn,
and it *did* show up again, but Nic didn't. And it wanted me
to go with it, and, well, I already knew what happened if you
didn't. So I did, and I didn't find Nic, but I got to the Goblin
Market—"

"And were lucky to escape unscathed," Melior said
sternly. He didn't ask how she'd managed to bring him back
from the dead—perhaps he didn't know how badly he'd
been hurt. Or maybe she was the one who was wrong about
the extent of his injuries.

"Unscathed," Ruth echoed unsteadily. "That *thing*—"

"The warwasp sought to kill you," Melior said bluntly, "and was dazzled by the bolder magic of the Sword. It is a creature of Chandrakar; I think Baligant wishes your death before you can be used against him."

"Me?" said Ruth. "Used against him? What am I going to do—miscatalog his books?"

Melior looked into her eyes, and Ruth realized with a small thrill of unease that he was deciding how much he should tell her.

"I want the truth," Ruth said flatly. "All of it."

"There is a court," Melior said after a pause, "which settles matters among the Houses of the Twilight—matters that are not the concern of the High King. I believe that Eirdois Baligant, the High Prince, works to harm us, and it is at the Twilight Court that I must tell the tale to the Earls and their vassal lords. But what is a tale without proof, in a time where I stand to be confirmed in my father's holdings, or have my rights set aside for another?"

"I don't know," Ruth said, feeling like a straight man. "What *is* a tale without proof?"

"Useless. But I *have* proof. You are my proof, Ruth Marlowe." He looked into her eyes and smiled, with the faint hint of self-mockery that told her he knew she wasn't going to like this, whatever it was.

"I think you'd better explain that," Ruth said, with sinking heart.

So Melior did.

It was in the World of Iron that Melior had discovered that Ruth Marlowe's soul was tangled somehow into the magics that had wrought the Sword of Maiden's Tears. Now Melior went on to explain that some wizard Ruth had never met was going to make a public spectacle of putting her soul back together and getting it out of the Sword while everyone at the Twilight Court watched. It would, he hoped, prove that Baligant was behind the plot to destroy the Treasures.

It sounded, if not actively painful, at least luridly public and humiliating.

"And what if I don't choose to cooperate in this?" Ruth said tightly.

There was a very long pause.

"Do not ask me that, Ruth," Melior said tonelessly.

Before she was quite knew it herself, Ruth was on her feet and out of the room, running down the hall just as if she had someplace to go. Running away before she said something she'd regret to the man who, last night, she was sure she'd die without.

And who now intended to use her as a pawn in some elphen chess game, no matter how she felt about it.

"Prr-RRING?" said the cat, from halfway up the stairs.

Ruth picked it up. The marmalade cat was a warm ecstatic weight in her arms, indicating by every means known to cat-kind that Ruth was surely the wisest of mortals to be devoting her time to *him*.

She walked the rest of the way up the stairs, cat in her arms, then down the hall to "her" room.

Once again there was a tub before the fire and clothes laid out, and this time there was the mouthwatering smell of hot venison pie and a bowl of candied chestnuts laid out on the table before the bow window. The cat leaped down from her arms and began making sure the accommodations were up to standard. Ruth stood and inhaled.

This time hunger overcame cleanliness. The cat jumped up onto the bed and settled itself to watch her eat, and Ruth, standing so as not to get guck on any of the furniture, wolfed the pie in large inelegant swallows, washing it down with mugsful of the hard cider provided.

It was better fare than that laid out below, she reflected.

"Don't like Melior much, eh?" she said to the cat around a mouthful of pie. The cat purred.

"Don't blame you," Ruth said generously. "Don't like him myself at the moment." She filled her cup with the last of the cider, drained it, and sighed.

"But I love him, I think. And he's *responsible*—to the Court of Twilight, whatever that is. To prove the truth to them about that other guy. Baligant."

The cat stopped purring, and regarded Ruth with gold oracular eyes.

Ruth pulled off the robe, folded it fastidiously, and climbed into the bath. "You see," she said to the cat, picking up the soap, "if he doesn't get back with the Sword, or if Baligant manages to get all the Treasures and screw everything up, that means Naomi died for nothing, doesn't it?"

The cat watched her.

"Or maybe I'm just crazy, talking to a cat. But I don't think so. I wish—"

Ruth thought of the garden and the orchard and the

meadow beyond. About the clean clothes and hot dinners; comfort, order, and civilization. About calm comfort, untroubled by love or politics. *I wish I could stay here.*

"But I can't," Ruth said aloud, and bent to wash her muddy, bloody hair.

As if it had already known her intention, the clothes laid out for her to put on were traveling clothes, even though the shadows stretched toward evening. Ruth tried to remember whether any of the rash and hasty half-promises she'd made yesterday included a promise to only spend one night here.

But whether or not she'd promised, whatever she'd promised, the house seemed disinclined to welcome Melior. And that seemed to mean they would have to leave tonight.

It did not occur to her to stay without him. She had no idea if she could really be happy with him, but the idea of not finding out was unthinkable.

And so, Ruth thought primly, she'd better get dressed.

There were knitted woolen stockings that gartered above the swell of the calf with bright braided ribbons, brown boots lined in sheepskin with stout formidable soles, an airy linen smock made opulent with tucks and pleating and delicate white embroidery over which Ruth, professional costumer, tied with ease one wool and two cotton petticoats followed by a sleeveless chemise of silk, which was in its turn surmounted by a soft, thick, serviceable and dependable double full circle skirted T-tunic in dark green wool.

The neck of her dress laced closed with a scarlet ribbon, and at the wrists and above the neckline the immaculate white embroidery of her smock could be seen. The neck, placket, and wrists of the dress, and a band eight inches above the hem, were brave with bright multicolored silk embroidery in designs that were vaguely Celtic, in the way the clothes she wore were vaguely historical.

But the twelfth century T-tunic did not go with the fourteenth century petticoats, and the sleeveless silk chemise was from no historical period.

Still, it was warm.

There were gloves, too, long gauntlets of supple green leather whose cuff-embroidery matched that of her dress. And a snood, of green velvet ribbons and lined in darker silk, that Ruth gratefully seized upon as an answer to the eternal question of what she should do with her hair.

There was a belt of green-dyed braided leather that she fitted about her waist, threading it through the drawstrings of the pouch she carried and returning the tasseled cord to the bed curtains. The free end of the long belt wove back and forth through D rings; Ruth folded the excess over and through, making it dangle properly.

The last item there was Naomi's Kinsale cloak.

Ruth was sure she'd lost it at the Goblin Market. She thought the matter over carefully and became positive. She'd been carrying it at the Market. She'd dropped it sometime there, as she certainly hadn't had it in the forest.

And now it was back.

Welcome to Elfland. The Lost and Found Department . . .

She picked it up and slung it over one arm. The cloak was heavy and it dragged, but she clung to it like a last lifeline to home. How many times did she have to leave safety and comfort and at least the semblance of normalcy, just to follow Melior? There ought to be a limit to what she was asked to give up, somehow, somewhere. . . .

You've buttered your bread, Ruth Marlowe, now lie on it.

She turned to the cat and held her hand out toward it tentatively. It allowed its ears to be ruffled and its jaw to be rubbed.

"Do take care of yourself, moggie. And I remember my promise."

But this time, talking to the cat, she felt silly instead of wise. She shrugged the cloak into a more comfortable position over her arm and went out the door.

It was no particular surprise to see Melior standing at the foot of the stair waiting for her, fully dressed. The Sword was slung over his back again, and he leaned upon a black walking stick as long as he was. His clothes were a match for hers, down to color, cut, material, and embroidery, save that he wore his own boots and the orange scaled cape.

And it was too soon for him to be up and around; he'd been dying the night before. She could tell he was hurt; his mouth was set firmly and his gloved hand clenched tightly on the stave.

"Looks like we're both ready to go," Ruth said, trying for the bright neutral tone that had served her many an hour at the Reference Desk.

"Yes. The Border should be easy enough to cross from

here; we might even find the Road again. But I confess my plans take me no farther than the nearest inn."

"Why—" Ruth began, but a gesture from Melior stopped her. She came the rest of the way down the stairs and followed him down the hall.

The front door stood open. And standing on the threshold, knowing she would never see this place again, Ruth felt a wild clutch of homesickness drag at her heart. This place was not home, she had been here barely a night, but somehow it was the distillation of all of Ruth's best times and places, and leaving it would be like abandoning all her happy memories.

"Come, Ruth." Melior's voice was abrupt with tension. Out of sheer inertia, she crossed the threshold and set foot on the path outside. Melior's measured pace was easy to match, even in her bulky unfamiliar skirts.

She would not look back. She held firmly to that resolve. She would not look back for a last sight of a place she could never go home to again.

The sun was setting, and despite the fact that it had been autumn here last night the sky was the pale crystal-white of clear spring sunsets. Dusk and the season made everything sharp and rainwashed and vivid, and tiny details leaped out at her, from the green of the moss overgrowing a rock to the even distinctness of the cobbles edging the walk. Bare bushes and early grass became trees within yards of the walk, and here and there Ruth could see clusters of spring flowers closed against the oncoming night. Melior's footsteps were loud beside her.

They came to the outer gate, the one that divided the house's grounds from the forest, a double recurve of weather-grayed wood. There were clusters of flowers at the foot of each post, and the garland she had hung the night before was still draped over the gate. The lamps were already lit, their candles feeble against the bright twilight.

She could still go back.

Even now, the house would take her back, and there would be long walks in the twilight, through the orchard and the meadow to the river beyond.

Melior put his hand on the gate, and it swung away from him as if it did not like to be touched.

Four steps would take her onto the forest path. And the gate would close forever.

It did not matter what she might have with Melior. What she was giving up here was real, and good, and precious, and she would miss it all the days of her life.

Ruth wavered. And Melior yanked her arm so that she stumbled forward, through the gate. She gasped as she heard it swing shut behind her with gunshot finality.

Melior looked down at her. "Some day I will explain, if you still wish to hear. You have been done great honor, Ruth Marlowe, in that place."

Ruth shook her head, blinking back tears, and wiped her eyes on the sleeve of her tunic. Melior held out his free arm and she put herself inside it, resting her hand on his hip and leaning her face against his tunic.

This was what she'd chosen. For better, for worse, with malice aforethought. This. Melior.

Then he shifted his weight, hissing a little to himself as he leaned his weight upon the stave, and the two of them began to walk down the forest path through the darkening wood.

Chapter 23

Between the Knife Edge and the Skin

There was a long time of pain and sickness, of wandering alone crying out for any of her own to find her, to answer her. She was hot and cold by turns, and fought the hands that held her back when all she wanted was to run.

At last, exhausted, Jausserande fell into dreamless sleep. Some uncounted time later she drifted toward consciousness, only to be lulled back into dreams by the familiar sounds of an armed encampment.

"—don't know why you brought her."

From somewhere outside the place where she lay, Jausserande heard voices, but it was too much trouble to wake to them.

"Everybody else got to bring home a souvenir. I didn't get time to shop."

Jausserande heard the words without caring. She felt weak; lazy. Every muscle in her body ached with past strain.

"The men won't like it."

"Then the *men* can go find somebody else to play with, Yarrow. I'm the Daddy; either they do what I tell them, or I'm taking my toys and going home."

How strange. She must have taken a head-hit in the last raid. That would explain everything. How Miralh would laugh.

Jausserande drifted back into sleep.

"Wake up, Tinkerbelle," a voice said, very close.

Jausserande jolted awake, fully conscious this time. Fatigue resolved itself into separate aches. Her head. Her leg.

The Harvest Home. *Fox.*

Fox was standing over her, holding a bowl. Jausserande lunged for him, reaching for his throat—

And was yanked back by the collar around her neck. Its leash was tethered securely to something that would not yield; her hands were prisoned behind her, in a carven yoke such as she had seen prisoners wear in wartime, half her life ago. She fought her bonds, gritting her teeth at the nausea and weakness that rode over her in waves.

"Quit thrashing. If Raven couldn't break that—and he tried—you can't. I thought you *aristocrats* were supposed to have a few brains," Fox sneered.

Jausserande stared up at him, violet eyes wide with shock as the full horror of her situation sank in. She was in the hands of the enemy. She looked around.

Jausserande lay on a crude pallet in a primitive hut. Her boots and her belt were gone; she lay on the pile of skins in her linen undertunic and drawers, with a large bandage wrapped high on one thigh. Through the squares of bark that formed the hut's outer covering, she could see chinks of daylight shining, and could hear the sounds that had mocked her with their familiarity. The sounds of an armed camp, yes—but the camp of the outlaws.

Fox stood over her—wearing, she noted with almost ludicrous indignation, her gray wool tunic over the same crude leathers she had seen him wearing at Dawnheart. His skin had darkened with exposure to the sun, as humans' skin was wont to do, and the hairs on his forearms were almost elf-silver by contrast.

And Melior's signet ring was on his finger.

Fox gazed passionlessly down at her, as if she were a litter of pigs he was deciding best how to cull. Then he squatted, setting the tray down on the floor of the hut within easy reach.

"Going to behave, Tink? You try to kick me, and I'll knock you silly."

Jausserande swallowed, through a throat gone suddenly dry. This was not clean war, where prisoners were ransomed. Fox and his losels had nothing to lose. He might do anything.

And there was nothing she could do to stop him.

It was a new sensation, and a year ago she would have fought no matter the odds, as blindly as an unbroken colt. But she was Cupbearer now, and the honor Jausserande had taken up so lightly held her more brutally than Fox's shackles could. She had responsibilities that stretched far beyond her own desires. She was Cupbearer; and while the Cup of Morning Shadows was safe still . . .

The key to the Cup was not.

"Lie back," Fox said, and reached for her leg.

Despite her best intentions, Jausserande flung herself away from him. Her arms were twisted awkwardly behind her by the shackle, and the leather collar at her throat chafed. The bad leg buckled agonizingly under her when she tried to use it and Jausserande bared her teeth at Fox in hopeless defiance.

Fox sat back on his heels.

"What? Afraid of me, a—what was the quaint native term again?—'mud-born'? Afraid of *something* at least, Tink? Finally? Fear, you know, is the beginning of wisdom. Mao Tse-tung said that, I think. You won't ever have heard of him."

Jausserande watched him, spellbound as the lark before the cobra.

"But maybe you've heard of gangrene? Stupid bitch," Fox added in an afterthought. "All of you damn elves think you're so irresistible. You just come waltzing in and expect everybody to be struck stupid by your ineffable beauty—and then you start putting the boot in. Well, the boot stops here, Tink. No more elves. No more magic. No more Twelve god-damned Treasures."

She had thought the situation was as bad as it could be, and had been wrong. It had just gotten worse.

The human was mad.

"What are you going to do?" Jausserande demanded, her voice harsh and low. "And what have you done with The Rohannan?"

"Who?" Fox's surprise was genuine enough.

Now it was Jausserande's turn to be nonplussed. Had he killed Melior and looted the body without even knowing his victim's name? She stared at Fox's hand.

He saw the direction of her stare and smiled, the sweet smile of a saint seeing Paradise. It transformed his face to something neither human nor elphen, and Jausserande did not care for it.

"Oh, the ring. He gave it to me, Tink, and that was his first mistake, and too bad for him not his last. But you asked what I was going to do, so in good villain style I might as well tell you. I'm going into the Vale and getting the Cup of Morning Shadows. Then I'm holding you and the Cup for ransom until I see if Melior is going to come and get you

back. If he does, I'm going to shoot him in the back and see
what a hammer and anvil'll do to his Sword."

The Sword of Maiden's Tears. Line Rohannan's Treasure—destroyed?

"You can't do that!" Jausserande gasped.

"Wanna bet?" Fox reached into a pouch dangling from his
belt and pulled something out. Jausserande desperately tried
to shut her eyes, but couldn't bear not to see.

Her cup. The *tainaiste*-Cup, that would find the true one.
In Fox's hands. The attack on the Fair had been a feint all
along. The outlaw did not seek plunder, but to strike at the
heart of Chandrakar itself. At the Twelve Treasures.

But who could be so crazed?

No one. Unless her cousin, whom she had thought mad,
was not. And the human, though mad, was not crazed.

"Tell your master the High Prince he will never succeed
in his depravity—not while any of the Treasurekeepers re-
tains his charge!" Jausserande raged.

The surge of fury left her weak. Jausserande closed her
eyes, and through the tide of weakness felt Fox's fingers at
the bandage on her leg, unknotting and unwinding. Almost,
she did not care.

"You'll live," he said, when the wound was bared to his
inspection. "Jesus, a five-year-old with a slingshot and a box
of paper clips could take over this place in twenty minutes.
Assuming he could get anybody to get off their ass and
rebel. How do you ever expect to develop any decent technology without iron?"

His words meant nothing to her, and his scornful manner
whipsawed Jausserande between fury and a hard, hopeless
fear. There would be no rescue for her here, and even the
small magic she could command was beyond her in this
weakened state. She tried to shut out the day, the place, the
sight of the *tainaiste*-Cup in human hands, Baligant's madness, to put all the Treasures so at peril.

The feel of a wet cloth on her skin shocked her to alert-
ness again. Fox was bathing her wound. She stared; it was
a short ugly violet gash, swollen and raised but obviously
healing cleanly. Such a small injury, to cause such agony.

Jausserande's eyes teared unwillingly at the memory. She
had ridden all day once with a bone-deep sword cut to the
leg, but the sword had been bronze, and nothing, *nothing* to
the pain of iron.

"I'm going to leave the bandage off so it can get some air. After all, you aren't going anywhere, are you?" Fox said.

Jausserande didn't answer. She turned her head away, dismissing him.

"And now, Tink, it's dinnertime. There's just one thing I'd like to share with you before I read you the list of tonight's specials. Look at me, elf bitch."

His voice had lost its light note of self-mockery.

Unwillingly Jausserande met his eyes. They were blue; pale blue and opaque, like expensive glass. His face was expressionless, his tone emotionless as he spoke.

"If you give me trouble, I won't feed you. If I don't feed you, nobody will. They're afraid of you. That probably sounds like a good deal to you, but it means my men won't come anywhere near you—unless, of course, Yarrow cuts your throat. He's that kind, you know; inclined to panic. And he gives up too easily—but on the other hand, you're tied up. Not much of a challenge.

"But since I know Yarrow's that kind of guy, I've got Raven keeping an eye on him. Raven wouldn't touch you with a ten-foot pole. He's kind of an idealist, you might say.

"So if I don't feed you, I don't think the rest of them are going to give it a real high priority. Think about that. You'll die of thirst in about four days, assuming you're anything like a human, and you know, somewhere along about your third day without water you'll be willing to do practically *anything* to get a drink."

The smile that followed that bland recitation of horror was all the more terrifying for its easy brilliance.

"So why don't you be a good Tinkerbelle, and cooperate, and we can all keep our illusions a while longer. Okay?"

He knelt beside her, watching and waiting, and all Jausserande could think of was that if she died here, the Cup of Morning Shadows would be lost to Line Floire forever. And Line Floire would in turn be lost.

And Baligant would win.

If fury could have cut her bonds, Jausserande would have been free. If desperation were a weapon, Fox would be dead. But they were not.

He was waiting for her to answer, Jausserande realized. And when he was tired of waiting, he would leave. He would not come back. And she would begin to die.

The need of her Treasure broke her own need before it.

"I accept your terms," Jausserande whispered.

If her capitulation pleased him, Fox didn't show it. There was none of the gloating or bragging Jausserande expected from a human who had captured one of the Morning Lords. Instead, he simply moved forward and helped her back into a sitting position. Her leg gave twinges of pain as she shifted, but she thought it would soon be strong enough to bear her weight.

And then she could get free. Get the *tainaiste*-Cup. Kill Fox.

Jausserande leaned against the post she was shackled to; a tree trunk, lopped and left rooted in the earth. Fox brought a waterskin and held the nozzle to her mouth; Floire Jausserande, Cupbearer and Treasurekeeper, gulped thin warm flat beer until the waterskin was withdrawn.

"For what it's worth," Fox said, turning back to her with a bowl containing boiled grain, "my plans don't include killing you. But you can kiss your Cup good-bye."

Never, Jausserande thought fiercely, but there was puzzlement in the thought. Didn't Fox know that the loss of the Cup meant death for every man, woman, and child of Line Floire? How could Fox think to promise her life and withhold the Cup?

"Whatever you have been offered to do this, Line Floire will match it, for my freedom and the return of the Cup. And more—Gate passage for you and all you choose to a land where humans rule," Jausserande said. Surely Baligant could be offering nothing more. "Think, before you cleave to your bargain with the High Prince. A lord who has betrayed one will betray all."

Fox stopped with the spoon halfway to her mouth. "Very pretty, and very noble. And you'd probably even keep your word, which is a nice gesture considering what we mean to each other. Too bad you got me wrong, Tink. I don't give a damn about the home rule situation in Elfland. I'm a freelancer."

Jausserande opened her mouth to protest. Fox filled it with a spoon of porridge.

Days passed. Jausserande brooded as her injury slowly healed, wondering how she could kill the outlaws' leader. In her captivity she saw no one other than Fox, though she heard his men on every side. He slept in the hut beside her, and in the darkness Jausserande would lie awake, listening to his breathing and watching the progress of the waxing moon through a chink in the roof of the hut. He had the *tainaiste*-Cup. She could not kill him until she knew where it was.

During daylight hours Jausserande had the hut to herself, Fox usually being absent on his mysterious business of rabble-rousing and thievery. She listened carefully to the careless talk that went on outside, and after a few days had collected a good idea of the extent of his following. The knowledge made her no happier.

Fox was the touchstone for every spark of foolish human disaffection in all her cousin's wide lands, it seemed, and had gathered about himself not only the brutal losels that one might expect to find accompanying a forest outlaw, but also men of a dangerously high quality.

Jausserande suspected that there might be women in Fox's band as well, and that was the gravest news yet. It meant that this band of Fox's was no summer rebellion, with disaffected serfs returning to their hearths and masters as soon as the first snow fell. If the women supported Fox, then he might find welcome and support in any village in Chandrakar.

Ungrateful, stupid creatures, to turn so on their overlords just as peace had come to Chandrakar at last. It was their great-grandsires who had first gone to war; surely they themselves should be grateful to put an end to it.

As she had been? Jausserande was honest enough to ask herself that question. If she could imagine no life beyond war, how much less imaginative might these short-lived humans be?

It mattered not. Their duty was to obey their overlords. There was no excuse for their rebellion. When Melior returned, he would not be allowed to be as soft with them as formerly. Line Floire would sue for Jausserande's blood-price, and Melior must pay it. Fox and all his band would die: gelded, hanged, and then beheaded to deck the Traitors' Gate of Dawnheart.

If Melior returned.

And even if Floire took its vengeance, what would happen to the Cup?

In the late afternoon after the night she had watched the full moon pace the sky Fox came to her. It was early for the evening meal Jausserande had come to expect from him, though he carried a wooden tray with food on it.

But instead of feeding her, today he untied her hands.

Freed, it was absurdly easy to untie the braided leather leash from the tree; Jausserande stood, holding to the post for support. Her muscles trembled with the unaccustomed exercise.

"Why?" Jausserande said, stretching to ease the stiffness of long stillness. She could kill him even bare-handed, she was nearly certain, but if she knew that, Fox must know it as well. She rubbed her wrists and eased her shoulders, not looking at him.

"Eat your dinner, Tink; we're going walkies. And although it's hardly necessary to mention it, I will: the Cup is hidden somewhere that only I know about."

Jausserande sat again and reached for the tray. There was bread and ale, proof, though she hardly needed it, that Fox had sympathizers in the local villages. She did her best to ignore him as she fed herself. His trick was only what she had expected. It was only what she herself would have done, had one of the other Treasurekeepers fallen into her hands during the war.

But today Fox was edgy, keyed up and minded to talk.

"The way I figure it, if you kill me, no Cup. If you escape, you can't dally to search every rock, rabbit hole, and tree. The only way you can think of to maybe get it back is to string me along. In other words, cooperate."

"What makes you think it means so much to me?" Jausserande said crossly.

Fox laughed, a short sharp bark such as his namesake might have uttered. "If it means as much to you as the Sword does to Melior, you'll do whatever it takes for a chance to get it back."

Jausserande nodded, slowly, acknowledging what was no more than the simple truth—and wondering, not for the first time, why the outlaw Fox seemed to claim such intimacy with her cousin. She reached for the wooden mug on the tray and then stopped, speaking almost without thinking.

"Fox, what do you truly want? Destroy the Treasures and you destroy us all, elf and human alike—you cannot want that."

"I want," said Fox, with the soft passion of a man at the edge of endurance, "to be able to sleep again at night. So I'll destroy Chandrakar? Fine by me. It's a damn shame Chandrakar didn't think a little harder about what it destroyed.

But it didn't—so Chandrakar—and its Treasures—and its elves—have me."

Another of Fox's brilliant smiles, which Jausserande was coming to distrust as the indicator of Fox's truly nasty temper.

"Like the man says. I'm not your judge, I'm your judgment. Get dressed, Tink; we're going for a ride."

He'd brought her most of her own clothes, with a heavy sheepskin vest to take the place of her lost tunic. He even brought her cap with the Ravens' badge, and Jausserande could not say whether such consideration pleased or discomfited her.

Since knowledge was the only weapon she had, she considered the matter carefully. Fox did not treat her with the respect a worthy enemy deserved. He was not cruel out of fear of her strength. He treated her with the distant kindness she used toward her human servants, as if he were so high above her that there was no way she could drag him down.

Realizing this, her eyes kindled, and she glared at Fox, settling the cap on her head. He regarded her with mocking acknowledgment.

"It's show time, Tink. C'mon."

"My name—"

"Is really, *really* unimportant to me, Tink. C'mon." He turned his back and ducked out through the hut's low doorway.

After a moment, Jausserande followed.

Her first view of the camp showed it much as she had imagined it would be. Shelters made of bent but still-rooted saplings roofed over with hides and squares of bark, small fire pits were scattered here and there, carcasses and food bundles hung from tree branches—all the signs of a long-kept base camp, yet so portable and ephemeral that an hour's hard work could erase it almost as if it had never been. She counted perhaps thirty men, and knew there must be at least half again as many that she did not see.

Fox led her to the edge of the camp, where, within a concealing lattice of branches, six horses stood, saddled and ready—fruits of Fox's raid on the Harvest Home.

Fox looked at her, a slanted sidewise knowing glance.

"See anything you like?" Fox asked her, still in that blithe untrustworthy mood.

Wait for your chance, Jausserande told herself. She spared a sweeping glance for Fox, the stolen horses, the outlaws standing around.

"Nothing."

Fox laughed.

He rode well, an uncommon skill in the mud-born. The horse Jausserande rode was the worst of them, easily caught by any of the others should she incite it to bolt, and haltered to Fox's saddle besides. Four of his men rode with them, and Jausserande had seen the flash of sword and dagger as they mounted. Fox led them with easy certainty onto the road that led into the Vale itself.

Jausserande watched Fox's back and the long tail of pale hair, and wondered who he was and what she should believe about him. Even if Melior's theory was true, she did not think that this one looked to Baligant Baneful.

But if he did not, *why* did Fox want the Treasures? They were of no use to the mud-born. Humans had no magic—*they* could not wield the powers of the Twelve Treasures. And, though the Cup of Morning Shadows was not so guarded, no human could even *touch* Rohannan's Treasure, the Sword of Maiden's Tears.

Yet if she could believe him, the Sword was more Fox's goal than the Cup, though he wanted the Cup as well.

Why?

For the first time Jausserande wished she had paid more attention to her lessons in the Art Magical—or, even better, had an Adept Major to consult. Because Fox said that his intention was to *destroy* both Cup and Sword, and Jausserande had no idea what would happen if he succeeded. Chandrakar would be doomed, that was common knowledge, but doomed *how?*

As her horse's hooves struck the white clay road, Jausserande felt a familiar warning tingle of sensation. This was the road into the Vale of Stars, where elphen magic could not be used, lest it twist itself and turn upon the wielder. Even the enchantment upon the Cup was a simple thing, a mere mechanism, related to the works of the Art Magical as a child's hobbyhorse was to a war destrier and thus safe from the power of the Vale.

Did that very simplicity mean that Fox would be able to use its magic as well?

The terrain rose around the mounted party in the gathering dusk, until they rode down a gleaming bone-white road between the steep dark walls of a great defile, and at last passed through into the Vale of Stars.

Beyond the walls of the pass the road dipped sharply, arrowing down into a tiny perfect valley. Though the sky was already dark, and the crowding hills shut out the sunset light, the Vale shone with its own illumination. There was a faint glow to the mist that hung over the vivid green meadow, and even in this season the trees were filled with pale flowers that gave off their own light.

All was perfect; Jausserande could hear the purl of a quick-running stream, see the flicker of grass stems bent beneath an evening breeze. To this place, unique in Chandrakar, the war had not come.

Until now.

Fox chivied his mount down the narrow track. Jausserande was pulled unwillingly with him, wondering if it was best to vault from her saddle and run before Fox could attempt to compel her help.

She didn't get the chance.

"Tie her," Fox snapped over his shoulder, and before the horses had stopped, Raven yanked Jausserande from her saddle. She fought him, but his strength was as great as Fox had foretold, and he was able to hold her as another of Fox's men jerked her hands back and bound them behind her.

Not enough to restrain her, save for the noose that went about her neck. Run and she would hang herself.

"There. All comfy now?" Fox asked, dismounting. The man behind her tossed Fox the free end of the halter. He caught it and looped it about his wrist.

"I will see you hanged from Dawnheart's walls with your own entrails," Jausserande grated.

"Why is it that people complain when others do things as well as they would themselves? Your problem, Tink, is that you get really bent out of shape when you start to suspect you aren't going to win."

Around them Fox's men were dismounting and picketing the horses, but Fox and Jausserande might have been alone. Her fury was a palpable weight, pressing against her skin until only gritted teeth kept her from panting for relief from it. For a moment she forgot even the Cup.

Fox turned away and strode off, pulling the rawhide leash

taut between them. A sharp shove between the shoulder blades sent Jausserande stumbling after him, muscles trembling at her narrow escape—though from what, she wasn't sure.

He does not know where he must stand. The realization broke through to her consciousness like a rock that she could cling to. How could he know, when even she had only Floire Glorete's handed-down directions to a place Glorete had never seen?

What had Glorete said? Jausserande frowned, summoning memory under unpromising conditions. *On the second day of the full moon*—that was now—*at moonrise, the presence of the shadow-Cup within the Vale of Stars would show the presence of the true Cup and, being thrust into shadow, bring the true Cup visible.*

Moonrise would be very soon. And when it came, the *tainaiste*-Cup would cause an image of the true one to appear for a few moments somewhere within the Vale of Stars. Glorete had told her to hold the shadow Cup within the image of the other one, but even Glorete hadn't been able to tell her what would happen then.

Could Fox do that much? Would he even see it? Would he ask her aid—and kill her when she did not give it?

For the first time Jausserande forced herself to think about what would happen if the Cup of Morning Shadows were lost here—not as a vague possibility, but as a real likelihood.

Chandrakar would still be safe, since the Cup would still be within the land. And perhaps Line Floire would send someone to the Vale to search when Jausserande was known to be dead. And perhaps that one would find it.

And if they did not?

On the day of the Kingmaking, with Eirdois Baligant in the High Seat, Floire would be called upon three times to present its Treasure. And when it had been called for the third time, and failed . . .

Line Floire would be no more. Before the sun had set, every man, woman, and child of the Line would have been driven beyond the bounds of Chandrakar, banished and attainted with no more possession than the clothes they wore. Landless wanderers, thrown upon the mercy of Lands that had none.

It could happen.

Fox stopped near the middle of the tiny valley. If not for

the luminescence filling this place, he would not have been able to see; overhead, the sky was dark indigo velvet powdered with bright autumn stars. From the corner of her eye she could see two of Fox's men in the distance, standing with lighted lanterns beside the horses. The lanterns' warm light clashed oddly with the cool illumination that emanated from the grass and trees.

She glanced behind her. There was Raven, the black-haired giant who—so Fox said—feared her. When he saw her look toward him, he looked away, obviously ill at ease, and it occurred to Jausserande that if she could manage to be alone for any length of time with Raven, she could probably bend him to her will.

Beside him was the man who had bound her hands. Remarkable among Fox's band, he was not marked or branded for thievery or trespass, but his eyes would mark him in any company: one blue and one brown, they gave his face an oddly unfinished look. He regarded her with a knowing disrespect that irritated Jausserande even as it worried her. Such irreverence toward their overlords was not natural to the mud-born.

"Well, Tink, here we are. Just you, and me—and this."

Fox reached to his belt and pulled out the shadow-Cup. Melior's signet ring flashed on Fox's hand as he raised it.

"You had it all along!" Try as she might, Jausserande could not keep the note of betrayal out of her voice.

Fox smiled and spoke—for him—with compassion.

"But you couldn't know that. And with stakes so high, you couldn't risk it."

"How can you know that—and still do what you do!"

"I'm just one surprise after another, Tinkerbelle," Fox said, turning away.

Raven came forward, making a wide detour around Jausserande. Fox handed him the end of her leash, and Raven looped it around his wrist.

"Don't drop that."

"Fox, shouldn't we—" Raven began.

"Once we've got the Treasure, Raven, things'll be different," Fox said.

"They'll be worse!" Jausserande cut in swiftly. "Let me go now and—"

"If I have to shut you up, Tink, you won't like it," Fox

said mildly, and the man still standing behind Jausserande chuckled.

Jausserande shut up.

Fox gestured, and Raven moved aside until the rope about Jausserande's throat was pulled uncomfortably taut. Now Fox lifted the simple pewter cup higher. The light from the meadow played along his jaw and the underside of his raised arm, but the darkness of his hand nearly blended into the dull pewter surface of the cup.

"Such a large area to search. And such a short time to do it in. Moonrise, isn't it?" Fox turned back to her, and his bared teeth were predatory.

Jausserande raised her chin and stood silent.

"And somewhere—some *particular* where—here in the beautiful Vale of Stars we swap *this* one—" Fox tossed the Cup into the air and caught it, "—for *that* one. I wonder where?"

But he didn't wonder, Jausserande suspected in growing horror. If he did not know—or think he knew—how to re- trieve the Cup of Morning Shadows, Fox could not be so gaily confident.

Surreptitiously she tested her bonds. Her hands had the numb tingle of having been tied too tight for too long, but as she pulled, she felt the leather cords creak and stretch.

She could get free.

She worked at the bindings on her wrists as Fox wan- dered, seemingly in random circles but actually covering a good amount of territory, as full night fell and moonrise drew nearer.

The pied-eyed man moved far enough away that Jausser- ande could watch as he unslung a crossbow from his back and held it ready, but she was still close enough to see that some of the bolts were tipped with a bright grayish metal.

Iron.

Raven's hold on her leash never slackened, but Jausser- ande had taken care to turn away from him and make no abrupt struggling movements. The leather bonds on her wrists continued to stretch. It began to seem that she had de- luded herself during the days she had spent in the outlaws' camp. The most important thing was not to get the Cup of Morning Shadows.

It was to keep the Cup away from Fox.

"Ah-hah." Fox spoke softly, but Jausserande was so keyed

up that the sound made her jump. The movement made the cords slide loosely on her wrists.

The moon hovered on the edge of the ridge, dispelling the luminescence from the Vale by its greater light. In the distance there was a spark of gold.

"Bring her along."

The source of the stream she had heard was a spring, round and perfect as the Cup itself, that bubbled up out of the earth at the crown of a small rise. Above it hung the faint balefire flicker of the Cup of Morning Shadows. The *true* Cup.

Jausserande stared, her heart hammering in anticipatory terror. In a moment he—

"Hold on tight," Fox said, but not to her.

Raven's hands settled on her shoulders in a crushing grip. Fox grabbed her arm and yanked. Her hand slid easily out of the loosened cords.

"Naughty," Fox said, but not as if he cared. And wrapped her fingers around the *tainaiste*-Cup.

She knew what he meant to do in the instant before he did it, but there was nothing she could to do stop him. She felt the hot callused roughness of Fox's hand over hers as he held her hand closed on the Cup, and Raven's grip on her shoulders was bruisingly tight.

And Fox used all his strength to force her hand, filled with the shadow-Cup, into the gleaming ghost-image of the real one. It would be her touch that retrieved it, not his.

Jausserande struggled until every muscle burned and her heartbeat was a hammering concussion in her temples. Her breath was a rasping repetition and there was the taste of blood in her mouth. Nothing had any effect.

And, at last, the Cup in her hands and Fox's passed through its golden mirror image.

The icy suction that Jausserande associated with High Magic pulled at the marrow of her bones, and through the Cup's gleaming illusion she could see the *tainaiste*-Cup catch fire, dull metal gilding.

And vanishing.

She felt it melt away in her hand, and for a moment she was as stunned as Fox. Raven released her and backed away, and she heard the words of a mud-born prayer against magic.

Magic.

Shadow and image both gone—and no Cup. But then she realized that Raven and her need to protect the Cup no longer held her, and the only hands on her were Fox's.

He was powerful for a human, but no match for elphen strength. Jausserande tore free and whirled away, only to slam into Raven's massive bulk. She knew he was stronger than she, but his fear of hurting her placed him at a disadvantage. In a moment she would be free of him, too.

"No, Hathorne—you'll hit Raven!" Meaningless words that she did not bother to listen to. Now Raven's grasp was loose on her wrists, and then she was running, a jagging path to baffle the crossbowman. The evening grass was cool on her legs as she ran for the trees and safety.

She did not hear the whistling arc of the slingstone that struck her unconscious.

Chapter 24

Queen's Play

In the space of one short night she had been maid and mare, leopardess and dragon, warwasp. . . .

And defeated.

Amadis could still not believe—could not *understand*—the moment when her carefully made plans had dissolved like sugar in hot wine. Though the mortal man she had left for dead had wounded her, the Wild Magic had rippled through her like pure power incarnate, obedient to her command, and even the death-metal embedded in her throat was only a minor handicap. It had been simple to follow the soul-anchor to the Goblin Market; one snap of her mandibles and the soul she had spun out like flax would be free to inhabit the Sword of Maiden's Tears for the rest of its eternal existence, and the *proof* that Baligant's rebellious nobles might bring against him would be lost, lost, lost—

Only that was not what had happened. The Swordwarden had been there, the magic of the Treasure that he bore blinding to her supernatural senses. She had lost her prey, but the Swordwarden's death would serve almost as well, and so she—

Had been defeated by him. By Rohannan Melior, and the Sword of Maiden's Tears, and a magic greater than her own. If she had not fled, she would have died there.

Which might, Amadis considered, have been better than what faced her now—to go and tell Baligant High Prince, her master, that she had failed. That Ruth Marlowe, who had been the trap to bring the Sword of Maiden's Tears into the World of Iron, was still alive, and must inevitably encounter—and be used by—the Sword and its bearer.

No. Amadis considered the matter carefully. To die was worse than having to make such a confession, it was true. But it was far better to be able to report success than to confess to failure. She had possessed the strength and wit to return secretly; Baligant would not know to demand her presence yet. But the little time before the need that measured the seasons of her life was once more acute was short, and when that time was gone, she must go to Baligant High Prince in hope of slaking it again.

Without success to offer him, Baligant would deny her. And though he would not deny her unto death, the long agonizing humiliation that stretched before her as the payment for failure was something it was worth any exertion to avoid.

So when Baligant asked of the outcome of her hunt, she must have a better answer for him then than failure. In the chamber set aside for the wizard's use in the tower by the sea, Amadis made her preparations.

In this chamber the floor was inlaid with lines of silver; the gross geometries of the true world and its Gates. All lines led to the center of the room, where a low black cube of glass supported an enormous alabaster bowl, also webbed with silver. These were the trappings of the High Magic, which any Adept Major might presume to master.

In Amadis' hands, these objects became something more.

She set the wards, which would confine the powers she raised within the cube of space defined by the walls of this chamber. She set another such binding on the white bowl, that it would retain its shape regardless of the energies poured into it.

Then Amadis gestured, and cold green fire gushed from her hands into the bowl. Her form and the form of all the room's contents became mutable, the shapes they displayed merely a consensus shaped by her will and by the Word. The bowl flared sun-bright all along its silver inlays, and the fire that filled it, refined by its own weight, became darker and quieter until at last the bowl was glutted with an emerald liquid dark as blood.

In this speculum, Amadis began to search.

She did not see the forest house where Ruth had sheltered, for sight of that was barred to such as she. And from the Market, paths multiplied in such bewildering profusion that it could take a very long time to search all the Lands they led to.

Amadis took the time, though she could not draw upon the Word for as much energy as she spent. That was her peculiar misfortune. But her need was great enough to spend herself so.

She had not only space to search, but Time, which shifted its rate at every border, spinning faster and faster until one reached the World of Iron and Time became a blur, snuffing out the brief lives of that world's mortal inhabitants in an instant.

And at last, because she must, she found the moment and the Gate wherewhen the Swordwarden and his heart twin, Child of Earth, crossed the border into Chandrakar.

There. She marked it: *there.*

The viridian phlogiston sank away into the walls of the bowl and vanished. The light left her hands, her body, the walls of the chamber, returning them all to this world: creatures of matter, with fixed and immutable shapes. The riptide of Wild Magic ebbed and ebbed and ebbed, until for a moment Amadis wondered if she had cast the spell that every wizard fears—the unrepaid outwelling of power that takes all with it, even the life force of the wizard and his Covenant with the Word.

But it wasn't. Not this time. Still in flesh, Amadis slid to the chill stone floor and lay there with her cheek pressed against the icy glass of the altar cube. And the hunger for the drug that was weakness, that was *power,* burned demandingly within her.

An hour passed, then two, before she recovered the strength to stand. She swayed slightly as she got to her feet, still graceful as a willow in the wind. Now to finish the task that Baligant had set her, and kill Ruth Marlowe.

She raised her arms, willing the transformation, but even as she did the impulse flickered and died.

Not enough.

She put her hand to her throat and touched the faint white scar where the lump of iron had lain. Gone now, but death-metal destroyed magic as rain quenched fire.

She must have time. But a hammering upon her door told Amadis that time was something she did not have.

"I trust you come to tell me that the Ironworld daughter is dead?" Baligant said.

"I *came* to tell you nothing," Amadis reminded him.

In contrast to Baligant High Prince's elaborate jeweled and embroidered robes, the gown Amadis wore was of unor-

namented silk with a surface so bright it seemed almost to
be made of the copper its color mimicked. Her hair gleamed
in coils against it, its surface only slightly less hard.

"Don't toy with me, wizard. I can be spiteful and excep-
tionally unjust."

Baligant sat at his ease in his favorite room, the one that
was crowded with treasure extorted from those whom
Baligant suspected of being better than he. Amadis stood, as
she had stood since Baligant's lackey had summoned her to
him.

"I merely remark that you demanded a report. I did not
come to bring you news."

"Did you or did you not slay the Ironworlder bound to the
Sword of Maiden's Tears?" Baligant snarled.

"Slain or not, Line Rohannan would retain the Sword,"
Amadis remarked, as innocently as if it were an observation
on the weather.

Baligant, like all clever men, could sometimes be dazzled
by his own cleverness. There might be something in that
which she could use, as Baligant used her. Amadis waited,
dispassionately hoping, and dreamed of revenge.

"Line Rohannan would retain the Sword," came Baligant's inflectionless acknowledgment. His scrutiny came to
rest on her, a slow weight. "Am I to understand, my . . . wizard, that you have *refrained* from slaying the earthling in order to bring me a greater triumph instead?"

"It is known that The Rohannan has obtained the Sword
but has not yet brought it to the Twilight Court. Nor is he
confirmed as the Lineholder. Now he is out of the world. No
man knows where. His own cousin will swear that he went
in search of the Ironworlder, and every servant in his castle
knows that he has thought of nothing else."

"And should he disappear, and the Sword with him . . ."

"Then his name would be remembered as that of a fool.
And another from Rohannan would go to seek the Treasure
Rohannan Melior had lost."

Baligant smiled. "Fail me twice, creature, and I will make
you beg for death."

He would, and she would. But she would not die, nor
would he cease to make use of her.

Baligant held out a filled and bloody hand.

And for a moment there was bliss; freedom from pain.
Power.

Chapter 25

Dress in Black and Lose Your Heart Beyond Recall

Once he'd recovered a little from the thrashing the dragon had given him, Nic circled the glade he'd awakened in until he found the unicorn's tiny split-hoofed prints.

He'd followed the tracks hopefully, but they led, not to Ruth, but to a stream he didn't remember crossing. He stopped, and drank, and salved his injuries as much as he could with the icy river water.

His head hurt. Also his arm, his back, and the rest of his recent injuries. The Hyborean Age was no place for a forty-year-old library director, no matter what he might have been once.

And if that much were true, then by extension this was no place for a thirtysomething librarian, no matter what she was now.

At least, not alone.

An hour later, unhappily satisfied of the unattainability of Ruth Marlowe or the main road, Nic sat down on a fallen stump to think.

About unicorns. Unicorns wearing handmade, man-made garlands. Unicorns right out of a medieval tapestry, unicorns that Miss Marlowe, who at least had some small familiarity with this place, had not recognized as familiar when she had seen them. Unicorns that appeared and vanished with suspect facility, and had a vested interest in herding him and Miss Marlowe straight down the middle of the High Road that led to Fair Elphame—to coin a ballad.

In the cold clear light of hindsight, it looked very much like Fluffy the Wonder Caprid had been a player, and, presented as he had been with such painfully real evidence of the existence of at least two sides, Nic wondered which side it had been on. The opposite side—or *an* opposite side—from the Dragon Lady, almost certainly. But that didn't mean it was on Miss Marlowe's side, whatever being on Miss Marlowe's side might constitute at any given moment.

Nic smiled ruefully. You could take the boy out of the country, as the saying went, but the boy would never stop expecting smoke and mirrors. He'd gotten too attuned to hidden meanings in his youth to stop looking for them now. The only thing he could be even sixty-five percent certain of was that the possession or destruction of Miss Ruth Marlowe was important to at least some of the sides.

Nic took a deep breath and held it, and blew it out, looking down at the split and ruined remains of his expensive leather wing tips. Suitable shoes for a life it didn't seem he was ever going back to.

It would be nice to know what was going on, not that *not* knowing what was going on had ever been much of a handicap in the past. You just kept going on until you made enough trouble that the other guy took his toys and went home, a tactic Nicodemus Brightlaw had found particularly useful at meetings of the Ryerson Library Board of Directors.

On the other hand, it didn't seem to be of much utility when he was looking for somewhere to spend the night. And Ruth Marlowe, come to that.

Nic got to his feet, took his bearings from the sun, chose a direction at random, and began to walk.

Melior had been perfectly serious about advancing no farther than the nearest inn, Ruth discovered. It had been a matter of only a half-hour's walk along the forest road until they saw the lights in the distance.

Why did it seem that she had come so far?

If not for the dense forest surrounding it, Ruth would have taken this place for the inn she and Nic had found their first day here. The same sloping roof, the same Brothers Grimm wood carving.

Maybe it was a chain, like Howard Johnson's. *Come to the Otherwhere Hilton, where you can check out any time you like, but . . . Oh, quit whining, Ruth Marlowe. You've got what you said you wanted. You're here.*

And somebody's trying to kill you.

"Come, Ruth," Melior said.

* * *

Melior entered the inn's common room as if he'd just bought the place on a long lease. The landlord scurried toward him as if he'd been included in the price.

"Dinner," Melior said succinctly. "A room. In the morning I will require two horses, one for my lady."

"Yes, my lord. At once, my lord."

And how are you going to pay for all this? Ruth wondered. Two locals—if there could be locals in a place like this—took their dice and tankards and vacated a table near the fire. Melior led Ruth toward it.

The inn was one room, so large that the black-beamed ceiling seemed very low. In one corner, enormous kegs were racked on their sides, bunged and ready for tapping.

So that's what a hogshead looks like. I've always wondered.

A board on trestles provided a bar of sorts, as well as a place to stack empty clay jugs, pewter goblets, and leather quart-jacks. The fireplace was large enough to store grand pianos in, and in addition to a roaring fire contained a covered clay pot as well as a whole roast sheep hanging on a spit swung out of the way of the flames. The opposite wall of the room was filled with an enormous oven, cold now.

The table was round, its thick oak planks polished satiny by years of handling. The chairs were three-legged stools with a cricket bat-shaped backrest.

It was all very odd.

Melior lifted Ruth's cloak off her shoulders and threw it across one of the chairs, then piled his own dragon-mail mantle atop it. He leaned the ebony walking stave against the wall. Then he sat down, and Ruth saw that one reason for the odd chairs was that their arrangement allowed a man with a sword slung across his back to sit down without removing it.

They must get a lot of wandering paladins here.

Melior arranged himself with his back to the fire, wincing as he eased his weight off the wounded leg. He pulled off his long gauntlets as the landlord hurried anxiously over with two pewter cups and a clay jug. Ruth ducked out of his way, pulling at her own gloves, sitting down next to Melior as the landlord set down the cups and began to pour.

"Have you no better vintage?" Melior demanded ungraciously.

The landlord stopped in his tracks and retreated, rattling

out a string of unintelligible promises. Melior rubbed his forehead wearily, face drawn.

"Rohannan is—*was*—known for its vintage," Melior said, as if that were an explanation.

"You didn't have to snap at him," Ruth said.

"His kind understands nothing else."

Ruth bit her lip to keep from snapping something unforgivable back at Melior. She was seeing a new side of his personality now that he was in his own world, one that she didn't think she liked. Not even arrogance: a matter-of-fact assumption of privilege that grated badly upon Ruth's republican ideals. *This* was her own true love? This ... *monarchist?*

"If you say so," Ruth said tightly.

Melior glanced quickly toward her, his eyes flashing golden-green in the firelight. "Yes. I say so."

The landlord returned, this time with a large, dusty, dark green bottle with a protruding cork covered in red wax. He cut through the wax and drew the cork, and a scent like summer flowers in honey filled the room. Melior smiled. The landlord looked relieved.

"And there is game pie, my lord, and new bread, and apples in honey for the lady. And a bath, should either of you desire—at your word I will have the tub brought up—"

Melior raised his hand and the man stopped speaking.

"Bring what I have asked of you, and that will be sufficient," Melior said briefly.

The landlord retreated once more.

Melior inspected the cups critically, and then filled them both, pushing one toward Ruth. He drank, and leaned back carefully.

"I hope you know some way of paying for all this," Ruth said sourly, not touching her own cup. The conversation seemed to be sliding irrevocably into one of those nasty snippy little fights she hated—and could see, here and now, no way to keep from having.

Melior glanced at her through lowered lashes and smiled faintly, and in that moment Ruth saw the man she'd fallen in love with such a very long time ago. Her mouth quirked upward in answer.

"Ah, Ruth, did you think I bought and could not pay? It is true that we do not *spin plastic* in the Morning Lands as you do in the World of Iron, but be sure that the innkeeper will receive his—certain to be outrageous—due." Melior re-filled his cup and drank again. "Magic is the coin between the realms, and he shall have what sorcery he asks on the morrow."

"You didn't have to be so rude to him," Ruth said, retreating to her original complaint.

"And is the friendship of Rohannan Melior such a desirable commodity, that you would offer it to every passing stranger?" Melior looked even more amused. "We are hunted—it is not hard to imagine by whom."

"B–Baligant," Ruth got out, remembering the name at last. She took a deep swig of the contents of her cup and choked, her nose and mouth filled with sugar and heat and the scent of summer fields.

Melior hissed slightly, a warning to Ruth to hold her tongue. The landlord reappeared, this time leading a girl dressed as if there were a Bavarian comic opera rehearsing next door. "Buxom wench" was about the only way to describe her, politically incorrect though it might be, with the tight red leather of the woman's gold-laced bodice thrusting her chest up and out in that uncomfortable-looking Playboy Bunny fashion.

The serving girl set a tray stacked with food down in front of Melior, and smiled in a fashion Ruth tried very hard to mistake for something else, and lingered in front of him to place the dishes on the table. In the firelight, Ruth saw that what she had first thought was glitter and then bad skin was actually *scales*.

She blinked, and tried not to stare. A tavern wench with scales?

I don't think we're in Kansas any more, Toto.

"If there is anything else," the landlord said hopefully.

Well, thought Ruth, *yes. For dessert we can always manage to get this place leveled by something out of a science fiction double feature.*

"The horses in the morning," Melior reminded him.

The landlord bowed and smiled and rubbed his hands together in a way that made Ruth wonder how expensive—or overpriced—those horses were going to be. Then Melior turned his attention to the food and so did she.

There were, as promised, game pie and new bread and apples in honey. Ruth, who had eaten well not that long ago, picked at a portion of apples. They tasted as if they had been boiled in honey, impossibly sweet. She pushed them away and concentrated on the wine, while Melior finished both servings of the pie, a heel of the loaf, and the rest of the apples.

"Ah," he said at last, leaning carefully back in his seat. The gem on the pommel of the Sword of Maiden's Tears glowed with opal rainbows in the firelight. Ruth regarded it mistrustfully.

"And now to bed, Lady Ruth. And tomorrow, home—or at least the Road," Melior amended truthfully.

Another of the inn servants followed them, to bring the cloaks and the half-finished wine, and to carry the candle and light them up the stair. Melior mounted the steps with apparent ease, and only Ruth knew how his hand tightened on hers. His injuries were far from healed; God knew what he was going to do with a horse tomorrow. God knew what *she* would do, come to that—Ruth had never ridden a horse in her life.

The room could be nothing but the inn's best, but despite that it was small, with a tilting ceiling and closed wooden shutters where glass windows ought to be. But there was a fire burning in the corner, and at least the place smelled clean.

And it contained a very large bed.

There was a thump as Melior dropped the bar into position across the door, and another as the head of his walking stick struck the white plaster wall beside it. Then the creak and pull of leather, as he unbuckled the harness that held the Sword in place.

Ruth sat down on the bed. And down, and down, and down, through featherbeds piled one on the other, because here at the Elphame Hilton the mysteries of the innerspring mattress had not been revealed unto them.

Melior regarded his lady, who was staring resolutely off into space, and wondered if he would have to manage his boots by himself. It was true that he could have gotten one of the lackeys to do it—if he had wanted to publish the fact of his injuries to all the wide world. It had seemed more desirable to have a barred door between him and them instead, but now he wasn't so sure.

Melior told over his memories of Ruth's world, and decided he would have to get his own clothes off. And then—

Return to Chandrakar as fast as they could, and hope and pray that the Twilight Court still sat. Summon Ophidias, unbind Ruth from the Sword, lay the evidence of Baligant's tampering before the convened Lords Temporal—

And, oh, yes, arrange to be confirmed in his lands and honors at the same time. Find some way to meet Ophidias' price. Discover what doom the Heartlands would call down on Chandrakar for the attack at the Goblin Market. Collect the taxes. Collect the harvest. Discover whether Jausserande had yet been successful in retrieving her Treasure. Sweep the forests for outlaws, and decide what to do with them when he caught them. Perhaps Richart would have some idea—many of them would be ex-soldiers, after all. Perhaps they could go to the guard, where a roof and a meal and a warm cloak would do much to discourage thievery.

Keep the sword. Keep his life. And, somehow, in all of this, incline his lady's heart once more to him. She had been willing to leave her own world for him once.

But that had been long ago, as mortals reckoned time. And if it were true that she no longer loved him, each day would be less bright than it might have been.

"Ruth?" Melior said.

She turned at the sound of his voice, and felt the corners of her mouth twist downward. But underneath the automatic pain was the unnerving certainty that her responses weren't *real;* that somehow she was only faking what a real person would feel.

Because she wasn't real. In the truest sense of the phrase, Ruth Marlowe was not "all there."

Against her will she looked toward the Sword of Maiden's Tears. That was where her soul was—the thing that would let her be real. Melior said he would return it to her. Until then, all she could do was pretend.

She got to her feet and went over to him.

"Need help?" Ruth said.

Melior smiled up at her and reached for her hand. His fingers were warm over hers, and she wished—

"I need to find Nic," Ruth blurted out suddenly.

Melior frowned and tightened his grip on her, as if he were afraid she would suddenly pull away.

"If he is here, it is wizard work, or do you think that the Iron Road is open to any who choose to stroll it for a day's pleasaunce?"

"I think I don't know where he is. I think he's in trouble and needs help. I hope you'll help me find him," Ruth finished in a strangled tone.

Melior lifted her hand and lightly brushed it with his lips. Ruth wanted to hug him to her; wanted to push him away. She stood perfectly still.

"I shall do all that I may to find your friend, once we are home," Melior said.

"But—"

"My lady, do you think we ourselves are safe?" Melior said gently. "We are in danger as great as the power of the wizard who hunts us. In my own place—" The last word was a drawn-out sigh, and Melior's head drooped a little.

"We'll be safer," Ruth finished for him. *Poor Melior; no wonder he's been so bitchy. If I knew what was going on, I'd be scared to death, too.*

As it is, I'm merely terrified.

"Yes," Melior said. He released Ruth's hand and looked down at his boots, and Ruth's imagination painted vivid holographs of the ragged tears and gouges that the warwasp had left in his flesh.

"Let me do that for you, okay?" Ruth said.

Though in the course of her association with the Society for Creative Anachronism Ruth Marlowe had been given occasion to assist both fops and fighters with that one item of garb which, when properly worn, it is almost impossible to remove unaided, it did not mean she was particularly expert at it. The first boot came off easily enough. The second, for all her determination, resisted until Ruth was tugging with all her might, whereupon it slipped free and sent her sprawling.

Still, it was probably easier on Melior than trying to remove them himself.

She looked up at him from her inelegant seat on the floor and grinned hopefully. And Melior, who had been trying hard not to laugh at her, gave up.

"So elegant a chatelaine," he teased, holding out his hand and smiling at her.

"I never claimed—" began Ruth.

"To be anything but my lady. My—dearest—lady. My heartsease."

He pulled her forward until Ruth knelt between his knees, her face turned up to regard him. And then he brought his lips down on hers; so slowly, so carefully, that she was mad with impatience by the time contact was made. It was as if the touch completed some circuit of power, filling meek Ruth Marlowe with a borrowed wildness. She reached up to put her arms around his neck, but instead of pulling him downward, the gesture raised both of them to their feet.

And finally, for a while, everything was all right.

She awoke near dawn, lying nestled in featherbeds with Melior's arm across her. At one point during the night he had opened the shutters, and from where she lay Ruth could see the faint proto-lightness of the sky. Mist overlay everything, so that only the sharp black-green tops of the pines protruded.

Dawn had always had the power to lift Ruth's spirits. To see dawn was to have survived the night, and there had been times when surviving was the only triumph Ruth had been able to claim.

Not any more. Now there was Melior. And if she was too old to believe that love could solve all her problems, at least she could believe that now she had an ally against them. That no matter what tricks of temper and imagination might intervene, there was no longer an invisible wall dividing the two of them. They were together, and all their future problems could come from that.

Ruth smiled to herself and nestled deeper into the bed.

All the mist had burned away and true morning had come when Melior escorted Ruth from the inn. The stave had been left behind; this morning Melior walked without it, and the effort it cost him was visible for no one to see.

An ostler led two horses into the yard for their inspection. Both were saddled and bridled. The dark gray one had saddlebags behind the saddle.

"Ah," said Melior, in rueful tones.

The large gray horse—as differentiated, in Ruth's non-equinephilic mind, from the small white horse—tugged at its lead rein when it saw Melior. He walked over to it, and it lowered its head to nuzzle him roughly, until he staggered. He grabbed at its headstall.

"This," Melior announced, "is Cobant."

Ruth looked blank.

"The horse I began with," Melior elaborated. "And lost."

"They sold him back to you?" Ruth said.

Melior shrugged, as though being sold one's own horse was no more than a wandering elf-lord could expect. "Assist my lady to mount," he said to the ostler.

After last night Ruth knew that Melior's injured leg would not bear the strain of her added weight, but she still wished he were the one who would be helping her onto the beast's back. She regarded her destination with wariness.

The white horse was really a pale gray, with dapples like rain spots across its shoulders and rump. It regarded her as if it had been expecting bad news and she was it. On its back was a carved wooden saddle with a high padded back and prowlike front, much as if someone had miniaturized an old-fashioned sleigh and then converted it to a saddle. The wooden stirrups were shielded by wide leather skirts, half flapping in the breeze like unhinged automobile cowling.

A second groom came forward with a mounting block, and there was nothing for Ruth to do but step up to it as if she'd been doing this all her life.

Two steps up, then a foot through the stirrup, then a hop and wriggle and Ruth was in the saddle, smoothing her wide skirts carefully back into place while her pleasant seat sidled mistrustfully beneath her.

The ground looked very far away.

The painted leather reins lay on the horse's neck, and Ruth, for something to do, picked them up. As if that were a signal, both ostlers stepped away, and the horse took a step forward. Ruth clutched at the curled saddle-prow before her and dropped the reins. The horse stopped.

Then Melior, without benefit of mounting block, swung himself aboard Cobant. He collected the reins and the horse moved as if it were merely an extension of Melior's will.

He tossed a handful of something that sparkled to the ostlers and moved his horse next to Ruth's.

"Ruth," said Melior in tones of sudden suspicion, "you *have* seen a horse before?"

"Sort of," Ruth said truthfully. Why hadn't he asked earlier?

Melior shook his head and smiled. Reaching across, he took the reins from her clutching fingers and unknotted them. He threaded one through a projection on the front of her saddle and wound the other through his gloved hand. He turned Cobant away. Ruth's horse followed on the lead.

"You ride like a basket of dead fish," Melior told her half an hour later.

"Thank you," Ruth replied sweetly. "How many baskets of dead fish have you seen go riding?"

It had to be admitted, though, that at the moment she *felt* rather like a basket of dead fish: walk, trot, and canter alike were bone-jarring, and she always seemed to be going down just as the saddle was coming up.

Enough to know that you greatly resemble them. It might be easier," Melior said, "did I take you up in front of me."

Ruth glanced sideways. Melior's saddle, though nothing out of a John Wayne Western (the sum total of Ruth's previous exposure to horses and riding), was still flat enough fore and aft that what he suggested looked possible.

"I don't want to hurt you," Ruth said.

"Cobant can carry us both this while. And I am anxious to strike the Iron Road and return home as soon as I may," Melior said. "By your leave, my lady."

"And find Nic," Ruth said, just to remind both of them, though in truth it was rather difficult to stay worried about Nicodemus Brightlaw after the things she'd seen him do. By now he was probably king someplace, just like Conan the Barbarian.

"And find your companion," Melior agreed.

The transfer was more easily accomplished than Ruth would have thought, and soon she was seated sideways across Melior's thighs, one arm around his waist.

Cobant broke into a trot, but this time, cushioned by Melior's body, the motion was fluid and peaceful. The road branched and branched again, and each time Melior took the wider of the branches. Her horse followed along behind.

There were any number of things she should ask about—the unicorn, the warwasp—but Ruth kept silent on all of them, as if to name events would be to acknowledge that they had happened. And she didn't want them to have happened. It was as if the time in the forest house had drawn an eraser across all

that came before it, and now the only thing Ruth wanted was
Melior and peace and quiet.

Then they came to a third crossroads, and Ruth, glancing
up toward Melior, surprised him sketching a glyph in the air.
The lines he had drawn sparkled for a moment and then
faded: faery-fire.

"You said you didn't have any magic," Ruth said, as if
he'd been deceiving her.

"*Small* magic only—and less than that in the World of
Iron," Melior corrected. "But enough to find our way. Now
we will stop, and rest, and perhaps strike the Road by evening."

They picnicked beneath a tree at the edge of the road—or,
rather, Ruth picnicked, the horses grazed, and Melior ate and
drank something beside the tree, the Sword of Maiden's
Tears handy to his hand, and kept watch.

It was a disturbing reminder of how far from home she
was. It was true that there was street crime at home, but
Ruth would never have gone into the worst neighborhoods
of home, let alone stopped to have lunch in a place as dangerous as Melior seemed to think this one was.

"We must give the horses ease, if we are to use them
later," Melior said, catching the tone of her thought.

"Where are we?" Ruth asked.

"In the Morning Lands, near the Iron Road. Once we
reach it, Chandrakar is not far, and Dawnheart a day's ride,
if that, from the Gate."

"Which tells me precisely nothing," Ruth informed him
helpfully.

Melior smiled. "Were you an Adept, my lady, I would re-
fer you to your ephemeris, but as you are not, I know not
how to lesson you. This is not the Last World, where everything is fixed and in its appointed place forever. These are
the Morning Lands. Things . . . change."

"Except you," Ruth said.

"As to that, my lady Ruth, perhaps some day even such as
I may learn wisdom, though not if wisdom means I must re-
nounce you. Come, if you are sated, and we will try if we
might make your ride a little smoother."

When they finally reached the Road, it was late afternoon.
The trail had been rising steadily since they'd stopped for
lunch, and the air had taken on an alpine sharpness. Oak had

given way to poplar and birch, then to pine, and Ruth was stiff and sore with the effort of keeping back straight, knees in, heels down, and wrists cocked. It was possible, she had discovered with pleasure, to not come down quite as hard—or as far—on the white horse's saddle as she had that morning, and the ground did not look quite so far away now that she was more certain of staying in the saddle. Despite—or because of—this, she was looking forward to tonight's inn with active interest.

"There," Melior said, and pointed.

Ahead the trail merged with a wider track. There was a tightness, an anticipation in the air, as if some enormous engine were running. The air above the wider track shimmered as if with heat, and the surface of the road changed and rippled in the wavering air—now claylike, now hot white radiance, now opaline gravel.

Magic.

"No!" Ruth cried. She hauled up and back on her horse's reins, and the beast obediently stopped. A cold chill of revulsion struck through her, and what had seemed so harmless when Melior used it to find their way, so reasonable when he proposed it in the morning light, was suddenly horrible.

Go on *that?* Ride along it, touch it, let it touch *her?*

"No," Ruth said, with what she hoped was more calmness. "Not on that."

Melior had reined in also, and sat regarding her with blank puzzlement.

"You can *see* it?" he said after a moment.

Ruth nodded miserably.

"A terrifying sight, is it not?" Melior asked.

"Don't humor me!"

"But it *is* a terrifying sight, Ruth—for any of the Five Races, let alone for a—" she saw him stop, and decide to go on, "—for a human, a Child of Earth, who has little experience of magic."

"I've had enough," Ruth said tightly, glaring mistrustfully at the sword Melior carried. *Enough to know that magic kills.*

He caught the direction of her glance. "But that explains it," Melior said. "You are bound to the Sword, and it lends you some of its magic." He looked back toward the Road. "I

swear you will take no hurt from the Road, Ruth. Magic is
not always baneful."

Ruth shook her head. How could she explain that it didn't
matter whether it was harmless or just as lethal as it looked?

"But it is the Road, Ruth. There is no other way," Melior
said helplessly.

"There has to be," Ruth said, with the irrational desperation of the phobic. "I can't go on that."

Even at this distance she could feel the presence of the
Road; a heatless proximity pressing on her skin. It felt as
Ruth imagined exposure to lethal radiation must feel—
insidiously toxic, destructive beyond death.

"None as certain, as simple, nor as fast," Melior answered
honestly, "and we are in desperate haste." He sidled his
horse over to hers and put out his hand. Ruth flinched away
from his touch, but he only covered her gloved hands with
his. "If I hooded you, or cast a darkening about the Sword
so you did not see the Road, would that serve?"

Ruth felt her eyes begin to tear from sheer stupid terror,
and fury at her own helplessness made her voice hard. "But
it would still be there, wouldn't it?"

"You see the Road as the Children of Air may see it—in
all places, and none; the silver cord that binds the Morning
Lands together."

Which meant "yes," she guessed. And there was no other
way. But—oh, God—to set foot on that road felt like be-
traying Naomi; making common cause with the magic that
had killed her friend.

And what would it do to *her?* To Ruth Marlowe—not fish,
not flesh, not good red herring? Gazetted Sleeping Beauty,
certified elphen pawn—would it fling her back into the
World of Iron and lock the door behind her?

Did she want to stay so much?

She opened her mouth to try to force the words of acceptance out, but as she did, Melior turned violently in his saddle, listening intently to something she could not hear.

Then he drew the Sword of Maiden's Tears.

It flashed like an airplane wing against the sky, and
hummed with the thin sweet croon of high-voltage power
lines. Melior's face was grim enough that for an instant,
watching him, Ruth forgot all her reasonable terror of being
trapped between the Iron Road and the Sword in the fear of
whatever made him look so frightening.

"They've found us," Melior said. He patted Cobant's neck absently, as if judging what reserves of strength the horse had left to give him.

"We must reach the Gate before they do—that is our only safety."

Ruth strained her ears, her eyes, her mortal senses, but the link to the Sword that had given her elphensight enough to see the Road gave her nothing more.

"Forgive me, Ruth," Melior said—and swung.

The flat of the blade hit her horse square across the haunches, and the horse, already infected by Ruth's fear, squealed and lunged across the little distance that separated it from the Road. Ruth, flailing desperately to stay in the saddle, felt the pressure of the Road crescendo; felt a heatless, lightless sizzle envelop her—then she was *on* the Road, and Cobant was crowding her horse to turn it along it. The mare bounced and shied; Ruth clutched at the saddle, afraid of being pitched beneath those fatal hooves.

The horse's plunging, kicking trot at last became first a canter, then a gallop, than a flat run. The hammer, hammer, hammer of the horses' hooves merged into a steady machinelike thunder, and now Ruth could hear sound behind them like the distant clamor of a mob—but loud enough to be heard over the jangle of bridle and thud of hoof. Ruth's new-learned horsemanship deserted her completely; she bounced helplessly in the saddle and focused all her will on not falling off.

That was all she could do. Her safety was entirely at the mercy of the muscles and will of a frightened animal running out of control.

Just as the car had been out of control.

The intrusion of the dream-memory into her waking fright was jarring. For a moment it blotted out the real world with its presence—

A back road, not very well lit. One in the morning, Prom Night. There was a flash of light in the road ahead, a coppery fiery light, and Ruth, straining her eyes, suddenly saw—

The creature that blotted out the sun merged seamlessly with the terror-image of Ruth's nightmare. It was dark against the sun dazzle, and despite its wide leathery wings Ruth thought of spiders and blind squirming eyeless things churned up out of the earth.

She barely had time to register its presence before it banked and dove for them. It passed low over her head, close enough for her to smell sulfur, blood, and the cloying scent of roses. Ruth crouched like a jockey, and the animal beneath her seemed to elongate, stretching its neck forward as if shrinking away from the monster above.

Suddenly there was a sound, a flash; lightning, thunder, nuclear war. She saw Melior's horse Cobant pass her, riderless and running flat out. Where was Melior? She wound the reins around her hands and pulled back as hard as she could.

Nothing happened.

Chapter 26

So You Want to Be a Hero

In the end, as it turned out, the unicorn was of some use after all.

In his circular sweep—looking for a road, looking for clues—Nic came upon the unicorn's track again, impossible to mistake. The print was slotted like a deer's hoof, but shorter and rounder, and in one place, where the tracks passed too close to a thornbush, there was a tuft of familiar white down caught among the twigs.

" *'Where are you come from, Baby Dear/Out of the everywhere into the here?'* " Nic quoted softly to himself. He followed the tracks, pushing the pain of his injuries as far into the background of his consciousness as he could. As it always had, a job to do settled Nic Brightlaw's mind wonderfully, letting him banish everything but the need to do it well.

It was the light that gave him his first warning that things were worse than he thought.

Ever since Christmas Eve, when he'd fallen through the enchanted bookshelf with Ruth Marlowe, the sun had behaved itself. It had risen, crossed the sky, and set in a reasonable fashion.

Not any more.

Nic stopped, and straightened out of his half-instinctive crouch, wincing as bruised muscles and torn flesh protested. He was in a spring forest with a heavy canopy, garden perfect: everything in new leaf and no sign anywhere of last autumn's leaves. The light was the rich mellow gold of late afternoon.

Just as it had been when he'd woken up—several hours ago.

Nic looked up. The leaves gave the view the aspect of a green and starry heaven—an ever-shifting, nearly solid viridian canopy through which light penetrated in white glittering chinks.

He turned around slowly, abruptly conscious of how unsteady he was on his feet; how dizzy, how likely to fall. There was no place where the sky, seen through the leaves, was brighter than any other. The light had not changed, or shifted, or dimmed, in hours. He braced himself one-handed against a tree trunk and continued looking for the source of the sunlight.

There was none. There was no sun.

Unreality washed over him in a slow wave of contused nausea. No matter what else had been strange, the physical world had always played by the rules. Now, it seemed, there weren't going to be any rules. Now, in the roots of his neglected soul, Nic Brightlaw believed he was in Faery. Where there was neither sun nor moon, only inhuman malice.

Perhaps he ought to have been frightened. But he felt, instead, a vast stubborn rage pushing at the edges of his self-control. He was here to do a job and *They*—whoever They were—were withholding information. Changing the rules.

It was an unexpected and not entirely pleasant thing to feel anger when the ability to feel anything at all had been dead for so long. To give it a focus—because anger, like lightning, needed a focus if it was not to destroy everything—Nic concentrated his anger on the unicorn. This was all Fluffy's fault.

He was going to find it. And once he got his hands on it—

A twig snapped.

Nic froze. He looked around carefully. Only his eyes moved.

There was a flash of white.

Fluffy the Wonder Caprid was back in town.

If this isn't the oldest trick in the book, it's certainly a main heading in the index, Nic thought with a flash of grim amusement. He knew how silently the unicorn could move. The noise it had made had been deliberate. Apparently he wasn't following fast enough.

But apparently, too, he was supposed to follow without knowing he was being led, and that spelled "trap" to Mrs. Brightlaw's little boy.

The nice thing about traps, Nic had always found, was that the people setting them were rarely paying much attention to anything else.

Nic blundered—gracelessly and with as much dramatic effect as he could muster—in the direction of the silvery flash. He caught a brief glimpse of Fluffy—*sans* flowers, but otherwise much the same as the last time he'd seen it—for one brief shining second before the unicorn plunged away.

Nic stopped. He was supposed to follow, of course. Instead, he headed off at right angles to the direction of the unicorn's flight. If it was smarter than a man, this trick wouldn't work. It might not work anyway, of course, but at least it would give him something to do.

When he was far enough away from where he'd seen the unicorn, he turned and walked parallel to its line, moving as silently as he could in his condition, looking for the right tree.

After a few minutes he found it: a massive, dense-foliaged oak, with a thick overhanging branch suitable for Errol Flynn to stand on while making speeches. Nic had other plans for it.

His first attempt to climb it made him abruptly aware that his right hand was entirely useless to him. He fell back, and found he'd reopened the deep gouges in his right arm. New blood seeped through the tight windings of Nic's makeshift bandage. The pain was exquisitely demanding, even overshadowing the pounding in his head. A fine countertrap he was setting here, lying on the ground waiting to be caught.

Hissing through clenched teeth, Nic rolled to his feet and hooked the useless hand through his belt before trying again, one-handed this time.

He made it onto the branch, but the pounding trembling weakness in every limb, the flashing light behind his eyes, told him how close to the edge of failure he really was. Catching the unicorn was his best and only shot.

It should come back for him. The unicorn was supposed to lead him . . . somewhere. Once it realized he wasn't following, it ought to turn back and try to draw him out again. When it didn't spot him on its back trail, it should circle to find him. Eventually, it would show up here. Nic stretched himself full-length along the branch and waited, hidden from watchers below by the dense overhang of leaves. One of the advantages of being the aggressor was not having to wait until the other guy did something.

Time was hard to judge without the sun to mark it by, and his watch had vanished long ago, probably in the fight with the dragon. In this woods there was only Now, and Now seemed to last forever. As he waited, Nic began more and more to think that this was not a place where human beings could safely remain. This was the dark side of Faery, deadly as poison, and Nic hoped, with the desire of one who dreams of a life free from complications, that he would not meet the rightful masters of these woods.

The unicorn came back.

Head up, pink nostrils flaring, tufted tail twitching like an inquisitive cat's, the creature minced into the clearing below Nic as if it were slumming royalty.

Nic slid off the branch and dropped on it.

It was only when he was in midair, unable to change his mind, that he spared a fleeting thought for the unicorn's exceedingly sharp horn. But its mind was on flight rather than attack. Fortunately.

Its legs buckled beneath his weight, and Nic twisted to grab it before it recovered. He was barely in time. The unicorn fought, all furious coiled muscles. It reminded Nic of wrestling alligators, the skills for which, once learned, were always with you, just like riding a bicycle. He clutched the unicorn to him, back to belly on the forest floor, his good hand clenched about the base of its horn, his other arm around its barrel just behind the furiously windmilling forelegs. It thrashed and squalled, but helplessly.

So he thought.

He was hoping it would run out of strength before he did, when suddenly the hairs on his forearm and the back of his neck prickled with some unsettling electrical charge. *Incoming artillery!* his idiot instinct yammered, and Nic threw himself sideways, still clutching Fluffy, to escape something that couldn't possibly be there.

And fell into a pit that couldn't be there either.

The fall was darkness and numbness—long enough for him to frame a coherent thought about failure and betrayal and dying alone. This time he landed on the bottom, and the pain that lanced through his skull made him close his eyes against the brightness. Then light returned, and he clutched tighter at the unicorn.

"Let go of that, son. I'm a thought fond of it, in my fashion."

Nic opened his eyes. He saw the biggest orange lizard he

had ever seen. And it had wings. The fact that it could talk, too, was almost an anticlimax.

Nic carefully let go of the unicorn. It didn't move, and for a moment he thought it was dead. Then it shook itself and rolled over, gaining its feet and staggering away from him— toward the dragon—shaking its head.

The unicorn collapsed beneath the shadow of one enormous wing, looking rumpled and tired, and closed its eyes with a sigh. Nic was absurdly reminded of Christian iconography, the lion lying down with the lamb. But Fluffy was no lamb, and this was no lion.

"That's a sight friendlier," the dragon said amiably.

Its hide had the satiny-rough sheen of sharkskin and the bright ruddy color of California poppies, Monarch butterfly wings, and fancy goldfish. Its eyes were burning pupilless gold, set in a long triangular head belonging to no known taxonomy—bird and beast and insect all blended together into something out of heraldry set at the end of a serpentine length of plate-crested neck.

It was lying on the grass, but even so, it could look Nic in the eye—and even so, it was much smaller than the last dragon he'd seen. Maybe that was why he didn't feel immediately threatened. Endangered, perhaps, but not threatened.

"I'm a friendly kind of a guy," Nic said mendaciously, glancing around unobtrusively. He was in open country, as manicured as a golf course, and the sun was a blessedly determinate point in the sky.

It took him a couple of tries to stand up, during which he kept his gaze warily on the dragon. He wondered if it could actually fly, or merely glided once it had launched itself from a height.

"Oh, I manage to get around," the dragon said.

"I'm glad," Nic said.

So it was telepathic, although it seemed to talk. On the other hand, it did not have the lips or tongue or palate to form those familiar English words he heard so clearly—just gleaming rows of teeth indicating a highly carnivorous lifestyle.

Outclassed. Game, set, and match to magic. Every muscle hurt, he was bleeding steadily, and the next fight he was in he'd lose.

Unless he could put it off long enough. A year or so seemed about right.

"I'm looking for a friend of mine," Nic began. "I wonder if you might have seen her?" *I wonder if you might have killed her, Puff, and if I can believe a damned thing you say, anyway.*

"Trust is a virtue," the dragon observed.

"Virtue is found only in Heaven," Nic responded.

"Does your friend have a name?"

"Ruth Marlowe. Do you?"

"Have a name?" the dragon asked, spreading its wings until the sun shone on Nic through a golden dragonsilk canopy. "Oh, many. But for the moment, you can call me Ophidias. It's a name much known in these parts," it added.

What, not Gandalf the Grey? "Okay, Ophidias, have you seen Ruth Marlowe?" Nic asked patiently. Although why he should assume that every talking dragon he met was a wizard—

"Not a dragon. Please. Dragons are such obsessive creatures; you wouldn't enjoy meeting one, believe me. I'd prefer you thought of me as a firedrake—or salamander, if you have a classical education."

Firedrake. Salamander. Creatures of fire. Creatures of Faery.

"Ruth Marlowe?" Nic asked yet again.

"My you are persistent. No, I haven't seen Ruth Marlowe yet. But I will." The dragon—firedrake—preened itself in the sun. The light struck golden rainbows from the chitin of its muzzle and crest and turned the unicorn's silvery coat saffron yellow.

So she was still alive. Nic felt a pang of relief.

"The question now is, what shall I do with you?" Ophidias pursued.

Here it comes. Nic tensed. He could see trees, behind him and to the right. Could he reach them before the creature reached him?

"No. The question, *firedrake,* is why *that*—" he pointed toward the unicorn, "—has shown up every other minute since Miss Marlowe and I arrived. And where it was leading me just now—and why. And while we're on the subject, you owe me big time for rescuing it a while back before Cruella DeVille turned it into unicorn *en brochette.*"

"Ah." The firedrake mantled its wings. "You want to buy."

"Maybe," said Nic. "But you still owe me."

Ophidias graciously inclined its head, agreeing.

"Where was the unicorn taking me?" Nic asked.

"To an inn where you would be fed, clothed, tended, and housed."

Nic started to ask why, and stopped himself. "Why" was something he could worry about later. There were more important things to ask.

"Where is Ruth Marlowe?"

"In Chandrakar, in mortal peril," the firedrake answered promptly, and waited.

Three questions were the traditional payment in fairy tales, and if Ophidias was a traditionalist, Nic had better not waste the third one.

"Can you take me to Ruth Marlowe?" he said carefully.

"Well," said Ophidias, after a long pause, "no. I can open the Gate for you, of course. But you're in no shape to go charging after her right now. Have some wine."

The firedrake spread its wing, and the unicorn was gone. Where it had lain, Nic saw a small table with a decanter and a single glass on it. Nic looked from the cup to the firedrake.

"Am I supposed to trust you?" Nic asked mockingly.

"Do you actually have a choice, Child of Earth? I could spin you a tale about being a great wizard unable to interfere directly in the affairs of the Morning Lands. I could go on about chess games of the gods, and grand illusions, and young Adepts reaching for powers they don't understand, and the mistakes of ancient enemies giving me the chance to thwart their plans, but the brass-nailed bottom line is, you either trust me for the hell of it and drink the wine, or hit the road just the way you are, Jack—if you can—but don't forget to look over your shoulder."

Nic walked to the table, poured the cup full, and drank it off without stopping to breathe. The sweet, raisiny taste almost gagged him, and standing this close to Ophidias was like standing in front of a roaring fire.

"That's no way to treat a fine vintage," Ophidias objected mildly, but Nic wasn't listening.

The wine slid honey-hot down his throat and set up a comfortable burning in his empty stomach. And as the warmth spread, his headache cleared; the aches of used and abused muscles dulled into the background and then faded altogether.

He flexed the hand that had been in the dragon's mouth.

The fingers moved, feeling returning to them in a tingling rush. Already guessing at what he would find, Nic peeled back the bloody makeshift bandage to look beneath.

The gouges were feverish, deep pink, and welted, but the fang marks were closed. There was no bleeding. As he stared at his arm, the color of the scars continued to fade.

"I trust you consider yourself repaid?" Ophidias asked.

"Yes." *If it lasts.* "Thank you."

"What a very suspicious young man you are. Now. Did you wish to bargain for passage to Chandrakar?"

Past overlay present with unwelcome suddenness. Sunlight. A crumbling sidewalk cafe in a city where the humidity molded your clothes to your skin even before you'd finished dressing. Across from him sat a smiling dark-skinned man, who smiled and smiled and offered his services in just such mild tones as Ophidias did.

Black market is black market, no matter where.

"Naturally I'm interested in listening to whatever proposal you care to make, but you'll appreciate that my resources are a bit limited at the moment," Nic said, falling into the old ways. He looked down at the cup in his hands, rolling it between his palms, then set it down on the table and took a step backward.

Nothing hurt.

"Well, son, I'm afraid your resources may turn out to be a bit of a problem. In fact, I don't think I'd be overstating the case to say that you really haven't got much to dicker with at all—except your life," Ophidias said in the bland tones of a Tennessee moonshiner.

If Ophidias had wanted his life, the firedrake could already have taken it with one snap of those long fanged jaws.

Don't listen to what they say. Listen to what they mean.

"So you'll put me in Chandrakar in exchange for my life," Nic said. "That doesn't do me a lot of good—unless you'd consider leaving me part of my life to use myself after I get there?" Nic said, equally blandly.

"You're good, boy." The firedrake flicked its tail and settled itself more comfortably, for all the world like an old hound dog in front of the woodstove. "How much time do you think the rest of your time is worth—once we deduct the cost of the travel?"

How the hell should I know, old man? Nic kept his face smooth. What was important here was the Mission Objective. Reality was for those who couldn't handle a good fantasy.

And Logic was the greatest fantasy of all.

"We haven't been talking about time until now. We've been talking about life. What will you give me for the part I've already lived?" Nic said logically.

Now Ophidias reared up on its hind legs, spread wings blotting out the sun. Nic didn't flinch.

"A *paladin*," the firedrake said, and now there was respectful amusement in its voice. "What do you offer?"

Nic considered carefully. What wouldn't he give, to lose the years and the knowledge he most needed to keep? But Mission Objective was paramount. What would he be, if those were gone?

"Leaving me physically as I am now, and with all the abilities I presently retain," Nic began carefully, "I offer you my life from birth until June 17, 1971—eighteen years—and from January 1, 1976 to December 24th of this year. That's a good length of time."

"Give me the five years you're keeping, and you can have the transport, plus a horse and weapons," the wizard countered quickly.

It was tempting. *But what is ability without memory?* Nic thought. He'd phrased the offer so that—as far as he knew—if it was accepted he'd jump straight from the end of his last tour to Christmas Eve, at least as far as his memory was concerned. He didn't know what that would do to him. But if he didn't keep his tours, he was just another civilian. He needed what he'd learned.

The horse and weapons would have been nice, though.

"No," Nic said. "The offer stands. How much is it worth?"

Ophidias seemed to smile, though the shape of its face could not possibly change. "Not enough. But don't worry, boy, you've got more. What about the life you haven't used yet?"

"What if I trip on a rock tomorrow and die?" Nic gibed.

"What if you do?" returned the wizard equitably. "Don't worry abut me, boy; I know the value of what I'm dickering for."

And I don't. Terrific.

Mission Objective.

"For transport, horse, and weapons—my choice—the life I've offered, plus what I have left, minus one year—"

"Seven days," the firedrake interrupted, with a flick of its tail.

"Six months," Nic countered.

"One month." Lash-lash, went the long whip of tail.

There was a pause.

"Okay. Minus one month of it," Nic agreed. "But including transport to hospitable terrain within, oh, five miles of Miss Marlowe and allowing me free access to her, that should be fair enough. And the time starts after I've reached Chandrakar and runs till it runs out. Without interruption."

The firedrake half-closed his eyes, thinking. Nic tried not to wonder how badly he'd been rooked, bartering his past and future for one month's grace. Still, if he couldn't reunite Miss Marlowe with her boyfriend in thirty days, he just wasn't trying.

Ophidias made up its mind.

"Remind me not to play poker with you, boy. Okay. For transport, horse, and weapons. The horse is my choice, and no discussion. The weapons are your choice from a selection I supply. A fair selection, my promise for that; no good ever comes of cheating a paladin anyway, even if I was of a mind to. You have one month from the time you reach Chandrakar. Then I collect. Deal?"

A choice from weapons the dragon supplies. Not a great offer, but probably the best I'll get.

"Firedrake," Ophidias corrected.

Nic took a deep breath.

It's like dying! a part of his mind screamed, and another part answered: *Don't be stupid. You died a long time ago.*

"Deal," said Nic Brightlaw, and held out his hand. Ophidias brought its wing forward so that the clawed tip—just—brushed Nic's palm.

There was a lightless flash, a chilling sensation of no-space, no-time. *Medic! Get a medic! I'm hit!* his mind screamed.

Then he was real again.

His mind staggered and groped; the cognitive analog of a man with both legs blown off trying to stand; the attempt to rely on systems no longer there, that habit insisted hysterically *must* be there.

Cautiously, with real fear, he tested what was left. Was it enough? He knew he'd sold the years of his life between twenty-four and forty in order to survive in never-never land. Was there something there he needed to keep to survive?

But he remembered that he'd survived them. That was enough. It had to be.

And his childhood, his parents, the town where he was born—gone. His first car, his first girl, the things that had brought him to the recruiting sergeant in 1971. Gone.

He didn't need them. Nic took a deep breath—wondering suddenly, with new and frightening ignorance, why the parents he must have possessed had chosen to name their son "Nicodemus."

Ruth Marlowe. The Mission Objective.

A brown-haired, blue-eyed girl with the bitter depthless eyes of a survivor. How long had he known her? Had they been lovers? Had she told him what had made her the way she was?

He'd have to ask her, wouldn't he, when he saw her again?

Find Ruth Marlowe. Someone was trying to kill her, and Ophidias had said she was in deadly peril. Stop the killers. And never mind "why." "Why" would kill you. "How" was what mattered.

Mission Objective.

"A horse, weapons, and a Gate," Nic said.

The wizard gestured, with one wide silk-sail wing, and Nic looked at what had not been there a moment before.

There was a horse that gleamed as if someone had spray-painted and varnished it. Its coat was as white as the unicorn's had been, as the fur of a very white cat, so white that its pink skin shone like pearls along its muzzle and around its dark watchful eyes. Its hooves were as pink as Nic's own fingernails, and there was a narrow white gleam of metal between the hoof and the ground; silver horseshoes. It wore a halter of pale blue velvet and a narrow rope ran from the halter to a brass ring bolted to a whitewashed post.

The post stood in front of a circular tent that looked like a miniature circus tent. It, too, was white and pale blue, and there was something faintly familiar about it. Not a real memory, or even a memory-of-a-memory ...

Ivanhoe. A movie. He'd seen it on base one night.

Nic glanced once more at the firedrake, and walked toward the tent. The horse stretched its head out to him as he walked past, and Nic paused to stroke its muzzle and neck.

The hide beneath his hand was glass-slick with grooming, hot with the sun, and its mane glittered with sunstruck iridescence; not like a horse's mane, but like a woman's hair. He ran his fingers through it.

Congratulations, Sergeant Brightlaw, you have just won a magic horse of your very own.

He gave the horse a last friendly slap on the withers and walked into the tent.

The thin fabric of the tent walls didn't keep the sun out. It was nearly as bright inside as out; a circle, perhaps twelve feet in diameter.

There was no floor. The tent's contents were laid carefully on the grass.

There was a saddle and bridle, he noted with relief. Either they counted as weapons, or the wizard was being generous. Then he looked further, and revised his opinions.

No guns, no rifles. No grenades, bazookas, no C-4, and certainly none of the more elaborate black budget dirty tricks that Nic was used to.

Seems like just yesterday, doesn't it? Nic told himself with gallows humor. He looked further. The wizard had promised him a selection to choose from, and so the contents of the pavilion were not simply what an Ivanhoe-knight would carry to tourney. Nic began to search, and to sort.

There was a huge triangular shield, painted to look like the Ace of Spades. Black and white, and a pretty redhead in black silk stockings and not much else superimposed on the center pip. It weighed nearly twenty pounds. He set it aside.

There was a sword in a scabbard of heavy, pale-blue leather, stamped in silver leaf with more spade Aces. Three and a half feet from point to pommel, with a blade three inches wide and sharp as his morning razor all the way up.

But he didn't know how to use a sword. He set it beside the shield.

There was a mace. Short. Light, after hefting the sword, but you still wouldn't want to stop it with your teeth. A possibility. He started a second pile.

Knives. Everything from a belt-knife Bowie point-heavy enough to use as a machete to delicate throwing knives that were each barely three inches long. Eight of them studded an arm's-length bracer that concealed one more surprise: the four silver knobs at wrist and elbow of the bracer could be pulled free, leaving you with a narrow, rigid, six inch long steel pin with a wicked point. Eight knives, eight pins.

A coil of rope, thin as climbing line and as strong.

A slingshot. A wicked cage of blackened bronze, held in the hand and braced against the forearm. The cup was leather, but the strap was strong elastic. The bag of shot with it weighed easily a pound and a half, small round lethal lead bullets.

Climbing hooks that could be used in the hands like claws, or attached to a rope and swung.

Caltrops. Spiky shapes that thrust at least two points skyward no matter how they fell. A horse that stepped on one was crippled. They'd survived past the days of cavalry, however: a car that drove over them was crippled as well.

A quarterstaff. Four feet long and lead-weighted. Nic slid his hand over the smooth wood and smiled.

A thinner coil of cord. It might support his weight. It might not. But what it *would* do, without uncertainty, was strangle a man. Or make a mighty fine trip wire.

A bow and its arrows joined the sword and shield. So did a crossbow. The crossbow had been the equivalent of the Saturday Night Special in its day: you needed very little training to become accurate, and it punched through armor as if it were swiss cheese.

But Nic didn't know how to use one, it had a limited number of bolts, and anything he might kill with it he could probably kill with the sling.

Spears and lance. Same objection as to the sword. Ax. Too big to throw. Looked easy enough to use. Might not be.

After some hesitation, Nic started a third pile.

The full suit of plate armor, complete with bucket helmet topped with dyed ostrich plumes, went the way of the sword without a moment's hesitation.

Good boots joined the mace, quarterstaff, and rope.

He hesitated for a long moment over the mail shirt.

Retro kevlar. It would stop a knife, probably stop a spear or sword. It felt like heavy velvet.

Then he hefted it again and heard the faint rustling jingle as it slid over itself and the links shifted. He'd never sneak up on anyone wearing that. It joined the sword.

He was drawn first by the leather shirt's false familiarity. It was not the "Come And Kill Me" blue of the sword's harness. The shirt was stippled in broad swatches of green, black, and darker browns. Breaking up the silhouette.

It had a round neck, and rawhide lacing all along the shoulders and outer seam. The sleeves looked as if they'd reach the elbow or a little below—these were the magical gifts of a wizard, and Nic didn't even have to question whether everything was in his size—and had a small notch at the cuff about an inch wide, edged with eyelets and strung with a rawhide cord. Pull it on and lace it tight, and it would fit like Superman's costume. Nic picked it up, puzzled.

It was heavy, so heavy he dropped it once. Then he flipped it inside out and saw that the dappled doe-leather shirt was entirely lined in thin pale chamois. He saw the careful marks of stitching, where thin pieces of metal had been sandwiched between two layers of chamois, assembled piece by piece into a silent armored jigsaw, until to wear the shirt was to be invisibly sheathed in metal.

Whoever thought this one up, I love you. You've got my kind of twisted mind.

He added the shirt to the pile of things he would keep.

There was another wrist-brace, similar to the first except that it had no concealed pins or sheathed blades. It was heavy enough that Nic was willing to bet it concealed another shaped metal plate. He took it.

There was a sack of coins, which any parfait gentill knyghte would have scorned. But money was also a weapon. Money was cooperation. Nic took the money.

He took a firebox: flint and steel, and a space for tinder.

He took a mirror, a polished square of metal the size of his hand.

He took a three-foot length of leather braided with horse-hair with a heavy ball weight on each end. Bolo.

He took a small wooden box with a sliding top that was filled with black grease and green grease. He tried them first, suspiciously, on the back of his hand and then with his tongue. They tasted vile, but he knew what they were, then. Camouflage.

He took the pants that went with the tunic. They were wool, not leather, and they didn't have metal plates sewn in, but they were lined with thick fleece, and there were shaped pieces of stiffer leather covering kidneys and groin. More protection than none.

There was a cape with a hood, longer than he was tall. It

was thin dark wool, shining with grease, and had wooden loop-and-toggle buttons halfway down the inside. Flap-covered slits let you poke your hands out when the cloak was buttoned.

Rain poncho.

He took a foolish-looking helmet that looked as if someone had mated a football helmet and the old *Wehrmacht* coal-scuttle helm. The cage on a pivot that gave it its resemblance to a football helmet could be hooked in place like a visor and protect eyes and nose, or swing down as far as the helmet would permit and protect the lower jaw. There was also a chin strap.

What is this? Wardrobe left over from Santa Claus Conquers the Martians?

And suddenly the voices from a time that ought to have been buried safely by almost two decades of living were painfully bright and close, and Nicodemus Brightlaw was gone. What was left was Sergeant Brightlaw of the United States Army Special Forces. "Saint" Nic.

Sniper, infiltrator, specialist in covert penetration and field intelligence. Field intelligence was walking through your lines and theirs, walking far enough that you'd have something to bring back. Papers. Prisoners. Intelligence. The truth.

Find the truth and the truth will set you free. Jesus on horseback.

Nic shuddered.

Let it go, Saint. They're all dead, and you are, too, and what Puff the Magic Dragon out there is counting on is that you're going to come apart right here and he scoops it all for free.

He added the helmet to the things he would take. He added a belt that incorporated a shoulder strap to distribute the weight that would hang from it, and pouches to hang from the belt because there wasn't a backpack and if you trusted the other man to carry what you needed the other man might just wind up raspberry roadkill and your stuff with him.

Then everything in the tent seemed to be sorted into those three piles. By now the illumination in the tent was less, and the tent's contents were harder to see. He didn't worry. Time started when he went through the Gate. And he had a month. In a month, Ruth Marlowe would be either safe or dead.

Nic took a last look at the ax and the mace and reluctantly added both to the pile with the armor and the sword. Too heavy. Everything he chose, he—and the horse—would have to carry.

He stripped off the clothes he'd taken from the man he'd killed in the clearing when he and Ruth had first arrived, and the last of the clothes left over from a life he no longer remembered, on a Christmas Eve that now never was. He remembered that day from its beginning; getting out of bed, getting dressed.

But the memories were slippery and senseless, hard to hold on to, because the day before that, his mind assured him, he'd been at in-country waiting for the Sikorsky that was going to medevac him back to the rear echelon country club, home, and Mother.

Away from the nightmare.

He looked at his body. There were scars where there had been fresh wounds day before yesterday. Old scars. Years old. And he was old. An old man of forty; impossible age to contemplate from twenty-two.

If you'd thought this was going to be easy, Saint old son, you wouldn't have done it.

He dressed in the firedrake's gifts, lacing and buckling everything carefully: heavy, calf-length boots that would protect the foot running or riding. Pants, gray-green wool lined intermittently with leather. The shirt was hard to lace down by himself but he managed. It was much less heavy worn than carried, and hugged his outline like a tight T-shirt.

He had a sudden desperate wish for a cigarette, even though he'd given up the habit the first week of his first tour. Charlie didn't smoke. Charlie could smell you if you did. End of incentive program.

Next came the bracers. Nic strapped the knife-studded one onto his right arm. He could throw left-handed, and he'd rather block with his left arm for a while anyway, magic healing drink or no. Nic fumbled the buckles awkwardly closed with his left hand.

The other bracer was easier. He strapped the heavy leather cuff that concealed the metal plate onto his left arm. It should foil any number of attacks. The edge of the bracers came to the cuff of the shirt, just as if someone had known he would select these items to wear from all that had been offered.

Someone had.

He swung his arms, stretching, trying to learn how the weight and constriction would hinder him.

Not too bad. He bent over and picked up the belt, noting how his center of gravity seemed to have shifted. Have to watch that. He straightened, buckling the belt around his hips, its tongue-and-toggle fastening eerily reminiscent of his web-nylon utility belt.

Bowie knife. Dagger. Sling and shot. Money.

But even that much weight made him waddle like a pregnant duck. Sapping his energy. Tiring him.

And God knew what the horse that had to carry all this and him besides would think.

He looked at the mace, the caltrops, the water bottle, the other knives. The claws. The bolo. The two coils of rope. The quarterstave. The cloak.

Triage time, dogbrain. Nic unloaded the pouches.

He kept the bracers; they were replacing a shield, as well as containing a number of samples of Sentry Surprise. He kept the big knife, and would at least until he could decide whether he'd need it to move through the jungle.

Forest. It's a forest here, not jungle. He kept the belt with its two deep pouches; he had to have a way to carry things. And it was something he could get rid of later. Ditto the poncho. Ditto the quarterstaff. Ditto the water bottle, because it was a forest-not-a-jungle, and there were fewer places to get water in a forest. He kept the claws.

He dropped the box of camo cream into a pouch. The memory of how much disadvantage a blond-haired white boy was at while trying to sneak anywhere in a jungle was still fresh.

He hefted the bag of lead bullets, then poured out half, dropped them in the pouch, and threw the bag into the first pile. He slid the slingshot into the pouch with the ammo. The right angle of the wrist brace protruded slightly, but it didn't look like it would fall out.

The caltrops joined the shot bag on the discard pile. Fun was fun, but there were other ways to sabotage a line of retreat.

He picked up the bag of money, easily as heavy as the bag of lead bullets. Trick question time. Did he need money or didn't he?

He poured the contents of the bag into his hand. Copper,

silver, gold, and some coins of a greasy gray metal that looked like polished pewter and hefted like lead. He picked those out and discarded them.

Copper for the working man, silver for the maid ... Something ... Something ... Gold for the ruler who sits in the hall/But Iron, Cold Iron, is the master of them all.

Scraps of Kipling danced through his head. Poet of Empire. Advocate of a rousing good brawl. But Kipling had believed there should be honor on both sides in war.

There wasn't. And cold iron wasn't what Nic wished for, it was hot lead.

In the end, he took less than half the money provided. Gold was for bribes, because Nic was betting that human nature wasn't that different here and a gold coin was a dazzling sight that could make anyone lose his head. Some copper, some silver, to pay for his own needs—assuming there was anyone to buy from. He put the money in the other pouch.

It clinked. Nic sighed. He retrieved the money pouch, poured the coin he was keeping into it, wrapped it tight, and stuffed it back in the pouch.

Blessed silence.

He picked up the tinderbox, and found that the slippage of the light was such that he had difficulty picking it out against the grass. Into the pouch with the money.

He picked up the coil of rope and the coil of line and slung them over his left shoulder, then picked up the cloak and stave, testing the arrangement.

Better. He'd worn heavier packs and carried more equipment, but he didn't have a pack and he hadn't seen a single example of lightweight, rot-proof, ripstop nylon superfabric since he'd gotten here.

He used the stave to hook the helmet up off the floor and let it slide down the length of the quarterstaff into his hand. He tucked the quarterstaff awkwardly under his arm and put on the helmet. He pulled the strap tight through its D ring closure and left the protector down, shielding jaw and throat with its leather-wrapped metal cage.

Thus burdened, he turned back to the saddle and bridle.

Here too, he discovered, a choice was offered.

There was the saddle that went with the plate armor. It looked like a rococo rocking chair and Nic grunted with the weight when he tried to lift it. The bridle that went with it had wide ribbonlike reins with tassels, and the bit was a complex arrangement of several hinged bars.

He reached for the memories that would tell him what this apparatus would be doing in a horse's mouth, and ran, once more, into the impervious blankness of lost time.

And Nic realized with a sense of grim amusement that his knowledge of horses and the ability to ride was a skill picked up in his vanished childhood.

Score one for you, lizard-breath.

But he'd bargained for a horse, and he had a horse, and he needed a saddle for the damned thing, that much he knew.

There was a stirrupless pad—two sheepskins sewn together, fleece out—with a braided circingle and D ring close. It went with a braided-leather line consisting of one rein ending in a loop that would slip over the lower jaw, and no bit at all. Maybe he'd been that good a rider, once. Not now.

The last available choice still looked like nothing Nic had ever seen, though it was his by default. It was the same streaky black and green—though what good camouflage would do him mounted on a horse that white was a mystery—and looked rather as if someone had incorporated a racing saddle into a throw rug; a rectangular shape of heavy felt that would hang nearly to the horse's knees on each side. On the horse side there were two leather straps and a sheepskin pad. On the rider side there was a covered wooden shape of teardrop-verging-on-oval that rose only very slightly at the back.

Short pieces of rope that Nic identified, after a moment, as cargo tie-downs fringed the saddle seat like tentacles. Two at the front, where Nic mourned the complete absence of a saddle horn, four at the back. The stirrups were nothing but long leather straps that hung down to the edge of the saddle skirt. The strap ended in a long blunt fishhook shape, and you made a place for your foot by sliding the hook end through your choice of holes in the strap. The shorter the stirrups, the wider the loop. Nic hooked them through the bottommost hole.

The only unrejected bridle had a straight bar for the horse's mouth with a ring the size of a bracelet at each end. There was a rope with one end woven unbrokenly over the ring; twelve feet of rope. There was also a strap attached to the ring, with the now familiar double D rings braided into it about a third of the way back from the free end. Between the D rings at one end and the bit dangling unanchored from the other, there was another strap. This had a flat loop at each end and slid freely up and down the strap until stopped by the hardware.

It took Nic some moments of puzzling until he decided that the bit went in the mouth, the long strap went up the horse's cheek, around the back of the head, through the free loop on the dangling strap (which would go under the horse's chin, Nic decided from hazy recollections of John Wayne movies) and down to the ring on the other side. The rope was obviously meant to function as a rein, but the only way Nic could see to make that work was to run it through the free loop on the other side and either tie it there or hold the loose end in his hand.

Fortunately saddle and bridle didn't weigh very much. Nic added them to his burden and walked out of the tent.

The horse was still there. But Ophidias was gone, and it occurred to Nic with the persuasive force of intuition that there was no Gate in his future to measure time from; he was already in Chandrakar.

Perhaps he'd been in Chandrakar all along. Perhaps only since he'd sealed the bargain.

Why hadn't he asked where he was, when he was asking questions?

Would it really have mattered, in the end?

"Great going, Puff. But where do I go to pay up?" Nic asked aloud.

Don't worry, paladin. I'll find you.

The voice in his mind had the fierce unreachable irritation of an itch beneath bandages. Nic shook his head violently to be rid of it. He turned back to the horse.

The tent behind it was gone.

Smoke and mirrors. "You sure you don't have relatives in Washington, big fella?" Nic said aloud.

This time there was no answer. Nic set his detachable possessions aside and advanced upon the horse.

There followed a brief interval where he cursed the firedrake and himself indiscriminately for his sudden lack of information that, as it turned out, he probably needed far more than he needed the memory of how to open a can of Army-issue beer with his utility knife.

He put the bridle on the horse. To do that he had to remove the velvet halter, and he had enough presence of mind to put a loop of the halter rope around the horse's neck, make a slip knot, and tie the horse to the post on a very short leash. Next stop, the bridle.

He got it assembled in place, but before he got it buckled the horse shook its head violently. The bridle went flying. Nic went and picked it up. He looked back. The damned thing was laughing at him. He was sure of it.

On the second try he got the bridle on and buckled. The horse shook its head again, and then delicately tongued the bit into Nic's hand. The bridle fell off.

Then he was ready to try again and the horse wasn't. It tilted its nose in the air, holding its head out of his reach. He had no way to bring its head down, and belatedly considered he should have put the rope-loop higher. But he outwaited it, grabbed it by the forelock, and held on grimly while he shoved the bit at the horse's lips one more time. The hand holding the forelock held the strap, while the bit slewed sideways and Nic groped for the throat-strap. Get the strap. Thread tab A into slot B. Then yank the strap through the bit-ring until the D ring hardware touched it. Thread the strap through. Tuck the hanging end between the layers of doubled strap. Wrap the single rein around the horse's neck and pass the free end through the empty bridle-ring. Tie it. Remove the rope. Recoil it.

The horse regarded him placidly, as if it had never moved in its life and didn't mean to start now.

Nic picked up the saddle.

The first miss was his fault; he got the saddle on its back and realized only then that the straps to tie it on were bundled beneath it.

Take it off and try again.

On the next attempt he let go of the saddle once it was on the horse's back. It shrugged—Nic would swear it shrugged—and the saddle slid off. The horse casually lifted one foot and set it firmly on the saddle skirts.

After some negotiation, Nic was able to lift the foot and kick the saddle out of the way.

Third try. He kept one hand on the saddle and crouched forward, looking for the straps. He'd never properly considered how wide a horse was when you were trying to get your hands on something hanging down on the other side of one.

It began to sidle away from him, edging around the post like a sweep second hand.

But in the end that maneuver hoisted it on its equine petard. After a couple of circuits it had wrapped the slack in its rein completely around the post. The front end of the animal had to stand still. Nic kept the back end from moving by finally getting his hand on the loose end of the back strap and pulling it toward him. He buckled it, drawing it as tight as he dared. The front strap was easier, now that he didn't have to hold the saddle in place.

Once the saddle was in place, Nic unwound the horse from the pole and decided he'd try boarding it. It looked easier on television. It had probably been easier for him, once. He grabbed a double handful of mane the color of moonlight and put his toe into the stirrup loop. He stepped down into the stirrup, swinging his other leg up—

The saddle slid unhurriedly in the direction of his weight. Nic fell, carried off balance by the unfamiliar weight of armor and weaponry. He sprawled on his back in the grass, looking up at the horse's undercarriage, and at the saddle slung beneath its body. He felt a moist caress on his cheek. The horse nuzzled him, dark eyes wide with innocent inquiry.

"That does it. Just hold that thought, Shadowfax; in another moment you're going to be singing soprano."

He got to his feet and grabbed the horse's reins in one hand while he shoved the saddle upright with the other. Then—as he should have done at first—he began hauling on the girths alternately, tightening them until the leather creaked and there was a faint but perceptible indentation in his mount's satiny white belly.

Nic backed away, panting with exertion. The horse looked at him innocently. It did not seem to be particularly uncomfortable with the saddle's tightness.

"All right. Good. Fine. I'm glad we had this chance to get to know each other," Nic muttered to himself. He put his foot in the stirrup again, and this time swung his leg across the saddle without trouble.

He looked around. From horseback the landscape flattened out. He could see farther, move faster, and—if he only had the technology and training—smite enemies in their hundreds with sword and mace, lance and shield.

The mounted horseman. The cutting edge of military technology for two thousand years. The cavalry that had smashed empires.

"Heigh-ho, Silver," Nic said without enthusiasm. The horse shook its mane, pulling on the reins.

He swung down again. He picked up his goods and chattels, and used the trailing lengths of rope behind the saddle for their proper function; to tie his cape and other possessions firmly into place. After some hesitation he lashed the quarterstaff on top of the pile, seeing no other way to carry it. It stuck out ludicrously on both sides. Wide load.

This time, when he mounted, he held the reins bunched in one hand and the mane in the other. His legs hung awkwardly, even in the stirrups that kept his knees bent—as if this were a Harley, not a horse—and he had no idea what to do with the reins, other than not drop them. But after some joggling and swearing he got the animal moving, and even pointed in the right direction.

Once he'd untied the horse from it, the hitching post had disappeared as soon as Nic took his eyes off it, but he ignored that. If he'd done all that he'd done in order to be able to find and protect Ruth Marlowe, then finding and protecting Ruth Marlowe was what was important—not magic tricks.

And after a few minutes a-horseback, he realized that the dragon had kept its part of the bargain. All the abilities Nic had possessed at forty were all still there, including the instinctive operator's manual for Horse (One), Single Operator Equine Transport Unit Mark One (Magic). If he didn't think about what he was doing and why he should do it, he was fine.

Now all he had to do was find Ruth Marlowe, and see what rescuing her required.

In one month.

Starting from now.

Chapter 27

Cold Steel and Chance Encounters

It was dawn in the Vale of Stars, and Fox the Outlaw Brigand was a man with a problem. The problem was his hostage.

He didn't particularly mind the loss of the Cup. Fox hadn't been after the Cup in the first place. Having it vanish was almost as good, for Fox's purposes, as having it himself. But since he didn't have it and couldn't either bestow or withhold it, he also had no particular control over his hostage. Even if he kept her tied hand and foot (as she was now), something would happen. With the cup gone, Tinkerbelle was a loose cannon; an elf bitch with nothing to lose.

Fox could almost sympathize.

His spies at Dawnheart had told him yesterday that The Rohannan—whom Fox had known as Mel the Elf—was still away, No one knew when he might return. Since what Fox really wanted was Melior and the Sword of Maiden's Tears, his hostage was no good to him if Melior was not around to be lured within reach. The logical thing to do was to get rid of her and try again later.

Logical, sensible, and safe.

Of course, there arose a question as to method.

It was not that Fox was a stranger to killing. He had killed—or helped to kill—five people already in his career: three humans, the elf on the Vale Road, and one hominid neither human nor elvish—though Fox was not prepared to say, even to himself, what it *had* been. He remembered every face, though he didn't know all of their names.

He made no excuses for himself. He knew he could kill again if it was necessary.

But was it necessary to kill Tink? *That,* as Hamlet said, was the question.

Hathorne rode ahead, his horse picking its way carefully up the trail that led to the pass into the Vale. Fox followed, leading the horse that carried the hostage. Behind them came Raven, then Ash and Otter. All present and accounted for.

Fox thought the matter of Tink through carefully and decided he did not have to kill her, providing he was prepared to take a few risks.

If he dumped her at Foretton, the village at the edge of the forest—across the valley from Dawnheart but well within sight of it—they'd fall all over themselves to return her to the castle. It was reasonably safe. She didn't know where the camp was, exactly, and it was time to move it anyway.

And now that Fox'd seen inside the Vale, he thought that its one pass could be properly defended by very few men. They could set up a free human village here, safe from elvish magic. He owed them that much, considering he didn't intend to devote his life to them.

It had seemed so impossible for him to succeed that he'd never thought past the moment when Melior was dead and the Sword destroyed. Now it seemed at least possible, and Fox, ever the clever general, tried to push his mind past that moment.

The few experiments he'd been able to conduct had indicated that he could not leave Chandrakar by the same sort of magic he'd used to bring himself here. Possibly he *could* walk the Iron Road again—but without magic, he couldn't *find* it. Without the magic to find the Iron Road, he was trapped in Chandrakar.

And in Chandrakar, Fox was a hunted—and, he prided himself, famous—outlaw. Even if he left Domain Rohannan and Canton Silver itself, Melior (aka The Rohannan), the Earl of Silver, and any number of other high-nosed elves would undoubtedly make sure that none of the other six Cantons would harbor him; at least, not for long. At least, not unless Fox could be of more use to them than Silver Silences' displeasure was harm.

Fox really, *really,* hated the idea of being of use to any elf. To any*body,* for that matter; he had always been remarkably evenhanded in his disdain for other sentient life.

Live fast, die young, and leave a pretty corpse, he thought philosophically. *Maybe I CAN start a full-scale peasants' revolt.*

It was something to think about.

* * *

An hour's riding brought the outlaw party to the place where they would leave the Vale Road for the sheltering woods that edged it.

"Here's where we kiss and part, gang. I'm sure you'll all agree that Tink here has been a great little hostage, but the clock on the wall says—"

Raven, Ash, and Otter stared at Fox like a field of grazing sheep. He sighed, and took a deep breath, and tried again, resisting the temptation to count out the words on his fingers.

"We don't need the elf any more. I'm going to take her back to Foretton and let her go."

"Not kill her?" asked Raven with guilty relief.

"Not kill her," Fox said. "I'll meet you back at camp. Tell Yarrow to get ready to move. Everything positively must go. This once in a lifetime, never to be repeated—"

"I'll take her," Hathorne said, interrupting.

Fox studied the man as if his own life depended on it— which it might. He knew little more of Hathorne than his name and his claim of being wolfshead—outside the protection of the law—but that was true of a number of the members of Fox's merry band of murderers, poachers, and thieves. He knew that Hathorne had done enough peace-breaking since he'd joined them to swing for it if Hathorne were caught, and he knew that Hathorne was as quick to speak against Chandrakar's elphen overlords as Fox was himself. That much being said. . . .

"No, I feel like a little jaunt," Fox said, smiling his sweetest smile.

"I really think—" Hathorne began.

"No, you don't," Fox assured him kindly. *And I do.* Any local boy who hated elves that much could hardly be trusted alone with one.

Fox swung down from his horse. "Raven, help me shift her. You can use the extra horse back at camp."

Between them, Fox and Raven shifted the unconscious Jausserande to Fox's horse. She would have roused hours ago from Fox's sling-stone blow, save for the sleeping draught he'd given her.

Sleeping draught, hell; nothing beats a Seconal dissolved in half a cup of wine for sweet dreams and no regrets. Boy, is she going to have a headache when she wakes up.

He swung himself back into the saddle behind his hostage,

conscious of Hathorne watching him. The man's mismatched eyes were brilliant in his weather-browned face. Fox wondered what he wanted with Tink—other than the obvious. Maybe he was overreacting. Maybe Hathorne was just thinking of going into the kidnapping and extortion business for himself.

"See you guys later," Fox said, kicking his mount into a canter. Hathorne watched him out of sight.

Something, Fox thought, was going to have to be done about Hathorne.

The first thing that returned to Jausserande was the pain, a dull, sick, jarred-loose throbbing in her head that meant she'd hit it very hard. Or had it hit *for* her.

There was a taste in her mouth as if she'd been eating river mud, and she focused on that. She would not think of the night just past, or the red murder waiting to be loosed in her one final time would find that its time was now.

If she didn't throw up first. She breathed deeply and steadily, forcing back pain and nausea and taking stock of her surroundings. She was somewhere in the open air, lying facedown across the withers of a horse. Its rider's body pressed her against the saddle. She smelled leather, horse, and grass, wood smoke and cut hay—

They must be near a village.

The horse slowed.

"This is your wake-up call, Tink," a hated and familiar voice said. "I'll spare you the conventional villain speeches, except to note that I'm sparing your life—which is more than you'd do for me."

The horse stopped. Its rider put his hands on her, lifting her away from the saddle. Jausserande struggled, and found that she was tied hand and foot. Fox heaved her off the horse as if she were a sack of meal and flung her to the ground. She landed hard and awkwardly in a pile of leaves, and by the time she had struggled onto her side and gotten her breath back, Fox's mount was a retreating flicker of motion seen through the trees.

Pure outrage gave her the strength to drag the buckskin strips from her wrists, oblivious to the pain. In a moment more, her ankles were free as well. Jausserande lunged to her feet, shaking with the need to kill something.

But there was nothing here to kill.

She kicked savagely at the leaves and looked around. Dawnheart was a white shape on a distant hill, brilliant in the late afternoon sunlight, and the sloping valley between it and the forest edge was a brown and gold patchwork of autumn meadows and harvested fields. Foretton. She remembered its name; it was the last village she'd passed with Guiraut before reaching the road that led to the Vale Road—

The road she would never need to ride down again.

The magnitude of her failure left Jausserande momentarily breathless. Where could she begin to repair the loss suffered by Line Floire? She strained her eyes to look across the valley, but could not see the scarlet-and-silver pennant flying from Dawnheart's tower that would tell her that her cousin had came safely home. But even if Melior were still absent, any of Rohannan's serfs would give her any aid she desired. If she could build a fire, she could even signal the castle directly—Richart's sentries still walked the wall, and after what had happened at the Harvest Home, the captain of Dawnheart's Guard probably had patrols out sweeping these woods as well. Help was as close at hand as the village below her.

But Jausserande didn't want help. She wanted Fox's throat between her hands. She shoved her hair out of her eyes, streaking her pale skin with dirt. She wanted Fox in her hands, at her mercy, with a passion greater than any she'd ever imagined—a passion greater than her need to possess the Cup of Morning Shadows.

Before anything else, Jausserande wanted Fox.

And she was going to have him.

Jausserande turned her back on the castle and began to follow the horse's track into the wood.

Blurred events taking only seconds seemed to stretch and slow with the deadly inevitability of a dream.

Ahead, Cobant pulled farther and farther away, and Ruth's own horse seemed determined to close the distance. A shadow occluded the sun as the monster passed overhead once more. Ruth looked up, blinded by her own whipping hair, and could not be sure what she saw.

The knowledge that Melior was lost and the realization that her horse was bolting came to Ruth Marlowe at the same moment.

"Stop!" Ruth screamed, dragging at the useless reins.

There was no response. Foam dripped from the animal's mouth and rose up from the sleek hide as if the white horse were a rug being shampooed. If the horse stumbled—if she fell off—Ruth Marlowe would be as dead as any car wreck could make her.

There was a sound behind her like baying. Something hunting. Something hunting *her*.

Ruth clung to the saddle, to the reins, trying not to think about how vulnerable she was on horseback. The pounding gallop began to be an active hurt; each hoof impact upon the road sending a stabbing pain through Ruth's knees and spine and head. She couldn't feel her legs, couldn't feel her hands; tears streamed down her face from the whipping of wind and hair and mane, and the world was reduced to blurred and meaningless light.

She even wished she were more afraid: fear seemed to have sharpened every thought and feeling to the point of pain; imagination raced even faster than her mount, painting vivid pictures of every possible way she could be hurt. Safety was over the border—but Melior had said it took magic to reach it, and Melior was lost.

The howling rose to a cheated crescendo behind her, and then, at last, panic might have come, save that pain came before it: pulling, tearing, sick fire in the marrow of her bones, twisting and burning and ripping until nothing, nothing, nothing was left. Ruth screamed in agonized protest through a jarred disjointed jolting that ended with falling and landing and left behind it only the memory of pain vivid enough to make her bones throb.

Silence.

The quiet was the first thing she heard. Quiet, and stillness—no baying hunters, no thundering hooves, only an odd rhythmic sound Ruth couldn't identify. She gasped blindly for air and got a mouthful of earth. Choking and gagging, she struggled to her knees. There was no Road and no pursuer anywhere in sight. She scanned the sky with anxious terror. There was no dragon either.

Ruth's horse lay on its side a few yards away. Her hind legs were outstretched and her forelegs tucked near her belly, as if she'd been shot while in full flight, but her side heaved like a working bellows and Ruth could now identify the sound as the high whistle of her gasping breaths. The mare's coat was covered with foam, almost steel-colored

with wet, and foam and drool streamed from her nose and
mouth. And down low, toward the hoof, one leg was twisted,
and shards of white bone showed like slivered almonds
through the blood.

"Oh, God. Oh, Jesus. Oh, God." Ruth tried to stand, and
fell, and crawled on hands and knees toward the horse.

"Well met, maidey," a voice said behind her.

"Please, can you—" Ruth began, turning.

The words died in her throat. It was the odd-eyed man, the
one who'd tried to kill the unicorn and Nic when she'd first
arrived in Elphame. He was alone, on horseback, and looking at her.

"Best to be saying your good-byes now, maidey," the man
said as he dismounted. He took a step toward her, one hand
down by his side.

He was holding a knife.

He reached her and hauled her to her feet, and Ruth,
scrabbling for balance, felt the lancing pain of a twisted ankle as she tried to stand. The pied-eyed man hefted her easily, pulling her back against him and raising the knife.

"Hathorne!"

The name rang out, sharp and imperious. The man jerked,
as if part of him wanted to respond.

But he didn't. He raised the knife.

"Let her go," the voice said again, so familiar that Ruth
was sure constant terror had unhinged her mind. "Let her go
now, Hathorne. If I shoot, I'll hurt her. But I'll kill you."

There was a moment where Ruth, nauseated with terror,
felt Hathorne weigh the usefulness of her death against his
own. Then he released her with an ungracious shove. Ruth
fell forward and scrambled onto her back in an unladylike
sprawl. Her ankle was a nexus of white fire.

She looked up.

"Hiya, Ruthie. Long time no see." The man known to his
followers as Fox smiled.

Ruth stared. She saw a blond man in a gray tunic, his long
hair pulled straight away from his face to fall in a silky tail
that hung forward over one shoulder. He held a crossbow
balanced on his hip. His pale eyes were startlingly blue
against the sunburnt brown of his skin, his forearms were
sculpted with muscle, and he stood with the unconscious arrogance of the athlete.

"*Philip!*" Ruth squealed, but Philip—if it *was* Philip—wasn't looking at her.

"This is Ruthie, Hathorne. She's by way of being an old friend of mine. I'd like to know what you thought you were doing."

"I wasn't going to hurt the maidey," Hathorne said unconvincingly.

"You weren't going to rape her either—not in that position," Philip/Fox said, completely uninterested in excuses. "What I want to know is why I had to tell you twice to let her go."

"Philip?" Ruth said, in a whisper meant only for herself. Could this be Philip LeStrange—this cold-eyed master of men? When Naomi had been alive and the five of them had been together, Philip Leslie LeStrange had been weedy, blond, short, twenty-two, and the product of respectable parents who were sure that his health was too delicate for anything more than a quiet career as a librarian. He'd worn bifocals and backpacks and the only weapon he'd been familiar with was words.

But she hadn't seen Philip in over two years. Things seemed to have changed.

"I meant no harm, Fox," Hathorne said again. "Didna thole the maidey was thy kith."

His Monty Python dialect was growing thicker by the minute. Ruth clamped her teeth shut over the urgent information that Hathorne had already tried to kill her once before. This wasn't the time to mention that. Not when she wasn't sure whose side Philip was on. Hathorne had called him Fox, which was just the sort of name Philip would choose for himself if he were picking an alias, but what did the fact that he was using it *mean?*

"Yeah, well, don't let it happen again. If you want a woman, go to the town and buy one. You know the rules: no messing with wives or sisters or girlfriends. It's stupid. The *elves* are our enemy, Hathorne—not humans."

There was another long pause. Hathorne bowed his head in acceptance.

"You okay?" Philip said to her.

Try as she might, Ruth could not reconcile what she saw with what she remembered. How could Philip have made himself so at home beyond the Morning in only two years?

And how had he gotten here?

"I—" Ruth began, and coughed. "My horse—" She gestured.

"Wait there," Philip said.

She watched as Philip—*Fox*—turned away and led Hathorne back toward his horse. She watched them talk, Philip gesturing. His head barely came to Hathorne's shoulder.

Well, he was still short, at least.

She saw Hathorne crouch by the horse's side, and look up at Philip. Their voices didn't carry. Philip made a chopping motion with his hand, explicit in any language. Hathorne knelt on the horse's neck to cut its throat, and Ruth, shuddering, looked away. She closed her eyes. Her fault. Her fault *again*.

"There wasn't anything we could do. Broken leg." The words came from above. Ruth looked up at Philip. No, at *Fox*. "Too bad. We can always use horses. Do you want the saddle?"

"The saddle?" Ruth said blankly.

"Yeah, Ruthie, the saddle. The part that goes around the middle of the horse; you sit on it?" he said condescendingly.

"Leave me alone," Ruth said wearily.

"I ought to," Philip said, still in that nasty sneering voice, "but you're too damn much trouble to leave wandering around loose."

Ruth stared at him in dawning disbelief.

"Get your ass in gear. This is not optional. In case you hadn't noticed, it's getting dark. And there's all kinds of things that come out after dark."

Ruth put her head on her knees again and closed her eyes. "Somebody wants to kill me, Philip. They're chasing me. There was a dragon, and we were on the Road—the Iron Road, you know?—I think it's got Melior."

"Where's the Sword?"

The question—simple, intelligent, cutting through everything else—made Ruth feel insensibly better. No matter what else might be true, this was Philip. Her friend, as much as he was anyone's, and the thing that Philip had always been best at was cutting to the chase.

"I don't know. We were together." She tried to remember whether the Sword of Maiden's Tears had been in its scabbard or in Melior's hand when the dragon had attacked and couldn't. "I think it's with him."

"Well, that's just fine," Philip said, so warmly that Ruth

stared at him in faint surprise. "We can work with that. Now come on, Ruthie—we gotta go."

"I hurt my ankle," Ruth said, knowing it sounded childish. She fought down the tightness in her throat. She'd die before she'd cry in front of Philip. Fox. Whatever.

"Don't worry, I've got the best MASH unit in all Elfland. Now come on. Put your arm around my neck. No, don't look over there; Hathorne's butchering your horse. Shut *up*, Ruthie, there's no sense in wasting meat. Close your mouth. Which ankle is it? No, keep your eyes on my *face*. Look at me, Ruthie, upsie-daisy. And don't worry; this is going to hurt."

Philip was right. He put her arm around his shoulder and his hands on her waist and lifted. Pain like lightning shot through her back and legs and she yelped.

"If you think that's fun, wait till we get to the part where you get on the horse. Here we go. Lean on me, Ruthie, I'm not going to drop you." Philip kept up the easy encouraging patter as she hobbled toward where his horse was tied. His arm circled her waist like an iron bar, easily supporting her weight. Her arm pressed down on the hard, well-built muscle of his neck and shoulders. Scrawny, unhealthy Philip was muscled like a kick boxer.

She was gasping with effort by the time they stopped. Philip wasn't even breathing hard. She looked up at the horse. It was bigger than hers had been; the saddle an impossible height from the ground.

"I'll boost you up across it. Swing your leg over, but don't put your feet in the stirrups. I'll get up behind you."

"Philip, I don't think I—"

"One-two-three—" Philip said, ignoring her. He put both hands on her waist and lifted her straight up over his head. It hurt, and when she grabbed at the saddle edge and used it to pull herself forward that hurt, too—just as he'd promised, a part of her mind reminded her.

But falling would hurt worse, so she scrabbled, yanking at her skirts and cloak, until she had one leg on each side of the saddle and was sitting more or less upright.

Philip vaulted lightly up behind her. "There we are," he said, as if to a backward child. "Now just sit here and let me do all the work." He reached around her to collect the reins.

Ruth was forced back against him as he settled in the saddle and shifted his weight forward. He reined the horse around and set it through the trees at a walk. He rode as if he'd been born on horseback, and Ruth tried to remember if Philip had ever mentioned horses when she'd known him before.

It had been spring on the Road, but it was autumn here, wherever here was. The trees had dropped most of their leaves, and what remained on the trees were as gaudy-bright as the contents of a box of breakfast cereal: raspberry red, lemon yellow, orange orange. The sun was at the right late-afternoon angle to slant through the leaves in translucent golden bars, yet, despite all the gold, Ruth was glad she had the cloak to pull around her.

"Philip—"

"Call me Fox." There was no hint of apology or embarrassment in his tone. "It's the kind of name they use here, for one thing."

"Where are we?" Ruth asked. "Fox." It wasn't that hard to say. What was hard was to think of him as Philip.

There was a pause of surprise behind her. "Chandrakar. I thought you knew. Dawnheart's just the other side of the valley; about ten miles."

"Dawnheart?" Ruth asked. "Your camp?"

There was a short bark of laughter; for a moment Fox sounded distinctly like his namesake.

"I wish! No. Castle Rohannan, you could call it. Mel lives there when he's home."

"Oh, God." Ruth leaned forward with sheer despair. Fox put an arm around her waist and pulled her back against him. "What am I going to do?" she whispered, not intending him to hear.

"Well, you could start by telling me what's going on. Start with how you got here and go on till you get to the end. We've got about an hour before we reach camp; I don't want to push the horse when it's carrying double."

"You've changed," Ruth said.

Another laugh, with nothing of humor in it. "I've changed, Michael's changed, everybody's changed."

"I haven't," Ruth said bitterly. Maybe only people with souls could change.

"No," said Fox noncommittally. "But you will."

Ruth began her explanation with Christmas Eve at the Ryerson and immediately received another shock.

"You got a job there? So did I. Intern the summer you graduated. They still talk about me?"

"Why?" said Ruth.

"Because I vanished without a trace—assuming they noticed. There's a Gate to Elfland down in the Second File."

For the old Philip, this would have been unusually talkative, but Ruth didn't pay any attention.

"I know," said Ruth, "I fell through it."

Fox snickered, and sounded exactly like his old self for a moment. "Of course you did. The Sword is on this side. The Sword fell to Earth to be near you, once upon a time. Then you fell to Elfland to be near it. Quod Eras Demonstratum, or, in the vernacular, thus always to tyrants."

"Not all the way. And not alone."

Ruth explained about finding the Gate and falling through into a place called Counterpane. About Nic Brightlaw, who had accidentally come with her, who'd saved her life and then disappeared.

"You brought my boss to Elfland?" Fox said in disbelief, and Ruth realized with a jolt that of course he would have known Nic if he'd worked at the Ryerson. The thought was disturbing in a way Ruth couldn't quite place.

"Wow. Old Mr. Brightlaw in Elfland. But go on, Ruthie. Jesus, you never did know how to tell a story."

"Well then it's just as well I wasn't going to be a J-librarian, wasn't it," Ruth snapped, nettled. She explained briefly about the unicorn, about reaching the Goblin Market, being attacked. Finding Melior, losing him, finding him again. And, now, losing him once more.

"And there's something else you ought to know, Fox. That friend of yours with the charming manners? He showed up almost as soon as Nic and I did. He said he was hunting a unicorn, and at the time I believed him. But now I don't think so."

"Hmm." Fox's breath tickled her neck. "So Hathorne's been walking the Road, has he? Have to be; aren't any unicorns in Chandrakar to hunt, and you saw one at the same time. Hathorne's been a naughty boy; I wonder who his patron is, and what his patron wants?"

"I don't know what you're talking about," Ruth said.

"It doesn't matter anyway," Fox said. "All that matters is finding Melior and the Sword. Oh, yes. At last. Thank you, Ruthie," he said prayerfully.

"I'm sure he'll help you, too," Ruth said, although she wasn't exactly clear on what kind of help Philip/Fox needed. "But how do we find him—where do we start?" Ruth said. "Oh, God, he's dead—I know he's dead." Tears would have been appropriate, but tears wouldn't come somehow, and her protests of Melior's death tasted like lies. She shook her head. Fox poked her in the ribs.

"If he's dead, he's still going to be dead when we find him. If it's a stupid elf vendetta, they probably want to talk him to death. And anyway, I know who's got him."

"Who?" demanded Ruth, trying to turn around in her seat to look at him. Fox prevented this.

"Jesus, Ruthie, use your head. Who hates Melior, who wants the Sword of Maiden's Tears, who screwed up your life in the first place? Eirdois Baligant of the House of the Vermilion Shadows, known to his friends, loved ones, and other intimates as Baligant Baneful. *He's* got Melior.

"And maybe even Nic Brightlaw, Boy Librarian."

CHAPTER 28

Love in a Faithless Country

He did not wish to wake, because the situation, in addition to being hopeless, was also perfectly clear.

Baligant had won. Line Rohannan was doomed.

Melior drifted just below the surface of waking, letting the eddies of sleep carry him where they would. Vertigo became the saddle of a horse, with Ruth's horse just ahead, and miles of undefended open Road to cover before reaching a Gate to any land, let alone to Chandrakar.

Then he was looking down on the running horses, as the cruel claws of the wizard-dragon gripped his arms. Saw Cobant running free as Ruth's inferior mount struggled valiantly to keep up. Saw the pack behind—not wizards, but wizard-called: hellhounds, creatures of magic who could run the Road and pull down any prey.

And then the pain, as the wizard used pure brute power to make a Gate where a Gate *might* be, but was not.

And then darkness.

Melior drifted deeper, seeking oblivion, and his vision took on the jangled logic, not of memory, but of dreams. He saw the *grendel* once again, but this time it was Philip LeStrange who held the Sword of Maiden's Tears to slay it. And who did not become *grendel* in his turn, but kept outward human seeming and changed within—into a creature far less human and more deadly than any *grendel*.

He saw the Cup of Morning Shadows, blazing bright gold and filled with power. But it was not Jausserande who held it, but Ruth—Ruth who cried as she held it, consumed by flame, for only that which was untouched might touch the Cup, and Ruth was his, his, his, his heart twin, his lady bright.

He saw Jausserande, her face in agony as she lost that which meant more to her than the Cup, and the pain was everywhere, burning, pushing him up out of dreams.

* * *

"It was time you awakened, Baron Rohannan." A woman's voice.

Melior roused to consciousness, and the burning came with him; a brand in the shape of a flower, angry garnet against his ribs. The woman holding the iron that had marked him stood watching, her sharp white teeth denting her full underlip.

She was as fair, perhaps, as the white Hermonicet—Hermonicet the Fair, whom Melior had never seen, and for whose sea-cool kisses the seven elphen Houses had gone to war. But this woman was fair as the sun, not the moon—as beautiful and deadly as sun fire; all the shades of gold and copper and blood. Hair the color of firelight rippled over her shoulders, eyes the hot color of burning coals gazed into his.

Mad eyes.

He tried to move and found he could not, hung in chains like any felon in his own dungeons. There was rough stone against his bare back, and his feet were bare also; his toes barely skimmed the floor. The pain in his shoulders of his unsupported weight was a burning pressure that would only grow worse with each passing hour.

The lady set the iron aside into the brazier to heat once more. Though her outward seeming marked her as one of his own race, the Children of Air, Melior knew she was not.

"I awake," Melior said, watching her. "What would you have of me?"

The lady sighed, as though his question wearied her unutterably. "Peace," she said.

Melior would have said more, but she turned away, circling the room, her fingertips running along the wall as if she were any bored child seeking to amuse itself. Her hair, unbound like a maiden's at her betrothal, hung in a rippling metallic curtain nearly to the floor.

Melior could smell the sea, and—if he turned his head—at a price paid in sickness and pain he could see a narrow window-slit set in the curving wall. There was another opposite it, and though the thickness of the wall denied Melior sight of the outside, he could see pale daylight against the stone.

Aboveground. Near the sea. He thought he knew where he was. Castle Mourning, the seat Baligant had chosen to occupy until his Kingmaking in order to be near his bride. The

Eastern Marches, then, and all Chandrakar away from Domain Rohannan of Canton Silver in the West.

But why?

"Yes-s-s-s" said the red-gold lady of Mourning, completing her circuit of the barren tower room and returning to Melior's side. "It is *good* that you are awake."

She picked up the iron, cherry red once more. She chose her site with care, and pressed the glowing metal home.

There was a soft groan from her chained victim.

"You to the Sword, the Sword to she. Then I have you all three, and my master's favor. What could be more desirable?" asked the mad lady of the sea-tower.

Five miles, more or less, was the bargain he had struck with Puff the Magic Firedrake, as he recalled. Five miles separated Nic Brightlaw from Ruth Marlowe at the moment he mounted the horse.

But in which direction?

There was a white castle on a distant hill, pat and perfect as something out of a *Boy's Own Paper*. He'd ride up to it as a last resort; in Nic's newly-abridged experience, wealth and corruption went hand in hand. Meanwhile, he rode through a world where everything was new, impacting on his senses with a vividness found only in the memories of childhood. These were the lands a child's eyes saw, unblinded by years of grinding dailyness.

As his eyes were now unblinded.

The road was well kept, the foliage cut decently back, white stone markers set at the verge, carved deeply with letters in some alphabet that Nic couldn't read. The air was autumn-crisp, and through the gaps in the hedge he could see harvested fields, orchards stripped of their summer bounty, vine stocks pruned and tied back in anticipation of winter. Tidy, prosperous, peaceful.

At least now. Because as he rode, Nic could see other things, too. A hillside that glittered as if it were covered in ice, although it wasn't ice—it was vitrified stone; glass called up out of earth and stone by some firestorm worse than a thousand lightning strikes. A swath of woodland burnt to charcoal. The place where a village had been once, and now only foundations remained.

Now that he knew what he was looking for, he could see the subtle irregularities in the plantings that terraced the val-

ley hills—plantings lately begun, plantings that attempted to
follow the outlines of those abandoned years before and
which could not match them exactly, because the memories
of the original husbandmen were bone and ash on the battlefield this once had been.

War. Miss Marlowe had said there'd been a war here. And
it was Nic's experience that wars were never over.

After he'd been riding for an hour on a road that climbed
slowly as it ascended the hillside, Nic came to a village. It
looked much like the villages that were still fresh in his
edited memory: a sprawl of huts made of sticks and grass
(some, here, of stone), a well in the dirt square that served
as the center of town. The wells he remembered had pumps,
of a sort, while this one had a crank and bucket, but there
was more sameness than difference.

He tugged on the rein and his mount obediently stopped.
Nic sat, and looked at the well, and wondered how to get
water out of the well and into his horse.

"Can we aid thee, lord?"

Nic instantly pegged the speaker as the village headman, a round brown individual wiping his hands on a leather
apron as he approached, looking understandably nervous. To
Nic's relief he was speaking English—at least, it *sounded*
like English, which was all Mrs. Brightlaw's favorite son
asked of life.

"Water for my horse. Beer. And some information."

The man look relieved, nodding. Nic dismounted, pulling
off his helmet, and the man's expression became confused,
wary. After a moment Nic understood why. *It's the ears. Mine
are the wrong shape. Elves are the bosses here. Pointed ears.*

"Do you come from the castle?" the man said carefully.

Saying "yes" could be checked too easily. And Miss
Marlowe hadn't told him nearly enough to be able to pass
here.

"Americal Division," Nic said, just as if it would make
any sense to his listener. Never mind that the Americal had
been disbanded in 1971, long before Nic's tour. "I'm on a
long-range recon; humint penetration and survey. I'm afraid
I got separated from my unit, so I'm looking to resupply and
hook back up. You can check that with Captain, um,
Ryerson, if you like."

It was nonsense, but it had the right sound. The headman
relaxed again. "No, that's fine." A child who had been

watching from the shadow of one of the houses came forward. "You can leave your horse with Wing, he'll take care of him, good master . . ." the headman hesitated, fishing for a name.

"Saint," Nic said. "Call me Saint."

From the tavern—a shed with three walls, a roof, some crude benches, and a roof that wouldn't leak so long as the weather was dry—Nic could watch as the boy Wing filled the trough for the horse one bucket at a time. A piece of silver to the headman brought grain for the horse and food and beer for Nic. The beer was warm and sickly-sweet. He drank it without complaint.

The other men of the village—close at hand, now that harvest was over—collected slowly beneath the tavern roof. Nic produced more silver, and paid a round for all.

And got, as he hoped, information.

There were brigands in the woods; a cunning band, led by someone called Fox. There'd been a raid on the Harvest Home, and the castle had been set afire. Arnaut the steward had sent to the Earl of Silver—Baron Regordane as he'd been, whose father had fought so bravely in the War—as their lord, the Baron Rohannan, was from home and the poor lord's sister not able to command by way of the injuries she'd taken. And his cousin the Treasurekeeper, who might have done aught, was gone this fortnight and feared murdered and slain by the same villains—

That you are sheltering, supplying, and spying for, Nic finished silently. He'd heard this song too many times in the past to mistake the tune. He wondered how many of the men here drinking with him raided with Fox—who would have to be his next stop, that much was clear.

"Your bandits are your problem, not mine," Nic said. "I'm not here for them. I'm looking for a girl." His description was simple: brown hair, blue eyes, a stranger. He didn't mention the unicorn. He wondered if this Fox had a useful taste for gold.

No one had seen a blue-eyed girl stranger. They were quite forthcoming on that point—and honest, too, since Nic had framed the question in such a way that the answer could exclude any mention of nonlocal men.

Then it was time to go. This time the whole town stood around to watch him: the men and boys in a body in front of the alehouse, the women and younger children from the doorways of their houses. Nic mounted his horse and turned its head toward the road that led into the forest. He thought a moment, hesitated, and then said the words that would set him on an inevitable collision course with the outlaw leader.

"There's a gold piece for whoever brings me the girl I'm looking for," Nic said.

Clucking to his mount, Saint Nic rode out of the village.

It had been early afternoon when Fox had dropped her on the hill above Foretton. Jausserande found and lost his trail a dozen times in the hours that followed—she and her Ravens had been cavalry, not scouts—but she continued without dismay. Every time she thought she'd lost it unrecoverably, some luck, some instinct, found it for her again, as if she and Fox were destined to meet once more.

Here he'd stopped a long time, to judge from the disturbance in the leaf-mold. And when he moved, it had been fast—she saw the deep gouges left in the damp leaf mass by the horse's unshod hooves. She looked in the direction he had gone, peering with sight far superior to her quarry's into the deep blue evening shadows that filled the woods as if they were a bowl.

That was when she saw the body.

It was all white ribs and blood, the roosting place of feasting crows. Such larger scavengers as remained in Chandrakar after a century of war had also been at the body—pigs and dogs, perhaps; it was too early in the season for wolves.

A horse.

Fox's?

She advanced on the carcass carefully, conscious that other predators might be doing the same. The crows launched themselves into sluggish complaining flight—alerting the whole forest that someone was here.

The horse was not Fox's. What hide and hair remained were gray, and Fox had been riding a bay. The gray had been skinned and dressed out, and after another moment she saw why: the shattered fetlock.

But whose horse was it? What other riders used these woods?

Jausserande circled the clearing. Here was sign that two horses had been here, there a clear point that told her Fox's was one of them, and the scraped branch where he'd tied it. She saw a glimmer of out-of-season color among the leaves and retrieved a green velvet snood. Jausserande ran it through her fingers and sniffed at it. There were strands of light brown hair caught among the velvet ribbons and the cloth held a flowery perfume.

Human. Some human girl lost in these woods, set upon by Fox's bandits and stolen away. It was almost a plausible story, save that the splendid hairnet argued that she was the daughter of some rich farmer or some hedge lord's petted mistress. Where, then, had been her escort?

Suddenly there was the sound of someone on horseback coming nearer.

Jausserande looked about for some place to hide.

By the time he'd left the village, Nic had figured out the other joker in the wizard Ophidias' deck. The lizard-wizard had promised that Nic would be no more than five miles from Ruth Marlowe at the moment he entered Chandrakar. But—as Nic had already figured out for himself—there was no guarantee that Miss Marlowe would stay put. Which meant that one direction was nearly as good as another—and there was always the bandit chief. It was Nic's experience that if you could only get in good with the hill bandits in any region, your job was half done for you.

Up ahead he heard the caw and flurry of crows. He pulled his horse to a stop, listening, then went forward at a slow walk. Ambush at worst, confrontation at best. Unavoidable, at least if he wanted to do something more than wander around in circles.

He entered the clearing where the butchered body lay. Deer, he thought at first, then, accurately gauging its size, horse. Dressed out as neatly as any deer ever poached—

And not a scavenger in sight. How odd.

"Come out, come out, wherever you are," Nic Brightlaw said, raising his voice slightly. And though he had expected it, even he was surprised when the woman dropped out of the tree.

It was the human warrior from her vision.

To be truthful, Jausserande had recognized the horse first—not the animal itself, but what it *was*. Creature of magic, and therefore being ridden by no human enemy.

Then she saw that she'd been wrong—its rider *was* human. He had ridden out of her dreams.

"What do you here in Rohannan's woods?" Jausserande demanded boldly.

The rider shifted comfortably in his saddle and looked at her, his eyes a clear and untroubled blue. She recognized nothing of his clothing and equipment, and he displayed no badge to say what lord claimed him.

"I might ask you the same question," the rider said. "Your horse seems to have met with a mishap."

His voice reminded Jausserande uncomfortably of Fox. This voice, too, held no proper note of subservience.

"I am Floire Jausserande, and hold freedom of the wood by my cousin's gift. The horse belonged to another. Come now, churl, and explain yourself or face my just punishment."

The stranger blinked mildly, as if surprised, and said, as if to himself, "If this is Chandrakar, I don't think Miss Marlowe is going to like it here." He turned his attention back to her. "I am . . . Saint, and I go where I damn well please. As it happens, I'm looking for a man called Fox. You wouldn't have seen him, by any chance?"

Jausserande's hand dropped to her belt, to the sword she did not currently possess.

"Ah," the stranger said in satisfied tones, "you *do* know him."

"I'm going to geld him, then skin him alive, then hang him in chains from the castle walls," Jausserande said flatly.

"First, catch your rabbit," the stranger said mildly. "For my part, I only want a short conversation with him about a friend of mine. You wouldn't have seen her, would you? Her name's Ruth Marlowe."

Ruth Marlowe. The Ironworld mud-daughter that Melior had formed such an unsuitable passion for. What connection did this stranger have with Ruth Marlowe?

And what connection, for that matter, with *her?*

"Well if you haven't, you haven't. A very good evening to you, Miss." He turned his horse to go.

"Ceiynt! Wait!" Jausserande cried.

He stopped, and looked over his shoulder at her. In the lengthening shadows his face and hands were dim blurs, his horse a white beacon in the darkness.

"How will you find Fox?" Jausserande said.

"I don't expect to," Ceiynt said. "I expect he'll come looking for me."

"He'll kill you," Jausserande said quickly, "and even if he had Heruthane, she belongs to my cousin, not to you."

Ceiynt turned his horse about, until he faced her once more. Jausserande felt the flicker of warning danger, but at least she had his attention.

"It was my understanding that Miss Marlowe belonged to herself. And since a number of rude strangers are apparently out to kill her, I'll trouble you for a declaration of intent. Lie if you like. I will mention that I don't think I can miss at this range."

She saw the paleness of his raised hand in the gloom, and, gripped between his fingers, the thin dull-colored feather-shape of death-metal.

It was too much. Jausserande sat down, not entirely of her own will, on the ground. "Strike then, upstart maggot! No doubt Fox will reward you for it. I don't care."

"Tell me about Fox. Tell me about why you recognize Miss Marlowe's name. Take your time." Ceiynt's voice was gently insistent.

"I have told you, mud-man. She is my cousin's—and she is *not* here, because if she were, he would seek her here, and he does not." Silence. "My cousin is the Rohannan," Jausserande said, impatient with Ceiynt's silence. "He has told me of his venture into the World of Iron, and of Heru—*Ruth.* And you also come from the World of Iron—do you come seeking her to take her back?" Jausserande finished, struck by a hopeful thought.

"Seeking her, at least." There was the rustle of motion as he sheathed the death-metal weapon once more. "And what are you doing out here all alone in the woods, Little Red Riding Hood?"

"Killing Fox." The words were muffled; Jausserande leaned her cheek against her knee and wished the mad mud-born would leave her in peace. That he would not, she already knew; this close to him her undependable elphensight burned bright and certain, lighting a few hours of the future. "And now you will say that you will ride on, and will not, and will offer me a share of your fire for my aid in leading you to this Fox—who has done that for which the Earl of Silver would hang him, did not Rohannan or Floire reach him first."

There was a pause.

"I suppose in that case, I'd better build the fire," Ceiynt said. "Do tie this thing up—or whatever you do with them," he added, tossing her the reins of his horse.

It was full dark when Ruth and Fox reached the outlaws' camp.

They'd stopped once so she could wrap Naomi's cloak around both of them. Fox's arms were around her, his hands on the reins, and it began to seem to Ruth that she had spent her entire life seated on one saddlebow or another. She heard the signal whistles as they passed beneath the trees, and Fox's soft snort of satisfaction. A moment later they reached the camp itself.

It was familiar as things imagined out of books are familiar—the scattered small fires, each with its tripod-hung kettle; the men in rough furs and leathers, with club or quarterstaff kept near to hand. Fox tossed the reins down into waiting hands and slid off the horse.

Ruth stared.

"Welcome to fucking Sherwood, Ruthie—now get off the horse," Fox said sweetly.

She'd forgotten the twisted ankle. Fox hadn't. He took her whole weight as she staggered and swayed, hissing in pain.

"Raven! You've got a customer! And where's Hathorne?" Fox called.

No one, it seemed, had seen Hathorne, but in answer to Fox's cry, Raven appeared.

He was the largest man Ruth had ever seen; well over six feet tall and with shoulders as wide as if he juggled cart horses every morning before breakfast. His hands were the size of gallon milk jugs, and curling black hair seemed to cover him everywhere. He wore a deerskin tabard with the hair still on, sleeveless, laced loosely at the sides. His brown eyes were mild.

"Raven used to be a blacksmith," Fox said, then, to Raven, "This is—"

"Don't you *dare* call me Ruthie!" Ruth hissed swiftly.

"Ruth. This is Ruth. Ruth is a friend of mine. She got hurt," Fox said blandly.

"And the highborn?" Raven asked. His voice rumbled, deep and slow.

"The highborn is *fine,* Raven. I let her go at Foretton.

She's probably up to her neck in a hot bath right now. What's for dinner?"

"Philip, what are you up to?" Ruth demanded in an undertone.

"It doesn't exactly matter, from your point of view, does it, Ruthie-Ruth? Come on, let's go to my office."

"Philip—" Ruth began. Fox's grip tightened, hard enough to steal the air from her lungs. No, not Philip. Not any more.

Between them, Fox and Raven got her to one of the little huts that ringed the clearing.

"I'm not going in there," Ruth said, looking at the tiny enclosed space.

"Raven," Fox said. She felt his muscles flex as he made a gesture she couldn't see.

She thought they were going to force her, and prepared to fight, but Raven simply went and began to cut the cords that fastened the green hides over the hut's wooden frame until it was no more than a shelter half, open to the night.

"Better?" Fox asked, in noncommittal tones.

Ruth felt tears of weakness prickle behind her eyes. "Yes," she said in strangled tones.

The hut-as-was was a little larger than a pup tent. Through the hole in its wall Ruth could see an uneven earth floor, scrubbed smooth, that supported two piles of skins and pine boughs. At the head of one of the makeshift beds was a tree trunk, lopped short, with a carved groove circling its trunk about six inches from the top. Fox helped her through the side of the hut and eased her down onto one of the beds.

She sat there, feeling every muscle reminding her of its recent ill-treatment, and watched as Fox lit a candle and set it inside a mirrored lantern-box that sat upon a plain wooden box. That was all that was here.

"I used the last of the Seconal on Tink. Is there any of the wine left?" Fox said to Raven. The blacksmith nodded and backed out through the low entrance. Fox rocked back on his haunches and looked at Ruth. The candlelight cast his face into harsh lines.

"Pray that ankle isn't broken, because if it is, we can't set it very well. For what it's worth, I don't think it's *that* bad, but first we have to get your boots off and see—*that's* going to take two strong men and a boy." Fox smiled with all the poisoned sweetness Ruth remembered.

"Why?" she said, tiredly puzzled.

"Because it's going to *hurt,* Ruth. There's no morphine here, no penicillin. Not even an aspirin. There's just *magic,* and mere humans don't get the use of much of that." Fox's voice was vicious, and Ruth recoiled from the bitterness in it.

"But I don't understand—why don't you just ask Melior to help?" Ruth said, bewildered.

The words hung in the air, and suddenly Ruth was conscious that she'd said something very wrong.

"Ah, here's the steward with the wine list," Fox said. "Sorry the service doesn't run to cups—" he went on, taking the leather bag from Raven.

"I brought my own," Ruth said with sudden remembrance, hoping she hadn't squashed it flat. She upended the belt-pouch, producing Nic's watch, the magic ring, the gold scissors she'd bought at the fair, a length of red ribbon, and the battered tin cup.

Fox took the cup and filled it with wine.

"Chug it down—when you've had that and another one, we'll see if we can get your boots off."

"But I'll be drunk!" Ruth protested, "and—"

Fox put a finger on her lips, effectively silencing her; Philip had never touched anyone, or liked being touched himself. She gaped at him.

"—and you're worried about your virtue," Fox said, picking up the thread of dialogue and twisting it effortlessly away from its original meaning. "Cheer up. I prefer sheep." He wrapped her fingers around the goblet and raised it to her lips. "Drink."

Ruth drained the cup—the wine had no particular flavor other than alcoholic harshness—and then, at Fox's bullying, another.

Rich warmth spread through her, as though her veins were filling with hot honey. Without any particular self-will she lay back on the pallet and gazed at the ceiling from a place where her body was only a distant inconvenience.

There was some tugging and prodding, nothing to do with her. The night air was cool on her bare feet and she curled her toes.

"Ruthie? You still alive?"

Scraps of talk swirled through her head like smoke.

"Christ, she's out like a light. Was that the wine with the hemp seeds in it?"

But she wasn't asleep. She was just floating.

"Is that it? Doesn't look too bad. Do we have any green hide to wrap it in? She can soak it off at the other end."

But what was the other end? *Journeys end in lovers' meeting,* but hers had ended in lovers parting.

She had to find Melior.

She felt some one winding something around her ankle. It tickled.

"There's elves hunting her, Raven. But I don't want anything to happen to her. Not yet."

Raven's response was an unintelligible mumble.

I was a child and you were a child, in a kingdom by the sea . . .

"Yeah. Out like a light."

No.

Yes.

Fox snuffed the candle and climbed out the side of the hut ahead of Raven. It was a good thing he'd dumped Tinker-belle this morning—he didn't think she and Ruth would get along.

And besides, Ruthie made a much better hostage.

Fox was clever, and, when setting out on a hopeless crusade, knew better than to scatter his shot. His goal had always been small and simple: to smash the Sword of Maiden's Tears while Rohannan Melior watched helplessly. No more than that, and, being a realist, Fox had accepted that what he actually accomplished might be less: to destroy or hide the Sword in Melior's absence, for example.

Or to kill Melior while the Sword went safely to other hands, although killing Melior was really his last choice. The dead didn't suffer nearly as much as Fox felt Melior deserved to suffer.

He had not considered the effect of his plans on Ruth before. Ruth, after all, was *there,* at the far end of the Iron Road, while Fox and Melior were *here,* beyond the Morning, and whatever happened, Ruth would never know.

Well, now she would.

Fox had been in Chandrakar a period of time he privately termed Long Enough—at least two winters, and he'd been somewhere else before that for a while—to know things about the place that their good buddy Mel apparently hadn't thought important enough to mention to Ruth. Like the fact that Chandrakar—seven Cantons, twenty-seven Domains, the Twilight Court and the Lords Temporal, the High Court and the High Prince, and the Holy College with its High and Low Adepts—was a hierarchical ladder that made Dark Age Europe look like an upwardly mobile love-in, and humans weren't even on the bottommost rung.

Mud-born. Or, if you were being kinder, Children of Earth—the only one of the Five Races that couldn't use magic.

Which wouldn't be so bad, if the elves' use of magic hadn't stopped medicine, engineering, and the rest of science dead in its tracks. Why invent the telephone when you had telepathy and teleportation? Why study pharmacy and surgery if you could set bones and take away pain with a touch? Why build better roads if you could fly—or print books when you would live long past the day when the book had rotted to dust?

If you were an elf. If you had magic. If you didn't care about what humans could do, providing only they did what you wanted and kept your vineyards and dye-yards running, worked your looms and mills, tilled your fields and bred your servants.

And remember, always, the inevitable expansionism of a race that lived forever—and still bred nearly as fast as humans. And so was now, despite the war, despite everything, not only displacing humans from society, but from the very world. Someday, perhaps, there would be lowborn elves who would toil as serfs in Chandrakar's fields, but by then all the human serfs would be extinct.

Two years, Ruthie'd said it'd been since she'd seen Melior last. Fox didn't know how much longer it had been for him.

It felt like forever.

But he looked cheerful as he wandered through the camp in search of a bowl of stew—or, more likely, cold meat, what with the camp being moved. He was looking in a desultory way for Hathorne, even though he didn't really expect to see him. If Hathorne was after Ruth with elvish backing, Fox wanted to know what Hathorne's backers really wanted.

But as he made his circuit, something else drove thoughts of elphen politics completely from Fox's mind.

"Yarrow, how come nobody's packing and all the horses are here? We need to send riders to Foretton and Black

Bridge and get a bird to fly to Avernet. We're moving, re-member? Bring the wives and kiddies."

Fox squatted beside the cookfire with its gently-steaming copper cauldron that should long since have been emptied and readied to move.

It was late—i.e., about two hours after sunset, and while sentries and a few others were still awake, most of the out-laws would be either asleep or preparing to be. A society without artificial light rose and slept with the sun.

"But you said that wasn't till next week, Fox."

"I sent Raven, Ash, and Otter back to tell you guys to move *now*," Fox said, working hard to keep his voice low and even.

Yarrow's brow cleared. "But then Hathorne said he'd talked to you later, and you'd changed your mind."

Fox took a deep breath. What a moron he'd been not to check *immediately* that his orders were being carried out. It was true that the camp had looked much the same when he'd ridden in, but all he'd really seen had been things they'd been going to abandon here anyway.

And if Hathorne had countermanded the order to move—

"When did he tell you that, Yarrow?" Fox kept his voice low and even. His control over his band was slight, usually consisting more of getting them to do what they were going to do anyway more efficiently than of overt innovation. Push or hurry them, and he risked losing any control over them at all.

"He rode after you and the highborn, just in case you needed help . . . an hour after Raven and the others got here, say."

Which, made it something Hathorne had done before he'd found Ruth—but a betrayal regardless.

"Yarrow," Fox said gently, "Hathorne *lied* to you. He's betrayed us. We've got to move the camp *now*."

Yarrow had lost both ears for theft in one of Canton Sil-ver's northern cities and didn't want any more elvish justice. He sprang to his feet, ready to bolt. Fox grabbed his arm and yanked him to a stop.

"Quietly. Together. Like we did it at the Fair." Fox stared into Yarrow's eyes. "Rouse the camp. Do it quietly. Every-thing's going to be fine." When he saw that Yarrow was go-ing to behave, at least for a few minutes, Fox let him go.

Rouse the camp. And send the men *where?* The Vale was

still the best choice, even though Hathorne knew about it, because magic would not work there.

Or so Fox had been told. But he recollected that he'd also been told that humans couldn't work magic—and he'd worked magic to get here. So had Ruth, from everything she'd told him. So, for that matter, had Hathorne, every time he walked the Road.

Fox hesitated, thinking fast. What he knew about the Vale might not be true, but even so, the elves believed in the Vale's legend. And there were some members of his band who could not simply blend back into the towns and villages of Domain Rohannan. They had to go somewhere. It would have to be the Vale.

The quiet camp began to resemble a kicked ant's nest as Fox's outlaws were roused and alerted. Fox had little time to think of Ruth. She was safe enough where she was. His men might steal her boots if they thought of it, but they wouldn't hurt her.

"Raven! Get me three horses—fresh ones. Stay with me."

He could send Raven off later. For now he needed his support here. There were beggars to outfit, plans to pass on—all the while knowing the plans would not be followed—food and spoils to share out so that every man would have an equal chance of surviving. He sent them on their way in twos and threes, knowing that any man traveling at night was suspicious, knowing that half of them couldn't read the sky to find their way, knowing that instead of this unplanned exordium they should have been settling into a safe place to winter.

Knowing that many of them would panic at the first sight of a pointed ear, and babble enough to get themselves hanged.

At his direction they tore down the skin huts and covered the fire pits. Maybe Hathorne would be confused if the place looked different enough. Fox didn't think so. *He* wouldn't be.

Damn Hathorne. And damn the inevitable for happening, right on schedule.

It was long after midnight. The last few of his band were sitting, talking, waiting for their turn to go. Waiting because too large a party of humans traveling together would rouse even more suspicion in their elvish masters. Fox stood, watching them, not really daring to sit for fear he'd nod off.

Last night he had been in the Vale of Stars, and he hadn't gotten any sleep then either.

Never mind. There'd be plenty of time to sleep when he was dead.

He went over to where Raven, a tree-tall shadow in the dark, stood with the horses Fox had reserved for himself, Raven, and Ruth.

"You could take one of them and go. If anybody stops you, tell him you're taking it to the smithy. It could work," Fox said.

And if Raven could get out of Canton Silver where he might be recognized, even the poacher's brands on his cheeks might not matter too much.

"And shall I leave my Dowsel and the hills where I was born? And you, Fox—what would you do without me?" Raven said, after a moment to think it over.

Dowsel had been Raven's wife. She was buried in an unmarked grave somewhere along the Dawnheart Road, and Fox knew from experience that when her name was invoked it was useless to argue.

Raven wouldn't go, and Fox felt a faint flutter of relief, even though the reality of it was that it meant he would probably watch Raven die. But Fox was weary to death of stories he didn't know the ending of. This ending, grim as it advertised itself to be, he would see.

And maybe God would let him broker a miracle. So he said:

"You always were the brains of the outfit, Raven. I guess you'd better stay."

"And the little earthling girl?" Raven went on, meaning Ruth.

"Earth girls are easy, so the saying goes," Fox said, his mind elsewhere. If Hathorne wanted Ruth, and was working for Baligant Baneful (Fox did not entirely rule out the possibility of another employer), then he probably had a way to track her by magic. If he didn't have magic, he'd come first to the camp and then to the Vale of Stars.

He would probably not go to Dawnheart.

"Come on, Raven. I've got an idea."

The man most recently called Hathorne—and who had answered to many other names in his life—roasted horse meat over a fire as he waited for true night to fall. This particular

item in the bag of wizard's tricks he'd been given to play
with did not work in sunlight.

His camp was among rocks, sheltered from the wind, and
to casual eyes—if there were any—he appeared to be no
more than a harmless traveler on innocent business. As he
waited, he thought about Fox.

Hathorne had always suspected that Fox had come, if not
from the Iron Lands, then at least from the Borders where
cross-traffic was known to be common. It was only the
worst sort of luck that Fox should come from the same
world as Hathorne's quarry did. Hathorne's orders were explicit and simple: get the girl and kill her without witnesses.
Bad luck, for now Hathorne must report to his master that he
had neither got nor killed the girl. Best to rely on the old
lag, that, seeing how complicated the game had grown, he
had done nothing rather than do that which his employer
would dislike. It might serve, and it might not, but what was
nearly certain was that he had lost as much of Fox's trust as
he had ever had, and with it, the possibility of using the outlaws whom Fox had gathered.

On the other hand, he could tell his master that Line
Floire's Treasure, the Cup of Morning Shadows, was itself
truly lost; that he himself had seen Floire try to retrieve it
and fail.

He could tell his master that.

At last the darkness was complete, and Hathorne took the
ring out of his pouch. He did not put it on, but took a clay
bowl out of his saddlebag and filled it with water. Then, hes-
itating for a moment as if he were about to do that which he
did not wish to do, he dropped the ring into the water.

The ripples it made entering the water did not die out, but
increased, shadowed and tipped in light, until the whole surface of the water in the bowl was a blinding chiaroscuro of
motion. Hathorne did not look away—he had learned better.

"Who calls?" The voice was honeyed-sweet, sexless and
inhuman, and as always the sound of it was like an ice dagger in Hathorne's guts. No face formed itself in the bowl
whose surface was now a liquid sheet of hot silver; but its
baneful glow dazzled the eyes, inviting them to embrace illusion.

"It is Hathorne," he said from a dry throat, adding nothing
as he had been given no honorific to add, though fear and
deference were explicit in his every tone.

*"My Hathorne. Have you brought me the news of where
the Ironworlder girl's grave lies?"*

And now it was agony to speak, agony to stare into that
fiery bowl—but the alternative would be far worse.

"She was where you said she would be—but you did not
tell me that she was Fox's trull of old. He has taken her back
with him alive to his camp, on the day after he failed to
achieve the Cup of Morning Shadows."

There. All said in one breath, and neatly, too, so that the
silver hellgrammite he served could not blame him for telling the one thing first and withholding the next.

There was a long, nerve-racking silence, broken only by
the sighing of the wind through the trees and the hiss and
pop of the tiny fire. Hathorne's eyes watered, and tears
streamed down his cheeks, but he kept his eyes fixed on the
bowl.

And now the blazing silver cleared, to show him the outlaw camp—not deserted, Hathorne had made sure of that,
but in a flurry of activity through which that white witch-
breed Fox stalked like a man demented.

The scene changed. He saw the Ironworlder girl he had
hunted so long and so fruitlessly lying in dimness in one of
the huts.

And then he saw a figure on a white horse—magic white,
white as a unicorn—with a rider whose face was in shadow. Beside him was the elphen maid that Fox had captured,
whose throat it would have felt so good to slit, and then fire,
fire, fire rose up to cover all.

*"Kill the Ironworld girl before they meet, or forfeit your
own life,"* the sweet metal voice told him. *"Kill her now."*

The bowl went dark, and in the blessed silence there began a stabbing pain behind Hathorne's eyes.

"There's magic about," Jausserande said, sitting bolt upright. In the fireless darkness, her face was a pale blur.

She was wrapped in Ceiynt's cloak, and had burrowed
down for sleep into a pile of leaves so that only her pale hair
showed. Now she was sitting up, staring out into the night
as if an explanation would be forthcoming from leaves and
branches.

The man Jausserande called Ceiynt felt it, too, although he
wouldn't have called it magic. What Nic Brightlaw would
have called it was "trouble"—the feeling of "something's

about to fubar" that presaged a sniper or mortar attack. The feeling of being in a suddenly discovered minefield.

He got slowly to his feet, crouching, cursing the absence of his M1 and the AR15 he'd swapped it for. Jausserande was standing blithely upright, staring into the dark.

"That way," she whispered, and Nic took off in that direction, moving silently through the dark.

He saw the flare of the campfire from a hundred yards away though it was built small and sheltered among the rocks. One man, one horse. The man was sitting cross-legged before the fire, staring into a bowl as if there were no hooligans in all the wide world. Light shone out of the bowl as if from an arclight, and in the blue-rinsed illumination Nic could see that his hair was curly, reddish, worn long.

He was talking.

No, that wasn't right. He was listening.

"Kill the Ironworld girl before they meet, or forfeit your own life. Kill her now." The voice made the high mechanical moan of a wet crystal goblet when you run your finger around the rim. Nic's hackles stood on end, and every instinct urged him to blot out both voice and auditor.

But he held his hand.

The bowl went dark and slid from the man's crossed ankles. It tipped and spilled, and water flowed into the fire, making it hiss and gutter.

Nic charged.

To capture a man without hurting him in any way that matters is a task more difficult than merely killing him. And when the 23-year-old mind attempted to command the body two decades older, it was inevitable some miscalculation must occur.

Nic's lunge fell short, striking the man about the knees instead of the shoulders. He felt the clench of seasoned muscle under his hands, and then the other attacked with a silent desperation that marked him as guilty in Nic's mind. Guilty as charged.

Neither dared to let go. They rolled across the fire, putting it out completely. In the midnight darkness they fought by touch.

Here was a rock, to gouge into the stiff complaining muscles of the back. There, an exposed tree root to batter the enemy head against. The other sought for every advantage, used every dirty trick that Nic had ever learned a counter for, and if they were evenly matched, how could he manage to hold the enemy without killing him?

There was the dull sound of rock against skull, and the desperate struggling man in his arms went limp.

"I thought I told you to stay where you were," Nic said.

"You did," Jausserande responded coolly.

Nic pushed the body off and she grabbed it.

"I hope you haven't killed him. He was talking to someone, and I'd like to talk to him," Nic said.

The darkness was absolute—no, not quite, because he could see Jausserande—no, more than see her. She was glowing.

As he stared, the white radiance increased until Nic's shadow straggled across the ground. Jausserande cast no shadow, being the source of the light—an incongruous glory, given her tattered and mudstained appearance.

"Magic," Jausserande said, though whether it was a dismissal or an explanation wasn't quite clear. She rolled the body onto its back. "Ah. His name is Hathorne. He knows where Fox's camp is." She worked quickly and efficiently, searching Hathorne's body, stripping him of cloak and vest and shirt.

Nic stared down at the man. He'd seen him before. This was the man who'd tried to kill him just as he and Miss Marlowe had arrived—and in this world, coincidence was no coincidence.

Apparently his elphen ally knew him, too. Nic felt no particular need to burden her with the additional information, however. Not when the Mission Objective was the only thing that mattered.

"And he'll lead us there?" he asked.

"He will when I've finished with him," Jausserande answered with quiet certainty. She pulled Hathorne's boots off and tossed them aside. Shadows flitted and danced in the silvery elvish light, but Nic ignored that, watching what she was doing with such innocent efficiency.

Victor Charlie did that with his prisoners. Barefoot Americans were at a disadvantage in the jungle—soft-footed, easy to recapture. Easy to track.

He could smell the war that had been here. He could see it in every move the elf-girl made, moving sleek and efficient through the forest as if she were a part of it. He was worlds and decades away from home, and nothing was any different.

"I need something to tie him with," Jausserande said peremptorily, raising one silver-glowing hand.

Nic looked at the pile of discarded clothing and held out his knife. Her reaction to that surprised him: she shied back, rather as if he'd offered her a grenade with the pin out.

"You do it," she said tersely.

Now this was interesting. Nic shrugged, and began reducing Hathorne's leather shirt to strips.

Jausserande prowled around the campsite. She found Hathorne's horse where he had tethered it for the night, and beside it, its saddle and pack. The pack had little enough in it: some skin-wrapped chunks of meat, salt, and a tinderbox—

And—victory. Jausserande's fingers closed over a thin wallet of silk, its surface rough with silver-embroidered designs. She slid it inside her tunic for later study and went back to where the fire had been.

Its place was now no more than a flat and muddy sprawl. The shards of a broken bowl were embedded in the mud, and Jausserande's study of them was rewarded by her discovery of the ring. She pried it out of the ground and picked it up.

A wide band of fine silver, the metal preferred by Adepts and wizards for its ability to hold the imprint of magic nearly as well as crystal. Around the band, inside and out, unreadable writing flamed into existence and guttered out as she turned it, radiating outward from a reddish stone the size of her thumbnail.

The power imprinted on the object made Jausserande's fingers tingle, and she frowned. Wizard work at the very least, but who were the Adepts of the Wild Magic to interest themselves in the affairs of Chandrakar? And, more than that, why use as cat's-paws humans and *losel* outlaws like Hathorne?

Fox had not lied when he told her he did not serve Baligant Baneful, so it seemed. But had he *known* what the real truth was?

It really didn't matter, since she intended to kill him anyway. But it would be nice to know.

Jausserande slipped the ring into the wallet with the other things. She went back to the horse and saddled it.

"Satisfied?" Nic asked. Jausserande inspected the work and nodded briefly.

"Bring him along." She was leading a saddled horse— Hathorne's—and, having delivered this last order, rode off, glinting like a distant star.

Leaving him, on foot, to carry the prisoner.

Nic looked down at his prisoner and shrugged. It was true that the lady was rude and condescending, but one had to expect that from one's allies. He bent and picked up the unconscious man and followed the glowing figure. Too bad Charlie hadn't glowed in the dark—they could all have been home by Christmas.

Expectation and reality met and quarreled in the unfamiliar strain on overtaxed muscles as he started down the slope with his burden. Was this what being old was like?

That wasn't important. What *was* important was that Hathorne's talking flashlight had told him to "kill the Ironworld girl."

And the only Ironworld girl Nic knew of in these parts was Ruth Marlowe.

CHAPTER 29

Hymn to Breaking Strain

His first perception was of heat, followed by the smell of wood smoke and the sound of a fire. Hathorne rejoined the world, knowing that something had gone wrong.

A pointed stick jabbed him in the stomach. He tried, reflexively, to bring his hands around to cover himself, but they were bound behind his back.

"Welcome to the world, Chucko." The voice was unfamiliar, but when he opened his eyes, the face was not. This was the man who had accompanied the Ironworld bitch through the Gate—the one Hathorne had been given no orders about.

Pity. He'd thought the *losel* wight was dead.

"You have the advantage of me," Hathorne said, wheedlingly.

"For a change," the man said.

"Stop coddling him, Ceiynt." The elf bitch—in the flesh this time, and not in a vision. He wished he'd killed her when he'd had the chance. Correction: he wished he'd worked harder to *make* the chance, and damn Fox's soft heart.

Something had gone very wrong indeed.

Strong hands hauled him upright. Violet eyes whose slitted pupils shone with the cat-green of elphenkind glared into his. She held him upright by one fist twisted in his hair, and smiled, and leaned very close, so that he could see the curved wolf-teeth in her smile.

"Ah, Hathorne—have you no brave words now?" Her voice was rough velvet, quivering with anticipation. Hathorne began to sweat. It was well known that the Morning Lords placed no value on *human* life.

The pointed stick jabbed at his naked and unprotected belly once more. "I would hear your voice," Jausserande said.

"My lady—" he began, and gasped as the stick jabbed and slid aside, scraping a deep welt along his ribs.

"So humble, now that *I* hold the leash! I do not ask you, Hathorne, but tell: you will lead us to Fox's camp."

"Yes. I'll do that. I'll do just as you say, Lady—" the words came out tumbled and too fast, but Hathorne didn't care.

"I have a couple of questions, if you don't mind," Ceiynt said. He yawned, and his boredom in the face of all this made Hathorne even more uneasy.

The elf bitch's eyes flashed as she turned to look at Ceiynt. "What matters? He will do as he is told."

"You're a trusting soul," Ceiynt said. "How do you know he'll lead you to Fox instead of just around in circles?"

"Fox's camp can't be more than two hours from here. If he takes longer than that, I'll cut off his thumbs," the elf bitch answered with sweet reasonability. The firelight flashed on Hathorne's own good knife—bronze-bladed and horn-hilted and very sharp—in her hands.

"Um." Ceiynt appeared to consider this. "What if he told you it was just a little farther, or that he was lost, or if he fell and pretended he'd twisted his ankle and couldn't walk?"

"I'll cut off one thumb," she said promptly. "And give him a chance to save the other."

"Suppose his job was to delay you until his reinforcements arrived?" Ceiynt said again.

The elf bitch sighed. "Ceinyt, what is your *point?*"

The blond man smiled, holding all of Hathorne's fascinated and horrified attention. He'd fallen into the hands of ghouls.

"I just want to ask him some questions," Ceiynt said reasonably.

Jausserande pulled out a whetstone and began to hone Hathorne's blade. "Ask him, then. It will pass the time until dawn."

The sound of metal on stone was loud in the shadows.

In the merry greenwood the night inched over the summit of midnight and began to slide down the other side. Everyone else was gone. Fox, wrapped in Naomi's cloak, halfdozed while Raven kept watch. The attack (if one was coming) would come at dawn. Therefore they would leave just before dawn.

And see what was following them, and if they could finesse or outrun it. A thousand possibilities, but, like Holmes, Fox preferred not to theorize in advance of his data.

He wished Ruth weren't here. Poor Ruth, sleeping ice princess, but sleeping was better because at least then you didn't feel. And when Melior had come along and opened little Ruthie's glass coffin, she'd had no waking defenses.

Everything that magic touched it hurt. And whether Ruth had ever gotten over Melior or not, if she'd stayed in the Real World at least she wouldn't have been hurt again. But here she was, hip-deep in Elfland, leading with her chin.

Fox dozed. And inside the hut, Ruth slept heavily.

"C'mon, Jimmy—we're going to be late!"

The dream, the memories began again, unspooling toward its predestined end.

Ruth fought them—the car, the dead children, the midnight slipstream carrying her forward to an unsolicited epiphany.

There was a flash of light in the road ahead.

"Shit," Jimmy muttered, thinking of cops, of tickets, of his dad's refusal to ever let him borrow the car again. But the lights weren't flashing red-and-blue. It was a coppery fiery light, and Ruth, straining her eyes, suddenly saw—

A nightmare in the road ahead; an undigested vision out of the Saturday Monster Matinee. Ruth had a confused image of mocking red eyes, of needle-sharp fangs in a gaping maw, of poison, ruin, and pain. She saw the monster spread its burning wings as the Oldsmobile rounded the corner; heard Jimmy scream as it reached out for him. . .

Felt Jimmy floor the accelerator, desperate to find escape for them all.

Heard the mocking laughter inside her head as the creature vanished.

Saw the tree—

—and, with the desperate strength of terror, broke free.

It was a mistake.

Blind. She was blind. Chill in the roaring void, more naked than an absence of clothes could make her. Hovering unsupported in a lightless abyss where pure information, disenchanted as computer code, printed pictures in her mind.

Will this work? A dark voice, brown, stinking of ambition. *I must be certain, wizard.*

See this? It is an Ironworld soul, still bedded in its mortal host. And I shall weave it to the Sword of Maiden's Tears and set the sword—so. If he but touches the Sword, it will fall through all the worlds.

This voice flared and guttered, flame-bright like burning roses, thick with decay. *It will fall. I have the soul here.*

The soul.

Her soul.

Her.

Ruth struggled to wake, struggled to run away, to hide from the newborn memory of lying helpless on the grass, flung free of the wreckage, awake and aware while a wizard out of Elphame tore out her soul.

But all she did was wrench herself into yet another vision.

"What do you want?"

Here there was light and sound, color and form and line. A room, visible, but with the shifting insubstantiality of a dream.

"What do you want of me?"

But it was no dream. She knew the man within it.

His legs had long since lost the power to bear him up. He hung from a beam in the center of the room by his shackled wrists, every muscle in chest and torso pulled taut.

"What do you want?"

His skin was mottled with the marks of whip and rod and knife, each pattern of horror left somehow unfinished, as if this torture were only the evil pastime of some easily-distracted child.

"I want nothing." In Ruth's dream she could not see the speaker, yet the voice called up a clear image of red-gold horror. *"My master wants the death of the Ironworld wench, and so he will have it. He would have the Sword lost to Line Rohannan, and so he will have that, too. All for my master, all, all, all—"* the mad little voice sang, swooping and skirling as if its owner danced.

"And what for yourself?" Ruth heard Melior ask, in a voice weary with pain. *"Is there nothing you want for yourself?"*

"All, all, all—" sang the voice. *"All, all, all—"*

"What do you want?" Melior cried.

Ruth awoke, struggling with monsters.

"Jesus, Ruthie—lay off, willya?"

Philip—no, *Fox*—the voice oddly unfamiliar in the dark. He held her pressed tight against him until she realized where she was.

And where Melior was.

It was like the knowledge that someone stands behind you; the burning intuition that makes the hackles rise even when you stand in a room you thought was empty.

"Fox! I—" she gagged on the New Age idiocy of the words but got them out nonetheless. "I had a vision. I know where Melior is."

She could see Fox outlined against the sky in the predawn light. The air was chilly, and when he let go of her and she kicked off the blankets she was colder yet, but she didn't hurt as much as she expected to.

"Okay," said Fox.

"No! I mean I can *find* him. We've got to find him—" Her throat closed with the Technicolor immediacy of her dream.

Melior was being hurt. And things that were only entertaining in lurid fiction or nothing to do with you in the dryly inaccurate report of a newspaper mattered desperately when they were happening to someone you loved.

Not a dream, not a hoax, not an imaginary tale—

"They're hurting him," Ruth finished flatly.

There was a pause, in which something that ought to have happened, didn't.

"So you can find him," Fox said, halfway between comment and question. He backed away on knees and toes and then stood.

"Yes. I think so. I mean—"

"Fine." Fox was not interested in eqivocations. "C'mon. Get dressed. It's time to go."

Ruth got to her feet, having forgotten about the ankle. Fox hadn't, and moved forward to support her, but there was no need.

She was fine.

Fallen leaves crackled beneath her bare feet. Experimentally she put more weight on the injured ankle.

Nothing. No pain. Fox stared at her.

"Okay. It wasn't as bad as we thought. So get your boots on and c'mon—unless you want to wait for Domain Rohannan's police to raid this joint—and trust me, Ruthie, they are *not* going to read you your rights and then let you call your lawyer."

"Raid? Fox, what's going on?"

"*Put* your boots on," Fox snapped, completely out of patience. He stepped through the hole in the side of the hut and stalked off.

Ruth sat down and groped about for her boots and stockings. She wasn't pleased with the thought that Fox had had his hand halfway up her leg last night—or with much of anything else she could think of at the moment. She ran her fingers through her hair and dislodged a number of leaves and brambles. Maybe Fox had a comb.

She unwrapped the sticky rawhide bandages from her ankle and brushed away as much of the residue as she could, then pulled on stockings and boots. The day was already perceptibly lighter by the time she was done—was it only yesterday that she had watched the dawn, safe and warm with Melior in the bed at the inn, and thought that everything would be fine now?

Oh, God.

Ruth followed Fox out into the camp and saw him standing beside some horses with another man—Raven, that was his name. The giant.

"Here." Fox threw Naomi's cloak to Ruth and went back to the shelter. He came back carrying the lantern and the box, with the skin blankets draped around his shoulders. Ruth swung the Kinsale cloak around herself, feeling the weight settle on her shoulders with a tug.

"Need a leg up?" Fox said.

"Where are we going? For that matter, what's going on?"

Fox sighed, and leaned his head against his horse's flank. "Ruth, I will answer any question you have—after we're moving. Now get on the damned horse." His voice was hard and adult, and he looked desperately tired.

Ruth got on the horse.

It was nearly true dawn by the time they were underway, Fox in the lead and Raven at the rear. Fortunately for Ruth, today's horse had few ideas, and all of them involved following the horse ahead of it.

"I don't see anyone," Raven said hopefully.

"Maybe I was wrong," Fox said wearily. "But if we're all alive next month, we can get together and sing about it."

"Fox?" Ruth said cautiously.

Fox half-turned in his saddle to look at her. "Poor Ruth,"

he said mockingly. "They should have said that no one'd be seated after the intermission."

"Just a synopsis, that's all I ask." The invisible Melior-compass in her head pulled Ruth east, toward the rising sun. They were riding at right angles to it. "And—we're going after Melior, aren't we?"

"Yes." Fox added nothing to that. "Which way is he?" he asked, and, when Ruth pointed, said, "thought so. We'll head that way eventually, but right now it's down to Foret-ton for breakfast, supplies, and gossip. Then we circle around to reach one of the main roads."

It sounded plausible, and that, from the man she had once known as Philip, was enough to make her suspicious. "The synopsis?" Ruth prompted.

"Well, in this unlicensed remake of Francis Ford Cop-pola's *Robin Hood: Men in Traction,* the Merries had just discovered a spy in their camp and are trying to get out of the way before whoever they were sold out to arrives to col-lect his new purchase."

Ruth considered this. She was cold and preparing to be hungry, hunted by wizards and tormented by a vision of Melior in agony, but she wasn't brain-dead.

Item: Philip was in Elfland. More particularly, Philip was *here,* in Chandrakar.

Item: Philip, now known was Fox, was the self-confessed leader of a band of outlaws.

"Oh," said Ruth inadequately. Something didn't add up. Ruth tried another question, with an increasing sense of the surreal. "Who's after you—us?"

"I wish I knew. Someone's backing Hathorne with serious magic, and I'd like to think he was just after you—"

"Thanks so much," Ruth snapped.

"—except for the fact that it's *my* group he infiltrated, *my* group he's been supporting with general rural lawlessness, and *my* men he's set up to get killed."

"But he was waiting for me when I got here. How could he do that if he was with you?" Ruth asked.

"Time's different here. A function of geography. If you take the right route, you can get somewhere before you've left. And then, there's always teleportation," Fox said blandly.

"You're kidding," Ruth said.

"Straining at gnats again, Ruthie?" Philip LeStrange had always possessed the power of being infuriating to the max, and he hadn't lost it just because he'd changed his name to Zorro (the Fox).

Ruth refused to dignify his comment with a reply, and as a result, they rode along in silence for nearly an hour while Ruth brooded. Because there were too many holes in Fox's story, too many stops and starts with convenient lacunae in between.

During the silence the sun came up and they struck a trail, a munificent throughway fully four inches wide and mostly covered in leaves. The icy autumn air gradually warmed, and everything was shades of gold, from the smoky barred sunlight to the drifts of leaves through which the horses plodded. Enough leaves still remained on the trees to color and soften the light, and break every vista up into a dappled Impressionist landscape.

Nothing gold can stay. Robert Frost said that.

Did she really need to know the answers Fox could give her? Why not? This was, after all, *Philip,* the annoying little cyberpunk eight years her junior. Without computers, what could he possibly be doing that would cause much trouble?

Don't answer that, Ruth told herself. The man who'd faced down Hathorne in the greenwood, who'd carried her back to his outlaw camp, was not the guy she'd gone to Library School with.

Too many unanswered questions.

If Philip had been here in Chandrakar, why hadn't he gone to Melior?

If he'd found a way to get here, why hadn't he taken her with him?

"Fox, what were you in the greenwood rebelling against?" Ruth finally asked.

Fox sighed and rubbed the back of his neck.

"The elves, Ruth. We're at war with the elves."

The questions Saint Nic had for Hathorne were many and varied, and kept coming back to the same one: who wanted Ruth Marlowe dead?

Along the way he learned that Miss Marlowe was, indeed, with Fox, that Fox was her kin from the World of Iron, that Fox wished to be High King in Chandrakar, and that Hathorne, for love of the true High King or anything else they pleased, would take them to Fox on the instant as soon as the sky was light enough to see the way.

"Lying mud-sucker," Jausserande commented, without interest. The knife had long since been honed to sharpness and she was whittling a long piece of fell-timber into a spear, holding the point over the fire at intervals to harden it.

"Well, yes, probably," Nic admitted. He hadn't even had to get particularly rough with Hathorne to get his answers so far; whatever else they were familiar with, the natives of these parts had no particular experience with the relentless disinterest of a field interrogation. Keep asking them the same questions over and over and they came all to pieces.

Of course, the fact that his partner—bloodthirsty little savage that she was—frequently offered suggestions as to body parts that Hathorne could afford to lose (without impairing his utility in the least) did not hurt matters, especially since neither Nic nor Hathorne had the least doubt that she'd do it.

"Then why do you keep talking to him, if you know he's lying?" Jausserande asked.

"To see what he says *this* time. And what would you do with him?—bearing in mind that we need him in more or less one piece to lead us to Fox."

Jausserande stopped what she was doing. A mound of pale wood shavings lay among the leaves at her feet. The weapon in her hand was some three feet long, one end sharpened to a wicked sturdy point. The whole body of it was scraped smooth, and midway down the shaft was ringed and checked to make a textured handgrip.

"Thumbs," said Jausserande, with whom this amputation was apparently an article of faith. "He'll sing then."

"He's singing now," Nic pointed out. "And if you take his thumbs off, what inducement has he got to help you?"

"If he cooperates, I kill him or let him go. If he doesn't, I take him back to the Castle to be racked to death. It isn't nice," Jausserande added, apparently moved by an impulse to accuracy in reporting. "But it works."

Hathorne had gone greenish-pale, his skin as wet as if he were drowning.

"Or broken on the wheel," Jausserande went on, "although you don't really break them *on* the wheel," she emended scrupulously, "you break their joints and their long bones—you can rack them first, that makes it easier—and then you hang them on the wheel to die. It does make them scream, I'll say that much; you wouldn't think they'd still have the energy for it, but they do. Dying can take days, especially if there's rain."

"Thank you for sharing," Nic said, modernist irony dredged up out of the memoryless void.

"Of course, I couldn't do something like that if he had a patron," Jausserande went on, apparently addressing her knife.

Nic held in a smile with an effort. *Little girl, I love you—you've hooked him, now play him.*

Jausserande looked up at Nic, her violet eyes wide and innocent. "Well, it's *rude,* you know," she said, as if he'd spoken. "Killing other people's mud-born. And we're at peace now"—a long sigh—"and the Rohannan doesn't want to start another border squabble. And neither do Floire or Regordane; no one in The House of the Silver Silences does, as a matter of fact. But I don't think any of the Silver lines is his patron. If he has a patron."

Nic glanced back at Hathorne. "Who sent you to kill Ruth Marlowe?" he asked gently.

Hathorne didn't answer. This time, Nic could see, it was an effort.

"Tell us who your patron is. We can't hurt you then."

Hathorne wanted to answer, Nic could see—wanted it desperately, in fact. But there was something that frightened him more than that little elf hellion did.

"His patron might be from outside Chandrakar," Jausserande offered. "That's probably it," she said, with the satisfaction of one discovering the answer to a puzzle.

The knife, apparently, was dull. Jausserande got out the whetstone again. "Among the Seven Houses of the Twilight, Rohannan would succor him—how not, if he rescued the lady Ruth? And Regordane gives ear to the Swordwarden. No harm to it—what's one thief more or less among the mud-born—so House Silver itself would stand his patron—if he aided Line Rohannan now."

Scrape, scrape, scrape went the knife on the stone. It was irritating enough to Nic, and he didn't have being broken on the wheel to look forward to.

"You heard the lady," Nic said—softly, insinuatingly. "Who sent you? Who wants Ruth Marlowe dead?"

It had been a good try; they'd played it just right, and they'd very nearly had him. But, looking at Hathorne's face, Nic could see it wasn't going to work.

"Or," said Jausserande, "we might just notify his patron now and save all the fuss."

She reached into her tunic and pulled out a ring, twirling it between her fingers. Snapshot identification came clear in Nic's mind. A ring like the one Miss Marlowe had found on one of the men he'd killed—one of Hathorne's partners.

The effect on the prisoner was even more dramatic.

"*No!*" Hathorne's howl was desperate. He lunged for Jausserande. Nic grabbed him. He struggled wildly, heedless of his bound hands. Trying to get the ring.

"No— Don't do it— You'll kill us all, Lady!"

Jausserande looked at Hathorne with eyes as flat and bleak as winter ice.

"I don't care."

It was easy enough then. Hathorne would do anything to avoid having his patron summoned; even tell all he knew. It was just disappointing, after all that buildup, that he knew so little.

He was a Borderer, from the Borderland called Cockaigne, but he'd left there long ago. Wizard-touched and lucky, he had the knack for slipping through some of the greater Gates (Jausserande seemed to find this part of the story unremarkable, and Nic didn't care), and eventually he'd come to the attention of his current patron.

Whose name, face, home, and race, Hathorne did not know. He had never met his patron, never seen or spoken to his patron save by magic. Couriers delivered his gold, and such other items as he might be supposed to require. He had an amulet that let him see the Iron Road, and once upon it he relied upon his patron's power to pass him through such Gates as Hathorne needed to pass. The ring, dropped into any vessel of water during the hours of true night, would summon his patron's attention. If his patron wished to summon him, the ring would grow hot.

He had been told to insinuate himself into Fox's outlaw band, and he had not found it too difficult. There had been other tasks, now and then, some that took him out of Chandrakar.

Then, one night, he had been shown Ruth Marlowe's face in the bowl and told that here was one he must kill. He had taken to the Road immediately and passed through, and when he had entered the inn to which he had been directed, he had found companions in the same service. There he learned that their task was to hunt the unicorn through the nearby wood—and slay it and the woman they found with it.

"Only no one said as you'd be there with the maidey," Hathorne said plaintively.

"It was an impulsive decision," Nic said.

After losing the girl and her unicorn and searching for them in vain, Hathorne had come back to Chandrakar and stayed with Fox until he'd been summoned again to meet Ruth Marlowe at Road's End. He didn't know why Ruth Marlowe was supposed to die, nor who wished her dead, and meanwhile he had been playing a double game of his own, passing information to Lord Richart at Dawnheart about the outlaws' movements in hope of winning gold and a free pardon.

"And passage out of this luckless land—aye, to the World of Iron itself, even, if that's far enough!" Hathorne snarled in disgust.

"Do as you are told and Line Rohannan will see you taken care of," Jausserande said. "Now. It's light enough. Take us to Fox."

Nic and Jausserande rode, with Hathorne on foot before them. His hands were free, but it was not as trusting an arrangement as it might appear, for Hathorne had one end of a coil of rope tied around his neck and Nic held the other end.

Whenever Hathorne moved too slowly or appeared to mistake his way, Jausserande would prod him with the end of her improvised lance.

They found the camp by midmorning.

"Gone!" Jausserande was cheated fury itself.

"Where?" Nic demanded, but Hathorne, exhausted, had sunk to his knees and did not answer. *"Miss Marlowe!"* Nic shouted, but no one replied.

"She'll be with him. Fox likes hostages," Jausserande said. She vaulted down from her horse and quartered the camp at a fast trot, reeling off her finds as she did so.

"Fires hours cold—huts here that they've taken down—half a dozen huts—horse lines here—they're not coming back before Spring, that much's clear—" she ducked inside the only structure still standing and with a small cry of satisfaction came out with a deerskin and a pair of green leather gloves.

"She was here!" Jausserande crowed.

They'd known that, of course, but it was nice to have proof.

"So where is she? Where are they?" Nic said. Just his luck, to get a line on the bandit king and arrive too late.

"Where?" Jausserande demanded, glaring down at Hathorne.

"Perhaps—they were going back to the Vale—" Hathorne began.

"No," Nic said suddenly. "I know where Fox is going. Where I'd go. And I know how to get there."

Jausserande glanced quickly up at him, then used the end of her lance to lift the loop from around Hathorne's neck and toss it to Nic.

"Then we ride," she said.

Nic kicked the magic horse into a jog trot—back toward Foretton, and what all good outlaw leaders, bandit kings, and rebel terrorists craved. Information.

Jausserande turned her horse to follow.

"Wait! Lady— Lady Jausserande, you said—" Hathorne gasped.

"Aye." She reached into her tunic and pulled out something, concealed in a fist. "Then go to Dawnheart, and tell Guard-Captain Lord Richart that you are to be housed on my word until I return."

She opened her hand, and Hathorne's ring fell from it into the leaves. "Or call your patron." Jausserande wheeled her horse again and took off after Nic.

Fox's raids on the road were based in Foretton and the other local villages; their return to camp with their spoils was a matter of two days on foot. On horseback the journey took a little over five hours. They started at dawn and reached the hill overlooking Foretton a little before noon.

But instead of riding down into the village as Ruth expected, Fox dismounted and pulled Ruth down from her horse. Raven led all three animals into the deepest cover the autumn forest provided.

Fox looked at Ruth's clothes and sighed. "You show up too much. Wrap up. And stay back."

Ruth glanced down at her dark green dress, brilliant against the dun leaves, and pulled the gray cloak around it as much as she could. She thought of the first cloak she'd seen Melior in, back in the World of Iron: its spotted, mottled gray-green coloring would have been perfect camouflage here.

She looked at Fox dressed in ragged grays and browns and a deerskin tabard still covered with its previous owner's gray winter coat. He pulled a corner of the blanket up to cover his pale hair, and knelt in the leaves near the edge of the drop and seemed to stop moving completely. Raven came back and sat down, back against a tree, waiting with that same patient immobility.

Ruth found an appropriate rock and sat on it. From this vantage point Ruth could see across the valley, and on the southern hill the terraces, planted with fruit trees, that led up to the distant white castle. Dawnheart. Melior's home.

"What's going on *now?*" she asked several minutes later, keeping her voice low and hoping she sounded patient. Melior's presence was a maddening tug eastward, and they didn't seem to be heading that way any time soon.

"We're watching to see who's in town." Fox spoke without moving.

"We could always go down and ask," Ruth pointed out scathingly, although if Fox were a hunted outlaw—and wasn't *that* the culmination of a lifelong dream?—that was the last thing he could do.

"Sure. Only in these current middle ages, Ricky over at the castle's going to know we don't belong in the village. They don't issue travel visas—mostly because most people can't read or write—but the point-ears sure as hell want to know what you're doing when you're off your land."

"You don't make the place sound very nice," Ruth said, after a while.

"It isn't very nice. Humans are *serfs* here, Ruth. Peasants, bound to the land. And every single one of them belongs to one elf-lord or another."

"But Melior said—" *He said he wanted to marry me.*

There was a long pause, then Fox spoke again, sounding reluctant. "Mel might have been tenderhearted, or stupid, or

optimistic, or buttering us up because he needed us. He
might even have thought he was telling the truth."

"But he wasn't," Ruth said flatly.

"No," Fox said simply. "Feudalism isn't pretty, but it gets
downright ugly when you add in racism."

"Melior said there was intermarriage," Ruth protested.

"Maybe. I don't know. I only know what I've seen."

And what is that? Ruth wondered. *"Feudalism isn't
pretty,"* Fox said, and he was right. Hangings, beheadings,
brandings, maimings, murderous taxes, and no law, no justice, no protection for the lower classes, whose only hope
lay in not being noticed. Justice for the rich. Obligations for
the poor.

If Fox was telling her the truth. And if he was . . .

Where did Melior fit into this? Where did *she* fit?

And . . .

"Fox," Ruth said carefully, "what would you say if I
asked you what you wanted with Melior?"

The silence stretched.

"In about an hour we should know whether Ricky the
Rodent—that's Guard-Captain Lord Richart to you—has
eyes in the village," Fox said, his voice perfectly even. "We
can go down then."

Nic's and Jausserande's goals were actually in reasonable
agreement: he wanted to see Ruth Marlowe safe from her
enemies, Jausserande wanted someone named Fox dead.

Nic could not recall Miss Marlowe mentioning someone
named Fox. And as for the matter of murder, his own hands
weren't so clean that he could sit in judgment on someone
else's hobbies. And so they circled around and came up into
Foretton by the main road a little after midday.

"Company," Fox said, looking down into the village. "Jesus, what did he do, *bleach* that horse?"

"It's a magic horse," Raven rumbled, craning forward to
look. "Shod in silver. They come purpose-sent, and go in
their own time."

"I don't like this," Fox said.

"No more do I. Fox—"

"Shhh-h."

Ruth stood up and peered, but she couldn't see the village from where she stood.

Abruptly Fox scuttled backward and stood up.

"Raven, get the horses—that's Tinkerbelle down there, and it looks like she's got some high-ticket help. Come on, Ruthie. Hoka-hey."

Hoka-hey. It's a good day to die. It took Ruth several minutes to trace the quotation to its source: Sitting Bull. The Trail of Tears.

Did Fox expect to die here? Had Melior brought her all this way only so *she* could die here? She tried to remember what he'd said about her *surviving* the plans he and his wizard had for her, and couldn't.

And the memory of that other wizard, that other magic, froze her like the memory of a rape. She would *not*—

They did not go down to the village, but circled around it, heading east at last, paralleling the road along the heavily-forested top of the hill.

Roads are where they are for reasons. The road on the hill leading to the valley below was the easiest path; here above it their way was blocked by boulders, rock slides, fallen trees, and deep-cut dry creekbeds. Fox and Raven were leading their horses, but Fox had insisted that she stay mounted, and Ruth was just as glad not to have to try to climb over this stuff in a long cloak and heavy full skirts. After an hour of that, they stopped to rest.

"If they catch us, Ruthie, don't fight and don't run. Just tell them you belong to Melior. Say it early and often. They should back off."

"But Melior's—" Ruth said.

"Captured. But it won't make a difference to them where he is if you belong to him. Try to get away, though. For immortals, they've got short memories," Fox said. He was talking as if he expected to be caught, and it scared her.

"Tell them you belong to him, too, then. Fox—Philip—he was our friend—"

"He wasn't my friend. And it wouldn't work anyway."

"Philip, you can't blame him for Naomi's death. I know you loved her—"

Fox glanced up sharply at Ruth; she had the disturbing feeling that she'd finally gotten his attention. "It isn't like that," Fox said, with the flat patience of one whose emotions are long dead. "People fall in love and one of them dies; there isn't any point in making a federal case out of it." He took a deep breath.

"But this is different. Melior used all of us: you, me, Michael, Jane—to get the Sword back. Because the end justified the means, in his eyes. Do you understand?"

"No," said Ruth tightly. The horse shifted under her.

"The end does not justify the means, Ruth. The means *are* the end. The way you travel determines your destination, and sometimes you can't get there from here."

"So you think Melior was wrong."

Fox sighed. "No. I think he was neither right nor wrong. But if I . . . disapprove . . . of the means, the only appropriate response is to punish the end."

"You mean, destroy the Sword?" Ruth asked, baffled but knowing it was vital to figure out what Fox was telling her.

"If you like. Think of it as free-market economics: an item has no intrinsic value. An item's value is set by a free market. Right here, right now, magic is more valuable than human life. But if I devalue magic, that changes."

"But if you destroy the Sword—"

"Yeah, yeah, yeah—I've heard all the arguments, too. Baligant would kick all the elfie-welfs out on their collective ass. Chandrakar would, um, let me see if I have this right, 'cease to be.' " Fox snorted eloquently.

"As for point one, if they just cooperated with each other for ten minutes, they could all refuse to leave the party, and what exactly could Baligant do about it? Intrinsic value, Ruthie—a thing has only the value people place on it. And as for point two, get to the part where I care."

Fox stopped talking and looked away. He seemed to be finished. Ruth stared at him.

"You're nuts! You— Thousands of people would die!"

Fox smiled at her, very slowly. "Are you sure, Ruthie? Are you really sure?" He turned and walked off, leading her horse with him.

"They haven't been here," Nic said.

Jausserande looked around the village. The headman was desperate in his desire to satisfy, but unable to produce what wasn't here.

"You said they'd be here," Jausserande said.

"I said they'd come here. But if they saw us coming—"

Both of them stared upward, to the hillside above the village. A perfect vantage point—and very near the place where Fox had left her the day before.

Jausserande wheeled her horse and spurred it along the forest path. After a moment Nic followed. His horse easily overtook hers, and only a few minutes took them to the hillside overlooking the village.

"They were here," Jausserande said grimly, and even Nic could see the scrapes and mars of horses' hooves in the leaves.

"But where did they go?"

"Come on," Jausserande said cryptically. "We'll make faster time on the road."

"Fuck it," Fox said, some backbreaking time later. "There's the road. If they're behind us and we can reach Black Bridge, maybe we can lie low long enough to lose them."

She really hated being scared without knowing what was going on, Ruth thought crossly. Fox and Raven were trying to get away with desperate haste, that much was clear. But she could see no one following them.

"Heads up, Ruth. Elevator going down."

Fox tossed her the rein and started down an incline, that rapidly became, as far as Ruth could see, a sheer drop. Her horse lurched and slid, jerking Ruth from side to side in the saddle and making muscles that were trembling and weak from hours in the saddle ache ferociously. When they reached the road, she was shaking.

"You did that on purpose!" she said accusingly.

Fox didn't answer. He got on his horse.

"I'm not going with you!" Ruth said wildly.

"Go on, Raven. I'll talk to her. We'll catch up," Fox said, in that soft, reasonable, *lying* voice.

Raven favored both of them with a troubled look eloquent of his doubts, but turned his horse down the road and set it to trot.

Fox walked his horse back to Ruth's.

"You *hate* Melior. You blame him for Naomi," Ruth said. "I'm not going to help you find him just so you—"

"Fine," Fox said. "Then who's going to help *you* find him?"

Ruth stared at him. Fox shook his head, as if marveling at her stupidity.

"Mel is back and Baligant's got him. You and I know that. And you might be able to get Tink to believe you—if she didn't cut your throat first. But no one else. Baligant's their *king*. Nobody's going to pay attention to *mud-born*."

"I've only got your word for that, you know," Ruth told him shakily. Strong emotion scared her. It always had. And Fox's passion burned like acid.

"Fine. Go to Dawnheart. Shout it from the rafters." Fox smiled unprettily. "See what kind of help you get."

"Whatever you've got in mind for him, *Philip*, isn't help."

Fox took a deep breath. It occurred to Ruth, belatedly, that if she was afraid of Fox on Melior's behalf, perhaps she ought also to be afraid for herself.

"Political Science 101. It doesn't matter what my wishes for England are. With me, you have a better chance of reaching Melior than without me. Along the way I could change my mind and be nice to him. You could kill me when you have no more use for me. You can abandon me *later*. Or you could be your own sweet normal stupid self," Fox finished nastily.

"I got this far by myself," Ruth lied stiffly.

"Fine. If you change your mind, leave word at the Gallows Oak in Black Bridge." Fox wheeled his horse and galloped after Raven.

Ruth sat there, listening to the hoofbeats of Fox's horse fade into the distance and finally die away completely. Overhead the afternoon sky was a deep October blue, and high in it she could see the faint shape of a circling hawk. There was a scent of wood smoke in the air, and, in the distance, the faint tolling of a bell.

But other than that, silence. Silence, and solitude, and in the absence of frenzied escape attempts, the call of Melior's pain burned bright and insistent—and, unfortunately for Ruth's pride, from the same direction Fox had gone.

Maybe Fox had been right. Maybe it didn't matter what his motives were, as long as he was useful.

The cold-bloodedness of the calculation pulled her up short. That the end justified the means was a trap and a lie. But she didn't know what else to do. Nic was gone. She'd driven Philip away and, if she could trust a single thing he said, she could expect no help from any of Melior's friends.

She looked back over her shoulder to where Dawnheart was a white shape on the hill.

Item: she needed help to rescue Melior. Going by herself was almost the same as not going. The people who held him prisoner wanted her dead. They'd be delighted to have her show up, wouldn't they?

Item: she should be able to get help at the castle. All else aside, it was Melior's castle, and his retainers should be loyal to him—shouldn't they?

Were they?

Going to Dawnheart was the only sensible thing to do. She wouldn't have taken Philip's advice in New York. She wasn't going to take Fox's advice in Chandrakar.

With reluctant resolution, Ruth kicked and shoved at her horse until she'd turned it toward the castle, and then kicked it some more until it began to walk.

What Fox had not expected was Raven's response to the news that Ruth had elected to leave them. Raven reined his horse to a stop and stared at Fox with a level accusing gaze.

"She has no more sense than a babe unborn. You should have brought her, Fox."

"Yeah, well, how?" At least they wouldn't hurt her, if she had the sense to open her mouth. Everyone in Canton Silver knew that Melior'd been trying to get his mortal maid out of the World of Iron ever since he'd gotten back.

"Tell the mortal maid you meant her lord no harm," Raven said reasonably.

"*Raven!* I'm trying to *kill* him. How could I tell her that?" Fox said in exasperation.

"Lie," Raven said simply. He sat his horse unmoving and gazed at Fox.

Fox ran his hand through his hair and looked back in the direction of Jausserande and her wizard, who might be less than an hour behind. He ran his hand through his hair and clung grimly to his temper.

"Let me get this straight. You want me to go back there, backtrack, catch up with her, and tell her I've *changed my mind?*"

"I will do it," Raven said with hurt dignity. "And happen she will come with me, and we will meet you at the Harp in Black Bridge."

"*'Happen'* she won't believe you," Fox said. "Look. You go to Black Bridge—"

"Thou'rt a poor tale-spinner, Fox. We shall both go, and I shall say I lessoned you to prudence."

His two choices, it seemed, were letting Raven ride back alone toward Tink—who would recognize him instantly as a member of Fox's band—or go with him. To talk sense into Ruth. *Ruth.*

He should have coldcocked her. He should have brought her along bound and gagged. He shouldn't have rescued her in the first place.

Raven was right. He should have lied.

But he hadn't wanted to lie to Ruth.

One more social taboo about to be broken.

"Come on. Maybe we can find her before she falls off her horse and breaks her neck," Fox said.

"How much traffic is there along this road?" Nic asked. They were moving at a trot, to spare Jausserande's unmagical horse—and, privately, Nic doubted his ability to stay on if Shadowfax II elected to gallop.

"Some," Jausserande said. She'd told him there was a market town called Black Bridge about two leagues down the road. If Fox was on the run, he'd head for someplace with more people, where strangers would be less noticeable. Besides, Black Bridge had a garrison, and Jausserande could enlist them. "Not as much as in the spring," she added. "No caravans—and the great lords are at Court until the moon rides full again."

The moon had been just past full the night before, as Nic recalled. So the great lords were at Court for the next month.

And a month was all he had anyway.

"So—" he began.

"Hist!" Jausserande hissed, hauling her horse to a stop. Nic reined in and listened, but it was several minutes before he heard it.

Hoofbeats.

Ruth was getting the hang of it now. Horses were just like cars, except instead of shifting and stepping down on the gas, you kicked them in the stomach until they were going as fast as you wanted them to.

At least in theory. At any rate, she'd gotten it going faster than a walk, and the staccato bu-da-dum rhythm its hoof-beats made gave her the illusion of doing something.

And it got her away from Fox.

She had just gotten used to the relief of feeling she was doing all she could do to move matters forward when she came around the bend in the road and saw the riders. One of them was on a horse so white—

The white horse Fox had been talking about.

The people he'd been running from.

She hauled back on the reins, and, to her surprise and relief, her horse actually stopped. It took a few steps backward, shaking its head, but when she loosened the reins, it remained blessedly still.

The man on the white horse stayed where he was.

The silver-haired boy on the brown horse walked his mount forward. When he was halfway to her, Ruth realized that "he" was a she, and she was an elf. Ruth moistened her lips nervously and wished she didn't look as if she'd slept in her clothes. Well, now she could test her theories against Fox's.

"Name yourself, human woman," the elf-maid said. Where Melior's eyes had been cat-green, hers were a shade of violet found only in expensive underwear. Beneath the scrapes and dirt and the tattered clothing she was exquisite. Her silver hair gleamed like polished metal in the sun, for all it was pulled back into a rough horsetail and hadn't seen comb or brush for far too long. But that didn't matter, apparently. There were no bad hair days if you were an elf.

"I— I'm going to Dawnheart," Ruth said.

"Aye, very likely," sneered the elf. "And your escort lost along the way."

"I didn't have one. Look, do you know a man named Melior—"

It was as far as she got before the elf grabbed her by the front of her tunic and dragged her off her horse.

"Tell me what you know of my cousin!"

"Let me GO!"

Fox and Raven heard the scream from the bad side of a blind corner. When they rounded the corner they saw—in no particular order—the white horse and its rider, Jausserande, and Ruth, stuck unrescuably in the middle.

Fox swore.

Jausserande looked up and saw him. He could see the color of her eyes plainly, even at several yards' distance. She dropped Ruth, who sat down in the road. Fox kicked his horse into a turn and headed back up the road at a hammer gallop. He could hear Raven behind him.

And behind that, a ululating howl of delight.

"Let me go!" Ruth demanded, and, abruptly, the stranger did. Ruth sprawled backward in the road, only dimly registering the sound of several horses leaving.

"Fox!" She started to her feet.

"Miss Marlowe?" a voice above her head said.

She stared up. Stared for an instant at yet another large hostile stranger in weird clothes before she saw—

"*Nic!*" She clutched at his arm. "Nic! Oh, God, it's you— I'm so glad you're here! I thought you were dead—we've got to stop her—she's after Fox."

He smiled faintly. "The lady's name is Jausserande, and I don't think that anyone interfering between her and Mr. Fox is going to have much luck," Nic said. "I think she means to hang him and cut off his thumbs—I'm not particularly clear on the order, but—"

Miss Marlowe stared at him as if he was crazy. Nic reminded himself firmly that this was a *civilian;* she hadn't been there.

"Oh, God. He was right. He was telling the truth. Nic, you've got to help me help him get away! He's my *friend!*" Ruth said with agitated inaccuracy.

This presented an unfortunate conflict of interest, if true. "Come on, then." Her horse had wandered a few yards away and was unconcernedly browsing. He ran to it and led it back, tossing her up without asking if she needed the help.

"Follow me," he said, and turned his horse in the direction Jausserande had gone.

And a pillar of fire rose up out of the center of the wood.

Fox couldn't believe his luck—all bad. Ruth was caught and Tinkerbelle was on their tail. Tink had Hathorne's horse, from the markings, and that meant Fox's horse might be able to outrun it.

But Raven's horse, with its greater burden, couldn't.

Ambush time.

He turned off the road into the wood, knowing that Raven would follow. Spotted a likely looking tree, kicked free of his stirrups, and did a flying dismount into a pile of leaves. Rolled to his feet, barely escaping being trampled by Raven, and scrambled for the tree. A second later Tink appeared, too hot in pursuit to think clearly.

Fox jumped.

And the world exploded into flame.

Fire. The first spell, the simplest spell. She had little power and less interest in the Art Magical, but for days Jausserande had lived in fire, fire waiting to burn.

She nearly had them; moments more and she could throw the giant from his horse. And then something hit her, and the Word was ripped from her very bones, following the outlaws as she could not. Fire. She heard a horse scream.

And then she was down, but the spell had distracted her attacker long enough for her to gain the advantage.

Fox.

She twisted, bringing Fox's body under hers, and struck hard at his face with the butt of Hathorne's dagger. He fell back, scrambling out of reach. In a moment he would be gone. She gazed wildly around herself and then thrust to her feet, running away from him.

Toward the fire.

What burned now had been dead already; a lightning-blasted oak, tinder dry. It had gone up like an oil-soaked torch at her Word. The giant's horse had shied, and the giant was no rider. He lay sprawled among the leaves like a stunned ox.

Jausserande vaulted him and set her knife to his throat.

"Don't!" Fox shouted.

Nic's horse stood fast, its ears swiveled away from the sound of burning. Ruth's tried to shy; she hauled back on her reins like grim death until it danced in a circle. The pillar of fire was visible through the autumn trees, lethal and unnatural.

"What?" Ruth said, staring anxiously from the forest to the sky and back. But there was nothing to see but the fire.

"I don't know. Come on—we'll go around. *And find out who called in an air strike later.*

"Why not?" Jausserande asked. One hand was fastened in the unconscious outlaw's black hair. The other held the blade, razor-sharp, at his throat. The pressure of his pulse fluttering against the blade had already made it break the skin, and a thin gaudy line of red trickled along its edge. "You're outlaws. Your lives are forfeit," she said, as if Fox needed reminding.

"What about a trial?" Fox said. Jausserande snorted.

"You'd rather have me than him," Fox pointed out. She couldn't see him any more, only hear his voice. The heat at her back made her skin itch, but she hardly noticed. Her gamble had paid off—Fox was trying to bargain for his companion's life.

"I have both of you now," Jausserande pointed out.

"Kill him and I run for it," Fox said promptly. "Want to bet I catch one of the horses before you do? And I'll be back—but before that, the story of what a jerk you are will be *samizdat* from here to the border."

Jausserande didn't know what "samizdat" was and didn't care. "Ceiynt will grind your bones to powder. The ears first, I think, to wake him." She lifted the knife. The mud-born in her arms began to stir.

Fox appeared.

He was crouched on an overhanging branch about ten yards away, and half his face was masked in blood from where she had struck him. In his hand was the iron knife.

Jausserande flinched; she couldn't help herself. Fox saw it and grinned.

"Checkmate," he said.

Raven groaned. "Fox?"

He opened his eyes and froze. From where he was Fox saw all the color drain out of Raven's face. Jausserande smiled down at him, tender as a new mother.

"Yes, mud-born. You are going to die. But not here. I don't need to kill you here. You'll come back to Dawnheart; they'll rack you sweetly on *my* word, no matter where my cousin bides. And you, Fox, I'll run to earth another day."

She got to her feet and pulled Raven to his knees. He stared at Fox in miserable terror and Fox knew there was no fight in him. Raven would go like a lamb to the slaughter, just because Jausserande was *highborn*.

"Let him go," Fox said flatly. "Let him go and I'll surrender. You won't have to wait."

"Fox—no! They lie, the highborn; their promises are like smoke," Raven cried. Jausserande snarled and jerked his head back.

"Well, I've taught you that much," Fox said. "Think fast, Tink; if you kill him, there goes your shield—and I kill you."

"I will not pardon him," Jausserande said through gritted teeth. She held the point of the dagger to the side of his throat; one shove and Raven was a dead man.

"Pardon, hell. Just let him go and he can take his chances. You can hunt *him* down another day. Right, Raven?" Fox said bracingly.

"Fox, I—"

"All this damn time and you haven't learned to follow orders yet? *Run away,* Raven. It's a chance, at least."

"Drop the knife." Jausserande said, growing impatient.

"Let him go and I will," Fox said.

"All right. Surrender and he goes free this day. My word on it."

It was weakness. He was throwing away his last chance—for nothing. All he'd gain Raven was a head start, and it wouldn't be enough. And if he couldn't escape before Tink got him back inside Dawnheart, he'd bought a one-way ticket to hell.

He'd known how it would end. But after everything he couldn't bear to watch Raven die.

Fox's knife dropped from his hand, into the leaves below. The sound was muffled by the crackle of flames in the burning tree. *One more social taboo broken.* He jumped down after it, and stood, staring at Raven.

"Kneel," Jausserande said.

Fox dropped to his knees.

She stood up and away from Raven, releasing him, and took a step toward Fox.

"Find a horse and go, Raven," Fox said. Raven got slowly to his feet. "Go *on,* goddammit."

Raven stared at Fox for one last frozen moment then turned away. He could have attacked Jausserande, but Fox knew he would never think of it.

"On your face," Jausserande said, and Fox lay down. She walked over to him, yanking a length of leather out of her tunic, and knelt on his back to tie his hands.

There was a sound of hoofbeats—a pair of riders. Fox jerked convulsively where he lay.

"No," Jausserande said, "he goes free. If they bring him to me, I will free him." She stroked Fox's hair. "Your life for his this day."

The smoke and fire from the burning tree was probably visible for miles, and its sparks would almost inevitably start other fires soon.

"Would it do any good at all to tell you to stay here?" Nic asked.

"I don't think so," Ruth admitted.

He dismounted, his eyes on the figure silhouetted by the blaze. He tied his horse to a tree and took the quarterstaff from its packs. He tied Ruth's horse to another tree, and helped her down.

"At least let me go first," Nic said. Ruth nodded. He moved off, quarterstaff in hand. Ruth followed.

Jausserande got to her feet when she saw them, and pulled Fox up with her. He looked like a splatterpunk special effect, half his face covered with blood and dirt.

"Welcome to the party," Fox said. "Hi, Ruthie. Welcome to Introductory Social Science. Who's your wizard friend?" For a man in so much trouble, Fox sounded remarkably cheerful.

"He isn't a wizard—he's Nic Brightlaw from Earth!" Ruth said.

There was a pause as the two men stared at each other.

"Philip," Nic finally said, sounding more puzzled than anything else.

"Hi, Mister Brightlaw," Fox said with fulsome smarm, sounding for an instant remarkably like Wally Cleaver. The act collapsed. "Good. Great. Fine. *He* can help you find Melior."

"Let him go," Ruth said to Jausserande. "I mean it."

Jausserande looked at her and laughed. "So you are my cousin's Ironworld heart twin, Ruth? I wish him joy of you."

"Melior's in trouble," Ruth said quickly. "We were coming here, and he was captured—by Baligant and a dragon. Him *and* the Sword. You have to help. And let Fox *go*."

Jausserande sighed, as if the news had aged her. "I will bear that news to Dawnheart, and evil news it is, but the fate of The Rohannan is Line Rohannan's business, and this rebel brat is mine, so—" Jausserande raised her dagger.

"He's got the Cup," Fox said swiftly.

Jausserande stopped, lowering the dagger, torn between hope and the certainty that anyone in Fox's position would lie. Ruth started forward and Nic stopped her with a hand on her arm.

"Think about it, Tink," Fox said quickly. "I don't have the Cup. You don't have the Cup. It wasn't in the Vale of Stars in the *first* place, remember? When Mel was on Earth, he told Ruth and me that Baligant's master plan was to get his hands on all twelve Treasures. Now, sweetcakes, where do *you* think the Cup is?"

Jausserande turned and backhanded Fox—hard—across the face.

He struggled to keep his balance, but couldn't with his hands bound. He fell back and sideways, unable to break his fall. When he was down she kicked him. Her boot landed solidly in his ribs and Ruth heard his gasp of pain from across the clearing.

"No!" Ruth tried again to fling herself at Jausserande; Nic held her arm tightly while she jerked and struggled. "Let him go—let *me* go—leave him alone—*what kind of animal are you?"*

"Satisfied now, Tink?" said Fox breathlessly from the ground.

Jausserande stood over him, only a little less breathless than he. "So Baligant has the Cup—your word on it. I thank you for this advice and will act on it once I have hanged you."

"Nic, what's the *matter* with you—it's Philip—make her let him *go!"*

Jausserande turned toward Ruth, the knife heavy in her hand and a feral triumph in her eyes. Ruth backed up against Nic, feeling the hardness of metal against her back even through all her layers of petticoats.

"I wouldn't," Nic said mildly to Jausserande. "After all, we know *her* patron."

"She's his proof," Fox said. He'd managed to get to his knees and shook his head to clear it. Blood sprayed from his gashed mouth and spattered the leaves; he spat. Jausserande jerked back around and glared at him.

"Mel needs her. She's his proof," Fox repeated. He got carefully to his feet, never taking his eyes from Jausser-

ande's face. "When they were together, he told her, and she
told me. There's a spell that ties Ruth to Melior's sword, the
Treasuresword; the Sword of Maiden's Tears. He's found a
way to undo it and prove who cast it. Ask her."

"He must go before the Court of the Twilight,"
Jausserande said slowly, reasoning it out. "And until then I
will seal his Ironworlder in Dawnheart to keep her safe. And
I will kill you," she added.

"Fine," said Fox, leaning against a tree as if he hadn't a
care in the world. Where Jausserande had struck him, his
face was purple-red and swollen, and the split lip blurred his
speech—but only a little. "Enjoy yourself. Of course, Mel,
the Sword, your precious day-glo Dixie Cup—and ten other
exciting Treasures—are all lost. Somewhere. I don't suppose
you're planning to look for any of them? And have I mentioned that Ruth can lead you to Melior? She can."

"Don't. Fox—don't," Ruth begged.

There was a pause, and when Jausserande spoke again, it
was in a voice false and rich with mockery. "Oh, Fox. Dear
little Fox. Are you actually pledging to aid me to find my
cousin in exchange for your life?" She laughed, as if he'd
told a joke she found particularly amusing.

"No." Fox made an aborted motion, as if he'd wipe his
bleeding lip and had been prevented by his bonds. "I want
to find Melior myself. Ruth can do it—she's still tied to the
Sword, in case you'd managed to forget that. And she isn't
any safer in the Magic Castle than she is with us—there's a
wizard trying to kill her. If you find the Sword, you'll find
the Cup. Or that's the way to bet."

Jausserande hesitated, her face a study in betrayed bewil-
derment. She raised the knife again, her face set, and it was
plain to all three of the others that Jausserande intended to
reject all this talk of plot and counterplot for something she
could understand.

"*You* took it from me. I'll kill *you.*"

"Look," Nic's voice was quiet, as nonthreatening as he
could make it. He knew her kind now; her war wasn't over.
Didn't Philip realize that? Or was he as crazy as she was?
His memories of Philip LeStrange were blurred and unreli-
able; memories of memories from a Christmas Eve that
seemed to have receded into legend.

"Getting Melior and the stuff back is the main thing. You

can always kill Fox later. Where's he going to go? And we might need cannon fodder some time," Nic said reasonably.

"Cannon?" Jausserande said blankly.

"No cannon," said Fox, and now his pain and weariness showed in his voice. "No cannon, no gunpowder, no *iron*. Catapult and crossbow. And, of course, *magic*."

Jausserande dropped the knife to the ground and stalked away toward the burning tree. Nic let go of Ruth and she ran to Philip/Fox.

"Oh, *God*—" Ruth said. She blinked; tears spilled down her face.

"Untie my hands," Fox said. He half-turned, leaning against the tree for support, and offered her his bound hands. They were already bluish, the dark leather biting into the flesh.

"I— I can't. It's—"

"My knife's on the ground somewhere here. It's steel. Find it."

Ruth scrabbled on hands and knees around Fox's feet until she came up with the blade. She sawed through the leather until it was raveled enough to break.

Fox sighed and worked his shoulders, then looked down at his swollen hands. "Keep the knife. It's iron—well, steel. It burns them—elves. Badly. I think I'm going to sit down now," he added, and did, leaning back against the tree.

Ruth scrubbed at her stinging eyes. "Was it true?" she asked.

" 'What is truth?'—to quote Pontius Pilate." Fox rested his arms on his drawn-up knees, working his hands

"Where's Raven?" Ruth asked guiltily. She looked all around, but didn't see him.

"He's got a head start. I wish he had the brains to use it, but he doesn't. He's dead meat, Ruthie; we all are." Fox leaned his head back against the tree trunk and closed his eyes.

"How could—" Ruth stopped. There were just too many questions. She looked behind her. Jausserande was standing staring into the burning tree. Nic was standing near her, talking.

"You were right, Fox. I'm sorry," she said. "Maybe Melior— I'll *make* him change things."

Fox laughed, then swore at how much it hurt. "Jesus, Ruthie, he's got the High King trying to kill him and you want him to take up civil rights, too?"

I want him back. Alive, Ruth thought. "Maybe," she said aloud. "Fox, what do we do now?"

"It depends on them. I take back what I said earlier, Ruthie. It's never a good day to die."

The Court of Illusion

In the Castle called Mourning, at the edge of the world, Eirdois Baligant, who was beginning to realize that he had surrendered more than he knew for the privilege of being named High King of Chandrakar and husband of Hermonicet the Fair, waited upon the pleasure of his wizard to attend him.

That was not how it should be.

Nothing was as it should be.

A human lifetime ago he had begun his conspiracy. The Seven Houses were at war, and so the matter was a simple one: steal the Twelve Treasures of Chandrakar, the entities which held within themselves the power which maintained Chandrakar's existence in the Morning Lands, and by their absence gain both ultimate power for himself and destruction for his enemies—for whomsoever did not present the Treasure that was his Line's to guard at the Kingmaking, he and all his Line would be banished beyond the bounds of Chandrakar and stripped of all they owned.

Why wasn't it working out that way?

Baligant paced. Simple equations, as rational and reasonable as the columns and figures that had occupied him as a clerk in Rainouart's Instrumentality of Taxation: The Sword of Maiden's Tears, Line Rohannan's Treasure, had been spell-trapped by Baligant's wizard to fall into the World of Iron when its Treasurekeeper touched it—thus its Treasurekeeper would be lured to his death and the Sword remain lost to Line Rohannan. The Cup, the Lance, the Harp, the Crown—Twelve Treasures lost, stolen, or strayed, leaving Baligant the victor.

Only Rohannan Melior had not died. He had retrieved the Sword, he had come back to Chandrakar, and he had brought with him *proof* that Baligant's wizard was the one who had tampered with his Treasure.

Baligant's wizard.

He would like very much to blame her—he *did* blame her, in fact—for the calamity he saw looming before him; but unfortunately he was also clearsighted enough to see that it was *he* who was in trouble no matter who was responsible.

What would he do? What could he do? Proof was proof, no matter what; his complicity would be undeniable.

Surely they would deny him the High Kingship then.

Or . . .

. . . would . . .

. . . they . . . ?

Where was his wizard?

"I am here, my prince," Amadis said.

She was, as always, beautiful—in the way that swords' edges and fire and high places are beautiful—a taunting, deadly, and inhuman limmerence that obsessed even while it threatened. Her hair was a fall of copper fire, her eyes were garnet sparks, and she wore the shadow of elphen beauty like a fatal cloak.

He had sent her to kill Ruth Marlowe, for Ruth Marlowe of the World of Iron was Melior's proof that the Sword had been tampered with, and, when she had failed, had sent her forth again. She should be desperate now for what only he could provide.

"You are tardy enough in coming," Baligant growled.

"Perhaps," said Amadis insolently. Baligant glanced sharply toward her.

"And, having taken so much time, you naturally have progress to report," he went on with heavy irony.

Amadis smiled, small and secret, and said nothing.

Baligant gazed around his treasure room, buying time to put down his growing unease.

Amadis was his wizard, mistress of the Wild Magic, and, like all such Adepts, paid a high price for her power in those things she might and might not do. Such prices were kept secret by their disbursers, but Baligant knew hers, and that knowledge was part of his power. What had shaped the spell that held her, and molded her to his will, and made its necessary flaw the bone-deep addiction to the ice roses unique to Chandrakar's heights.

And not the flower alone, but the flower mixed with the blood of Chandrakar's High King. Without them both she would expire in agony.

In which case, why wasn't she dead?

Like the clerk he had once been, Baligant was meticulous in details. His blood alone could keep her alive, and he did not wish her to grow too independent. He kept her closely; she should have been begging his favor long since to replace the power she had expended in doing his will. Even if she had done nothing, she ought to have reached the limit of her endurance by now.

He turned his back and walked to the window. The Eastern Marches stretched flat and silver to meet a polished pewter sky, and in the distance he could see the tower wherein his bride dwelt until their wedding day. The wind off the marches was cold. Winter was coming. Soon the Twilight Court would rise and the Lords Temporal return to their kingdoms, and the Morning Court would sit and the Prince-Elect tend to his taxes and his pleasures.

If there were to be any pleasures this year. And next autumn . . .

He gazed at the jar that held the dried roses, their petals still supernaturally pale.

"Would you hear what I have done?" Amadis asked.

Baligant turned. *I would hear more than that.* "No doubt you will tell me what you see fit to relate," he said dourly.

Amadis folded her hands upon her flat belly. "I have made a trap, and set out my bait, and the Ironworld girl Ruth Marlowe is even now drawn to my lure. I have made certain that she and Rohannan Melior will not meet, nor that he may wield the Sword against you. And she will die."

So Ruth Marlowe was being drawn to Amadis' lure, was she? The girl was human; she could not make a Gate-crossing unaided; Ruth Marlowe must be already in Chandrakar if Amadis trusted her to walk into her trap. And Amadis had also said that the Sword and the Ironworlder would be drawn together—so where was the Sword, that Amadis was so certain they would not meet?

"I told you to kill her," Baligant reminded her. *So why do you not tell me that she is dead?*

"And so I shall kill her," Amadis said with some impatience.

"Do you wish to displease me?" Baligant began—and stopped at the sight of the indifference in his wizard's eyes. "I think you are not being entirely forthcoming with me," Baligant observed mildly.

"What must I say?" Amadis said. "I have captured Rohannan Melior, and he, his Sword, and what pitiful magics he possessed are in my chamber room even now. He is the lure, and soon Ruth Marlowe will come that I may kill her," Amadis said with innocent satisfaction.

There was a pause.

"You ... did ... *what.* ... ?" Baligant said hoarsely.

No. He must have heard her incorrectly. Not even a wizard of the Wild Magic could be so unworldly and inhuman as to arrange such a way of fulfilling the orders he had given her. He had told her to kill Ruth Marlowe. That was all he had told her.

"It is what you asked of me," the wizard said.

And he had. Oh, he had—now Baligant saw the disaster he had made for himself—he had told her to kill Ruth Marlowe by any means. Any means at all.

He had *not* told her *not* to kidnap The Rohannan, head of Line Rohannan and Swordwarden, and imprison him in Baligant's own tower. He had not told her *not* to steal the Sword of Maiden's Tears—which was now known to be in Melior's possession—and hide it here in Castle Mourning.

He had not, in short, desired her to refrain from a number of actions she, being thus unrestricted, had straightaway committed.

And if they saw— And if they found—

"I will see you dead," Baligant gritted.

"No," said Amadis, as calmly as if venturing an observation on the weather. "I have what I need."

Baligant's hand ached with the need to strike her, but on the day that he touched her with anger or lust his control over her would end, and he did not know what her vengeance might be on that day. He clasped his hands together and ground them closed until the gems on his hands squeaked and squealed with the pressure.

"Go from my sight," he said hoarsely. "And stay within the place appointed you until I summon you again. Work no wiles; abstain from the Art—do *nothing,* do you hear me?"

"I hear and obey, my lord," Amadis said. She bowed very low, but as if it amused her, not as if she meant it. Then she turned, and left, and only the solid sound of the bronze door sliding home again marked her exit.

She looked remarkably healthy.

Baligant sat down upon his carved and cushioned throne.

About The Rohannan's presence here in Mourning something would have to be done, perhaps involving a slender dirk and a body left to fatten the pigs, but he would let that wait until he was certain what the best course might be. In that matter, in the matter of the Sword, he had time.

And what of the wizard?

"I have what I need," Amadis had said. But if he had shed no king's blood to slake her hunger—who had?

ROSEMARY EDGHILL

☐ **THE SWORD OF MAIDEN'S TEARS**   UE2622—$4.99
It was Beltane Eve when Ruth Marlowe stumbled across the
elf Melior Rohannan of Elphame. Melior knew that he must
reclaim the magical Sword that muggers had stolen from him,
for any mortal who wielded the blade would be transformed
into a monster. But in a city with as many hiding places as
New York, what hope was there for finding the unstoppable
evil that had stolen Melior's treasure?

☐ **THE CUP OF MORNING SHADOWS**   UE2671—$5.99
When Ruth Marlowe found a Wild Gate in a library basement,
she ventured into Elphame in search of her lost love, Rohannan the elf. What she found was a land beset by human-
caused trouble. Knowing that what humans have caused, humans must fix, Ruth had no choice but to take up the challenge
of halting a rebellion that could forever overturn the natural
order of Elphame.

IRENE RADFORD

☐ **THE GLASS DRAGON** UE2634—$4.99
Dragons have recently become an endangered species, more part of legend than of life—and with their swiftly diminishing numbers, the source of all magic is fading from the land of Coronnan. But within a realm which has always been protected by its magicians, and in a kingdom whose ruler's own life is intricately linked with that of the dragons, the disappearance of these magical beasts could well see the land fall to invaders.

☐ **THE PERFECT PRINCESS** UE2678—$5.50
Rogue magic had long been banned within Coronnan's borders, but as dragon magic waned and finally vanished, those who had mastered these forbidden spells saw their chance to seize control of the troubled land. And without the dragons and their magic to back his claim to the throne, Prince Darville—only recently freed from an enchantment that had kept him imprisoned in the form of a wolf—might soon see his realm lost to these enemies.

GAYLE GREENO

☐ **THE GHATTI'S TALE:**
  Book 1—Finders, Seekers   UE2550—$5.99
The Seekers Veritas, an organization of truth-finders com-
posed of Bondmate pairs—one human, one a telepathic, cat-
like ghatti—is under attack. And the key to defeating this
deadly foe is locked in one human's mind behind barriers even
her ghatta has never been able to break.

☐ **MINDSPEAKER'S CALL**
  The Ghatti's Tale: Book 2   UE2579—$5.99
Someone seems bent on creating dissension between Cand-
eris and the neighboring kingdom of Marchmont. And even the
truth-reading skill of the Seekers Veritas may not be enough
to unravel the twisted threads of a conspiracy that could see
the two lands caught in a devastating war . . .

☐ **EXILES' RETURN**
  The Ghatti's Tale: Book 3   UE2655—$5.99
Seeker Doyce is about to embark on a far different path—a
ghatti-led journey into the past. For as a new vigilante-led reign
of terror threatens the lives of Seekers and Resonants alike,
the secrets of that long-ago time when the first Seeker-ghatti
Bond was formed may hold the only hope for their future . . .
